DROWNING IN FIRE

DROWNING IN FIRE

CRAIG S. WOMACK

The University of Arizona Press

Tucson

All royalties from the sale of this book go to the Muskogee Creek Nation Language Preservation Program.

The University of Arizona Press
© 2001 Craig S. Womack
All rights reserved

www.uapress.arizona.edu

Library of Congress Cataloging-in-Publication Data
Womack, Craig S.
Drowning in fire / Craig S. Womack.
p. cm.–(Sun tracks ; v. 48)
ISBN 978-0-8165-2168-5 (pbk. : acid-free paper)
1. Creek Indians–Fiction. 2. Young Men–Fiction. 3. Gay youth–
Fiction. I. Title. II. Series.
PS501 .S85 vol. 48
[PS3623.06]
810.8'0054 s–dc21
[813 /   2001001221

"Fancy" by Alex Posey, unpublished poem from Posey papers in Gilcrease Museum, Tulsa, Oklahoma. Reprinted in *Alex Posey: Creek Poet, Journalist, and Humorist,* by Dan Littlefield, published by University of Nebraska Press, 1992.

Manufactured in the United States of America on acid-free, archival-quality paper and processed chlorine free.

Contents

ACKNOWLEDGMENTS

To Barbara Coachman, 1919–2001. The last time I saw you, in the old folks home in Lodi, California, you walked out of your room, turned back toward the door, and announced, as if an afterthought, "God is Creek," then disappeared down the hallway. I tell you what's the truth, Aunt Barbara: In all my years playing fiddle and guitar, I've never ended a solo on quite as interesting a note as that one. Hadam Chihacathlis.

To Gerardo Tristan Alvarado, for our life together.

To Joy Harjo, a sister in the journey.

To Geary Hobson, for friendship and keeping the faith. In your own words, "Roam on, brother!"

To Jeff Bloomgarden, Janet McAdams, and Joy, once more, for excellent readings.

To the members of New Tallahassee Ceremonial Grounds, for a place around the fire.

To the people of the Blackfoot Confederacy, for their beautiful land, exceptional kindness, and incredible patience in putting up with an Okie Indian.

To Lori Snaif, Mike Womack and Barbara Stanton, Lisa and Rick Timmermans, and their kids, for places to work in the last stages of this novel.

To Dan Littlefield, for his meticulous historical scholarship, specifically his article in the *Chronicles of Oklahoma* on the "Crazy Snake Uprising," which helped me pin down some of the history in Chapter 10, "The Colors of Fire."

To Coy and Wilma Womack, the best of parents, without whom none of this is possible.

To Ashley E. Harjo, Morgan A. Harjo, Brittany Roothame, Kelsey Marie Proctor, Alyssa Narcomey, Erin Floyd, Sarah Lena Sands, and Jacob Thomas Flood, winners of the Alexander Posey Literary Festival in the year 2000, and for the winners in the years to come. We're counting on you all.

DROWNING IN FIRE

ONE

Hitchi

JOSH HENNEHA, WELEETKA, OKLAHAMA, 1964

"Don't worry, son. Your Aunt Lucille knows what to do when it hurts." I put my arms around his neck, and he lifted me from beneath the covers. I held one hand over my throbbing ear and tensed each time I felt the pulse of pain.

"Shh ... shh .... You'll be all right." My uncle patted my head, and I leaned over and lay against his neck, wiping my tears on his shoulder. "Lucille's already up and sitting in her chair waiting for you. She'll make you better." He patted my head again, and, when we got to Aunt Lucy, seated in the kitchen, I unwrapped my arms from around him. She reached out, clutched me, and sat me in the middle of her lap. I turned around to face her while my uncle left the room.

"Son," she said. "Listen. Stop fussing with that earache." I had my hand clapped over my ear. She put my hand in my lap, and I looked at her hands, calloused and rough like a man's, always moving while she spoke. "I reckon I'll just talk into your good ear then," she joked, pulling on the one that didn't hurt none. She lit the Marlboro and breathed in the smoke, looking past me into the darkness outside the kitchen window. I turned and saw nothing. I bent to the side, turned my face toward her, and she moved close. She breathed deeply, and the red end of the cigarette lit up her face in the dimness. For a moment only, I saw her eyes, brown, nested in furrows, looking straight at me. She exhaled a long stream of smoke into my ear; I felt a hot wave against a bank of pain. Aunt Lucy, breathing smoke and stories into me, said, "Mama useta say, *hofónof,* long time ago, that in the beginning it was so foggy you couldn't see nowheres, not even anyone around you."

"I don't want to hear a story," I protested. "You done told me that. Get out your trumpet and play 'Stardust.'" I loved the sound of that dreamy old tune.

"I can't go playing trumpet here in the middle of the night. Your uncle has work in the morning."

"But everybody says you play all night in the bars," I tell her.

"Who says that?" Lucy asks, annoyed.

I figure I better not tell. She might not be happy to know that my mom, her own niece, says such things.

"I may play in bars, but does this look like a beer joint to you?"

I never have seen the kind of place she's talking about, but I sure heard people go on about it and how a woman has no business there. According to some of them I shouldn't even be staying over at Aunt Lucy's house.

I felt her legs, so much bigger than mine; her muscles relaxed beneath my fingertips as she began to speak. Lucy pulled me closer, deeper into her lap, until I could feel her breathing in and out, each exhalation in rhythm with her voice. The smoke floated with her words through the kitchen, and a cloud settled around an old tube radio on a high shelf above her head.

"Josh, are you listening?" she asked. I stopped tugging on her robe and looked up at her. She continued. "See, a mighty fog had covered us after we'd settled in our new home. You know, we'd just moved there after the earth had opened up and spit us out in the beginning. We'd come a long ways. For a long time we wandered about in darkness. And we all—some way or other out in the dark, I s'pose—got lost from one another; couldn't see nothing, and we got real scared.

Whenever we heard someone we knew calling, we followed their voice and held fast to that person, so we wouldn't be separated."

I wrapped my arms around her waist until I could feel her flesh beneath the robe. I clasped my hands together behind her back.

"Anyway, we stumbled about every which way, forming groups with those we touched. Even the animals were lost, wandering about, making their different cries for help. Bumping and running into each other. Out there in the dark listening to who was in the distance, who was near. The animals had grown so tame—from terror, I reckon—that they had no fear of us, and they throwed in with the various bands of people. Many people and animals were wounded and in pain from falling and running into things they couldn't see, and you could hear their voices, full of hurt."

"Did any of the people get bit by the animals?" I asked.

"Aw, maybe a little bit. But not enough to amount to nothing." She tried to hide a grin, turning her mouth down and looking straight into my eyes. She pointed out the window. "When the wind swept the fog away, the band of people on the east that first come out of the blackness became the Wind Clan. They had no animal near them, but, because they first saw the light, they became the leading clan. So the first animal that the other groups saw, they took the names of whatever birds or animals they found with them when the fog broke. We agreed never to desert our clans. Now, listen to me. These is our ways. The first animal our family spotted was *yaha,* the wolf. We saw him first, so we call him Grandfather. When the fog lifted, he was standing in the shadows among the oaks, resting after having loped all frantic-like from the thick haze. Of course, they's no more wolfs today."

"Yeah," I say, "but I hear coyotes at night off behind the pasture. Are they afraid of fire? Because if I was on a camping trip, and they came up around my sleeping bag, I'd shake the lit end of a stick at them."

"I mean they aren't no clan by that name. They aren't no more actual wolfs, either, to my way of knowing because when all the WPA was to put in big dams during the depression they drownded out all that wild country where wolfs and cougars and even bears lived in.

But we still got sweet potato, alligator, tiger, and winds. Wolfs was an old clan that died out. The others is still going. You get them from your mom's side of the family. Like ground membership." My mind drifted off, and I imagined a big black bear living down in the storm cellar back a long time ago when Lucy was as little as me, a hungry bear opening up jars of preserves and licking sweet jelly off his fingers. I seen that once in a book, but it mighta been honey.

"So it was this here particular wolf who tangled himself in a bramble bush, and his ear was tattered and bleeding. And here we come up the trail, all of us that had joined together in the darkness. When we saw him, trapped in thick vines next to a creek, we helped untangle him. We all held on as gently as we could, one on each leg, one on his back; one held his muzzle shut. The *hilis heyya,* medicine man, spoke words over him, kinda explaining like, so he wouldn't bite or be frightened. Mama told me, she says, 'Lucy'—she always called me Lucy 'stead of Lucille—she says, 'Lucy, these are the words we said over the wolf:

> *on the path he is lying*
> *stretched out we see him*
> *he calls out crying*
> *hurt we see him*
> *roaming in the darkness we see him*
> *stretched out we see him*
> *on the path he is lying.'*

We turned him a-loose, and he stood looking at us before he trotted off into the woods."

I reached up and felt my ear. It still throbbed. "Lean towards me," she said. "One more time and it'll stop hurting." She blew another thin stream of white smoke straight into my ear. I relaxed and turned loose of my grip around her waist, resting my hands in her lap. I watched the dangling gray ashes about to fall from beyond her fingertips. "Aunt Lucy," I said, "how do you say 'cigarette'?"

"In Creek? *Hitchi mokkeycha* for 'cigarette,' or just *hitchi* for 'tobacco.'"

"Please, one more story. It still hurts."

"This time, Josh, don't be daydreaming. Put your mind on the story. This one is about your uncle when he left Oklahoma for a while to pick cotton and work in the oil fields in the San Joaquin Valley. This happened around Dos Palos, California."

"Where is Dos Palos?"

"It's a flat place with huge fields of alfalfa and cotton, bigger than anything you've ever seen. It's close to a town named Visalia, and a lot of us had to go there and work when our farms went dry. Those of us who hadn't lost them already. A lot of them, like your uncle, was working on shares, farming other peoples's lands. That's the way poor folks, white and Indian, made their living. Our promised allotments slipped through our fingers when Oklahoma figured out ways to cheat us out of them. They forced us to take these allotments because they've always wanted to take away the one thing they hate the most—the fact that we exist as a nation of people, the Creek Nation, Muskogalki. This is what we always been, before they ever came here, these white peoples. We always been a nation. This is what we still are. Our family had to make another long trip. Again. We headed west."

"Oh," I said, and listened.

"But we was to come back to Oklahoma eventually. Your uncle just needed some work. Anyway, one time the boss-man on one of the Californey ranches your uncle worked on—well, he had a new Ford coupe—he said to your uncle, 'Glen, I want you to clean that car.' So, he did. The work boss had it parked up against an irrigation ditch next to the cotton rows.

"I tell you what," she said. "This ole boy—the boss-man—dipped snuff, but he didn't use no can. He spit it right on the floorboard of that new Ford. Like I was saying, he made your uncle clean it up."

As she speaks I see Uncle scrub up the brown stain and wads of shriveled looseleaf tobacco from the front seat of the car. Uncle has on a floppy fishing hat to cover up his bald head because it's hot where he works. I bet it's even hotter than Oklahoma in July next to the lake. Uncle wipes sweat off his face with a white handkerchief. It's even worse inside the black car than in the fields, the sun bearing down through the windshield, making the seats and the dash like an oven. Uncle don't let on like he's mad, but he *is* mad, madder than a bee with its stinger pulled. Madder than when I walked through his radishes, except he let on mad then for sure. The boss-man leans his flesh against the metal of the Ford and guards Uncle. The cotton bolls are waving roads of white clouds separated by water. While peering into the window, the boss opens his mouth and stuffs his cheek full of a large wad, then spits hissing brown streams into the dust at his feet. Meanwhile, Uncle quietly bends over the floorboard and scrapes, never looking up, dreaming of the dust patch he left that still holds him, its roots burrowing from eastern Oklahoma red clay to San Joaquin Valley black silt and surfacing somewhere outside Dos Palos, California, grabbing him by the ankles.

Lucy raises her voice. "Your uncle come home and said, 'I'm gonna kill that son-of-a-bitch-of-a-boss.'" That night I made beans and cornbread for supper and, afterwards, your uncle went out back of the tenant house they had for those of us that worked in the fields. It had already gotten dark out. I couldn't see him out there at night, but I could hear the whine of a saw he had brought to California with him, biting into wood. He cut out a beautiful prancing pony from an old piece of plywood and nailed it over the doorway of the shack we useta live in. It's a trotter, like the kind they got at the races out there that pulls a single-man cart but cain't never break out in a full run. We still have it. You'll see it from this window when morning comes. We've got it hung on the fence over the garden. In the years that it's been up there, the varnish has dried and cracked, but you can still tell it's a racing pony."

I looked out the kitchen window and squinted into the darkness, waiting for the first light. I could see Uncle coming in from his sawing that night, walking in the house, sitting before this woman of shoats and swill and dung and strong hands that had pulled down life from milk-heavy teats. And then used those same fingers to play a trumpet on Friday and Saturday evenings in the bad places. I saw Uncle crawl

up onto her lap and clasp stained fingers around her waist while she
held on to him in the darkness, lit the Marlboro, and directed wisps of

curling

white

hot

smoke

into his ear. After he straightened his back and pulled himself closer
against her, she spoke: "In the beginning we were covered by a mighty
fog."

Then it was me in her lap again, and I felt silence enveloping me
once more as my uncle lifted me away, carrying me into the bedroom.
I felt him pull the covers over me, but he already seemed far off, as I
retreated back to the safe place inside my mind. "The boy don't hardly
say a word around no one but you," Uncle seemed to be saying, back in
the kitchen. "Always daydreaming."

Lucy laughed, snubbing out her cigarette. "It's a sight on earth the
things you mens worry over," she said, the last of the blue smoke
drowning out their faces as I drifted off.

TWO

The King of the Tie-snakes

JOSH HENNEHA, EUFAULA, OKLAHOMA, 1972

I spent my days that Oklahoma summer fishing with my grandfather or traipsing after my cousin and his friends through hills covered with blackjacks and post oaks, cicadas humming in my ears, chiggers at my ankles, following as they scouted dark places to smoke their cigarettes and gather their secrets. My cousin, Lenny Henneha, barely tolerated me, the ties of blood hardly enough to admit a sissy into his circle. This resentful inclusion was a step up, actually, from school, where I spent my days on the edge of the playground, watching the scrabbling bodies weave in and out, frenetic blurs of girls jumping rope, clumps of boys playing soccer, bobbing up and down over a lake of asphalt. As for me, I waited for the misery to end when the bell would proclaim relief, when the teacher would call roll, singing out "Josh," and I would at least have the comfort of hiding behind a book back in class, its hard cover held before me like a Jesuit missionary's crucifix. But that was another world, and I had two more months left of sweating and barely being able to breathe the dripping Oklahoma air before returning to school in the fall.

• • •

"I can't swim out that far," Josh said, shaking while beads of water ran off his chin and dripped onto his chest. He had started out toward the raft and turned back, the other boys urging him on, already halfway out in the lake. He stood ankle deep in a mossy bed of lake weeds under a bright blue sky, his shoulders sunburned and peeling. He turned, climbed out of the weeds, and headed up the embankment in the direction of the dam.

"You fuckin' pussy," Sammy Barnhill hollered from the lake at Josh's retreating form as he made the blacktop road at the top of the hill.

"Come on, Josh," Lenny yelled in exasperation. "We ain't taking you anywhere else with us."

Josh shrugged and kept walking.

It was Jimmy Alexander's turn. "It ain't that far. Look, you can swim out on that intertube." Jimmy pointed at the boat dock where the black tube was swollen on the top of the hot concrete steps. Josh paused and considered Jimmy's advice. Before long he had the tube untied, dipped on both sides in the water to cool it off, and he was kicking his way toward the others, the willow trees leaning over the lakeshore becoming farther away each time he cast a backward glance, the dam road at the top of the hill a distant blur, the Texaco station in front of the dirt access road that led down to the lake now invisible as he kicked through the water, the sun burning overhead.

He and the boys swam out toward the old raft anchored off the shore of Lake Eufaula, racing to see who could get there first. Sammy pulled himself over the moss-covered sides, and, one by one, as the boys tried to grab onto the ladder and climb aboard, he kicked them back into the water. He announced, "Let's play king of the raft." As Sammy defended the ladder, Jimmy swam to the other side and hopped aboard. Josh, floating on his inner tube on the opposite side, watched Jimmy coming up out of the water. As Jimmy pulled himself aboard he seemed to rise out of the lake in an unending succession; his wiry arms and upper body kept coming and coming, followed by his swimming trunks and long legs, like a snake uncoiling. He was taller than the rest of them. Jimmy's eyes met Josh's just before Jimmy stood fully erect on the slippery wooden planks. Jimmy quickly turned away and snuck over to where Sammy stood, occupied with kicking Lenny back into the water, and Jimmy shoved Sammy into the lake. "New king," he said to Sammy, who came up spitting water and calling Jimmy a motherfucker.

Jimmy grew tired of using his superior size to keep Sammy off the raft, and he pretended not to notice Sammy mouthing off. Jimmy was shaking water out of his ears when Sammy climbed back up. The raft pitched a little, and Jimmy lost his balance, falling to his knees.

"Dumb nigger," Sammy taunted. Jimmy grabbed Sammy's ankles and sent him sprawling on his ass. He landed with a loud *thunk*. Jimmy stood above Sammy. Jimmy's short-cropped hair glistened in the sun, and he seemed to Josh bathed in light after emerging from the murky lake. Jimmy was more mature than the rest of the boys, the athlete of the bunch, a basketball player obsessed with the Lakers and his hero, Kareem Abdul-Jabbar. Jimmy, like many Creeks, had black blood and features, a fact the other boys held against him and used to discredit him since he could beat them at sports. Josh pretended to watch a ski boat passing by, back and forth, but he was using each opportunity to check out Jimmy, who was now lying back, hands folded behind his head, taking in the sun. The water was drying on Jimmy's chest in mottled streaks that ran down his belly to his swimming trunks, an old pair that was missing a button, pinned at the top instead.

Josh had secret words with special powers. Each time he followed the ski boat's pass between the raft and the shore, and his eyes swept over Jimmy, Josh sent out another message. The way it worked was that only the right person would know he was receiving the thoughts that Josh had stored up inside his head. Not very many people would know what the words meant. In the wrong hands the message could be deadly, or the recipient might turn on him. Josh watched Jimmy for a sign that the signals had registered, but nothing seemed to be happening.

Josh carefully unknotted a plastic bag, which contained inside it another knotted plastic bag, which he also undid, retrieving its contents.

"You brought a book with you?" Sammy said scornfully.

"Give him a break, man," Jimmy said. "What you reading, anyway?"

Josh held up the cover. Jimmy squinted, reading the title, *The*

Happy Hollisters, then laughed. "What do you get out of a story like that?" he asked. Josh couldn't explain that the Happy Hollisters were so far away, and he took comfort in that. Jimmy let it drop when Lenny interrupted by pointing out a school of crappie darting up to the raft's ladder.

Josh knew the sting of being last at everything. During school recess, Miss Manier, whom the boys all called Miss Manure, would have the kids line up to choose teams for kickball. Each day she would send one of the girls over to fetch Josh from his lone perch near the tetherball poles. Miss Manier began by saying, "Okay, children. Which one of you boys wants to volunteer for team captain?" One of the more athletic guys, usually Jimmy, would speak up first and stand there with his hand up in the air. But Miss Manier always picked a white boy to lead the teams. And next time Jimmy would volunteer again. Josh wondered why Jimmy didn't give up after a while. Didn't he get it? Alone, Josh dreamed of advising Jimmy about the ways of Miss Manier, inviting Jimmy over to his house where Josh would take him up to his room. Jimmy would sit on Josh's bed, and Josh would sit at his desk and say, "Jimmy, what you wanna do is watch close while captains are being picked. You might notice that Raymond gets picked every time, and he hates being team captain. Wait until we get out on the field, and offer to be last up if Raymond will let you lead the team because Raymond lives to bat." Jimmy would clap Josh on the shoulder and say, "Thanks, buddy, I never thought of that." Maybe afterward they would lie on Josh's bed, and Josh would casually pull out a *Sports Illustrated* with Kareem on the cover, and Jimmy would pick it up and explain to Josh all the mysteries of basketball.

Or Jimmy would toss Josh a ball lying in the corner of the room. "Hold it like this," he'd say, walking over and standing behind Josh. "Here, put your middle finger over the air valve," he'd add while helping Josh position his hands, and they would both slowly raise the ball together, time and time again, until Josh had it down perfect.

Out on the playground, Josh wondered why Miss Manier didn't just have them number off and separate into teams, sparing them all the daily humiliation. What was her game? But she was a white lady, so who knows? Not only did Josh never get picked for team captain, since he was Indian, but he got chosen just after the last boy was picked and before the first girl, because he was the least athletic of the schoolboys. Miss Manier never did anything to stop the girls from being picked last, either. She pretended not to notice any of this. Or maybe she really didn't see it. Hard to say. She looked busy pushing her glasses farther up on her nose when she wanted not to hear or see things.

The boys called him faggot. All the time. Every day. It might be summer vacation, but there was no vacation from that, and it had become like a second name; "Josh faggot" was as familiar to him as "Josh Henneha." He couldn't understand their world, either, whether they hated him because he read books or because he "walked like a girl," which they chanted to him in singsong voices on the bus rides home. Would it be any better in seventh grade? On the playground, Josh liked playing the girls' games because he didn't have to endure the burning shame of choosing teams. The girls simply took turns playing hopscotch or tetherball, and he felt more comfortable apart from the boys' cutthroat competition. During recess, when the kids could play with whomever they wanted, he knew that none of them would choose him for their team anyway. So he either joined the girls or stood alone at the edge of the blacktop watching the others.

Jimmy took a lot of shit for sometimes putting up with Josh. When Sammy would see Jimmy talking to Josh, he would say, "Jimmy, now we know. You're one of them, too. We see you got a new little girlfriend." Occasionally, Jimmy would convince the boys to let Josh throw in with them, although they complained about having him in their presence. Josh would join them only after relentless teasing. "You pussy. Playing with the girls again? Want to borrow my sister's panties?"

Today, though, Josh had figured out a way of making himself useful to Jimmy. From the bread bag, Josh pulled out Jimmy's pack of cigarettes, which he'd tied inside with his book before they swam out. Josh handed the pack to Jimmy. Jimmy passed each member of the gang one of them, and he demonstrated his awe-inspiring ability to light up even on the windiest days by holding the match with his thumb and forefinger and cupping his hand around the burning flame. Smokes were important, and Josh had managed to get them out to the middle of Lake Eufaula, an accomplishment that no one on the raft could deny. He'd used his head, he thought, even if none of them would admit it.

Lenny spoke up. "Let's have a diving contest." The first one to bring up a rock from the bottom of the lake would win, he explained.

The boys argued about who would go first. Josh sat alone on the edge of the raft staring wistfully, trancelike, over the side, his feet dangling in the water. They chose the diving order. Sammy would take the first turn, of course, then Jimmy and Lenny. They all agreed that Josh would go last, since, as Sammy said all the time, "He ain't no count nohow." Josh said, "You go ahead. I don't feel like diving just now." They met his statement with the usual jeers describing Josh's mother, words about unmentionable acts performed on close kin and the family dog, comments about his female relatives' sexual activities with ancient white men in overalls who sat on the town bench in Eufaula by the old Palmers Grocery and spat long streams of tobacco juice, and concluded with the final touch, without which any string of insults lacked finality: "I bet you're chicken, faggot."

Josh had an idea. He thought, "I'll see if Jimmy can receive my messages from beneath the water. I'll count to three after he dives and begin transmitting. I'll call to him from on top of the raft; Jimmy will answer back from below the waves. Maybe if I can't send my thoughts when we're sitting so close together, what about when I'm above the surface, and he's below?" It could be that brain waves can only be sent from opposite worlds, and only received if Jimmy is underwater, cut off from air and sunlight, blindly making his way deeper and deeper toward the sunken realms where big cats and largemouth bass lay hidden in sinkholes under fallen submerged tree trunks. When Jimmy returned and opened his hand, the rock would be a sign.

Sammy began the ritual by giving a sermon on deep-diving techniques. "You have to blow all your air out," he said, "and make your ears pop." Then, plugging his nose like a sailor jumping from the heights of a sinking battleship, he leaped, penetrating the surface and sending out waves that lightly rocked the raft. Feet first, the wrong way, Josh thought, if you wanna reach bottom. But he didn't say anything. The boys peered down into the light reflecting off the surface of the lake and tensed as they waited for Sammy to come back up. Finally, a hand shot from beneath the water, and Sammy's clenched fist broke through the glassy film, projecting toward the blue sky.

Sammy, pale and shaking from barely having enough air to make it back up, climbed onto the raft and didn't say a word in spite of the others' questions. "Did you reach bottom?" they asked. After he caught his breath, Sammy slowly opened his fist and proclaimed that he had dropped the rock shortly before reaching the surface. This explanation burned in Josh's ears.

"I'm going next," Josh said suddenly. He looked like he had just awakened from a long sleep. The boys looked quizzically at one another, wondering why Josh, who usually responded only at the last minute to their dares, took it upon himself to be one of the first divers. But Josh just had to go now. When Jimmy entered the lake waters, Josh wanted to have his dive over with so he could devote all his concentration to transmitting his message to Jimmy rather than having to worry about whether or not he would be the one to emerge with the rock.

Josh had listened attentively to Sammy's sermon on diving, but he jumped headfirst into the lake, unlike Sammy, then he blew the air from his lungs and pushed as hard as he could with his legs, grabbing desperately at the water, pulling himself down farther. He would finally show them. Maybe he couldn't kick a ball over second base, but he would come back out of the water with that rock, and he pictured shooting above the surface with it in his hand as the boys stared in amazement. He would climb the ladder one-handed, all the while holding the prize above his head like he had just won a new world title. He wouldn't say anything, just set the rock in the center of the raft and step back and smirk like he thought nothing of retrieving rocks from twenty feet below. Leading the contest would allow him to insist that Jimmy go right after him, bringing them even closer to each other's secrets, ready for Josh's messages. Maybe he and Jimmy would be the only ones to make it from the lake's depths with something to show for themselves, and they'd be united as winners. His lungs burned for air as he pushed deeper and deeper through the murky water, but he kept the image of claiming his victory before his eyes, urging himself on because it was a test, and his messages to Jimmy depended on it.

His hand struck soft mud. He couldn't believe he'd actually made it when even Sammy hadn't been able to reach bottom. He felt around until he clutched a slimy, moss-covered rock. He held it to his chest with one hand, embracing it like a mother holding her child, and he began grabbing at the water with his free hand and kicking his feet.

He broke the surface and gasped, but his hand had struck something solid just above his head, and he heard the thump resound like the inside of a kettle drum. He pulled in mouthfuls of air, but they smelled of dank mold. When he opened his eyes, he saw darkness, and he felt confusion, like having awakened in the middle of the night not knowing where he was. He wanted to call out, but he knew that would make him look chicken and spoil the effect of having retrieved the stone. He began to hyperventilate and panic, and the thought of winning the contest left him, replaced with the fear of surfacing in this unexpected world, breathing in darkness. He heard the voices of the boys above, and, finally, it dawned on him. He had come up under the raft. The others were sitting one foot above him and didn't even know it. They must have been busy chattering and not heard his hand strike the raft's bottom. He felt his way to the edge, ready to duck under and surface on the other side to show the boys his rock and claim his rights as winner.

Then he stopped. A single thought flashed through his mind and seemed to come from somewhere outside himself. "What if I just stay here? For like five minutes? Then when I come up, with the rock in my hand, I'll have proven I can stay underwater longer than anyone, beyond anything Sammy can explain. I won't tell them how I did it. And when I send Jimmy under, he'll be ready to believe my powers."

During those fishing trips with my grandfather at Lake Eufaula, I learned to row our old aluminum boat a little ways offshore and drop the cement coffee-can anchor while he got the poles ready. He was rigging up a pole he'd given my father for his birthday, but my father wasn't much to fish. "Don't tell Dad I never use this," my father had cautioned me when I left the house with the pole to go over to Grandpa's that morning. Grandpa would set things up in the boat before we got started. This arrangement seemed to work best since he easily became grouchy when he had to tell me which lures to try, how to work them in the water, and what to put on my line when I wasn't having any luck. The third time out he had snapped at me, "How many times I gotta tell you don't tie on a leader to that plastic worm." He spoke a kind of broken English I'd heard many of the old people use around there, especially on the days he complied with my grandma's prodding to go to the Indian Baptist church. At Grandma's church the deacon seated you in some kind of hierarchy I didn't quite understand, but it had to do with length of membership since the oldest people were in the front. The deacon would point his cane to the proper pew, directing men to one side, women to the other. The sermon was in Creek, little of which I understood, and afterward, when Grandma's friends came up to visit, they would speak English since I was from the younger generation. But I took it that Grandpa cared a good deal more for fishing than churchgoing.

After we got settled on the plank benches on our respective sides of the boat, he handed me my pole rigged with a bobber and minnow. He had given up teaching me how to jig the bass lure through the water and had given me over as a useless case, destined to use live bait forever. Which is the way most Indian guys fished anyway, my grandpa always complained, one hand on the pole, the other on the Budweiser. My grandpa, for some reason, had mastered all the nuances of bass fishing rather than just slinging a bobber with stink bait underneath it out into the lake. So I sat, elbow on knee, chin in hand, watching the red-and-white sphere appear and reappear in the waves of shimmering water, imagining it as a boat approaching a distant shore and I had stood years on the beach awaiting the return of someone on board. One day I had brought a book to read while I waited for a fish to strike, but Grandpa had glared at me with such disdain that I had timidly put it back in my lunch sack. I didn't say anything, but I pouted all morning. I was rereading all of C. S. Lewis's *Narnia* books and was completely taken with the notion of a wardrobe that was a closet on one side and a world of talking animals on the other, and the boy who could go get his brothers and sisters and bring them back with him, if only they'd believe.

Grandpa could cast his lure, send it singing in an arcing loop out across the lake, land it with a soft *ker-plop* over by a stump where he said the bass were, and reel it in, working it at the same speed with a gentle tugging motion that made it snake through the water. But what was really beyond belief was his ability to talk during these adroit maneuvers. When he spoke, all his words led up to a story; all conversation was a prelude. So I wasn't surprised when he said to me, "Hey, how 'bout it, this lake pretty big mess of water, ain't it?"

It was huge; even had we owned a motorboat, it would have taken hours, I imagined, or days, to boat all the way around it. "I used to farm right over yonder," he said, nodding toward the middle of the lake. "Before the dam went in. Built it in '63, I think it was. Started gathering water in '64. Now, water's all over. Little cotton, little corn, I growed some of everything, few hogs, too. Yep, had a house, right over thataway. Your daddy was borned there. Now you can't get nowhere around here on the same roads you used to. All covered up."

I was fascinated by the thought of underwater farms, barns, houses, pastures, and I could see kitchens with families of bass and crappie darting in and out the windows and under the legs of dining room tables.

"There is something white man has never saw or caught," he went on, "something in the water. Their head is shape like a deer. If you are by water it has a power and will pull you in. It don't pull just anyone in water, just certain people. If you ever see a whirling water in the river you better get out of there. It makes a sound like a big snake then rises up on a sheet of water. If you ever see the strange monster, someone dies. White man never did catch this tie-snake. They have horns like a deer and all kinds of color, kinda greenish and red. Long time ago, they old Indian medicine doctor use to make them things come out and catch them. When they catch them, they use to cut the ends off their horns and hunt with them. They would throw something doctored with Indian medicine, throw it in four times in the whirling water, and make tie-snake come out. One time my daddy said he went fishing and he kinda got a funny feeling by the river, like scared, and pretty soon he heard a growling sound in water and after a while it started bubbling so he got out of there fast. I heard he told about it. It was near Gaines Creek south of here."

Grandpa reeled his line in and tied on a new spinner. I had been dangling my arm over the side of the boat. I pulled it back in. Grandpa started back up. "One man name Curtis Goolman, kin of yours, he told me one time ...."

"I bet he's got the rock in his hand right now," laughed Jimmy. Sammy threw in, "Naw, he's probably got something else in his hand." All the boys laughed. Thirty more seconds passed, and a smothering silence fell over them. The boys began to take deep drags on their cigarettes and looked down at their bare toes. They coughed nervously and listened to the water slapping the sides of the raft. Sammy tried to kill time by blowing smoke rings, but the wind swept them out over the water.

Finally, Lenny spoke. "What do y'all s'pose happened to him?"

"I think we ought to swim to shore," Sammy said coolly.

"We don't know for sure if he drowned. We can't just leave him here," said Jimmy. "We gotta at least stay until we know what happened."

"What are we gonna tell everybody when we get home?" said Sammy. "We better get our stories straight or his folks are liable to blame us. It ain't our fault the dickhead can't swim." The other boys looked over at Sammy and saw that they were supposed to laugh again.

Jimmy said, "I'm staying here for a spell. Not that I'm afraid of getting in trouble or anything. I just wanna see if maybe he comes back up." Lenny sided with Jimmy and decided to stay on the raft. Sammy said, "Well, while y'all are sitting here getting cold in the wind, I'll be stretched out in the sun on the bank." Sammy slid into the water, and swam for shore.

Baa-rump. Baa-rump. Baa-rump. Under the raft, Josh heard the buoy bumping against it up above, steady as a heartbeat, and thought that he had better come back up before he stretched his miraculous powers too thin and the boys went home, leaving him for drowned. Then he wouldn't get to test his secret messages to Jimmy.

Josh dived and ducked under the raft. Just before he broke the surface, he felt a sudden tug on his leg. A clump of fishing line had wrapped around his ankle, and when he swam up he had pulled all the slack out, binding the entangled mesh tightly. He felt with his hands, unable to see in the murky water. The other end of the line was twisted around the cable that anchored the raft to the bottom. He dropped the rock. Had it been a single strand of line, he could have broken it easily since fishermen used light test weights for the bass and crappie in the lake. But with the whole clump wound around itself, the strength of the line was greatly magnified. Each tug dug into the flesh of his ankle with a sharp little searing that he couldn't exactly call pain. He almost wanted to laugh, then, panic-stricken, he placed both feet against the cable and pulled with his hands.

Josh strained and jerked. "Oh God! No. Please. Let me get loose. I won't try another trick like this," he thought, as he pulled at the line. He started to cry out in terror and swallowed some water. He began to choke and cough, fighting to keep holding his breath. He cut his palms on the thin strands, and, in desperation, he felt around, sightless in the murky water, to locate the individual strands. He began breaking them one by one. He had torn apart five or six of them when something brushed past his chest. Josh felt his arms flailing in the water around him. He opened his eyes and saw the underwater city where he was tethered to the spokes of somebody's wagon wheel parked on the street in front of a building. A large channel catfish with a Fu Manchu mustache was swimming in place just between the top porch rail and the roof of the building, making underwater burbling noises that sounded like garbled words. The fish darted inside the front window, and Josh watched him enter. A painted sign above the door stoop read:

GRAYSON BROS

DEALERS

IN

GENERAL MERCHANDISE

Josh could hear the catfish inside the store singing a jingle about seed, harnesses, farm machinery, groceries, "not to mention," he sang, "traveler's supplies, prints, hosiery, boots, shoes, hats, caps, and all the etceteras requisite to a first-class Western business house."

Josh looked down at his leg. A balled-up coil of snakes had wrapped themselves around him, from ankle to knee, and they moved in and out of each other, swaying in the lake bottom current and weaving between the wagon spokes. Just when they felt like they had loosened their grip on him, he'd pull and they'd tighten back up. He had gone off to the underwater world, but he couldn't get back to his . . . *the bathtub water drains slowly down and I feel my body grow heavier Lucy scrubs my back the warm water goes galump galump galump down the drain as she blows the smoke in my ear in the beginning we were covered we were covered we were covered don't go near swirling water they got horns that make powerful medicine the bubbles this is a trade I'm trading my air for water air for water water for air it's not fair that rhymes water is heavier than air but they are both free we were covered by a mighty fog in her lap kicking that ball clean over third base out over the chain-link fence off over the housetops and Jimmy cheering while I run those bases at a slow dogtrot and he makes hook shots from center court those slimy bastards will wish they would have picked me first look at the bubbles it's not a fair trade air for water breathing smoke into me covered by a mighty fog and hold on to each other so they don't get lost I'll hold on to Jimmy and maybe he'll wanna hold on to me too if he gets my message.*

On top of the raft, Jimmy shouted, "Oh my God. Look at all the bubbles coming up!" He jumped to his feet and pointed toward the water. He leaned over the raft and noticed the tugging was coming from beneath, not from the waves. "It looks like he's just below the surface." Jimmy dove headfirst toward the troubled water. Josh saw a snake, with horns, swimming toward him. Jimmy bumped into Josh after having just barely broken water. The giant snake was trying to wrap itself around Josh, and he was too weak to stop it. Jimmy placed both arms around Josh's chest and tried to swim back up, but he couldn't budge him. He followed the length of Josh's body with his hands, feeling everywhere until finally reaching the entangled mesh of line around Josh's ankle. Jimmy popped above the waves and pulled himself back on the raft, shakily grabbing a pocketknife they kept stuck in the wood planks for fishing. Jimmy dove back below, grabbing handfuls of knotted line, and he kept sawing through whole bunches of the mesh. Finally he felt Josh drifting away as he sawed through the last of it. He grabbed him again below the arms and swam toward the raft.

Josh was awkward and heavy, and his legs and arms flopped limply while Jimmy pushed him against the ladder, keeping him in place by standing on the bottom rung and holding him with one arm and pressing against him with his body. Lenny grabbed Josh's arms while Jimmy shoved from behind. They pulled him onto the middle of the raft, where Josh lay pale and motionless. Jimmy kneeled over him. He hoped Lenny wouldn't notice his hands shaking. He tried to control his voice, but he got dizzy and thought for a moment he might pass out. "You know how to do that mouth-to-mouth thing they taught us at school?"

"I ain't kissing no guy," Lenny said. "Let's just swim back and get help."

"He'll die, you fucking idiot," Jimmy said. "You're going to help me right now!" He grabbed Lenny by the shoulders and slammed him down by Josh's side. "Just help me keep his head tilted back," he said. Jimmy leaned over Josh, plugged his nose, and boosted his head up, then began breathing into him. Lenny stared in horror at Josh's strange, pallid hue. "What are we gonna do?" he whimpered. "I wish we had never swam out here. Oh, God, I hope this works."

Josh coughed, and his body began to twitch. He threw up all over himself, and he rolled over on his side and started spitting out mouthfuls of water. Jimmy and Lenny threw lake water on him to rinse him off. Josh just lay there and sucked in big gulps of air. The two boys stared down at him. The color started to come back to his flesh, his skin returning to brown. "Do you reckon he can talk? I never seen anyone drown before," Lenny said.

"I don't know," Jimmy said. "Josh. Say something."

"I had it. Dropped it. Really, I had it in my hand," he sputtered.

"Sure you did, buddy. You almost drowned. We thought you were a goner. Josh, can you swim back? Um, I mean me and Lenny could help you if you need us to," Jimmy said. Josh tried to stand, but his legs crumpled underneath him, and he sagged back down to the floor of the raft.

Lenny helped Josh stand up. He placed one arm around his side and slowly pulled him to his feet. Lenny draped Josh's arm over his shoulder and helped him stand while Jimmy climbed down the ladder and stood on the bottom rung in the water. They helped Josh over the side. Jimmy wrapped his arm around Josh and said, "We'll take turns swimming him to shore." Jimmy started out, holding Josh with one arm while swimming on his side. Josh felt strange, his arm draped around Jimmy's cold, wet neck, Jimmy's legs accidentally kicking him as he tried to convey Josh toward shore, their bodies shivering together in the cold water. Jimmy and Lenny kept trading off until they reached shore and climbed out on land.

My back was sore from sitting on the wooden plank, and I was getting bored and hot. After popping open a Coke, I reeled in, watching my bobber skip across the lake, planning to check my minnow, but my line was crossed over Grandpa's, and, when I pulled up my hook, I had his line in my hand, too. He glared at me and said, "Watch where you're casting that thing." The way he said "that thing" made it sound more like I had a gaffing hook and I was such a fishing disaster that I might jerk his head off his shoulders with my next cast.

"Anyway," he grunted, "your Uncle Curtis he told me all about that tie-snake. Me and your Uncle Glen, Lucy's husband, and Curtis was always drive over to Muskogee together and go bowling. Glen wore a floppy fishing hat all the time, even at the bowling alley. Now, there's a man could work a lure like nobody's business. Me and him hit every spot of water around here. Couldn't hardly bowl to save his life, though. Curtis always give him a bad time about his bowling. If Glen wasn't with us at the bowling alley, Curtis says you might as well just tell stories because they's no one to laugh at. Long time ago, Curtis says, two men out somewheres hunting together. Camping and hunting, out in the woods. So it gets time to go off to sleep, and the two lay down on opposite sides of the fire and after a while the one of them is sleeping hard but see that other old boy gets hungry, him, and he thinks how much he likes fish real good and how fish fry sound tasty 'bout now. Just then he notices water dripping from the top of the tree a-splashing down on the ground, just falling *ker-plunk* in a puddle from those stripped branches 'cause it's wintertime, no leaves. He waked up his friend who wasn't any too happy about leaving his snooze and says, 'Hey you ain't gonna b'lieve this nohow. Look yonder,' and his friend rubs his eyes. The man who like fish real good says, 'I go up and see what's causing all that commotion.' Up in the top of that tree he found some water and fishes swimming in it up there splashing every whichaways from dashing around.

"That ole boy get a big grin and says, 'How 'bout it, that's what I been wanting,' and throwed him down some of them catfishes to his buddy. Then he climbed down the tree and cleaned them up and getting ready to dip them in flour and cornmeal and fry them fishes when his friend says, 'There may be something bad wrong 'bout fish found way up in a tree thataway.' That old boy too hungry to worry, and he eats them fish all up so good even clean his teeth with the bones afterwards. His friend won't touch a one of them. So now he's full sure enough but not feeling so hot no mores thinking maybe he kinda overeat too much and he stretched out and said his bones ached little bit. His buddy says, 'Well, I told you they might be no good,' and they both finally go to sleeping on their sides of the fire.

"So this here one who ate the fish woke up in the middle of the night and couldn't b'lieve his eyes and shook his friend real hard and hollering, 'Look here what's the matter with me?' His friend looked and jumped back now seeings how his buddy's legs glued together. 'Well, I told you 'bout that fish. I don't reckon there's nothing we can do,' and he went back off to sleep, that other one. 'Bout the middle of the night he wakes him back up and now his body head down is tail of a snake. Come daybreak, he wakes up his friend one more time and saying to him, 'Look at me now,' and he's completely a snake then, laying there in a big coil.

"So the snake says—he could still talk—'Friend, you gonna have to leave me, but first could you take me over to the water hole?' The snake slithered off into the hole when his friend turned him loose on the bank and that hole commenced to cave in on itself and getting bigger and the water to whirlpool around right fast in the middle. Snake raise up his head out of that rush of water and says, 'Tell my parents and sisters come down here an' visit me.' So his friend brought back to the spot same place all them ones who is kin. They stood on the bank, and the snake showed himself in the middle of the pond. He come up there and crawled out, crawling over the laps of his parents and sisters where they sat on a log next to the bank, him shedding tears while he crawled. He couldn't talk no mores, so he wasn't able to tell them his story. Then he slid in the water, and they went back home."

I had sat down in the gunwale of the boat to rest my back against the bench, keeping one eye on my bobber, the other on Grandpa as he told his story. I had half a dozen questions, and often his stories ended like that, with no explanations. "How could water be in the top of a tree?" I asked him, "and how did the fish get there in the first place? What happened to the snake afterwards?"

Grandpa said, "Hush up, gotta little bite," and readied himself for the next strike. As I wondered if this was the real thing or an avoidance of my pesky curiosity, he jerked his pole back, and it bent over in a wide half-arc while he started steadily working the fish toward the boat.

When they climbed up on the bank, Sammy stood on top, laughing. He had watched the whole thing from shore. "I see the rat didn't drown after all. Hey, Jimmy, I didn't know you liked teaching little girls to swim. Yeah, I seen you lean over and kiss him on the raft. What's the matter, Jimmy? Ashamed of your new girlfriend?"

On solid ground, Jimmy suddenly realized the way he was standing with one arm around Josh's waist, helping him to remain on his feet. He looked down at his arm with revulsion and let go; Josh sagged to his hands and knees in the grass. Jimmy started talking fast. "I just thought I'd dive down and check. I mean he probably can't even swim, what the fuck? I couldn't just let him die." Jimmy spit out his words. "Do you think I liked watching him puke all over himself? I just didn't want to get in trouble. What do you think his folks would say if we left him there? Good thing I dived down when I did." Jimmy kept talking faster, all the while explaining, getting hoarser, looking into Sammy's eyes for some reassurance.

Josh quivered and pulled himself to his feet. His eyes burned from way back, and he snarled, "I didn't need your goddamn help. I almost had that line unwrapped myself. Anyway, I could of stayed down there another couple minutes. I knew how to swim before you were crawling around on the kitchen floor. I could have if I wanted to, goddammit. I was just about to get it untied when you messed me up and I ...."

Josh began to weep as the words drifted away from him like smoke. The other boys turned away disgustedly and walked up the bank toward the road, Jimmy the last one to leave. Josh heard their voices, laughing, like the small rasps of a steel file against wood. As they moved up the grassy hill, playing and shoving each other back down, Josh felt himself float out over his own body. He could see his skinny brown frame; it looked no more than an outline, a wisp of smoke that could easily blow away out over the lake. The boys, joking from the hillside, sounded like their voices came from deep within the belly of a cave where words dripped down red-streaked walls and echoed through caverns full of meanings he could not grasp. Confusion washed over him.

He watched Sammy and Lenny walking down the road that led home. Jimmy paused for an instant and turned back toward the lake. He approached slowly, and he stood off from Josh, looking down at him from the top of the bank. He waited until Sammy and Lenny were out of earshot. He stared at his feet as he spoke. "You know the guys. They're just playing around." Josh did not reply. The waves patted the shore in rhythmic claps. "Well, you know how it is around them, don't you?" Jimmy coughed and lit a cigarette. He waited for Josh to say something. He looked out toward the raft. "I didn't really

mean it. I just didn't want them to think, well, you know how they
tease you if they think you like someone too much."

Josh couldn't find the right words for his rage. He felt all the words
flaming up before his eyes and burning away like stubble before he
could use them. In church he had heard Jesus' words to the centurion:
Speak the Word and you shall be healed. He no longer believed. He
wished he could pick up words like stones, rub them to make them
smooth and polished, and put them in his pocket to save and use during moments like this one. He longed for the comfort of those stones.
He wished he had collected all kinds of them—agate streaked with
red lightning, hard quartz pounded into indissoluble rage, blood-red
hematite formed around secrets, yellow amaranth rained down by
tears. He would put all the rocks in his mouth and find his voice in
their swirled streaks of sky, fire, water. But there were no such rocks
and none of them contained secret messages and there was nobody to
send them to even if they had.

Jimmy snuffed out his cigarette on a broken willow trunk, flicking
the stub into the grass. "Well, I guess I'll be seeing you around," he
said. He turned and walked off toward the road.

"Yeah, I guess," Josh said.

Lord of the losers that summer, I lived inside my imagination and
often felt myself floating away, as others talked, into my private world
of dreams. But not when Grandpa launched into his stories, which
demanded some kind of listening akin to physical participation, and he
cast his voice in such a way that drew you into the presences his words
created. Bored on the boat with no place to go, bored with staring at
my bobber ride up one hill of waves and down the slippery slope of
another, bored with trying to will a fish into hunger for my minnow or
dangling night crawler, Grandpa's stories were a welcome, if strange,
respite. And if I wasn't fishing with him, my grandma would send me
over to my cousins to "play with boys your own age instead of being
locked up in that room with those books of yours."

Grandpa strung his bass on the stringer, running the clasp through
its mouth and gill slit and closing it, then tossing the chain in the

water, the only catch of the day. Maybe that very fish had been violently jerked out of its underwater home, from the barn or farmhouse my grandparents used to live in before the lake covered up their former residence. He settled back into the bench, and I saw his eyelids flutter and his head start to nod off. I couldn't believe it; even he was bored with fishing. Afraid that he might fall over, I said, loud enough to rouse him, yet tentatively, knowing how much a pain in the ass I was on fishing trips, "Hey, wake up."

"Ain't asleep," he muttered, and when he surfaced from his nap, he came up in the middle of another story as if he'd never stopped talking. He tied a bass plug onto his line while he spoke.

"A *micco* one time he send his son out with a message for another chief. Sent him out with that message in a clay pot so the chief would recognize him. His son stopped to play with some boys—he was carrying that clay pot you know—who were throwing stones into the water. Pitching and throwing. Making them rocks skip. Chief's son wanting to show off a little bit maybe he can do it better than all them other ones, so he throwed that vessel on the water, but it sank. Like this here."

Grandpa laid down his pole for a second and tossed an imaginary pot in an easy underhanded curve out into the lake. "That boy 'fraid to go to the neighbor chief without his father's message, more fraid to go back home and tell his father he lost him his pot. He jumped into that stream and got to the place where it sunk and dove down under there. His playmates waited a long time round that creek for him to come back up but never did. They went back home and told everyone he died.

"Underneath that murky water tie-snake grabbed a-holt of him and drug him off to a cave where he lived. Inside, tie-snake says, 'See that platform over yonder? Get up on there, you.' Up on the platform was the king of the tie-snakes." Grandpa dropped his voice and sounded commanding when he imitated the tie-snake ordering the chief's son.

"The boy didn't like too good what he saw; that platform was a heap of crawling snakes. Oh, they was just crawling around. Slithering around. Sliding around. Weaving in and out of each other. And that king sitting big up on a ledge right over there on that platform.

"Well, this boy walked up there anyway trying to not let on how scared he was. Plumb frightened. He lifted his foot to get up on the platform, but, as he did, it just rose up higher. He tried again, same thing. And a third time. That tie-snake said again, 'Get up yonder, boy,' and on the fourth try he got up there. King invited him come sit down on that ledge next to him. 'Better than them wiggling snakes all round my feet,' the boy thinks. King says, 'Over yonder is a feather; it's yours,' pointing to a cluster of red tail feathers from a hawk. That boy went over and reached out and every time his fingers went to grabbing those feathers they disappeared. But on the fourth try he got it and held to it.

"He goes back over to tie-snake who says, 'That knife over yonder is yours.' Same thing again. It rose up on its own every time the chief's son raise up his hand. On the fourth time it didn't go nowheres, and he laid holt of it. The king said the boy could go back home after four days. King says, 'If your father asks where you been gone, say, I know what I know, but no matter what don't tell him what you know. When your father needs my help, walk toward the east and bow four times to the rising sun, and I will be there to help him.'

"Tie-snake took the boy back after four days, up to the surface where he first dived under and put the lost vessel back in his hands. The boy swam to the bank and went home to his father who was right happy to see him seeings how he thought he was dead.

"Boy told his father about tie-snake king and his offer to help, but he didn't tell his father what he knew. His father heard about enemies planning an attack, and he sent his boy off to get help. The chief's son put the feathered plume on his head, grabbed up his knife, headed towards the east. He bowed four times before the sunrise, and there stood tie-snake king in front of him.

"'What do you need?' he asked.

"'My father needs your help,' the boy answered.

"'Don't worry none,' tie-snake told him. 'They will attack but nobody get hurt. Go back and tell him I'll make it all right.'

"The boy went back and delivered the message. The enemy came and attacked the town but no one got hurt. It came nighttime, and there were their enemies on the edge of the village all caught up in a tangled mess of snakes."

Grandpa was pulling up the coffee-can cement anchor since it was starting to get dark out. Crickets were chirruping on shore, and fire-flies flitted here and there over the water. I burned to know the boy's secret, what he withheld from his father, what lay buried beneath the shadowy water, but already Grandpa was set on rowing, rowing toward shore.

THREE

Whippoorwill's a Widow

LUCILLE SELF, WELEETKA, OKLAHOMA, 1911

Well, what if I did see something when I woke up after hitting my head on one of the beams in the pole barn? I don't rightly know if what I told Daddy was lying, but I didn't turn them loose. I might walk around a little at night in my sleep, but I didn't wander out to that pen. Anyway, I might have told him the truth if he wouldn't a-yelled at me so early in the morning. The hardest part of recollecting is that I was to tell it before I was to grasp all its meanings. So much come on me all at onced that each memory I spark touches another one off until it's all part of the same blaze.

"Lucille, wake up!" he had said, standing over my bed that morning, shaking me until I rattled.

"Daddy," I answered, acting like I just come out of a deep sleep, "I told you. I didn't turn those pups loose." He hit me hard across the mouth and then turned so red I thought he'd catch a-fire.

Now, I ain't exactly saying that I might or might not know who unlatched that gate, pulled apart the hogwire, and shooed those cubs out. Fact is, I ain't saying.

"Where's my snuff can?" Daddy screamed before breakfast that same morning as he grabbed one of the mule harnesses hanging off the post on the front porch. He threw it in the door at Mama and said, "Rachel, have that boy Dave hitch up the one-eyed mule." Mama only said *"Ihey,"* bent back over the cornbread, and turned it over quickly, so the yellow cake slid out steaming from the iron skillet. I looked out into the yard where I seen Dave bent over the pump, working the handle. Dave paid Daddy no mind, as if he didn't hear him bellowing in the kitchen, but I believe he done that just to get under Daddy's hide. Because he was smiling as he drew water, and I don't believe that was on account of joy over watering hogs. I have a mind for such details.

Like at dawn, just before daylight, is when I take a lot in. I sit on the porch, and I hear them in the dark. They make those little flapping explosions of air, flitting away on rounded wings like the puff of a large brown moth. They break the silence as they light out from the ground beneath the stand of oaks next to the field where Daddy plowed. The whippoorwills. Listen to them close and you'll hear it, too. They say "whippoorwill's a widow, whippoorwill's a widow." Now, don't go asking me how those poor whippoorwills could all be widows, but that's what they say before daybreak.

"Lucy, stop daydreaming and get in here and hep with breakfast," Mama said. I hopped up, got inside, and washed the dirt off the potatoes and sliced them; I watched them plop, hissing, into the lard. I set them on the table next to the pitcher of buttermilk and said *hombaks jay* to get everybody gathered up to eat. I heard all my little brothers, the whole den, come into motion, and they commenced to wiggling out of their beds, slithering into their overalls, their bare feet thumping the floor.

But that's not what I was fixing to tell you. All this trouble started when I had the dream, just a few hours before daylight when Daddy woke me up, stood over my bed, and carried on, shaking all the stuffing out of me. I have the same one over and over. At night I dream the devil's shadow. Satan is sitting on top of me, a-straddling my chest, burning me into a deep sleep, a heavy weight that presses down. He wants to slip inside me. I fight him with everything I have. I claw at his eyes, bite his cold white arm, kick him in that one place, but he has me pinned. He smells of coal oil and smoke. I try to find the flames, and I look up and see a kerosene can in his hand with fire licking the top and spilling down the sides. I hack and cough for want of air; I rub my eyes from all the smoke. I notice his eyes. Look white and blank, like he's got a lot of nothing in his head. I almost think I recognize him, someone real familiar, but I can't quite say who. It's a face I've seen before, almost within reach, a passing blur, blank and without form. None of my fighting does any good, and I know, in order to get him off me, I have to say the right words, throw off the dream, come wide awake with the fluttering of my eyelids. I quote all the scriptures they learned me over at the Sunday school Daddy made me go to at Willow Creek, that is until their white people come over of a Sunday afternoon and said we needed to stick with our own church and our own kind and go to the Indian Baptist. We just was to quit, though, no Indian Baptist or Indian Methodist 'cause Daddy waddn't about to go to Indian church.

At night I start in a-working on that devil in my dreams: For God so loved the world, then I hit him with the wages of sin is death, and get in a little for all have sinned and come short of the glory of God and keep shouting them verses, I mean just a-getting it, until I finally dry up my supply of Bible. I wake up in a sweat and hollering, but that particular evening I woke up unable to scream, and when I come out of it, I was plumb over to the pole barn!

Well, what could I do but make my way back into the cabin and try to get what little sleep I could before sunup when Daddy would wake me for my chores?

That's when I saw Dave crouched in the dark by the wolf pen. Daddy was guardian for a little Creek Indian boy who come into a bunch of oil money the year after statehood. An orphan who lived with his grandma until Daddy petitioned the court. You know, like Daddy said, them full-bloods ain't got enough sense to take care of their money when they get a heap of it, so they need white people to watch over them. Daddy didn't like him much 'cause when Dave and Mama talked that Creek, he didn't understand all of it. Sometimes

Daddy said he never woulda married an Indian woman if he'd a-known she'd be whispering secrets all the time. One time he said to me, "Lucille, what does that boy tell you about being over at his grandmother's? What are they messing with over there?" I just told him, "Aw, he just goes to hep that old woman chop wood. She's too old to do it herself." Letting on like I didn't know much. He said, "Lucille, don't turn your back on that boy 'cause you can't trust him. You know him and that old woman are Wolf Clan. Way out there away from everybody, don't even come out of that hole in the woods of theirs to go to church. We try to help him when all the time I reckon he's over by the spring with that old woman, where no one can see them, making medicine against me."

'Course, I may have forgotten now and then to tell Daddy one or two things I overheard Dave and Mama saying. Like this one time I heard Dave telling her about a couple of men he seen over at the stomp dance. These two men live together way back in the sand hills, away from everybody, without any women. Dave said, "Mizzus Self," on account of Daddy made him talk to Mama like that—"Mizzus Self," he says, "my Uncle Tarbie comes down to the stomp dances, and he's always with the same man. The young boys giggle when they see them two in camp, but the old ones always frown and tell them to show respect."

Mama just said, "Dave, those two are good men. Them old folks is right."

Now, Mama is always going on like that—talking careful. When Daddy kills squirrels, Mama cleans them. She waits until he ain't around and takes some of the hair from the right feet of them squirrels and buries it out yonder in the front yard beneath the catalpa tree, saying a little prayer to them, explaining that we are sorry for having to kill them, and we mean no disrespect. Just that we need them for our family to eat. Do you ever wonder if squirrels can understand how much folks like squirrels and dumplings? Maybe not enough to make up for being shot. Seems more fair for us than for them. That's the kind of thoughts that sometimes burns my mind.

Now, like I was fixing to tell you, at the store where we trade in Weleetka, where we go of a Saturday, where the menfolk gather, where they chew and whittle, where they stand around and swap their

stories, Daddy throws in right there with them. He knows about them
men Dave was asking Mama about because he's heard the white men
at the store whispering and talking about them. Sometimes Daddy
grabs up Mama's broom and pretends to be those fellers doing
women's work around the house. When he takes to prancing about
and making fun of them like that, Mama gets real scared and says,
"Ihi, show some respect. You don't know what you're doing."

Like this one time Daddy had an old mule named Sally, and she
was pretty near worn out. She'd get in the harness and lollygag right
in the middle of the field. Come noon, Dave used to wait for Daddy
with a bucketful of cool well water on the edge of the cotton patch in
one of the end rows, just like Daddy told him to except for one thing.
Dave would just stand at the end of the row; he waddn't about to
bring the bucket to Daddy out in the field, and he had that water-
pumping grin on his face, making Daddy wait like that. Well, Daddy
could see he was just about to get to the end of the row and get his
dipper of that sweet, cold water when the old mule Sally lay clean
down in the middle of the furrow. Daddy was already mad considering
Dave didn't come all the way down the cotton row with his drink, and
Daddy threw a terrible fit kicking that mule and hitting her with the
reins, just whupping the tar out of her. He shouted himself hoarse,
"You old whorish Jezebel, get yourself up." He called her an old nag
and just about anything mean you could say that had to do with a
woman, all of what no woman is allowed to say. Finally, he lifted up
the end of that old moldboard plow and dropped it on her haunches.
Sally just layed there a-bellering and all the time Dave hollering in
Creek for Daddy to leave that mule alone.
Daddy stomped off to the shed and come back carrying a can of
kerosene and Dave grabbed a-holt fast of Daddy and screamed *"Manks,
manks,"* and Daddy drug him behind in tow and dumped that kerosene
all over Sally, and Dave run off into the woods crazy-like and crying
and Daddy lit that poor old mule on fire and I never heard the like
what with Dave running through those sand hills near the river howling
and Sally bellering and the smell of burning hair and flesh my God.

Later that evening, Dave come out of the woods and took to mulling about in the yard over by the well while Mama give Daddy a haircut on the front porch. I was fixing to go out there and try to get Dave inersted in a marble I'd won off my little brother, but Daddy motioned me to come back when I stepped off the porch. I was always trying to get Dave to talk, and Dave was always wanting to get away from me and my natural-borned curiosity, and Daddy didn't like me around him none either. Dave used the hair shearing as a chance to disappear behind the barn. My little brothers was all lined up behind Daddy, making faces and pulling on each other's suspenders, fighting over who had to get shorn next. Daddy had just got in from plowing, and Dave had reappeared over by the squirrel and coon hides that was nailed up to the wood shed. He kind of just stood around out there while Mama tried to clip Daddy's hair. Daddy hollered out to him, "Boy, ain't you got no work to do?" Dave didn't say anything; he just held up some harnesses he'd been trying to piece back together without even looking up.

Mama forgot to sweep up the hair clippings. She didn't remember till after supper, and when she went out to the front porch, all the hair was missing. Blowed by the breeze, we reckoned, but Mama sure looked hard for it. No one had seen Dave later that evening, but when we all got bedded down on our pallets, he slipped in and told me he had been to his grandmother's. Daddy don't like Dave leaving any-where off the place where he can't keep at least one eye on his where-abouts, and he come in there and asked Dave where he'd been.

"I been to my grandmother's," Dave said. He didn't lie, and he acted as if he'd never heard Daddy forbid him to leave the farm, like Daddy spoke a different language he waddn't able to understand, even though Dave talked fair to middling English, and Daddy could talk a little Indian. Shy as he was and given to his long bouts of silence, he showed no fear around Daddy.

Did I tell you here I was clean out to the pole barn in the middle of the night half-asleep and still shivering from that dream I'd had? I could barely make out someone in the darkness. It was Dave sticking his hand through the hog panel and petting one of those wolf pups.

Now, I wouldn't a-seen him a-tall, but the moonlight shined on the farmyard that night, and I could see all the way to the edge of the fence where the cow pasture ended and the woods started up. The cows had bedded down along the fence line. I recognized Dave right away 'cause he had on that old pair of overalls Daddy made him wear, and he was hunkered down on his haunches like he always did around that wolf pen. Everybody else just stood against the fence to look at them pups, but Dave got right down there with them.

Daddy got them pups out hunting last winter. Not many wolves left in these parts; we hear of a few that have run deep into the hills and up into the Ouachita Mountains. Even though a bounty's out for the handful of them left, Daddy just enjoyed chasing them; he didn't kill them. Just liked to run his hounds after them. He'd get out there in the woods and lay his head down of a log and listen to them all night long. He could tell who was a-leading and who was a-bringing up the rear. If it's a hot trail or a cold trail, he could tell you. He found him some baby cub wolves, and he brought them home and built a little pen out here where we live at the edge of Weleetka. Daddy loved them wolves more than anything else on the farm, and he spent more time in that pen chasing and playing and working out his meanness than he did in the field.

So, I'm out there that night fixing to step out of the barn and say to Dave, "What are you up to?" and I open my mouth to say it when I go to thinking. Daddy told me that if I didn't stop sleepwalking, he was liable to make me start sleeping down in the storm cellar with the door locked. Maybe it's better if I leave well enough alone and keep quiet, I said to myself. Nobody needed to know I'd been out there.

Of course, now I'm wide awake what with this new development, and I decide to stay put and see what Dave's up to for my own curiosity's sake.

And what do I see but Dave talking to those wolves? I always suspicioned he wasn't quite right, and with the moonlight kinda shining on the pen, and those pups at that awkward, half-growed, gangly-legged age, loping up and down the length of that hogwire growling and snuffling a little at Dave's hand, and him speaking like he's talking

to someone across the table, I start to get a little spooked like maybe I
shouldn't be watching this after all. Dave starts in and lifts his face up,
and suddenly I can see him there in the half-light, his boyish face with
those sad, deep eyes set way back against his near-black skin. I think,
my God, him looking up like that, surely he'll see me, but he didn't.
I can't quite get the words right to tell you how it all sounded with
his voice rising in the moonlight, but it went like this here:

Yaha tecakkeyet
pocha
yaha
omalka atekes
cen-thlo co-pe-ya-thles
esponwikas
matafopke hue-thle tan chey-yachet
ometat pohossatos
ne-thle ha-thle se-homen-cen
haken aka wapas.

Chen-thlo co-pa-thles
momis thla-la-ketskathles
he-ya hote tokon
hatam che-he ca-thles
nethle anthlawan wakayof chen hanken pohayof.

Now, I'm just telling you what I heard in the middle of the night
out there after I woke up from my dream. Something in his words,
some meaning of sorrow within them, saddened me, and I felt like I
shouldn't a-been watching, much less spying. It went something like
him calling them brothers and grandfather and kinfolk the way I
understood it. He said he felt sorry for them. Or, I guess I should say,
he was apologizing for them being all locked up and for everyone forgetting how much they liked to stand on the edge of the woods and lift
their voices in the moonlight. He ended, I reckon, by promising them
that he would see them sometime again. Then Dave turned the wolves
a-loose. He got in amongst them and chased them out of that pen of

Daddy's. The pups were loping around the yard, running up to Dave and crouching before him, sniffing at his overalls, but, at the same time, they kinda looked at him like even they wondered what he was up to. They even loped around the yard for a spell like they wasn't quite sure whether they hadn't oughta stay. Just the opposite of me, because I was always looking to get off the farm, bound off, catch a wagon ride to town with somebody, or get off in the woods. I just knew the wolfs would get in the chicken coop or scare up the cows or come sniffing around me and wake everybody up, and then I'd be in for what's for.

Bounding over to where the fence line walled out the woods, they shot under the bottom strand, then they stood at the edge of the oak trees for a while before trotting off. I watched them disappear into the shadows and felt envious that they was able to run away. Dave snuck back in the house and got up in there where the rest of the boys was all laying around on those pallets sleeping. Morning was coming on; the first of the whippoorwills started to call out like I told you they do before daybreak, so I gave Dave time to fall asleep and snuck back in.

After that morning when Daddy woke me up screaming about those pups a-missing, I kept away from him for a long time. Anytime he come around me after that, I bounded off like a skittish cat. I need to tell you something I ain't let anyone in on yet. Until now, I couldn't speak of it, and I'm still a-studying it. About two weeks after Dave run them pups back into the hills—I remember 'cause a hard freeze had come and Daddy had waited for weeks for the ground to thaw a little so he could get the corn in. He was laid up so sickly that he couldn't get out in the field nohow, nice weather or not. There had come an influenza with the cold weather, and so many of them that lived around us got it. No one took ill at our house but Daddy. I went into his room to change them drenched bedcovers, and there Daddy laid white and pale, looking no more than a little dried-up branch in the middle of those sweaty, yellowed sheets. Sweat dripped off the end of his chin, and he motioned for me to come close. Just kind of rasping out "Lucy" seemed to drain all his energy. He looked too weak to even talk, and he wanted me to change the wet washcloth from his forehead.

I noticed something funny about his eyes—they glowed like coal embers. Out of his head with the fever, I reckoned. So, I started to take off the washcloth, but when my fingers brushed that flaming skin, I jerked my hand back like I had burnt it on the stove. Before I even knowed it, he raised up and grabbed a-holt of my arm with a grip like a snapping turtle. With strength I would a-never expected in his condition, he pulled me up against him. I shuddered at the feel of his clammy flesh and wet shirt and tried to wiggle free from his arms, but he had me pinned. His lips brushed against the back of my neck, and then I felt his hot breath in my ear. At first my mind went blank; the words slipped away from me, the words that would break his grip, get him to turn me loose, to leave me alone. Gritting my teeth and finally throwing off my speechlessness, I sputtered, "Turn loose, you old devil, or I'm a-telling Mama." Then I leaned over and bit him as hard as I could on his shoulder. He bit his lip, until I thought it would bleed, to keep from shouting out, and I dropped the washcloth. Here I run, my legs just a-hooking it out of that house. Mama said, "Oh, Lord. What in the world's got into that girl now? If she ain't walking in her sleep, she's running around like a wildcat." I stood trembling behind the outhouse: crouching, listening, wide-eyed, and rigid. After Mama hollered from the front porch, "Lucy, go off into the woods and look for some *hoyanica,*" I gladly gathered myself up and hurried out toward the trees.

The shadows of dusk coming on and me out looking for willow roots for Daddy's fever. But that was better than back at the house. From the edge of the woods, I could see Mama out in the front yard, bent over the log section, beating her last root with a wooden mallet. I headed down towards the flat place by the creek where the cows go to drink, next to where the woods start up and the fence ends, 'cause I knew about a stand of willows over yonder. We've had a little dry spell, and I had a lot of trouble digging up those roots, but, as I pulled them from the ground and put them in my apron, I got to studying the situation. I thought maybe I could use a little medicine of my own. Dave first give me the idea. Whenever we seen Daddy off out of earshot, Dave and I used to talk. He spoke a little easier that way, when it was just me and him. I says, "Dave, what do you think?" I never let on about what because I was working my way up to it slow.

Dave looked down at his scuffed-up black shoes, a pair of Daddy's old throwaways. I had to bring Dave back from the place where he was always off inside his own mind, daydreaming. It don't pour out of him natural like it does me, stays inside, hidden. His light, hidden under a bushel. "Do you know how a storm cloud can tell you who it is you are to marry?" I asked him. I had no more seen my husband in a storm cloud than a preacher in a jar of moonshine, but I was drawing him out, see.

Dave didn't look up, and he didn't asked for no more of what I meant. I was surprised when he said, "Lucy, I think you have a bad case of *Lokha. Lokha* is spirit animals that lives in a person. It goes out of the person's mouth at night and changes into the form of a chicken. Shifts back and forth between a chicken and a person. It practices witchcraft and steals and eats people's hearts. You can tell if a person has a *Lokha* by the way they breathe 'cause the *Lokha* sounds just like a chicken clucking. You know when the *Lokha* are around and trying to get inside people because you'll see a chicken go out into the hot sun, stretch its wings out, and lie down. Them *Lokha* is having a fever when they do that. That's a real bad sign when them chickens have a fever spell like that."

Dave was working at twisting off a plug of Day's Work all the time he studied the ground and talked to me. He made it into a lot bigger job than it was, just to give himself something to look at where he could put all his shyness into that tobacco twist. I knew how to listen without acting too inersted and scaring him off, but this time he'd scared me some plenty. Was he mad at me for all my pestering, trying to put the fright into me?

Dave up and decided that *Lokha* was most likely the problem and said I could take care of their bad medicine by burning some cedar leaves and cudfoot on the fireplace coals, burning them together on top of the wood stove, burning the mixture and breathing the smoke, burning and breathing to ward them off: "If anyone comes in your room and leaves signs of their presence," he said, "use those herbs. Let the smoke rise and hold your hands above it like you do when you warm them over a fire. Smoke them real good, rub the smoke all over yourself. Then lean over and breathe it in four times, so you get some inside you, too." Now, when he first told me that, I thought, what with those clannish full-blood ways of his and what they told me over to the church before they was to dismember us about Indians making idolatry out of weeds and dumb animals, I just figured not to think too seriously on it. Not to mention all the times Daddy warned me about staying away from Dave. But out there by the willows I got to recollecting on the advantages of having a little medicine of my own and smoking myself and the room where we all slept to keep anything bad from happening. Dave never showed a lick of meanness towards me and Mama, and he seemed to be trying to help me, even though he scared me some at first. I hadn't had too hard a time finding them willow roots, and I knew if I looked hard enough, surely I could scare up a mess of cedar leaves and cudfoot, too.

It ended up not as easy as I suspicioned; like I told you, we had kind of a drought-like, and I found myself getting deeper into them woods and further away from the cabin. I looked behind every rock, tree, and bush for that medicine, but I found none, and it kept getting darker. Now, I ain't afraid of the dark, at least not while I'm awake, but I couldn't see very well to hunt for those plants. I seen both cedar and cudfoot plenty of times 'cause Dave had pointed it out to me on our trips when Mama sent us off to hunt kindling. Who could miss a cedar tree? Dave always taught me things like that, how to use plants and such. He knows the woods; he knows where roots and leaves are to be found—sumac, wild grapes, gum trees—and which plants set things right with the animals. Well, anyway, I'm clean over to the spring by Dave's grandmother's, and I knew with all this dryness that I might have a little better luck over there. Sure enough, I spotted a cedar stand, and I got up amongst them trees, and, Lord, that cedar smell got to kind of calming me and making me feel better because I could smell it on my fingers from the leaves I'd pulled. That might sound a little exaggerated, but I smell things like that out in the woods. I even managed to find some cudfoot growing closer to the spring.

From down by the water where the path started up that led to the
cabin, I heard some voices when I was just fixing to leave. Sounded
like some older men talking in Creek and discussing something
important like at a meeting. I ain't so sure about these stomp-dance
kind of Indians, the ones Daddy always warns me about, ones like
Dave and his grandma, the ones who don't go to church and all. So, I
decided to kind of sneak up there where I could have a look and they
couldn't see me. Next to the path that led up to the house grows some
tall cattail reeds, and I got up in there amongst them and hunkered
down just enough so I could see to where I had heard the voices
coming from. Now I know you must be thinking didn't she get her
feet wet and her shoes muddy? Shoot, I hardly knew what a shoe was.
See, I was barefoot long after others growed up and got their feet in
shoes. Not very lady-like according to some.

Four men were standing around. One was directing the others,
and he kept gesturing, instructing them how to build a fire, pointing
here and there while they picked up things and placed them where he
wanted, telling the others where to set the logs. I recognized him—he
was one of those two men who live together who Dave had asked
Mama about. The man who lives with him was one of them helping
out. I had seen them come into the store together in Weleetka, so I
kinda knew what they looked like. A bundle hung around the man's
neck from a rawhide strap, and in one hand he held a turtle-shell rattle.
He didn't have them build it just any old way; he had them men to
place the logs so each one pointed in a different direction—north,
south, east, and west, like four opposite wagon wheel spokes. I could
only make out a little bit, but I heard him say, "Seborn, leave a little
space in the middle of them logs." It beat anything I ever seen. Dave
and his grandmother sat, kind of watching all the goings-on, outside
the circle, on a felled log behind the fire the men got started up. The
blaze looked kind of puny, but it burned real steady-like.

The one giving directions nodded at Dave, and Dave got up
quickly without saying anything and headed towards the shack like
he knew exactly what the man wanted. Before I hardly even knew he
had left, Dave come back, and I liked to jump up out of them cattails.

Dave had a-holt of something Mama had been hunting for months—
Daddy's razor strap. I strained to hear what these mens was saying to
one another, but I only caught the sound of them all beginning to
chant together at once. Their voices, soft, rhythmic, rose up with the
smoke of the fire. The men directed their words towards the fire as
they stood in a circle around it. The one in charge throwed Daddy's
razor strap into those flames. I heard a *whoosh!* and a suck of air, and
they all leaped back a little as that fire blazed up until I thought it
would catch one of those men a-fire, but it didn't. Those blackjack
logs just a-blazing. Now, I know about blackjack 'cause it burns with a
hot, even flame. Mama always has me hunting it for the stove. Next
thing, Dave's grandma asked the man in charge to excuse her; he
nodded his head in agreement; she headed off for the shack. I watched
her disappear down the path, and I figured she must of got too hot
around the fire. But she emerged back into the light of the circle in less
than a minute. She faced the men and opened her fists, and this time
I did jump and gritted my teeth to keep from screaming. She had
handfuls of blond hair, and I knew it couldn't of come from none of
them around there. Then it hit me. That haircut of Daddy's out on the
front porch. As the three men looked on, Dave's grandma handed the
hair over to the leader. Then she untied her apron and commenced to
pulling out bits and pieces of what-have-you: an old pocket watch that
had stopped working, a piece of busted plow line, fingernail clippings,
and they all belonged to Daddy!

The leader begin to throw the stuff in one at a time; with each
handful he took to shaking that turtle rattle a little faster, and them
small pieces hissed and made black smoke when they hit the flames.
Every time he turned loose of a fistful of them knickknacks, the fire
got higher until the flames leaped so far above them menfolk's heads
that I could see the shadows dancing off the cedar stand where I had
gathered the leaves. I thought, my God, how can those little pieces of
personal belongings make a fire jump like that? Turning, all at the
same time, they faced Dave's grandmother standing, by then, before
the log seat. She nodded, turned around, and lifted from behind the
log something in a tow sack. They started to chant even louder; their

voices rose when she raised off the burlap. One of them whooped.
There stood a crude human doll, made out of clay, about a foot in
height, and they had stuck some of that blond hair on top of its head.

Each of the four men positioned hisself around the fire so that he
stood in one of the four directions facing the logs, seated himself on
the ground facing inward, and the leader sat at the west. From the
edge of the fire, he scooped up a glowing red coal and raised it to the
bowl of a small clay pipe and lit it after having stuffed it with some
tobacco from his pouch. He nodded, and said, "Here, Seborn," passing
it next to the man he always come in the store with. Each man took it
and blew smoke towards his direction—north, south, east, or west.
Dave handed the doll between the men, then went back to his seat,
and they all gazed upon it. The leader announced the purpose of the
ceremony: They had gathered to punish someone whose meanness
had took more than one awful turn. They all nodded in agreement.
I strained to hear their exact words—something about a relative of
theirs being stolen might have been part of it. Seborn heaved the doll
in the middle of them flames. That doll landed perfectly upright and
stood in the center of the blaze in the space between the logs. As the
men stared at the doll, the fire burned brighter and brighter, and the
flames crawled up the side of that little clay man. I smelt burning hair
and watched the blackened blond wisps catch on the wind and light
from the little feller's head, slowly floating up over the cattails. The
clay doll turned a fiery red until I thought he would melt or blow up.
I tried with all my strength not to stare at that doll, but I could feel
him pulling my eyes towards his.

The more I gawked at that fire, the less sure I was of what I saw.
Like I said, my story swirls together. The logs started to look like
barns or outbuildings with flames shooting out the sides. I thought I
could hear voices screaming and hooves pounding and wood crashing
and splitting. That doll in the middle looked like someone in one of
those buildings trying to fight his way out of the flames. The man in
the fire seemed to be moving, yet, at the same time, standing still. The
burning barn glowed in the background. As if to beckon me towards
the flames, its roof, a collection of many swirling orange-red claws,

reached out and clutched and motioned me inside. Everything happening: voices shouting, feet running, embers crackling, the barn beckoning, everyone in a desperate hurry, yet blindly stumbling about, all of it making me wanna see more.

The whole picture, as I stood and gazed, seemed unreal, yet more real than the cattails around me. I could of sworn the little man tried to jump out of the fire, and the men watching looked frightened for a second like maybe they thought he could get out, too. They wanted to back up, but the man giving directions motioned for them to stay put where he had seated them.

I could see so much, so many faces, such great motion, like no other fire I'd seen before, and the picture got bigger as those oak logs cracked and popped. I might as well have been standing in front of it instead of out in the cattails; I felt as though I'd have to back up from the heat. I didn't know how those men could stand it up there so close. In the fire I could see some people trying to help put it out—looked like they had just got there—running back and forth between the well and the barn which had flames a-climbing up the sides of it like wild grape vines creeping up a tree.

I gasped and stood still as a fencepost, watching the fire from out there in the cattails. The flames shot out the roof of the barn and cast a hazy glow that lit up the ground all around, so I could see it framed brightly, like a painting, against the dark woods, and Lord it was beautiful. I remembered Dave saying that his people purified everything by starting a new fire at the beginning of the year in July. They kept the fire sacred and rekindled it before eating the corn harvest. They done that at their Green Corn ceremony. That was a lot to talk about for somebody as young and quiet as him, but that's what I remembered. Someone like that, what little they do say, you tend to take note of.

Daddy never let us go to any Green Corn, but Mama had told me plenty about it. All that church stuff commenced to running through my head like weeping and gnashing of teeth and unquenchable fire where the worm perisheth not, but I felt peaceful-like as I stared into the flames and listened to the cicadas singing off in the trees.

Then I finally laid a-holt of the picture dancing beyond reach in the flames. My mind kinda turned loose of something and let it all come flooding in upon me. That clay man flickering in the fire was Daddy. His white thin frame looked as scraggly as the young peach tree he was leaned up against in the front yard, and, like the tree, he was fixing to fall. Mama had throwed a comforter over his bare shoulders, and she tried to hold him back. Somehow, I heard their voices swirling around in the flames as I stood watching. She begged, "*Ihi,* you're too sickly to go into that fire. Let the neighbors work on it; you can't do anything."

But Daddy's meanness was limitless and so was his strength, so he cursed Mama and threwed her down into the dirt and run into the barn before any of the neighbors knowed what happened. He got in there and started opening them stalls. He grabbed up a driving whip and beat those mules silly to get them to come out, but they just bunched up in the corner and started kicking the sides of that barn until old One-Eye finally kicked a hole clean through the wall and backed up and lunged against it, but he couldn't get through. Mrs. Fixico, our neighbor from the next section over, screamed, "Throw a tow sack over their heads so they can't see." Daddy hollered back, "Damn your hide, woman," and took to beating them mules harder while they threw themselves furiously against the barn wall.

I saw one of the main beams give away and heard it crash as it hit the floor. The near side of the roof sagged and the barn sloped like a little hill. Daddy got in that stall with those plunging mules, and Mr. and Mrs. Fixico had to hold Mama back to keep her from lighting out and dragging him out of there. Daddy laid a-holt of old One-Eye by the halter and had got him dragged out of the stall, but he stood and balked at the barn door with that burning beam laying in front of it. Daddy tried to coax him over and One-Eye kind of bunched and squared himself up like a horse does just before he gets ready to hop a creek. One-Eye cleared the beam easy enough, but he caught his rear hoof and landed off balance and rolled with Daddy underneath him still holding on to his halter. That old mule got back up like nothing ever happened and run out of the barn over to where the cows were mooing and running the length of the fence at the edge of the woods.

When the rest of the mules seen One-Eye take the lead, they all
followed suit and charged out like a battalion of soldiers, all hopping
over Daddy, pretty as you please. Daddy kept flickering and dancing
in and out of the shadows of the fire, and one minute I thought it was
him laying in that barn, and the next I could of sworn I was looking at
that little clay man standing upright in the center of them burning logs.

Suddenly, it got so bright that I felt like it might hurt my eyes to
look anymore, like staring at the sun, but I still couldn't turn away. I
heard something almost like a gunshot, and that little clay man blew
apart into pieces and collapsed in the flames. The blackjack logs
popped loudly; sparks flew and rose up into the night air; a rising
column of burning embers and molten clay floated out over the spring.

I seen about all I could bare to look at, but I couldn't hardly force
myself to leave. The darkness had completely swallowed up those cattails until I could barely make out the grandmother's cabin down the
path in the distance. Keeping in sight the cedar stand for my bearings,
I pushed them reeds back and headed for the trees. The quarter-moon
swung out over the sky like a trotline when the river falls and all the
hooks are bobbing up over the current. I felt a stinging slap when I
run into a tree branch. From back towards the fire floated a little
smoke and some dying embers, but the voices had fallen silent. They
had all gone on, I reckon. The sound of cicadas humming filled the
air, and I walked faster towards home to avoid the strong pull of the
blaze behind me.

I reached the end of the woods where our grass pasture starts up,
held apart the bobwire strands, and pulled myself through the fence.
I stopped. Time was swirling around me like smoke, and I can't quite
tell it—but it was like those pups housed up and the pen they was
jailed in and Dave running them out of there shooing them off
towards the woods and that doll out in the thickest and blackest darkness of the trees and the mens that was attending to this business and
Mama back home who sent me out there in the first place and Dave's
grandmother standing back and watching all this what Daddy would
call devil work and the mule that got set afire like Daddy turning all
his hatred toward any laid-down womanfolk and me running off

while he was burned up with fever—it was all of one piece. The part I couldn't tell Mama was that I was of a right smart mind to just stay out there in the woods while my brain sizzled and sparked. Dazed by the fire, having looked into it so hard, my mind was clean addled. Maybe I'd never get rid of the flames in my head.

The willow roots spilled out of my apron, and I was fixing to pick them up when I heard voices from the farmyard—what sounded to me like neighbors. I knew nobody come to visit us much. Daddy didn't allow none of Mama's people over to the house. I pulled my apron back together and hurried on when I felt something. For a minute there, I thought it had come a little rain. It had started falling before I reached up with my hand and touched my hair, and like a rain, it continued to fall as I pulled back my fingers, covered with black, dusty soot. I thought, well, I didn't notice that back at the fire at the spring. The barn set in a low spot, so I could never see it until I got real close, but I could hear those voices getting louder and the sound of running footsteps around the farmyard.

It felt far too hot for a spring evening. When I noticed a column of burning fragments rising, small pieces of glowing wood splinters slithering up the night sky, I began running; I had to see. The house appeared before me, then the pump, the tree, the yard, the barn. The whole bunch stood around him, my little brothers out there in their overalls, shifting from one foot to the other with their hands in their pockets. Mama was sitting down on the ground coughing, and I reckon she must have busted loose and pulled him out of that fire by his feet. They stared down at Daddy, who looked so small and white against the orange fire swallowing the rest of the fallen barn. One of my sisters tried to put his workshirt on him, but he lay motionless as she pulled his arms through the sleeves and buttoned it up. Mr. Fixico climbed on his mare to go fetch the doctor. Behind them the barn gave a final groaning sag and caved in on itself, sending sparks that shot up over the front yard.

I turned my back on the whole brood of kin and neighbors and looked towards the woods. I heard no more voices from the front yard because they had carried Daddy into the house, only the sound of the crackling of the last barn embers. Everything else had gone silent except for out by the trees. I looked at the fence where our pasture ended and the woods began. The fence line had come alive with motion. The cows, running back and forth from one corner to the next, confused and looking for a place to get out, threw themselves, again and again, against the wire strands until they finally found a weak spot where they charged through. I heard them crashing through bushes until their bellowing grew fainter as they ran deeper into the woods. Old One-Eye didn't even bother to go through the cow's hole; he got a running start and cleared the top strand without even touching it. He sailed over the fence, mane and tail flying, back feet extended, forelegs ready to land and light out towards the woods, and all the while that quarter-moon shining directly above him.

From the trees, the humming of the cicadas grew louder until I thought my ears would split. I saw those wolf cubs on the other side of the fence at the edge of the woods, near the hole where the cows had jumped through. Looked like they had been encouraging them cows on as they busted down the fence. The last couple of weeks the cubs had come up at the edge of the trees, and Daddy had left food in their pen every day to try to lure them back into the farmyard. The pups stood together in a circle facing each other, and I could see their upturned muzzles and gray necks as they started their long wails into the night air. Their voices rose higher and higher until I thought they would burst if they didn't stop, separate notes, rising sharply together; their chorus echoed from the hills and filled the woods. Then their howl began to taper down into a quiet, steady tremolo that grew softer and softer until I could barely hear it—no more than a purr from a cat.

From over towards the direction of the spring, I heard an answer— a steady yelping, a high squeaking yip-yip-yip, almost playful-like. Then she spoke for all of them, and I strained to hear it right this time, listening with everything I had, as she called me. I told you I listen to her in the morning singing, "whippoorwill's a widow," except now I swear I hear her saying "whippoorwill's Lucille," and I know she's speaking to me. I laid on my back in the cow pasture and soaked up the call of that widowed bird, a voice from the night woods.

FOUR

Burning Jimmy's Jacket

JOSH HENNEHA, EUFAULA, OKLAHOMA, 1973

"Why do we have to fish on top of this rock heap?" I thought, but I didn't say anything to Jimmy. Or to anyone else. I could have killed him for bringing us out here. We'd passed picnic tables, shady groves, boat docks where we could have sat with our feet dangling in the lake watching brim nibble at our toes as the sun went down and the marina where the white people kept their fancy ski boats tied up and you could go inside the gas station to get a Coke or a candy bar. And for what? This ugly pile of rubble.

Sammy had been arguing with Jimmy the whole way as we'd climbed around rocks and trees, following the shore of the lake toward the setting sun, chasing it before it disappeared between the hills toward some spot Jimmy claimed was the best catfish hole in the lake. I found a cement block with a slab behind it for a backrest. Battling with a wiggly night crawler, I finally speared him on my hook, then rigged up a bobber above that and slung the rig out as far as I could cast it. I sat down and stuck my pole between two pieces of old rebar poking out of the concrete, pulling out the book I'd jammed inside my tackle box, *The Arabian Knights.*

It even smelled bad, this spot Jimmy had chosen. The dried-up skeleton of a dead carp lay washed up near shore, rising and falling gently in the shallow water. Its red gill slits still glistened as if it had been alive only moments before, the rest of it no more than a skeleton, fragile as a puff of dust. I imagined the carp's last turn, writhing in the water, his final gasp before he gave up and rose toward the surface, his memory of his former life falling away as he drifted toward land.

I pretended to read, but I watched Jimmy as he tried to shed his leather jacket. He'd extricated one arm from a tight-fitting sleeve, his face sweaty with the effort. He got it pulled off and stuffed it into the crook of a waterlogged tree stump whose branches had all fallen away, a faint reminder of the natural shoreline before the concrete rubble. Seemed like a lot of trouble just to look good.

"How come you wear that nigger jacket in the middle of summer?" Sammy said, throwing a rock at Jimmy's feet to get his attention.

"Shut up," Jimmy said, clumsily making his way over the concrete slabs toward the water.

"Nigger jacket that stinks nigger cause a nigger wears it. Like that old dead fish. *Fumbee,*" Sammy said, holding his nose.

"These bugs are eating me alive," Lenny said, trying to bait up and keep mosquitoes off himself at the same time. Nobody seemed too happy about Jimmy's choice of fishing spots.

Jimmy ignored them. "Throw some of that stink bait down here," he said to me.

But Sammy wouldn't let it go. "Throw your jacket in," he said. "Niggers like carp, so carp must like niggers. That'll bring all the bottom fish over here."

"That's an Indian jacket," Jimmy said. "An AIM jacket."

"Well, I *aim* never to be a nigger Indian," Sammy leered.

"I aim to climb up there and beat your ass," Jimmy said. He laid down his pole and started back over the concrete slabs. Sammy started throwing rocks, and one struck a glancing blow off of Jimmy's shoulder. Jimmy, who'd been taking his time, sprung over the remaining concrete slabs toward Sammy. Sammy yanked the jacket from the fork of the tree stump and ran off with it, leaving his dilapidated pole where it lay and disappearing around the first bend in the lake.

"My dad gave that to me, man," Jimmy complained. "I'll get it back."

"Who's these AIMs, anyhow?" Lenny asked.

"I don't know, just crazy Indians." Jimmy was settling back in, his pole between his knees. "My dad was partying with some city Indians who came down from Denver. They stole a car in Oklahoma City to get down to Anadarko for a 9er. They went into the liquor store at Lawton to get a twelve-pack while my dad waited in the car. He'd been driving them around since they weren't from around here. When the cops pulled up they seen my dad behind the wheel and was jerking him out of the car to arrest him. The AIM dudes used that as a chance to run off. My dad got off eventually as only an accessory, but he went looking for them AIMs to jump their ass since he took all the heat when they hightailed it outta there. Dad beat the tar out of one of them in the Indian bar in Muskogee, and the other give him his jacket in order to get out of a good ass-whupping."

Darkness had fallen on the water. In the moonlight, the white concrete looked like a field of giant molars, a graveyard of teeth. In an old bathtub, cemented in between the rocks, floated the cast-off hulls of cicadas, on a thin film of green water. Someday I would step out of my secrets, too, and leave them behind, and Jimmy would be the first person I spoke to.

"Time to go home," Jimmy said. "I can't even see my bobber."

"We just got here," Lenny complained. "Let's fish in the dark. I wish we had some beer."

"Nothing happening," Jimmy said. "It's all this wind." On the long walk back, I watched Jimmy's long arms swinging as he hiked toward town, pole in one hand, tackle box in the other; Jimmy first, Lenny behind him, me last. It made me mad the way Jimmy walked with such confidence, how no one could get to him, not even Sammy. When he said he'd get his jacket back, I knew he would.

When I got home and the screen door slammed behind me, my

mom said, "Hurry up and eat; your supper's been cold for two hours. Here, leave your fishing stuff on the porch." She smiled as if boys fishing made up for rules about dinner. She was a good mom. It wasn't long before I was in bed.

Well, not exactly in bed. Sometimes I could fly, not very high, but I levitated above the earth on a magic carpet. It was my secret; I hadn't told anyone. It was a little hard, you know, climbing out a windowsill onto a flying carpet, but I kind of just tumbled aboard, rolling toward the middle. I sat up before it took off, so I could get a good view of the town. The magic carpet banked high in the air, a hard southeastern turn, and passed over Eufaula Indian Baptist Church, then flew in the direction of the railroad tracks toward town. But first I took a side trip over Greenwood Cemetery before the carpet cut over in the direction of the old stone-built city hall building and nearly rolled me off when it turned toward Bundine Farm Supply, where I regained my seat and squinted to read the sign: "Pecans Bought and Sold. Custom Cracking Peanuts." Sure, I was kind of zigzagging around up there, but I had to go wherever it took me. I couldn't just climb off, and I never knew where it would touch down. I looked ahead at the National Guard Armory, which was coming up on me fast, and passed so close to the cupola on the Foley Building that I touched it when I flew by. Up that high, naturally, I had a good view of the lake, and the water, turned red from a recent rain, glowed in the moonlight, the red rivers of silt washing in and out of the blue circles farther from shore. The carpet hovered in place for a minute over Eufaula Indian Boarding School, there on top of the hill, then came in for a landing, descending in front of the white-pillared arch of the library, where I climbed off and walked toward the alley that led to Jimmy's back fence.

I crouched down, hoping to catch a glimpse through the board slats of Jimmy in his bedroom window. I waited until my calves hurt, crouching like that, but I could see only his shadow moving back and forth, deep within the room, and he would rise up like smoke, over to the window, a mere outline. Could he feel my presence behind the fence, gazing as I was through a tiny gap? When I thought I could stand no more, he dissolved out of the light, a snuffed-out silhouette.

Did he catch my image from the corner of his eye, image of me burning? Felt it as flames down his neck before he receded into the room, oblivious to the wall of heat before him?

Oh, the trips I'd taken! How I yearned for him to stumble out his back door into the moonlight, and stand in his backyard as if he'd just climbed out of the lake to meet me where I waited on the shore. I hated him for not coming out of his room. He could have at least given a sign that he knew I was out there, watching. On the flight home I had to circle my parents' house a few times, waiting for the lights to go out, so I could return unheard and crawl in through my window screen, which I'd left unhasped.

I slept without dreaming and morning came far too early. School was especially dull since I had a substitute teacher in my favorite class who didn't know anything about history except what the book already said. I liked history because it seemed like a dream. There was the book, and what everybody agreed happened, and then there were the secrets that no one talked about. Only a few people understood the secrets.

After school, I walked over to where Jimmy, Lenny, and Sammy usually played touch football on the street in front of their brick HUD houses. Valeria was sitting on the hood of her family's blue Mustang, filing her fingernails. Valeria Talamántez was a big high school girl, a tall girl with long, shiny black hair and black eyes. Her parents were the only Mexican family in Eufaula, and the only non-Indian family on this street of BIA houses. All the white people in town thought they were Indians, a point they always disputed, claiming to be Spanish. All the Indians disclaimed them as relatives, pissed at the town rednecks who couldn't tell Indians from Mexicans. I stood on the street corner, trying to catch a glimpse of Sammy and Lenny, which usually meant Jimmy was somewhere nearby. I didn't want Valeria to see me.

Valeria had spent the previous year ambushing me on the way home from school. She used to throw me down to the ground and tickle me until I cried. If she caught me alone on the street, she would put me in a head lock and pin me over the hood of her family's Mustang. She would hold my hands above my head and grind her crotch into mine. "*Chica.* Just like Jimmy," she would rasp.

I knew she said that because she hated him. I had watched the two of them fighting so many times you'd have thought they were brother and sister. Jimmy hated her just as much, but Jimmy, not skinny or shy like me, was a match for Valeria in size and in verbosity. They were like two tomcats strung up over a clothesline. Valeria had a litany of names to draw upon in their duels: *"Indio," "puto," "maricon," "señorito," "joto."* Lithe and muscular and mouthy, Jimmy could dodge or counterattack her flying fingernails as well as her venomous name calling.

Valeria's mother, though, had been especially nice to me. When she noticed me walking home from the school library loaded down with an armful of books, she would exclaim, *"¡Qué estudiante tan serio!"* When Jimmy, Sammy, and Lenny would be tossing a football out in the streets and she saw me watching from the sidewalk, she would call me over and ask me if I wanted any *dulces,* inviting me in. Under her mother's watchful eye, Valeria was restrained. Although I was afraid of Valeria, she was fascinating because she was so different from her sisters, who liked me to come over and asked me about schoolwork, and because at home she seemed so docile that I wondered if she was the same girl who chased and tormented me. Two of Valeria's sisters were in junior high, and I got along better with them than the boys at my school. And their mom encouraged me. "You keep up with those books and you'll be okay," she would tell me during these visits to their house.

I had always observed Jimmy's and Valeria's bouts from a distance. She and Jimmy seemed to be competing in a contest over who was most beautiful: Valeria with her long, black hair swinging down to her waist; Jimmy with his lanky basketball build, slowly changing from all clumsy arms and legs to muscle and grace. And Valeria's nails, my God! Her proudest asset, her fiercest weapon, those little pink daggers. She was always calling Jimmy over to show them off. From my hiding place, I saw Jimmy come out of the front door of Sammy's house, holding his leather jacket.

Valeria climbed off the hood of the car. It was a movie I was directing inside my head; Valeria stepping off, as if on cue, just as Jimmy came out of the house while I watched all of it unfolding from

the sidelines. Valeria walked up on Sammy's front lawn, showing the
two of them the latest spurt of growth from her fingertips. Surely she
knew what was coming, I thought, but she seemed to thrive on these
catfights. Jimmy infuriated her by claiming they were fake and saying
in a mincing voice, drooping his wrist like a wilted lily and blowing on
his nails, "*¡Qué uñas más bonitas!*" Valeria erupted into motion, legs
pumping the sidewalk, hands reaching for Jimmy's throat, hair trailing
behind. He danced and whirled in and out of his taunting words, just
beyond her grip, laughing and screaming in falsetto while rolling his eyes,
"*¡Chiquita! ¡Tranquilizate!*" His leather jacket twirled all around him
like a woman fancy dancer's shawl. Jimmy knew Spanish because I'd
sent it to him in one of my secret messages.

I watched the whole thing, stricken with admiration as Jimmy
poked words into Valeria like a picador's lances and mimicked her by
twirling his imaginary long black hair, flipping it behind his shoulders.
Jimmy could have never done this without my help.

But sometimes he stopped listening, blocking the gifts I sent him.
This is when I hated him the most. So I figured he got what he
deserved when he fell. Jimmy hadn't noticed a football someone had
left on the sidewalk, and he backed over it and hit the cement, hard.
Just the moment Valeria needed. They rolled around, a blur of hair
and scrabbling arms. Valeria couldn't keep Jimmy down long, though.
He easily wiggled out from beneath her and regained his feet. Not
having time to think where to run, he grabbed his coat and rushed up
to where I was standing, there on the corner, directing.

Valeria had broken one of her nails, and she was screaming in
rage. Evidently, she didn't want to risk breaking one more in another
tumble with Jimmy, and she retreated toward home howling, her curses
hanging in the air like smoke. "*¡Chingada! ¡Pendejo! ¡Hijo de puta!*" She
didn't even stop for air; they poured out of her breathlessly like a
demoniac's sermon: "*¡Métete el dedo entre el culo! ¡Mal parido! ¡Come
mierda! ¡Vete al diablo!*"

I watched Jimmy catching his breath, his chest falling in and out.
"Some show, huh?" he laughed. "What about that bitch, man? Valeria.
Jesus." Jimmy's cursing excited me. I never cussed. Well, in my head,

but not in front of my parents. My folks were afraid of their son's bad behavior getting back to the white Baptist church they attended, and they'd be kicked out. And, besides my limited cussing, I couldn't play basketball, either, like Jimmy—I could shoot okay, but not run and dribble at the same time. Neither was I able to escape Valeria—I would lamely wiggle out from under her when she'd pin me, breaking away finally but not triumphing as Jimmy always did, subduing her *and* getting in the last word. There he stood on the street corner, with his hand on his hip, about to speak.

So I helped him out a little since he was so close to noticing me.

"Hey, how about if I show you this really tough swing over on Gill Creek? You'll like it; you swing out so high you can jump off on the other side." Maybe it was cheating, making him say it like that, but in only a matter of time he'd be doing it on his own. The next few days we hiked over to the swing in the afternoons and hung out until we got bored. Just me and him. Then we would walk over to the waterfront and check out what had washed up from the lake or watch people fishing on the pier. That Friday, walking back home from the creek, he said, "Sammy and Lenny are sleeping over at my place this weekend. Wanna come?"

It took a lot of pleading, convincing my mom to let me spend the night over at Jimmy's. "I don't know; you know how those Talosis are," she said, fidgeting with her curlers. I couldn't even remember how Jimmy might be related to the Talosi family, since his last name was Alexander, but I did know all their sins, which my parents had recounted for me often. It all boiled down to my granddad selling one of them corn liquor forty years ago, and the Talosi boy getting thrown in jail by the county sheriff, then released after leading them out to the still in the woods where Grandpa made his brew. Up until then Grandpa had a pretty good little trade going back and forth to Muskogee.

"I know, Mom, but it's just down the block," I begged. "You talked to his mom and dad before." She relented, and I had gone eagerly over to Jimmy's with an extra shirt, toothbrush, and clean pair of underwear. After lying around watching TV that afternoon, we spent some time digging through Jimmy's record collection—Santana,

Moody Blues, a little Credence, unlike any music we had at my house.
My dad played the guitar, but only in the key of C, and he sang Hank
Williams and Jimmy Rogers songs, playing in C and singing in some
other key. I'd heard some of these rock-and-roll things like Jimmy's
records on the radio, as much as we could pick up from Oklahoma
City and Tulsa that wasn't strictly hillbilly music.

Jimmy's father kept hollering from downstairs, "Turn that goddamn thing down!" and my mouth hung open in disbelief when Jimmy
shouted back, "You're too deaf to hear it anyway, you old bastard!" I
was waiting for his father to come charging up the stairs to annihilate
us, and, when that didn't happen, I expected the walls of the room
themselves to cave in as a result of this sacrilege. On Jimmy's wall was
a black-light poster of Jimi Hendrix setting fire to his Stratocaster,
standing over it in supplication. The mirror on the back of his chest
of drawers had a cutout page from a magazine taped up in the corner,
Kareem Abdul-Jabbar, with his famous goggles, moving in for a layup.

"This is boring," Sammy complained, tossing one of Jimmy's
Sports Illustrated magazines into its pile in the corner of the room.
"Let's go to the liquor store and see if we can get someone to buy us
a twelve-pack." Lenny was lying on Jimmy's bed, shuffling through
baseball cards and arranging them in order from lowest to highest
batting averages.

"My dad ain't about to let us go out this late," Jimmy said. "Hey,
man, you all wanna smoke a joint before we go to bed?" He asked this
as casually as if he wanted to know if we'd all like a glass of milk. I was
scared to death; I'd heard all about dope and hippies from my parents,
and I knew they were both connected, inexplicably somehow, to Charles
Manson, or maybe the kind of AIM Indians who Jimmy's old man had
whupped ass on. Trying to save face and decline at the same time, I
said something totally inane like, "No, I don't feel like it right now."

"Cool," Jimmy said, as he started fishing around under his mattress, until he pulled out a little plastic bag.

"Can I see it?" Lenny said excitedly.

"What's the matter? Ain't you never seen dope before?" Sammy
picked up another magazine and yawned.

I wondered where Jimmy got the weed, who sold such stuff, and the secret signs between those who wanted it and those who had it in this forbidden world I knew nothing about. Maybe it came from someplace really far away like Dallas. I imagined Jimmy in a dark city alley, reaching his hand into the coat pocket of a white man and releasing a twenty-dollar bill, who knows, maybe even more, their eyes locked, the handsome stranger, in turn, taking Jimmy's hand out of his pocket, turning it over while still gazing in his eyes, uncurling Jimmy's fingers, and placing the bag of weed in his palm, a prayer without words, shared only between the two of them.

When they passed the joint around, I was too scared. "Won't your dad smell it?" I asked. Jimmy just shrugged.

"What do you know? He can talk! Why'd you have to invite this butt-wipe over?" Sammy said in disgust. But Jimmy got up and turned his window fan toward the screen, exhaling the smoke out of the room. He did this for me. I knew, though no one else could tell. And next he got up off his bed and put a towel at the bottom of the door.

"That oughta do the trick," he said. "We gotta go out in the garage and get some sleeping bags." As we thudded down the stairs, I worried that somehow Jimmy's dad would know we'd been smoking dope. Dope made people jump off buildings and kill themselves, dance in the middle of parks, lie around in public places making love out in the sunlight like the hippies and perverts out in San Francisco. I didn't really know what it would do to us going downstairs to fetch a couple of sleeping bags.

Jimmy's dad was stretched out on their brown shag carpet, letting the living room fan blow over him as he watched TV. He didn't look like a guy who could beat up a bunch of rowdy Indians. He was kind of short and skinny, and when he got up to go in the kitchen, he treaded delicately like the carefully placed footsteps of a cat, unworried but aware of everything around him. He looked a lot like the side profile featured on the blue Bob Dylan album cover we'd been looking at earlier that afternoon: same big nose, same curly hair, just a whole lot darker. Without coming out of the kitchen, he said, "Don't make a mess out in that garage."

The sleeping bags were stored in an aluminum rowboat with an outboard motor up on a trailer. Like Grandpa's. I wondered if they ever used it. I never heard Jimmy talk about fishing with his dad. Jimmy got inside the boat, moved around some orange life jackets, boxes of old magazines, and a lamp shade, and started tossing sleeping bags to us. Mine had that army-green smell of musty canvas or damp tarp. After digging all around in the boat, Jimmy came up with only one more sleeping bag, which he tossed to Lenny.

"Where's mine?" Sammy complained.

"That's it," Jimmy said, climbing out.

We passed through the living room again where Jimmy's dad was sitting on the sofa, eating sliced cantaloupe on a paper plate. He didn't look up as we traipsed back up the stairs.

"Do you mind if we sleep with the radio on?" Jimmy said, back inside the room.

"Where am I gonna sleep?" Sammy asked.

"Up here on the bed, I reckon," Jimmy replied.

"No way, man," Sammy said, yanking my sleeping bag out of my arms. "I ain't sleeping with no guy."

"Well, sleep on that dirty old bag, then. I don't give a shit." Jimmy was sitting on the bed, facing the window, pulling off his shirt, then his pants.

Sammy unzipped his sleeping bag. "I'll just sleep on top of it."

Lenny had already unrolled his. "Good idea," he said. They both plopped down on opposite sides of the room, didn't even take their clothes off.

That left me standing there. So I sat down on the opposite side of the bed, and I pulled off my jeans down to my underwear, the breeze from the open window giving me goose bumps on my legs. I could have stayed dressed, like Sammy and Lenny, but I figured I was supposed to take my clothes off, like Jimmy, since we had the bed. Nobody said anything about it, so it must have been all right. "Turn off the light, Josh," Jimmy asked. I got up, aware of my skinny brown body in my white Fruit of the Looms and, sure enough, I couldn't hit the light switch before Lenny snickered, "It's a scarecrow."

"Maybe he'll scare off that big black crow he's sleeping with,"

Sammy said. Sammy and Lenny spent the first part of the night doling out their usual string of insults at each other. Jimmy kept telling them to shut the fuck up. I heard their voices, but paid little attention as I lay beneath the covers, my heart racing as I tried to guess whether or not Jimmy had slipped his briefs down those taut brown legs of his while I had been undressing with my back turned on the opposite side of the bed. My hands were shaking beneath the covers.

Jimmy soon began to breathe deeply, but I couldn't sleep. I was burning up. He tossed in his sleep, and his leg rubbed against mine. I was a flame, flaring up, uncontainable. Words drifted through the room from the radio, *"Oye como va."* And then the static interruption of a commercial bleeding over from the country station, the price to pay for poor Eufaula reception so far from the city. "What dad wouldn't like a pair of all-leather Tony Llama boots? Tony Llama, what every dad wants for Father's Day." Jimmy's arm was flung above his head on the pillow, and I could see his chest rising and falling, illuminated by the soft moonlight from the window.

Sammy and Lenny's verbal combat had long ceased, and I could hear them breathing softly below me. My mind raced, a chorus of voices, like echoes from within a deep cave. I remembered what seemed like centuries of Sundays in the malingering air that hung motionless and fetid over the pews in the Southern Baptist church I went to with my mom and dad. My folks were especially proud to be members there because it was one of the very few white Baptist churches that allowed Indians who looked like us, like full-bloods, so it was worth it to my parents to drive all the way to Muskogee on a Sunday. Most of our people, if they were Christians, went to their own places, the Indian Baptist and Methodist churches. But not us. Every Sunday we sat in the white Baptist church, fanning ourselves off with bulletins and sweating as the red-faced preacher droned on, inter-minable, a man who lived for the sound of his voice:

"Know ye not that neither liars, nor adulterers, nor fornicators, nor murderers, nor the effeminate shall inherit the kingdom of God? As the apostle Paul says, they give over the natural use of their bodies for that which is unseemly. Men with men, lying together, women

with women. Not considering their eternal destiny, the wages of their
sin, their inheritance in Gehenna, the lake of fire." I knew I was a
freak, a grotesque, a rampant sinner, and as I lay in Jimmy's bed, his
body against mine, I burned, I burned, I burned.

I didn't dare move, dreading leaving the warmth of his flesh,
terrified not to. After a long while I finally began to drift off. I was
awakened later when I felt a heavy arm across my chest and Jimmy's
fingers moving. He must have thought that I had fallen asleep. I knew
I should act like I was coming awake to ward him off, but I wanted to
just lie there. His hand began to explore, creeping down my stomach
toward my shorts. My heart was pounding; I began to sweat. His
fingertips slipped beneath the elastic band, and I felt a fire, a hot
blue flame lapping and dancing over the surface of my skin when his
hand grasped me, hard as a rock. I gasped and rolled over, afraid of
the hot rising of my blood, afraid of the unknown, afraid of hellfire,
afraid of what thrilled me. I lay there motionless, and I could feel him
throbbing against my ass. I pretended to be asleep, and I rolled all the
way over on my stomach, staying on my far side of the bed, paralyzed
with fear.

I stayed there all night, listening for the slightest rustling of bedcovers on the other side. How do you wake up with your eyes already
open, a circle of dreaming and waking? I remember coming to con-
sciousness facing Jimmy, an awareness of the fierce sun blazing in
the eastern window, the fan already blowing hot air over my sweaty
chest and arms. The covers were thrown off the bed in a twisted heap.
I didn't remember kicking them off or shutting my eyes to sleep,
either. Even with my back turned, I had studied Jimmy all night long,
the memory much stronger than the image now directly before me as
I lay turned toward him while the sun poured into the room, making
me squint and stare, Jimmy's white undershorts barely discernible
from the rest of his brown body, Jimmy no more than an abstract glare
framed against the bright light.

A panic rose up in me. How could I ever face him? What would
happen when we awoke, rose out of bed? What would he say to me?
I had relied on signs, signals, secrets. Patiently, I had waited for Jimmy

to answer back. Enduring much shame, I had stood on the shore of betrayal, watching Jimmy walk away. The messages I had kept to myself, free of danger, safe from discovery. If Jimmy knew enough to touch me, could he also sneak inside my imagination? Maybe he was the one who really controlled the secret messages, not me. I'd never planned what I would do if the messages worked.

When Jimmy's eyes opened, his whole body came into sharp focus. I turned quickly away. I wasn't ashamed I'd been caught staring at him but more afraid he might know I was thinking about him.

Sammy was the first to stir. He picked up a sock and threw it at Lenny. Lenny groaned and rolled over on his side. Jimmy rubbed his eyes.

"Are you two married now," Sammy asked, "since you spent the night together in the same bed?" Jimmy sat up.

"Naw, that was you I heard all night long begging Lenny to give up some of that booty. Did you have a hard time zipping up your sleeping bags together?" Jimmy was facing the window, blocking the sun. "God, my old man's out early," he said. "Burning trash, looks like. Josh, check this out, man."

Jimmy had spoken his first words to me, the message after awakening from the previous night. Things seemed the same to him as before we went to bed. I made my way over to the window, and Jimmy got up and went to his desk, picked up a *Sports Illustrated*. I looked out. Jimmy's dad was dressed up like a bug exterminator. He held a pump canister and a wand, patiently spraying the flames of a trash heap of brush and garbage he'd made in Jimmy's front yard. "What's he doing?" I asked.

Sammy was standing next to the window by then. "Duh, he's keeping that fire going with kerosene, dumb ass."

Now Lenny was up and looking. "Yeah, but what's up with the bug suit?"

Jimmy laughed. "He just dresses up in that shit, man. Says it keeps the flames off him. Crazy. I think he likes the way it looks when people drive by on the road and see him. An Indian in a space suit, burning down Eufaula. My old man says, 'If just one Indian dude, on every single reservation, synchronized their watches and struck a match all at the same time, we could burn down America.' Talking shit, man. I don't know."

At breakfast, Jimmy was even more talkative than usual; as usual I was silent. They argued about what to do with what little precious time was left of the weekend before having to return to school. I couldn't tell them the huge sense of relief I would feel when classes started back up on Monday morning, and I could once again take up the private world of my books.

"Let's ride our bikes across the dam," Lenny said.

"What do we do when we get to the other side, genius? I know, we can ride back. Count me out." Sammy stood up and walked over to the stairs, sitting down. "I was thinking more along the lines of visiting the drugstore on Jefferson Avenue."

"The drugstore?" Jimmy was pouring milk into his cereal bowl.

"They got two new Schwinn ten-speeds out front. Check it out. They lock them up to the bike rack. You and Josh could keep the clerk busy inside the store while me and Lenny ride the bikes off."

"Like you said, they're locked up. It'll never work," Jimmy said between bites of cereal.

"I know where I can get some bolt cutters," Sammy replied.

"Like no one's gonna notice four Indians walking down Main Street, and one of us is carrying a big ole set of bolt cutters. It ain't like you can stick them in your pant leg or something. Then you rip off the bikes, and everyone knows me and Josh here were inside the store when they were stolen. Gee, I wonder how long it will take them to figure out we were in on it? We'll be the first ones they suspect, two Indians in the store. I say we get up a little game of two-on-two down at the schoolyard."

"Hey, that's a good idea, ball boy. Who's gonna play with the fag? It ain't gonna be me," Lenny said.

I felt sick. Not being called faggot; I was used to that. Nothing panicked me more than being thrown a basketball and the transformation when the ball landed in my hands. The moment when everything that comes next matters so much. Should I keep it? Get rid of it as soon as possible? Lop it over the sidelines like a live grenade in order to save myself? Everyone becomes your adversary, those trying to steal the ball away and your own teammates who turn on you, count you as a liability on the court, consider themselves cheated because they were forced to take you on their side. You can't control the game because so much depends on other people. And it was on a court, between two hoops, not inside your head. I would stand out there thinking, "Please, please, don't pass the ball to me," unlike my other teammates running around the court begging for it, pleading for their chance to shine. I followed orders, mostly relegated to guarding players. "Stay on him," that's what they always told me while the real players worked their strategies, which I knew nothing about.

"He can play with me," Jimmy answered. Not out of kindness, I suspected, but because Jimmy could beat any combination of the three of us.

"Fine by me," Sammy shrugged. I knew Sammy. He might stick with the game five minutes, then find some excuse to run off and raise hell elsewhere, most likely blaming me or getting on Jimmy's shit until Jimmy ran him off. At least it wouldn't last very long.

"Let me go grab my jacket," Jimmy said. He got up and opened the sliding door of the closet near the front entrance, rummaging around for the coat.

"Damn, man. Were you born in that thing or something? It's like a baby with her blanket."

Jimmy didn't pay any attention to Sammy. "It ain't here," he said, puzzled. You see, I knew a secret. It came to me when Jimmy had woken up that morning and saw me staring at his body. It was kinda like flying. You didn't want to soar high across oceans and circle the globe, that would be crazy. You could get up just high enough, brush the treetops, where nobody could hassle you. You might give yourself time to think there, where the sun touches the crowns of trees, the crests of hills, in the evening; that's the place where no one can bother you with everything happening below you on land. That morning, as the sun was rising, the secret I discovered in Jimmy's eyes was that the AIM jacket was the only thing his old man had ever given him. Someday Jimmy would let me take care of that jacket for him, trust it to my safekeeping. Once I had it, he would never dare turn on me again.

In my mind, I could see Jimmy's dad handing him the coat.

"Here, son."

"Are you sure, Dad?"

"Yeah, who needs an AIM jacket, anyway? Those guys come around here mostly just to make trouble. They don't know anything about us, and they want us to take up with them and raise hell across the country. They can't understand the way we think. We got enough problems of our own without worrying about manning an occupation off somewhere else with a bunch of college kids who don't know their butts from their gun barrels." I had been staring at Jimmy's uncovered body that morning when he saw the desire in my eyes and turned away, but not without letting this secret message slip out from him to me.

And what happened next proved it. He said, "Josh, could you run out on the porch and see if I left it out there? I'll go upstairs and look around." I headed outside right away, proud that he'd asked me, not Lenny or Sammy.

"Look at him jump up," Sammy said. "Just call him steppin' and fetchin'. I thought that was your job, Jimmy." I wondered why Jimmy didn't tell him to fuck off, at least for my sake. It didn't seem to bother Jimmy, one way or the other, and Sammy seemed to know just how far to dish out the bullshit before Jimmy would chase him down and beat the crap out of him. Being Oklahoma and all, I knew this wasn't the first time Jimmy had heard such shit. I got enough of it myself, but the silent kind: the eyes that followed me around the grocery store waiting for me to slip a candy bar in my pocket; the teachers who called on the white kids first, leaving us in the back row mostly ignored; the books we read in class that generally left us out but included us just enough to make sure everybody was good and afraid of us; the stares as my family walked to our pew in the white Baptist church every Sunday, constant reminders that we ought to stick with our own. But this year, especially, it was in the air, the fear, the possibility, that good Oklahoma Indians who'd always minded their own business might take up with the uppity hell-raisers in South Dakota. White folks were waiting for an explosion in a state where poverty was quiet and hidden out behind the scrub oaks where no one could see it.

I looked around the porch. There was a blanket to sit on, there on the wood swing, but no jacket anywhere in sight. It was a nice-looking porch, the floorboards painted a foresty green, the rails white, an old Creek home that had stood in Eufaula since Reconstruction after the Civil War. I looked out in the front yard. Jimmy's dad was bent over, refilling his canister with kerosene. The brush pile was smoldering behind him. One of the white neighbors across the street had come out to water his lawn, and he kept eyeing the smoke cloud floating off toward town.

I noticed something poking out between a mass of green, smoky willow branches. Somebody's arm? That can't be right. I walked past Jimmy's dad, who was screwing the lid back on the canister, and stood before the burning heap. He hauled his rig over and stood beside me, pulling down his plastic visor and snapping it in place on his hooded suit. He didn't say anything, just commenced to feeding the flames, which needed a lot of fuel to keep going, everything being so green.

But something in the middle of the pile was burning good, real good, where the arm had been sticking out. A big wind came up and blew some of the smoke away long enough so that I could see that the willow branches were piled on top of Jimmy's jacket, one sleeve protruding from the smoking leaves curling up around it. I looked at Jimmy's dad, searching for some clue as to why he had set his son's jacket on fire, but he seemed happily occupied just keeping his fire going. The willow branches were in such a tangle that a great fireball had risen up in the center of the heap, and I had to turn my face away. No time to lose. I ran in the house. Jimmy was still upstairs, so I bounded up the steps and burst into the room. "Your dad is burning your jacket on the brush pile!"

"What?" Jimmy looked at me like I had just announced the moon was blue cheese.

"Your jacket. I'm telling you; it's burning up!" A moment of recognition dawned in Jimmy's eyes, like when he woke up and caught me staring, except this time he didn't turn away. "Don't tell what you know," I thought, realizing I had spoken, but Jimmy had rushed past me down the stairs. I sat on the bed next to the window, there where Jimmy had undressed the night before, the very place where he had sat and watched his dad building the fire as morning poured into the bedroom. That way I wouldn't have to get too close; I could control them from up above.

Sammy had come out into the front yard, and he was doubled over howling with laughter watching Jimmy, who had grabbed a rake and was trying to get close enough to the fire to push over the willow branches and fish out his jacket. He would rush the swirling fireball and make a single mighty shove, then have to back off. The whole brush pile would quiver, sparks would fly in the bright sunlight, soot would come down like rain all over the yard, but the branches were hopelessly tangled. Jimmy would be able to do nothing more than let the fire run its course.

Jimmy turned toward his father, rake in hand. I thought he might club and impale him with the spikes. "What the fuck are you doing?"

His father shrugged, the same shrug I'd seen from Jimmy as he patiently endured Sammy's abuse. "I thought you hated that jacket."

"You don't know a goddamned thing about me, what I hate and don't hate. You're such a fuckup!" Jimmy kicked the kerosene canister and sent it flying across the yard, where it made a dull thud when it hit the front porch rail, leaving Jimmy's dad standing with the wand in his hand.

I had my hands on either side of the windowsill. Now Jimmy knew what it felt like, too, a gift given, only to be taken back by its giver, and I thought of that day at the lake, his arm falling away from my side once we'd landed on shore. I had drowned; Jimmy had saved me. He had come up out of the water with me in his arms, me gasping for air at first, then, him breathing into me on top of the raft. I had given him this chance, this moment when everything would pass between us. He had let Sammy and Lenny steal away the secrets only Jimmy and I shared together.

And now touching me in the middle of the night. He would have to wade back into the lake if he was going to escape the flames. The wages of sin. A kiss was drowning, a fire that took your breath away, sucking up oxygen, smoke that filled your lungs. He hadn't kissed me, but I wanted him to. Maybe it was our fault the jacket had burned. The fire began with his fingers running over my body, his touch as I lay there without moving. The likes of us would never inherit the kingdom of God, that much was for sure.

I came downstairs and walked out into the front yard. He watched me as I left, but said nothing because he was afraid of how much I knew. I walked home alone.

The next day at school I ran into C.A., the only junior high loser even worse off than me. Every day after classes I would rush out, having arranged my books and pocketed my pencils in perfect synchronization with the long hand of the clock striking 2:30 and the bell sounding. I ran down the playground ramp, shot full of dread, not looking back, wanting to get home before C.A. caught up with me. Ah, but why didn't I mention C.A. earlier, you ask? He exists in my memory as a suffering servant, a locust's cast-off shell, a tall, skinny, transparent no one. My classmates and I, behind the eyes of our hard little bodies, saw him as our punching bag, and since I was no good at punching, I avoided him altogether. I tried to push ahead on the crest of the wave of junior-highers spilling from hallways, C.A. just at my heels, dodging bodies and skirting the crowd, about to catch up. He was my only real friend, but I was ashamed to be seen with him. One day my mom had noticed me walking home with C.A., and she had sat me down on the living room sofa. She looked worried.

"Now, honey," she said, while fidgeting with her curlers and dropping down to sotto voce, "you know if you hang around that boy, people will start to say the same thing about you that they say about him."

His name was Clarence Albert, but everybody called him C.A., or C-gay when they were being mean. C.A. was extremely girlish, a real fem. I knew what my mom said was right, and I was just as eager to avoid him, because of what my classmates would think, as she was to have me not seen in his presence. What everyone knew about C.A., no one guessed about me. I wanted to be like Jimmy. Jimmy was a force to be contended with. Jimmy could play football. Jimmy could slam the kickball across the gym in games of slaughter and dance out of harm's way, an impossible target when the ball was thrown back at him. Jimmy could talk back; Jimmy could sass; Jimmy could create a whirl of words that surrounded him like a protective shield. I got made fun of but mostly because I was no good at sports, I was silent, and I hung out in the library and got good grades. I got called a "pussy," and even a "faggot," but C.A. was the one who actually acted like one, confirming everybody's suspicions, whereas I just wore the epithets. C.A. was a loser all the way around, and he tagged along behind me like a lost puppy even though I was always trying to ditch him.

He wore sweaters, and he pulled the sleeves down past his hands while he talked. Jimmy was the only person who spoke to C.A. for any reason other than calling him faggot. Jimmy seemed immunized from the guilt by association that the rest of us feared. Denial, in his case, being hopeless, C.A. bore his legacy of names and suffered quietly. And today he had thwarted my effort to outrun him. He jumped in front of me to catch my attention when I kept on walking. "I know a secret about you," he said, waiting for a response. I tried my stoic routine. Sometimes ignoring him worked. "Jimmy told me about this weekend," he blurted out. "He said you had a hard-on when he was trying to mess with you in his bed."

I stopped walking. Then I walked faster, trying to get away, but C.A. was still behind me. "No way, man!" I stuttered. I couldn't think of a convincing defense. "Hey, look, man. I've got to go to the store for my mom," I said, dashing up our front steps, slamming the screen door behind me.

I was taken by surprise, unprepared. At the mercy of things out of control. C.A. had named the unnameable. I couldn't believe that Jimmy had told, that he wasn't ashamed. I had feared what me and Jimmy would say to each other afterwards; I'd never imagined anyone else would be in on the secret. I was afraid of more than what we had done, the touching. Jimmy knew, and now C.A. knew, what I had *wanted* to do because my body had given me away, but, unlike Jimmy, I'd lacked the courage to join desire and deed. It didn't matter who had the story right. This seemed worse than lying or betrayal, this fear, but I wasn't sure what to think. I hated my longings, yet I had no power to escape them, and I was terrified of my potential to give in to this burning. And this secret I could tell no one. I couldn't be one of *them*. I might have temptations, but they would pass if I just had faith, remained stalwart; resist the devil and he shall flee from you.

At night I began having dreams. My grandpa wakes me up in the middle of the night and speaks Creek to me, most of which I don't understand. He motions to the edge of the dark tree line at the end of his property, outside the window. Leads me out of the house and off toward the woods where the cicadas hum in the trees, the roar of insects in my ears. He brings me to a clearing among the blackjacks and begins to wander here and there, picking up small branches of wood, setting them before my feet. He disappears into the shadows and comes back dragging a cedar sapling by its trunk. He pulls off a few sprigs of the cedar and crushes the purple berries beneath his fingers. He holds out cleansed hands before me, cedar fragrance; I sniff the sharp scent. He hands me a box of matches; I let them fall to the ground. He doesn't give up. He points to the tree for me to start chopping. An ax appears in my hands. I swing it, but it bounces off the little trunk without making a dent.

I remember the dream as the kind you have where you wake up afraid to go back to sleep, but as you drift away the dream takes up where it left off, a continuing series that lasts the night. Or, did I dream this at different times? Sometimes it feels as if I didn't dream it at all, and the vision lies in the deepest recesses of my memory. Whatever the case, suddenly my father surges up before me in my grandpa's place. "You swing that ax like a little four-year-old girl," he hisses. I raise the ax over my shoulder and come down on the tree with all my weight, but when the red blade strikes wood, I have cleaved asunder a black Bible. I begin hacking at it; every ax stroke makes sparks, until the white pages begin to catch fire. They curl, black wisps of fire words, and catch the wind and float out above the oaks, fading away among the insect din. I want to give up, but it is my grandpa in front of me again, pointing at the burning pages, urging me on. The pages pop and spit like crackling logs. The fire sucks the air around us, creating a draft of wind that whips at my clothes.

"I can't finish," I scream above the roar. "My arms are tired." My grandpa doesn't seem to understand any English and answers back only in Creek. I know I have to find the right words to make him realize I cannot go on.

His face becomes a vague mask, and then I see two men standing in front of a fire, throwing something into the flames; it flares up and lights their faces, but dies back down before I can tell who they are. The fire spits and stutters. Others begin joining them from the woods, standing around the fire in silence. Waving hands of flame rise up from the fire in the center. My Aunt Lucy and my grandpa are among those gathered, and Grandpa is watching me, repeating the words in English of the two men who continue to throw handfuls of objects into the fire, watching the flames leap.

One of these men says, "Seborn, help the boy out; he's never done this before," and he motions for me to step within the circle. I think I've heard Aunt Lucy mention this man's name before, but I'm none too sure, and since he's a stranger, I shout back at him, "Leave me be. I told you! Leave me be," and I throw up my hands in front of my face to block out the flames. Instead of falling in with the rest of them, I begin to shout Bible verses back at him, a rapid-fire succession of every writ of scripture I can think of. "For the wages of sin are death," I scream, but he continues motioning for me to join them. "For all have sinned and come short of the glory of God," I yell, but this man has endless patience; obviously he's willing to wait until I step forward. The fire in the middle becomes a round orb, the sun itself, and, though I fear harming my eyes, I cannot resist gazing upon it. The sun is the face of an aged old woman, hollowed cheeks sunken over orange embers that glow beneath her skin. Its rays are fingers making shadows on the people gathered around it. I know I have to find the right words to shake off the dream, to come awake, to put out the flames; my scripture verses have no effect. The more I quote, the more muted my voice becomes until, at last, I wake up groaning, unable for several minutes to articulate words.

And then, during the day, I began imagining scenarios where Jimmy and I became the best of friends even though at school I was running off whenever I saw him. In these daydreams I was transformed into a boy who spoke, a boy with a voice, a boy who fashioned things out of words. I would have to pray and ask Jesus to forgive me because my mind would drift, and I found myself in Jimmy's arms where he held me endlessly. Fantasies where we were lying together, and I could not get enough of him against me, our limbs interlocked like pieces of the same puzzle, our bodies making shadows on the wall. Every place I touched Jimmy in my mind flared up between my fingers and became words I could not say.

I always tried to fight it off. I quoted Bible verses. I thought of cute girls in my class I should like. I retreated into my favorite book. I dreaded the sight of Jimmy, afraid of having to look him in the eyes, yet I felt the need to touch him, to feel him swimming beneath my fingertips like cool water streaming from cupped hands.

My grandpa had to go to Oklahoma City to get some prescription blood pressure medicine for my grandma that couldn't be bought in the Eufaula drugstore. I volunteered to go with him. It felt good to get away, and I imagined his pickup as a space shuttle that had been jettisoned from the main pod that sat up on Honeycomb Bluffs in the hills outside of town. We arrived on the new planet at a point driving west on Highway 9 where the rolling hills of the cross timbers between the upper and lower forks of the Canadian River, densely covered with post oaks and blackjacks, flattened out into the pastures and fields of wheat and corn, dotted with farm ponds. Red-tailed hawks perched on the telephone lines or, hidden in the trees, occasionally lifted off and hied over the road, silhouetted against the sun as if it meant to touch fire to their wing tips. The cricket choruses hummed incessantly in a minor key, and I heard them as the voices of galactic councils, negotiating interplanetary peace talks, out in the trees.

The roadsides on the new planet were a charnel house. I couldn't help thinking that the armadillos, ran over and lying in the ditches, looked like little cartoon characters since they always seemed to die with all four feet sticking straight up in the air. Others were more grotesque. My grandfather grimaced at the sight of a decapitated red fox, its head in the middle of the road, its body in a ditch. Many turtles were smashed, and their surviving kin would plod obliviously across the shimmering pavement. Whenever my grandpa saw one, dead or alive, he would say, *"locha,"* and swerve the pickup to miss the turtle.

At the drugstore in Oklahoma City I bought a postcard with a picture of the Cowboy Hall of Fame on it. I thought about sending it to Jimmy, but I didn't know what to say. I paid for the postcard and stuck it into my shirt pocket and followed my grandpa back out of the store. Clad in overalls, clutching the bag of blood pressure medicine around the top of the sack, he lumbered along and swung up into his dented Ford pickup.

On the ride back to the house he broke the silence. "Grandson, you ever hear about ole Rabbit?"

"What rabbit?" I asked. I'd heard about lots of rabbits; what could he mean? He ignored the question and launched into one of his stories.

"One time Rabbit heard 'bout stomp dance, real good one, too. He took a notion he might try to steal him some fire from that dance. So he went—see, he's real tricky, Rabbit is—he went and rubbed him on the top of his head some pine tar. Maybe his hair stand up pert, near straight up, too, like pork'pine. Anyway, he gets there, you know, and the people say to him, 'Rabbit, how come you don't lead 'cause we like the way you dance real good.' Rabbit says, 'How 'bout it, okay.'"

Grandpa started singing Rabbit's song as he steered the pickup. "He gets the thing a-going with a low 'Yu-wooooo!' and the people in the line behind him answer with a 'Yu-woooo, hey!' and when he gets to 'He he aye,' he takes to dancing and everybody falling in right there behind him. Circling and dancing. Like I say, he starts that song, and the rest fall in right there after him."

Grandpa shifted the truck into a lower gear as he got off of I-35 to get on state Highway 9, and when he came around the bend, he was back into his story.

"Only thing was, Rabbit took to dancing real funny, and everybody say, 'Hey, what's got into Rabbit, him carrying on thataway?' See, he's dancing closer and closer to the fire and leaning his head way over like this here." Grandpa bent his neck at a crazy angle and leaned toward me in the pickup.

"Hey, watch where you're going!" I said, worried about the oncoming traffic as Grandpa merged into the two-lane, but he only laughed.

"Some ole boy says, 'Aw, Rabbit he dance kinda goofy like that nohow. When he leads he acts thataways.' But before anybody knows what's going on, Rabbit had dipped his head in that fire, and he took off running, I mean just a-hooking it. Everybody after him, that pine tar blazing atop of his head. Shouting and running and him dodging and shooting between our legs and skirting under bushes and fences. Finally, he disappeared clean out of sight. Everywhere he had spread that fire all around, see.

"The people made it rain for four days, and on the fourth day it put out them little spread-out blazes. But Rabbit's tricky, remember? He'd hid in a hollowed-out tree stump where he kept some of those coals alive. Not wanting his fur to get wet in the rain, and some nice friendly embers to warm him. Sun poked out and here comes Rabbit climbing out of that stump. Well, Rabbit commenced to setting more fires. Rains come again, but this time they couldn't put out all them fires completely. People started gathering up that fire and running off with it, bringing it to their kinfolks and friends to cook with and warm themselves. When that rain finally let up, fire was there for good."

Grandpa fell silent and concentrated on his driving. The road ran between the dark hills, and I imagined Rabbit touching his head to dry branches, scooting through brambles, gathering up piles of leaves and rolling in the middle of them, tossing them up into the air, laughing with abandon, and recklessly scorching everything in sight, one step ahead of his pursuers. When we walked in the front door Grandpa and I were both grinning, and Grandma said, "Lester, I hope you ain't been telling that boy those silly old-timey stories. He's too old for make-believe." He just handed her the blood pressure medicine and went out to check the cows.

Grandpa busted open a bale next to the fence and threw over a couple flakes of alfalfa. Uncle Glen often came over in the evenings to help him feed, and he was out there driving the pickup to the other end of the pasture. He got out and pulled a bale out of the back and tossed it over the fence. He went in the pasture through the gate and spread the alfalfa out. Him and Grandpa had their different ways of feeding. Glen had on his floppy fishing hat, and he waved at me. Grandpa motioned me over. "I got something for you," he said. "I'll give it to you while Glen's finishing up." I could never get away from Grandpa's without him pawning off some junk he wanted to get rid of which my parents were sure to complain about as soon as I got home. All our relatives said he treated them like a storage bin. He ambled off toward the shed. I helped him pull open a heavy tin door on rollers, and Grandpa reached up and pulled a string. When the light came on, I saw all manner of rusty and busted-up tools hanging off of hooks and nails: a two-man saw with no blade, an ax handle without a head, some vacuum cleaner hoses with no attachments, all of it rather neatly arranged considering it was all junk that didn't work, as if another tool shed might exist somewhere with all the matching missing parts arranged in the same orderly fashion. Grandpa walked over to a sawhorse that had a saddle blanket thrown over it but no saddle. Balanced lengthwise on the blanket sat an archaic bicycle pump. Grandpa handed it to me. "Can you use this?"

"Does it work?" I asked, looking at it skeptically.

"That'll work good for you," he said, as if everything in the shed was brand new. Grandpa put it between his legs and gave it a few vigorous pumps while I held on to the nozzle and felt the air come out. He looked really pleased with himself. When he dropped me off at my folks' house, I walked up the stairs slow, then sat on the top step, waiting for him to disappear around the corner. I found myself float-ing away from the porch, my feet barely touching the ground, the way they do just before flying. My feet and heart were racing one step ahead before my guilt could catch up as I found myself walking toward Jimmy's house. The sidewalk in front of Jefferson Davis Elementary School carried me like an escalator in a department store, and I felt myself drowning, going under, until I stopped struggling and gave in. I was propelled forward by the jackknife scream of my desire. There was nothing I could do that would stop me from speaking to him. At the edge of his yard I stopped and looked at the brush pile, now just a heap of ashes in a sunken depression where many such burnings had taken place. It all looked really ordinary.

I ascended the front porch steps. I rapped on the door's brass knocker. While I waited, my stomach sank, and my knees started knocking so hard I had to back up and lean against the porch railing.

Jimmy opened the door and just stood there, resting against the frame, in a pair of old Levi cutoffs. He had on a tank top, and he was eating a hot dog. "Dad's been barbecuing," he grinned. I waited for a sign of recognition, a signal that he'd broken the code between us. He wasn't looking at me. "What're you doing with a bicycle pump?" he asked.

I looked down at my hand. I'd forgotten to set down the pump before my flight over. So I handed it to him. A peace offering. Jimmy took the pump, puzzled. I couldn't just stand there. I had to say something. He waited, still leaning against the door frame and stuffing the last of the hot dog in his mouth, for me to speak.

"I'll show you," I said, taking the pump back. I put it between my legs, just as Grandpa had done, and pushed up and down on the handle. I handed the nozzle to Jimmy. "Here, hold on to this." He felt the air come out, flipped the valve back and forth to stop and release the outflow. "See, that'll work good for you," I said.

Jimmy laughed. "Hey, I'll go get that half-flat ball in my room." I waited on the porch and with the door open the setting sun had bathed the stairwell in the last of the day's light. Jimmy leaped up the stairs and plunged into his bedroom. When he appeared at the top of the stairs again, the sunlight lit up a big grin as he smiled down at me, holding the basketball out like a big round *yes*.

That was the summer, the summer of my dreaming. The summer I danced alone, hot nights in the darkness, leaping away with stolen flames. The summer of the suffocating silence, the tears of smoke. The summer I spent hoping for words to descend upon me as cloven tongues of fire, so I could speak my own language and be understood. I carried with me a story ember, waiting for a chance to touch the spark to tinder, to dance around the fire.

FIVE

Catching the Moon

JOSH HENNEHA, EUFAULA AND
OKLAHOMA CITY, 1978

I had given up dreaming for now; flying had become a burden and my
gift had taken wing, flapping away, leaving a gray unimaginative sky
behind it. Maybe I'd grown tired of my teachers telling me to come
down to earth. "Excellent imagination," read the English essay I held
in my hand, as I tried to discreetly eye the grade of the person in front
of me, "but a little closer attention needed to matters of organization."
Or the preacher's weekly promise that the way of the cross leads home,
a home I'd flown away from so often to my world above the treetops.
Then weary of my dad, who'd been taking me to his job site, instructing
me that "men took pride in their work," as I helped him pull conduit
in the houses he wired in Nichols Hills in Oklahoma City, the likes of
which he'd never own, yet he labored away, proving to himself, if no
one else, that he wasn't a lazy Indian. I just wanted to go home and
read a book, like all those younger Saturdays when I'd relished my
freedom to read and daydream.

A silence had enveloped me and Jimmy since junior high, and the
more he tried to draw me out, get me to say something, or beg me to

step in and even up a team for one of his street basketball games, the more I avoided him. And the more I avoided him, the more we'd run into each other.

High school held all the same prohibitions as childhood with the deadly new imposition that it all had to be taken so seriously, as if it were real. I put my B– essay back inside my folder. I'd noticed that all the white kids had a comment sheet attached to their papers, with the idea in mind that their drafts bore potential for revision. Indian students weren't given much encouragement to write; everybody knew Indians didn't write, even Indians, and the silence written all over the uninscribed pages of our returned papers let us know that our teachers held to the general assumption. The B– mark was a terminal one, the end of the trail, no hope for a better paper with a little hard work.

Which is how me and Jimmy ended up sitting at a table together in the back of our senior English class. "Revision groups," our teacher announced, clapping his hands to get our attention. Cloetus looked over at me. Me and him always ended up in the same group in the back of class, ignored, while the teacher circulated among the others, making comments and raising questions about the contents of the papers. Cloetus's family lived way out in the country by Glen Springs, and his mom waited tables at a diner in Okemah. His dad stayed home and ran a few cows and calves on pastures he rented. Cloetus's mom sewed all his clothes, and even though Cloetus was white he got made fun of because his homespun pants and shirts always bore the mark of some earlier era. The unrelenting teasing, being called Jed or Jethro or Ellie Mae every day, seemed to leave Cloetus in a constant state of distraction. He usually didn't finish his work, and his papers always came back with the two cryptic words "No conclusion."

Our teacher, Roy Hillabee, was the only Indian teacher in our high school, a mixed-blood Creek whose family had moved to Glenpool. Mr. Hillabee doubled as high school basketball coach and English teacher. Mr. Hillabee had put everyone in groups of four, which left me and Cloetus still sitting at our desks waiting while the rest of the class had moved over to the tables to work together, passing around the revision guide sheets the teacher had placed there. In order to avoid prolonging the suffering, I got up voluntarily and headed toward our place in back, motioning Cloetus to come with me. I knew the rules, especially the unspoken ones.

Before we got seated at the table, Jimmy came into class. "Sorry I'm late," he mumbled, but he didn't sound sorry. With Jimmy, laughter always lurked underneath an apology; a grin didn't lag too far behind anything he might say. Mr. Hillabee hesitated. Jimmy usually sat with the favored groups. His work was the opposite of mine, focused on a single topic, usually one of his basketball heroes, but riddled with grammatical problems. His papers, at any rate, had more red ink on them than mine did. I never could make any sense of the very few remarks Hillabee had written on our essays. All three of us were "problem writers": Cloetus never finished, I couldn't stick to the facts, and Jimmy didn't know how to put a written sentence together; yet Jimmy would always end up with one of the groups that got Mr. Hillabee's full attention. Maybe being on the basketball team had lifted him from anonymity; given the team's success these last two years, it would be hard for Hillabee to be anything but pleased with its players. Or it could have been that Mr. Hillabee didn't know what to do with Jimmy's dogged confidence, Jimmy's hand perpetually in the air with an opinion or an answer, even to questions Hillabee hadn't asked. Or maybe having one black-looking Indian kid in the white groups rather than with his own kind was Hillabee's concession to equal rights. I think he just gave up on putting Jimmy in his place. It was too much work.

Jimmy stood inside the classroom, waiting for Mr. Hillabee to direct him to his group. But Mr. Hillabee was frowning, irked at Jimmy's tardy disruption, and he had to save face. "You go with Josh and Cloetus," he said.

"But that makes a group of three," Jimmy said, razzed at the change of routine.

"That's all right," he answered, growing more impatient, "you can give them extra help. You'll have to read two essays."

Jimmy came over and pulled up a chair next to Cloetus. "You sure pissed him off," Cloetus remarked.

"He's gonna really be mad," Jimmy said, "when he hears I can't make it in time for the bus to the game tonight. He likes to keep all the players together rather than separate transportation. Less likelihood of no-shows."

"How come you can't make the bus in time?" Cloetus said. We had the class hour to ourselves. At the other tables, Hillabee had busied himself interpreting written comments for their recipients. Our papers had nothing written on them, other than a visual assault of red ink that indicated the mysteries of punctuation in some secret language known only to Hillabee himself. We had to fill out a sheet that said if our essays were well focused, if the introduction caught the reader's attention, if the body of the paper was well organized and contained sufficient references to reliable sources, and if the conclusion summarized the main points in the body of the paper without repeating them. I pondered how you summarized something without repeating it, but I took Jimmy's paper, nonetheless, and read it a little before answering no, no, no, and no. It was about why Kareem Abdul-Jabbar deserved his Most Valuable Player title. I wanted Jimmy to know that his writing sucked and that I'd also pissed on his hero. After all, he'd pissed on me more than once. But when I filled out the sheet, my hand wrote yes, yes, yes, and yes. It was much easier: A "no" meant you had to come up with some answers explaining why the writer had failed you; the guidelines read "If no, explain why not." With Jimmy, I didn't know why not.

Jimmy took my comments but didn't look at them. He told Cloetus, "I can't make the bus because I gotta go with my dad to court. He got arrested for throwing rocks and busting out the streetlight in Stidham."

"Was he drunk?" Cloetus asked.

"No. He's mad at the mayor," Jimmy said. Jimmy had Cloetus's essay in hand. He read the title out loud, "The Bermuda Triangle: Fact or Fiction."

Cloetus shrugged. "You gotta write something. Stidham has a mayor?"

I didn't know Stidham had a streetlight, I thought.

"Yeah, the mayor's buying up lakefront property and building houses in Eufaula. Dad's original family allotment used to be there until his brother sold the last twenty acres to the mayor. Dad says he's gonna tell the Baptist judge at the court that the goddamned mayor oughta stay in goddamned Stidham. My dad just wants me there to witness his little protest. He raised hell when he heard I had a game. But we oughta be out of court by five. I just have to find my own way since the bus will be gone.

"Josh, gimme a ride, man. You got a car on weekends," Jimmy pleaded. Jimmy was a charmer, used to talking his way into anything. But I knew his tricks. My dad had started letting me take the family car, our old Plymouth Barracuda, out on Friday and Saturday, as long as I had it back by midnight. I had a special trip planned—a new bookstore had opened in Oklahoma City, they said the biggest one in the state. You couldn't buy books in Eufaula. I didn't want to go to a basketball game.

"If I drive to Oklahoma City, my dad will make me promise to stop at my Aunt Lucille's. And he'll call and check," I said, lying. My parents didn't bother much about making sure someone visited Lucy. They'd just as soon keep me away from her, in fact.

"It'll be okay. If we get out of court by five, we can visit your aunt a few minutes and still get to the game on time."

"Yeah, but I have to get the car back to Eufaula by ten," I said, moving up my curfew a couple hours.

"Right, Cinderella. Remember, last weekend, at the drive-in? I know you couldn't have gotten home until midnight." God, I hated small towns. I'd forgotten. After *Carrie* finished, and I'd just about jumped through the front windshield when that hand came up out of the grave, I went to the concession stand before the second feature. Jimmy had been standing in line with his girlfriend, his arm slung around her waist, about to step up to the cashier, his girl loaded down with popcorn and Coke. I went back to my car and climbed in, slamming the door behind me. I sat there, arms folded, alone. What was taking so long for the next movie? That's when I heard a rapping at my window, and Jimmy's stupid grin contorted behind car glass. I opened the window, but just halfway.

"We seen you getting in your car," his girlfriend said, stuffing her face full of greasy popcorn.

"Hey, Josh," Jimmy said. "By yourself? Wanna join us?"

"Naw, that's all right." Just go away, for godsakes, I thought. The movie credits were starting up, and the two of them walked off, finally, passing a monstrous Coke back and forth between them.

So Jimmy knew I had the car on weekends. He'd seen me out late. Maybe I could drop Jimmy off at the game and go on to the bookstore. I wondered what time it closed. He could get a ride back with his teammates on the bus. Whatever. It felt good to have something he needed, for a change, even if it was only a ride.

Mr. Hillabee took back our work at the end of the class hour. "Indian giver," Jimmy said, under his breath. Cloetus laughed. "Only me and Josh get to laugh at that," Jimmy said. He was just giving Cloetus shit, but Cloetus didn't need any more intimidation. He got enough from his own kind. How far did Jimmy want to take this brotherhood, anyway? We didn't have much in common, my flight into my books and his life on the basketball court. I was desperately searching these books, looking for some clue, any clue, that there was someone out there like me. And I'd come up empty-handed, but I couldn't quit. I'd rather keep looking than find out I was alone. I didn't know what Jimmy got out there on the court, if he was looking for the same thing or just loved to play.

Hillabee clapped his hands again. "Listen up back there," he said in his coach's voice.

Whatever came after that I didn't hear. Jimmy had leaned over so close to me that his elbow was digging into my side. I felt the sharp little jab and thought about how easy it would have been to slip my arm around him, feel it rest slow and casual over his strong shoulders, my skin rubbing against his curly hair when he leaned back in his chair. Except it really wasn't that easy.

"Pick me up at the courthouse," he whispered, and I felt myself almost rising out of my desk, about to fly, like the old days.

That afternoon as I gunned the Plymouth down Eufaula's streets, I spotted Jimmy's dad in front of the brick building just as my car died making the corner. Jimmy's dad had on a short-sleeve Hawaiian shirt tucked into black slacks and blue Nike running shoes on his feet. The crowning statement was a Southwestern bolo tie with a huge chunk of deep blue turquoise lying against his dark chest, his shirt unbuttoned way down.

I started the ignition again and pulled up in front of the courthouse. Jimmy hurried his dad toward the car, hoping to get him inside before anyone saw them together, no doubt. He let his dad sit up front, much to my relief; at least I had a little break before the long car ride to the city where I was sure to find myself tongue-tied around Jimmy. Jimmy's dad was pulling papers out of a manila folder, handing them to me as I headed for their house.

"He's driving, for godsakes," Jimmy said.

"Oh, yeah," Jimmy's father said, taking back the papers. "This here's an allotment certificate from 1905. That's Indian land," he said, pointing the handful of papers toward the lake construction sites where the trees had been cleared and foundations laid. Soon me and my dad would be over there pulling conduit after the walls went up. "My brother got no right to sell that," he said. "Belongs in the family."

"But weren't you in court for throwing rocks?" I asked. "How'd you aim to win?"

"Rocks got nothing to do with it. Just wanted to scare 'em a little, make 'em listen to an Indian for once." Jimmy's dad looked pleased even though he was holding some kind of citation in his hand.

"God, Dad. It's a wonder they let you in the courthouse at all wearing that getup."

"That's my squirrel-hunting outfit. I scare them dead right out of the trees. I don't wanna have to even touch my trigger." Jimmy and his dad both laughed at the insane threat. His dad was loosening his bolo tie when I let him out of the car in front of their house. Jimmy got up in the front seat.

"Leaving the country," he said. "Oklahoma City." Like I was his chauffeur or something. Or maybe he just meant we were headed toward civilization. I could never figure him out. Or his dad either, their vacillation between all-out war and shared laughter.

Passing the Texaco station that marked the edge of town, floating above the treetops, just out of harm's way, the evening sun touching the western edge of the lake, a burning planet fixing to dive under choppy waters and resurface the next morning on the opposite bank. The morning sun would call the world into life as raccoons followed its rays down to shore and fished the shallows for crayfish, pulling black, webby fingers out of the water and into the warm morning air, their breakfast squirming before them. My pursuers left behind in the mad world below me. All these memories of flying had dimmed until some days I swore my feet had never left earth. Other times I knew I'd actually flown. The Plymouth floated past Raiford, the road spinning out behind us, and Jimmy was recalling the Okmulgee game they'd barely lost the previous weekend when a piece of gravel ricocheted off the windshield, forcing the tires of the car to touch down on the road again, and Jimmy's voice to come back into focus.

"We were off to a hot start," he was saying. "I put all these ball fakes on their defense, had them tripping all over themselves. You know they got all those really tall black dudes over to Okmulgee. They got pissed we were outfoxing them all night. Toward the end they started putting their hands right over the ball like it was some kind of Ouija board or some shit like that. None of our shooters could raise the ball clean or take a jump shot or even make a pass 'cause they was all up in our shit like that. That's when they started catching up to us. There was a lot of movement, but we couldn't get anything in the air. It all come down to that last shot at the end when I swooped downcourt and swung it to the open man for a quick shot. It was a gamble. I fucked up.

"You know any jokes?" Jimmy sighed. "I need some luck for tonight."

Don't put it all on me, I thought. Like I'm supposed to reach into my pocket and pull out some kind of good luck charm for you to wear around your neck during the game. Take off that fucking ring your girlfriend gave you, maybe that will bring you some luck. What kind of luck had he ever passed on to me, anyway? Jimmy had the pregame jitters, and he couldn't keep quiet or sit still on the seat. But I had no winning secrets; I barely understood the game. During Jimmy's street games it was all I could do to figure out when the ball needed to be taken out when playing half court.

"Where'd your aunt move to, anyway?" Jimmy asked.

Jimmy had remembered. I'd roped myself in when I said my dad wouldn't let me take the car unless I stopped in to see Lucille. This meant even less chance getting to the bookstore before it closed. When we got close to town we had to cut over to Del City to get to Lucy's.

Aunt Lucille was anything but refined taste or moderation. Her pink stucco house, neat as a pin, with its candy cane white trim, had such a profusion of rosebushes of every variety that even though she constantly fought them back, they were always swelling over the brink of her chain-link fence, their many-colored blooms pushing passersby walking the sidewalk out into the street. The yard featured a painted cutout of a windmill nailed up to a sycamore tree's first fork, so it could be seen from the street over the rosebushes. The windmill blades were spinning when we pulled up, which set into motion a man milking, seated bent over on a stool, a handkerchief in his back pocket, his hands moving mechanically up and down to simulate the tits of a cow being squeezed. It couldn't have been any more gross unless real milk squirted out into the painted representation of the tin pail.

"Lucille," Jimmy said, stretching out the syllables, just as his dad had done. Likely as not they'd heard the wild stories about her. We got out of the car. I fought the rosebushes and managed to get the gate pushed open. I knocked on her metal screen door but only managed to produce an inconsequential rattle.

"Knock on the wood door," Jimmy said.

"I can't; she's got the screen latched," I replied, annoyed at being instructed, like a kid. I looked through the blinds. Kitchen deserted, TV off in the living room, no lights on. If we hurried, we might get lucky and make it outta there before she got back. I'd get Jimmy dropped off at the game and see if the bookstore was still open.

"I hear somebody in the garage," Jimmy said.

"I don't hear anyone." But no sooner had I spoken than the sound of metal sliding on concrete could be heard, like a tool box being pushed out of the way.

A muffled voice inside the garage said, "Josh, help me get this door open." It was a big wooden garage door, one of the really heavy ones. I walked over and pulled on the handle, and Jimmy hoisted the thing up. A dusty beam of sunlight fell on Lucy, standing next to a band saw.

"Here," she said to Jimmy, "come over and help me with this." Lucy was wearing men's overalls with a pencil protector in the pocket. She had on a men's pair of black-framed nonprescription glasses. She got on her hands and knees and pulled out boxes stashed beneath the band saw, trying to get to an old leather case on the bottom. Jimmy helped her up and got the case out for her.

"How you'd know we were coming?" I asked, watching Lucy wipe her hands off on an old oily rag.

"Your dad phoned," she said. So, he was checking up on me after all. I felt better about my little lie to Jimmy about my dad verifying whether I visited Lucy, but noted that I might want to watch myself in the future. Make note they're keeping track, I thought. Could be they simply didn't want me over there around Lucy. I didn't introduce Jimmy. One way or another, Lucy was bound to know him since he was from around Eufaula. She'd ask and figure it out.

"How come you was to lose that game against Okmulgee?" she asked Jimmy. "You all had the ball but couldn't do a thing with it. Lester told me it beat anything he ever seen." Before Jimmy could defend himself, Lucy went on. "I sure do remember your daddy play-ing. He was so skinny the uniform barely hung on him. I see you filled out right smart, though." I repressed an embarrassed groan. Lucy was famous for flirting with young guys, one of the reasons the family refused to take her anyplace in public.

"Here we go," Lucy said, flipping open a metal hasp on either side of the case. I was curious to get a look. Jimmy came over and stood next to me.

A white polishing cloth lay neatly over the valves of an old trumpet whose gold plating had worn down to the dull silver metal that shined through in mottled blotches underneath. The horn was resting inside the cool red velvet lining of the brown leather case.

"God-a-mighty," Lucy said, rummaging through the case's compartment. "Valve oil, cleaning snake, rag, everything but the mouthpiece. I ain't got no more lip for it," she went on, picking up the horn lovingly with the polishing cloth, "but I was of a mind to test it out. If you boys are going to Oklahoma City anyways," Lucy said, eyeing Jimmy suggestively, "maybe we could all make a trip to the music store. You know I don't care to drive much since Glen passed last year. I'm gonna have to force myself, eventually, I reckon," she sighed.

"I got a ball game," Jimmy said, looking at his watch.

"I know that," Lucy said, putting the horn back in the case. "My air kindy give out on me, too. I'm playing mostly mid-range these days. You know, Chet Baker, some of the West Coast stuff; breezy, not too many notes. It's only over here on Southeast 29th. I just never could get used to the feel of that new horn. Valves too loose. I shoulda known an outfit that makes motorcycles ain't about to turn out a good trumpet."

"What's on Southeast 29th?" Jimmy asked. I was used to Lucy's outpourings, having to rearrange the jigsaw puzzle pieces of her stories.

"The music store where I'm gonna take back this Yamaha horn. I'll just pick up a mouthpiece for the old one, get that one going again. Maybe have the old horn dipped and cleaned. I ain't opened the case in ten years until you boys showed up. Waiting for a special occasion. You don't worry. I'll just leave it there at the store and pick it up later. You won't have to wait; you can run me right back home. The way you fellas played last weekend, I wouldn't be in no hurry to get to that game anyway," Lucy said, giving Jimmy a little smirk. "Maybe you oughta take up trumpet. Want me to teach you?"

Jimmy turned red.

A simple trip alone to the city, the one night a week I had to myself, and I seemed to be picking up unwanted passengers at every stop. I looked at Jimmy and tried to catch his eye, shaking my head no. If I could rely on Jimmy for nothing else, I knew he would always speak up, especially if a basketball game were at stake. Judging by his unusual silence, Lucy seemed to exert some kind of sway on him. "We don't even have to go inside the house," she said, pointing him toward the garage steps where a new black vinyl case sat. "Here's the horn I'm gonna exchange. I'm all ready to go." And Jimmy picked up the two cases and loaded them into the Plymouth, without a word of protest, as though he were Lucy's personal valet or something. I watched the two of them. Jimmy had climbed in the front seat, and Lucy had scrunched up against him and already had the passenger door shut. They both looked at me, standing in front of the garage, like, "Come on, what are you waiting for?"

I got in and eyed the two of them suspiciously. "Why don't one of you get in the back?" I said. Nobody moved. We looked pretty foolish, the way Lucy had managed to get all squeezed up lovey-dovey against Jimmy, and she had him all pushed up against me, too. Why he'd sat in the middle, as tall and long-legged as he was, made no sense, but I just chalked it up to the old woman.

"Turn north here on Sunnylane," Lucy said. "It ain't that far." Jimmy kept eyeing his watch. So why hadn't he discouraged her?

"This is Southeast 29th," I said. "Which way?"

"No, go past the interstate. It's up here on Reno."

"You said Southeast 29th," I insisted, trying to get her attention, but Lucy was talking to Jimmy, and the two of them were ignoring me.

"I tell you what's the truth," Lucy was saying, "that was a sight the night I started blowing for the Oklahoma City Blue Devils. I had plenty of air back then."

You've got plenty of air now, I thought.

"Tiny Bixby was playing first trumpet, and when he stood up to take his solo the sweat come off him until he hit a high C on 'Basin Street Blues' and fell flat on his face dead drunk. He'd snuck off to the bathroom during every break; he'd nearly finished a fifth. He hit the floor hard, too; he musta weighed upwards of 300 pounds. I know the musicians felt it 'cause I could see everyone grabbing for their sheet music even from back there where I was sitting with Glen. Back in those days we liked to come in and drink a little hooch of a Saturday evening, and it give Glen a chance to get out on the road and open up his new Oldsmobile he bought when the money was good working in the oil fields. The tenor sax man took over Tiny's solo, and before the band had even played the final bar of 'Basin Street,' Walter Page, the bandleader, had fired Tiny on the spot. 'Tiny, you sick sonofabitch, go dry out somewhere a long ways from my bandstand.' 'Course, Tiny was clean passed out, didn't hear a word of it."

"How much further is this place?" Jimmy asked, eyeing his watch again. We'd passed Barnes Regional Park, and we were headed away from the city. "We need to get there in the next few minutes or forget it."

"I'll just run in and out," Lucy said. "I'll tell you what. You won't even have to bring me back by the house. I'll go to the game with you all." I looked desperately at Jimmy, counting on his usual assertiveness. He was sitting still, his arm over the backrest, and Lucy leaning into him talking and talking and talking and all traces of Jimmy's pregame jitters gone. If anyone was going to stop Lucy, I'd have to do it myself.

"And then they limped along the rest of the evening with that second trumpet," Lucy said, "and he managed to just shut down the dancing after that until the floor was swept clean of dancers and nobody drinking. The trumpet guy would stand up to solo, but he couldn't hit a lick to save his life without a piece of sheet music in front of him. And even then he'd land straight on the eighth notes while everybody else was trying to swing. He got to landing right on the beat like that until he finally started to thump along right regular like an old flat tire. Walter turned so red I thought he was going to lay into him with his orchestra stick. The boys was getting paid a percentage, and when the crowd stopped dancing and drinking, the take shrunk considerable.

"Me and Glen seen the whole thing, the dance band come to a grinding halt, the trumpet player on straight eighths while everyone around him was swinging hotter than a Sunday picnic. So I went up to Walter, and I says, 'Walter, let me have a hand at that trumpet part. I'll take over, and you can send him packing before he drives all the customers outta the club.'

"'I already fired one SOB,' Walter says, 'and that's enough for a Saturday night. I'll just retire him, not fire him, and we'll do without trumpet. I'll let the square head sit in his stand and follow along with the sheet music. He can diddle his horn as long as he don't blow her. Besides, Lucille, you might could pass as colored, since you're darker than some of these high-yeller horn boys, but you'll never pass for a man.'

"'You ain't seen me in overalls,' I told him.

"'We don't wear overalls,' Walter said. 'The club won't let us in here without these God-blessed band uniforms. Pretty soon management gonna get so fussy about our appearance, they'll make us wear these penguin suits even when we're out cattin'. Now, if you was a singer, Lucy, that would be another story entirely. They'll 'low that. But you can't play a horn on the stand 'less you got one in your britches, too.'

"Walter didn't talk to me like a lady, but I was used to that. Some might have called me cruel back then for dragging Glen to them all-black speakeasies of a weekend after he'd worked his tail off out in the field, but that's where the jazz was. I'd been inching my way closer and closer to the bandstand, and I waddn't about to give up."

Jimmy took off his wristwatch and handed it to Lucy. "Here," he said, "put this in the glove box." I couldn't figure out what for. Maybe he was just anticipating the game when he'd have to suit up. But he'd been worried about getting there on time.

Lucy took the watch from Jimmy like a gift just for her. "Thank you," she said, thoughtfully, studying the face of the timepiece before opening the glove box and tossing it in. Jimmy nodded, like, "don't mention it." I just kept driving, wishing for some way to get Lucy back to the house and bust up their little party.

"So I come up with the best gol-durned thing that happened that night as well as the move that kicked off my career in first trumpet with the Oklahoma City Blue Devils. Me and the second trumpet grabbed a-holt of an arm and leg each and hauled Tiny behind the band promo partition that seconded as a place to change outfits and the like. I picked up Tiny's horn from where it had hit the floor and give it the onced over. The valves waddn't stuck or nonesuch even though the bell was bent a little. The crowd thought we was just laying Tiny out to rest until he could come to. But I stayed back there

behind the partition. And before he climbed back on the bandstand,
I told the second player what to do. I says, 'Every time you're supposed
to blow, stand up and fake it, and I'll let loose with Tiny's horn here
behind the wall.'

"Now, that's where I got all my wind from; I had to blow twiced
as hard as any trumpet player of my time, hidden off behind the bandstand like that. We got back in the swing of things that night as soon
as I took over; the dance floor filled back up, and the wine and liquor
started to flow. Walter waddn't about to let go of his new invisible
trumpet player, nor his old square-head trumpet player who couldn't
swing even if he was in a fistfight, but he turned out to be a mighty
fine actor, the best fake trumpeter from here to Kansas City."

Lucy turned to Jimmy and asked, "Hadn't we oughta be getting to
the game?" Jimmy nodded. "Aren't you all playing over at OCU?" she
asked. Another nod from Jimmy. "You better get us over there, Josh.
Quick as you can," she said, like I was the driver and they were Bonnie
and Clyde.

"You're the one who wanted to go to the music store," I complained.
What was next? Now, I'd have to go to the game and sit there and talk
basketball with the old woman. I'd have to drop her off afterwards,
and Jimmy would most likely end up riding back with me.

"Turn around and head back to town," Lucy instructed. We'd
passed a bridge over a creek, and we were coming up on a field of
cows next to some high red banks somebody had bulldozed to start a
farm pond. There was no way in hell there could be any music store
out this direction. I turned around in the field road. "Reno will take us
right over to OCU," Lucy said. Yeah, fifteen miles back, maybe.

When we finally backtracked to the city, we let Jimmy out, and
he headed for the men's locker room. After we got seated up in the
stands, Lucy popped open her purse. She'd emptied everything out of
it and packed it full of peanuts. This seemed mighty suspicious, this
purseful of peanuts, as if she'd known all along that she was going to
rope me and Jimmy into taking her with us.

"Not much of a game," she said, "without salted peanuts. Here,
hold out your hands." I obliged. Lots of kids from my school were there,

but none of them were sitting next to an old woman; they were all huddled together laughing and talking, waiting for the game to begin.

Jimmy started out kind of herky-jerky, it looked like to me. I didn't know the basketball term for it, if there was one, but he was taking mincing steps, as if his legs weren't quite hinged in the middle. He seemed to dribble with the flat of his hand like he was holding a two-by-four.

"Who are you watching?" Lucy asked, cracking open a peanut. Jimmy had the ball—was I supposed to be looking at someone else? I almost said, "Jimmy," then checked myself. Because Lucy made me realize I was watching Jimmy no matter who had the ball. I didn't know what to say, if you could admit watching a guy as long as it was a basketball game.

"What do you think about him?" Lucy said, continuing her line of inquiry. I started studying my peanuts, feeling my face turn red, like Jimmy's had earlier. Did she mean his game, the way he'd played that year? Or his moves that moment on the court? Maybe she thought I'd heard some gossip about him or his family. She sure to God couldn't want to know what I thought about *him*.

When I didn't answer she laughed at me. "You always was a quiet one. Just shut up tighter than a terrapin sometimes. It'd sure be nice to have some beer with these peanuts."

"Yeah, right," I said. "At OCU. This is Oklahoma, remember?"

"No way in hell to get beer at a high school game," Lucy sighed, "but it don't make you want one any less."

"Can I have some more peanuts?" I asked nervously. Cracking open shells would at least give me something to do with myself.

But Lucy had thrown all her attention to the court. "Wow," she said, grabbing my arm. "Did you see that? Jimmy just took the ball in the pivot and jumped and turned and stretched hisself out like a snake, unwinding until he let go with one of them long arms of his and dunked it in there clean as a whistle. He's beautiful, isn't he?"

I wanted to chalk the question up to her flirtatiousness, her interest in young handsome guys, but I couldn't. It seemed like she expected an answer. What was she trying to worm out of me, anyway? Maybe I

could get her off this kick of hers by tricking her into telling one of
her stories. She didn't seem to have any secrets, nothing she wouldn't
talk about. If she'd done it, she'd tell it. My plan had been to pick up a
book, sit and read it during the game, see if Jimmy still wanted a ride
home at the end or if he'd just go back with the guys on the bus. Well,
that plan was all shot to hell, but maybe I could at least escape from
Lucy's questions.

So I said, "Is that old trumpet in the car the one you took off of
Tiny the night he passed out?"

"What's Tiny's trumpet got to do with basketball?" she huffed.
Roy Hillabee had called Jimmy over, and Jimmy was hunched over on
the bench, breathing hard. Rivers of sweat ran down his neck and disappeared under his jersey, staining it dark. Hillabee was crouched
down, his hand on the back of Jimmy's neck, and he was giving him
instructions. Lucy was watching Jimmy getting coached during the
time-out. And then she turned and said to me, "You ever talk to him
about basketball?"

I knew she meant Jimmy. "I don't know anything about basketball," I said.

"Maybe he could teach you," she answered. I hated this. In
Oklahoma you weren't shit unless you could make some team. All
I asked was to be allowed to suffer my nonexistence quietly. But no.
I had to have people like Lucy remind me that my world counted for
nothing. Like a few lessons from Jimmy and by the end of next week
I'd be the star center for the Eufaula Chieftains.

"You could always talk about books, then," she said.

"He doesn't know anything about books. Aren't you missing the
game?"

"No," she answered, matter-of-factly. "I always had an eye for
everything that was going on around me." I felt like I had a vampire at
my neck, draining me dry. I had to get away. The game had barely
started.

"I'll wait out in the car," I said.

"Who ever waits out in the car at a basketball game? What did
you come here for, anyway?"

"You made me come here." Now we were quibbling like two kids.

"No, I wanted to go to the music store. You boys was already on your way to the basketball game."

And then she reached over with another handful of peanuts, and the second I opened my palm to take them, she added, "Together."

When I left, our team was still ahead, and Lucy let me go without a parting shot. Out in the parking lot, I rolled down the windows of the Plymouth and stretched out on the back seat. Mosquitoes kept biting my arms, and I could smell the freshly mowed grass of the football field. Some kids in another car were arguing about who looked old enough to buy beer at the liquor store. I could see one of those floodlights arcing back and forth across the city sky, probably a car dealer advertising a special weekend sale.

Jimmy lifted up his arms, and I helped him pull off his basketball jersey. I got the jersey off of him, and he floated away, sinking into darkness as bubbles floated up toward the surface. "Why'd you turn loose of me on shore?" I cried out, but the words made no sense underwater. I dived down into the black depths and pulled him from the bottom of the lake. We surfaced in a basketball court. He was worn out from playing so hard. "Thanks, man," he said gratefully, cupping his hand around the back of my neck, just as coach Hillabee had done earlier to him, except he pulled our foreheads together. He clapped me on my back, and I was just about to run back into the game, when he took my hand and opened my fingers and dropped kernels of unpopped popcorn into my palm. I stepped back, and it was Jimmy's girlfriend, stuffing the hard corn into her mouth. "Yuk," I said, throwing the gift down on the gymnasium floor, where each kernel landed on a little flame and popped, turning into basketballs that me and Jimmy pulled from the fires while his dad watched up in the stands.

"Wake up, Josh," Lucy said, "we're ready to go."

"I can drive," Jimmy said, "if you're sleepy."

"Sure, if you want," I answered, sitting up in the back seat and rubbing my eyes.

"How'd the game go?"

"Great, man. We're back full steam now." Jimmy had changed into his street clothes. His hair was wet from showering, and he smelled like he'd just put on deodorant or cologne or something.

"If you all keep pushing the ball like that," Lucy said, "and you can keep away a little more from all the contact and the whistle blowing, you'll be running circles around those guys. Nobody'll be able to touch you." Lucy gave me a blow-by-blow account all the way back to her house while Jimmy grinned during every word of her precisely recalled choreography of his movements. You'd think he was the only one on the team, to hear Lucy tell it. He let her out and carried her trumpets to the front door while she fished around for her keys.

He got back in the car and said, "I like your aunt, man. No matter what everybody says about her. She's a cool old lady. How old is she, anyway?"

"Ancient," I answered. "Just go to the interstate and cut over at Shawnee," I told Jimmy. I wanted to talk shop like Lucy had, say something smart about the game. I'd planned on sneaking back in before the game ended, not getting caught sleeping out in the car. I felt like a little kid who'd gone to sleep up in the bleachers, except I wasn't even in the stands when the grown-ups were ready to leave.

Jimmy still seemed buzzed from the game. He had his arm dangling lazily out the window, and he was searching all over the radio for some tunes to drive home to besides the usual Oklahoma hillbilly stuff. When we passed the I-40 exit, and he kept heading south on Pennsylvania, I asked, "Where are you going?"

"Oh, I've got something I want to show you," he said. "It's amazing. You wanna get some beer first?"

I shrugged. I didn't drink much. I had nothing against drinking like my parents did, but I was just too much of a loner to go out and party with anyone. I'd always imagined Jimmy as the healthy athlete. You couldn't play basketball or practice hard hung over. But then I'd known him to smoke a little dope, have a pack of cigarettes on him for a while then quit; now this. Unpredictable. I knew as little about drinking as I did about sports, so what did I know about beer and playing basketball? Outside the liquor store I saw the same kids who'd been arguing at the game, parked in front, trying to get someone to go in and buy for them. I knew it would be a helluva lot easier for under-age white kids to score some booze than two Indians pleading with white customers as they entered the beer joint. So I said, "Jimmy, give your money to that white dude. They're trying to pick up a six-pack, too."

"How'd you know that?" Jimmy asked.

"I heard them out in the parking lot at the game." I wanted to make myself useful, show that I hadn't been a total loser since Lucy and Jimmy had been running the show all evening, and I'd been caught napping during the game. The kid took our money and gave it to a grizzled old drunk who staggered into the store and came back with a grocery sack to distribute to the white kids and us. He'd bought us a fifth of Jack Daniels, of all things, and then he didn't have much change because the whiskey cost a lot more than the beer. He insisted on keeping the dollar and a handful of coins left over from the pur-chase for his "commission." We didn't argue because the store clerk had stepped out front to chase us all off, or so we thought, until he came up to me and Jimmy and told us to get the hell out of there while the white kids sat watching undisturbed inside their car, and the drunk popped open a can inside a paper sack in front of the store.

Jimmy drove south down Pennsylvania, kind of like we were headed toward the stockyards. "Here," he said, handing me the bottle of whiskey, "keep it low." I tried to keep him from seeing my hands shaking. I unscrewed the black cap, took a swig, and I couldn't believe the fire fanning out inside me as soon as I swallowed. Jimmy's easy-going chatter disappeared as I put all my concentration toward keep-ing the stuff down. I handed the bottle to Jimmy right away. And I thought sitting through the basketball game was going to be tough.

Jimmy parked the car next to a section of older, single-story stucco homes, and I figured it was so he could drink for a spell, but he got out of the car and said, "Follow me." He strode down the street with the bottle under his jacket, big confident strides that made him seem older. We were walking in the direction of Wheeler Park. He handed me the bottle again, and I took it reluctantly. The next drink came sur-prisingly easy, even though it tasted just as bad. We walked through the park, where Jimmy didn't have to hide the bottle anymore. "Just watch for cops driving by," he told me. Jimmy led me to a spot where the woods started up and a trail dropped down the bank into the darkness. He sure had gotten quiet all of a sudden. He kept looking back to see if I was still coming, and he seemed nervous at whatever it was he wanted to show me, like he might change his mind.

I couldn't imagine what it could be, but I felt the whiskey pulling me down the path. I was startled out of the haze when Jimmy took me by the hand and led me along. "How come you done that?" I asked him.

"I just don't want you to get lost," he said nervously, as he urged me farther down the path past broken tree trunks and across swampy places where the trail was covered with standing water. "No," I said, jerking my hand away, "I don't need to be led anywhere. I can find my way back." Was I *that* drunk? I couldn't believe he'd just done that.

"Okay," Jimmy said, "no problem." This wasn't the confident basketball star or the Jimmy who mouthed off to teachers behind their backs and sometimes to their faces. But he kept heading down the trail. On our right was a steep wooded bank and to our left, out in the middle of the north fork of the Canadian, fingers of moonlight brushed the ridges of a sandbar that was framed against the black forms of houses looming across the river.

Jimmy kept trying to hold my hand again as we stumbled along the path through a mist that had come in with the humid night air. So this is what drunks are like, I thought, always trying to grab a-holt of you. The mist reached from bank to bank of the Canadian, a ghostly white bullfrog stretching and billowing out in mid-leap over the river. I remembered how my grandpa would say "it sure is froggy out" on nights like this. Just east I could see a bridge and hear a few cars speeding across some overpass. Alone with Jimmy in the middle of an interminable series of trails that penetrated the mist along the river and coiled through trees and loped up and down wooded hills. The lights of the city, visible on the other shore, might as well have been across an expanse of ocean for all I knew of how to find my way back. But the whiskey seemed to keep me putting one foot in front of the other.

Jimmy broke the silence. "Okay, we're going to come around a corner up here. Just watch. And keep moving."

What the hell? I was scared of Jimmy's fear, the hesitation in his voice. He was the guide, the one who'd brought me here. The path took a sharp turn away from the river, and the open expanse of water was replaced by trees on both sides of the trail that created a canopy that blocked out all the moonlight. We were passing through a dark tunnel, and before we came all the way through it, men began rising up from behind copses and trees, approaching as silently as communicants. Though I'd never seen such a thing, immediately I knew what the men were there for. Lovers of darkness rather than lovers of light; I could hear the preacher's voice. Oh, my God, I thought, if I pass out from the whiskey, I'll be devoured by these ghosts, stripped to the bone like a carcass surrounded by vultures, covered by the black pitch of night, unspeakable acts taking place all around me. I wanted to fly away, but my feet wouldn't lift off the trail like in the old days, and Jimmy would grab my hand and pull me in deeper every time I hesitated. I'd see a little bit of light, regain my confidence, and pull away from him again, making my way on my own. "Yea, though I walk through the valley of the shadow of death," I thought, but I couldn't laugh, and I couldn't see Jimmy, so I reached for his hand and let him coil his fingers tightly around mine. They felt good in the dark, wrapping tightly around my hand.

Upright stumps formed vague shapes whose features became recognizable, on closer approach, as men, in groups of three and four, hands reaching for one another. One of these groups of ghosts glided toward me and Jimmy; they were rigid, expressionless, silent, and when I tried to run, Jimmy tightened his grip on my hand and wouldn't let me go. When they got close enough that I could see the looks on their faces, I could feel their hunger, their taste for flesh. They were searching for bodies they could take over and inhabit under the cover of darkness before the morning light drove them away after having escaped the woods unscathed, giving their names away to no one. Maybe it's better that way, I thought, out in the woods, no chance of recognition, no need for conversation.

We reached the end of the tunnel, and the path turned back toward the river. Jimmy took a pull from the whiskey bottle and relaxed a little. "You ever seen anything like that?" he asked.

I just shook my head. My flying had never taken me anyplace like this. The sky was free of this kind of darkness; only on land could something like this happen.

"I told you," Jimmy said. "It's like nothing you ever seen." How in the hell did he discover this graveyard? I wondered. "The first time I didn't know if they were real or the spirits of the river. They call it cruising."

Who calls it that? And how did Jimmy know any of them? He couldn't have talked to them out here since none of them seemed to speak. Did they have another life somewhere else? Yeah, *bothas,* bad spirits, I thought, the kind my parents used to warn me about before they became Baptists. Well, even after they became Baptists, except now they called it all superstitions.

"This is what I wanted you to see, I guess, because it's my favorite hangout. I like coming here after city games, just to watch the river go by—in spite of the ghouls you have to pass by to get here," Jimmy laughed.

So, he was talking again. We seemed to be on safer ground, having passed through the dark canopy of trees. Jimmy was back to himself, and we could see the Canadian. "Is there another way to get back?" I asked.

We sat down to rest on the riverbank. I watched a beer can circling in an eddy of debris and stagnant water, then filling up and slipping under.

Jimmy said, "I came here to tell you something." He tried to make it sound like no big deal, like the way he'd analyze one of his games. This was a helluva ordeal to go through just to sit and drink and shoot the shit. And he kept looking at the river, pausing, watching the water go by, as if the words he needed were getting away from him, rushing by in the current.

"I must have been about ten or eleven, and I had a friend who was different like I was," Jimmy said, pausing, searching for the right way to continue. I'd never seen him at a loss for words.

No way. He had to be lying. How could a basketball player who never shut up and kept people all around him laughing and listening to his jokes and watching his antics feel different? That was my story, not his. He must have meant looking black. But he was just an Indian to everyone I knew, even though a lot of assholes gave him so much shit for his skin color. But we all gave each other shit, as much as possible; that's how we knew who we were. Except for my silence, which made me even more suspect. I didn't know how to dish it back out without giving myself away, letting my secret out of the bag. Jimmy and I had touched in the water, touched in his bed, but I didn't know what it meant. I only hoped to God it didn't have anything to do with the darkness we'd just passed through and the hungry men rising up out of the bushes.

"I really remember him distinctly," Jimmy said, "because our families were friends, so we'd often go places together on weekends like camping and picnics. We were both really literate at a very young age, and we sensed something in each other; the way it worked is hard to explain." Literate? I thought. Do you call *Sports Illustrated* literate? If Jimmy had read anything, I'd never heard him talk about it. But I read books, and who did I ever discuss them with? Especially what it was I was looking for in the books I read. I couldn't tell anyone about that.

"Are you talking about C.A.?" I asked. But why C.A.? Me and Jimmy didn't have anything in common with that big sissy.

"Maybe," Jimmy said evasively.

I had no idea how to find my way back alone and Jimmy talked too damn much. "I still don't understand how we knew about each other," Jimmy said, "but I remember this one weekend in particular. His family came over and we were picnicking, and I used to have a Speak and Spell. It was one of those little toys where you would push the buttons, and it would say letters. We were alone and my parents were off talking and my friend spelled out, letter by letter, 'I am not like anyone else,' and I wrote back, 'Me neither.' We never really did anything;

he was fourteen, and I was only ten. It was like a secret between us for quite a while. We knew about each other, and it became an unspoken thing. He got in trouble and ended up spending a lot of time in the juvenile detention center, so he was taken away. I kind of missed him because he was the only one who knew what was going on."

I thought I was going to be sick for a minute, and I placed my head in my hands. I needed silence, time to think, not all this chatter, so many words. It was too much. We had to get back to the car. I had to have it home by midnight. I'd never even brought it back late, and I had no idea what my parents would do. Yet I felt a hunger; I wanted to hear more like I had wanted nothing else, though I couldn't tell if what I truly hungered for was a touch, a friend, a story. I wanted something that I couldn't explain or even imagine what it would be like if I had it. I had no words for it, only the flying, and that had left me.

I wanted to talk to Jimmy, to join him and his friends in the easy banter he surrounded himself with. I wanted my eyes to look into a sympathetic face, just once. I wanted to look into Jimmy's eyes one time without dropping my gaze to the floor, afraid of the glance that lingered a little too long, the smile that remained a fraction of a second more than it should, uncertain what Jimmy might do if anyone noticed me looking. Sometimes I felt the words rising within me, about to break through to the surface, as if I could almost reach down and help yank them from their depths. I felt them just within reach, when the words would sink back down before I could speak. If I ever brought forth these words, what would I first utter? I wanted words that moved like a wave, words that crashed against my dammed-up body, rising and spilling out, a great flood broken loose, beyond my imaginings, actual speech, words that would not return void but as a net of names, pulled back in, their secrets sparkling in the tangled weave. But my words, it seemed, would not suffice; they lacked the force to rise against the choking feeling when I began to think whether I was like the men I'd just seen approaching in the darkness.

"You all right?" Jimmy asked. He seemed afraid of me, of what I might do or say about where he'd brought me. "Are you gonna tell anyone?" he asked. I'd never had any power over him before.

"I just need to walk around for a bit," I said, and I tried to stand up but sagged back down to my knees. Jimmy got on his feet and took me by the hand, mistaking my meaning. He must have thought I wanted to continue farther down the trail into the woods. Together. I felt dizzy and lost, wanting to escape Jimmy, yet unable to find my way back to the car without him.

We passed another group of men, this time standing in the open just off the path, two upright, two on their knees. The darkness covered their features, and there were no sounds but the river flowing behind them. Jimmy said, "How do we know they're real since they never speak?" I had never seen anything like this before, so much sex, going on all around me, covered in darkness. I couldn't keep from looking; it was like a building on fire; I couldn't turn my eyes away. Nobody ever told me anything like this happened in Oklahoma or anywhere else. I had to watch these ghosts, these men—and I believed Jimmy that they might be either. I realized for the first time that I was far drunker than Jimmy, and I felt cheated. I wanted us both blasted beyond recognition. I took another drink from the fifth of J.D., hoping to see more.

The whiskey kicked in, and I felt my body begin to float away and drift off to the place of the men with no words. I saw this as some- where in space where all their unspoken stories piled up like bones, an accumulation of dust. The words hung just above the little circles of men until, with each act performed in darkness, enough words bunched together, and they flew off in clumps of silence to this land of gray ashes. The men had touched and not spoken, ignited fires that would only burn out by morning. Jimmy's jacket had gone up in flames, ignited by our sins. But Jimmy and me were still here, weren't we, neither stranger to the other.

I was too drunk. I could see a war of words, and it was going on inside my head. I hadn't thought that much about Grandpa's stories, or Lucy's, because the church stories were always at war against them, and I'd heard the church stories more often, every Sunday since I could remember anything at all. The church stories were a barrage in my head that never let up and blasted over my grandpa's and Lucy's

voices. The stories I heard Sunday after Sunday in the white Southern
Baptist church my parents had taken me to. The stories I needed
because they held off the devil. I could sometimes feel them coming at
me from all sides like rounds of gunfire. I couldn't protect myself from
the words dropping all around me, so fast, when I least expected them.
"For the wages of sin are death" would whistle past me, and, if I
dodged that volley, I would be hit with "For all have sinned and come
short of the glory of God," the words raining down upon me, or
turning and retreating, I would run from "Know ye not that the
effeminate shall not enter the kingdom of heaven." It never let up,
these other stories, constantly advancing, riddling me with sharp stabs
of pain, yet I was terrified of the prospect of not believing them, so
I lived with their chaos.

Once I'd gone with my granddad's brother to the Pentecostal
church. He went to a white church, too, like my parents, but one much
too rowdy and redneck for the likes of my folks, who were trying to
get somewhere in the world by hanging out with the right kind of
people. I stood in a healing line with my great-uncle, who'd stepped
forward because of the arthritis in his knees. A huge preacher from
Texas, wiping his forehead with a white handkerchief, prayed over my
Uncle Ernest first. "In Christ," he said, "there is no respect of persons,"
which I took to mean he'd pray for Uncle Ernest even though he was
Indian. My uncle was slain in the spirit, and he fell backwards under
the power of God. When the preacher stepped over my uncle and
moved on to me, he asked me what I needed prayer for. I mumbled
something vague about a personal problem. I knew better than to
name the real affliction, and I couldn't even say the word anyway,
whatever the word might be, not even to myself. The revivalist placed
both hands on either side of my head and shouted, "I bind you, Satan,
in the name of Jesus, and I loose the power of the Holy Spirit to be
manifested in this boy's life. I bind the spirit of confusion, I bind the
spirit of waywardness, I bind the spirit of doubt, and I release faithuh
in the name of Jesus! I release the poweruh of the blood of Jesus! I
plead the blooduh over this young man! Satan, you will take your

handsuh off this boy's life!" Electricity had shot through me like a bolt
of lightning, shaking me from head to toe.

The healing never took, so I figured that it was like a spiritual
flu—after a while it would go away if I just had enough faith, if I just
had a little more commitment; if I grew up and met the right woman,
she would take away these wayward feelings. It was this very trip to
the river with Jimmy; this was the kind of thing that would fuck
everything up. I would have to fight off the lure of these dark places.
Maybe it was good we'd come down here; now I knew what I was
up against.

At night I dreamed the devil's shadow, a burning weight that
pressed me down. The devil was thick in the air of my room, hovering
and trying to suck out my spirit like my grandma had told me a cat
could steal a baby's breath. I knew I had to find the right words to
come awake, to cast off the dream with the fluttering of my eyelids.
I would begin spewing forth a litany of Bible verses, all the ones I'd
faithfully committed to heart as a kid, my Sunday school verses. It was
a vital matter to chant them without pause, to throw up a shield of
words between myself and the devil looming over me. I would exhaust
my memory and find myself still writhing and weighted down and
lapsing into speechlessness, unable to form words. I would wake up
groaning and terrified. All my life I'd been searching for the right
words to wake up from a bad dream. I could not distinguish my own
voice from the voices of others which swirled around in my head.

I wanted badly for Jimmy to touch me, and the thought sickened
and shamed me. Ha ha ha, the ghosts would call at sunrise. From the
pale ashen place, the river's wandering dead would hiss and groan at me
from their shadows, unable to speak. I imagined the unspoken words
coming at dawn to carry me off to the place of silence. They would
arrive in a long procession, led by a blue-faced, cowl-covered word with
large bloodless hands that gestured wildly while its lips moved but
produced no sounds. I felt myself running backwards, away from the
words, but they rose up and flowed around me, carrying me swiftly
away. I would take the darkness with me then, a dream with no waking.

I looked out over the water to discover that the Canadian River was full of moonlight. A cool dew had begun to cover my skin. The moonlight slumped through the fog and was stretching out over the dark waters. I saw the moon five feet away, reflected in the river, and when I leaned forward to place my throbbing head in my hands, my own face was in the center of the watery moon. The moon wavered in the current, pausing for permission to hold my face against the shimmering light.

"Fuck it. I'm leaving," I said. "I'll find my own way back," and I swayed up unsteadily on my feet and lurched toward the trail. I wanted out of the woods, away from the river, far from Jimmy.

"Christ. Wait up," Jimmy said. "All you had to do was say something, and I'd have taken you back. Hey, you're going the wrong way!" Jimmy grabbed me and turned me toward the car, but when I faced him my hands were clenched fists, and I started pummeling him as hard as I could. I got in a misplaced jab that landed on his chest and even winded him, then I grazed his upper lip. Jimmy was bent over, holding his hand to his mouth and spitting out blood while trying to fend off my blows at the same time. I was swinging and sobbing, blinded by my tears until I was punching mostly at air. Jimmy grabbed me and pulled me tight against his chest in a bear hug so I couldn't use my fists. We both sank to our knees in the sand.

I couldn't stop crying, and I didn't know if we were still fighting when Jimmy started kissing my eyebrows and my forehead, whispering, "It's okay, shush, shh," as he ran his fingers down my neck. I fell backwards into the cold, damp sand of the riverbank, the wetness seeping up through my clothes. Jimmy touched my throat gently, and then put one finger to my lips. I lay back as Jimmy loomed above me. Jimmy slipped a hand inside my shirt and bent over and kissed me, and I could see Jimmy framed against the moon over the river, rising up and filling the circle of yellow light. I felt like I would soon break into a thousand shards, beyond my ability to piece myself back together. Jimmy, his face in the grass, whispered into my ear, "Take it easy. I'm on your side, remember?"

Jimmy held my face and pulled me closer. "I will never let anyone touch me again," I thought. I was too exhausted to flee, and when Jimmy's hands moved over my chest, we were falling into each other, and I gave in. Jimmy jerked me toward him by my belt so we were both facing each other on our sides, and we savagely fumbled at each other's pants; then we were together, flesh to flesh, touching everywhere, and I felt Jimmy on top of me, and I was lost inside the motion joining the two of us together as we rose and fell against each other.

Neither one of us said anything for a long while. My head was throbbing, and I was sobering up and shivering from the moist river sand. Jimmy broke the silence first. "I know you need to get going, but let's wait for the sunrise. I promise to take you back after that." I didn't have the strength to argue; my mind was focused on holding back the wave of nausea that was sweeping over me as what I had just done began to catch up with me, and I felt as if Jimmy had stolen my spirit.

"You ever try to catch the exact moment when dawn occurs?" Jimmy asked. "It's like all at once everywhere it's morning, and you can't say exactly when it started. Listen, like right now, first it's completely silent."

It was quiet, I noticed. No cars could be heard sweeping across the overpass anymore. "Hear the first sound?" Jimmy asked. I strained to listen and smiled weakly when I recognized the bullfrogs croaking from the riverbanks. "Look, the first thing you see, way over the water, is a kind of dull line where the black is softening into gray and the city is starting to spread out." I could see dark blurs becoming buildings. As Jimmy spoke, the sun rose. A dull red lapped up against the black clouds. I could hear traffic picking up in the distance. Everything else was still, and the sound seemed so far away. "Watch," Jimmy said, pointing toward the middle of the river. "Look at the red streak crawling on the water." I saw a finger of orange light advancing across the river. It lit up a snag in the middle of the current, and the rays splashed off a red Coke can that was bobbing up and down in an eddy around the branch. The water was no longer black but muddy red in the morning light. "Notice," Jimmy said, "how the mist rolls up off the river and you can see the tree line where we've been walking." I saw the east reddening up over the tops of trees, and I could make out the older homes in the neighborhood where Jimmy had parked the car and started down the trail, their porches bathed in light. All around me was the glow of the morning sky, the red radiance that touched the treetops and reached down in fingers of light to the ground, light that had appeared at sunrise when night and day had merged on the horizon. "Smell that breeze?" Jimmy asked. "It's different than the nighttime. Fresh. Not the river water smell of dead fish." The chilly wind fanned over me and gave me goose bumps on my arms. "Listen," Jimmy was saying, "next thing you know you've got the birds singing full blast and everywhere; here, the river, the city; it's morning and it has snuck right up on you by surprise. You never know exactly when it begins."

We got up to leave. On the way back to the car, the men were gone—no heads behind bushes, no huddled circles off the trail, no evidence they had ever been.

Jimmy wanted to stop on the way back to buy some smokes. When we got inside the convenience store, he didn't have any money. I paid for the pack of Marlboros, and the clerk threw them in a paper sack and pushed it across the counter to me. I picked up the bag and offered Jimmy the cigarettes. "Here," I said, holding out the bundle in my hands, "take this."

SIX

Once around the Lake

LUCY, EUFAULA, OKLAHOMA, 1990

I, Lucille, smoking words on my tongue, dreaming of whippoorwill
calls, casting swirled memories on the waters, has stories too dark
to tell. A life of talking, and I ain't told some of them to anybody.
Sometimes I've hidden my light under a bushel, covered my meanings
with smoke and fog. But in my stronger moments I know how to
make them laugh by holding back; I can bring them to the brink of
themselves. I play my words like a trumpet, let the space between
notes fill in the meaning. Like how Louis Armstrong done it, cut loose
and hold back in a slow blues. When he stops blowing, the song keeps
going. Or maybe how Bob Wills strung it out with his Texas Playboys
is kind of my style—"take it away, Al, take it away"—and Brother Al
Stricklin touches them piano keys. "Get it low, Al, you know what low
means." I can step in and out with my stories just like that; the band
rests, and I take my chance to solo, play my words against the piano,
bass, guitar, drums of the rhythm section while everybody else falls
quiet. And if they're listening right, if they take in the words, not just
hearing them with their ears but soaking them up through their body

openings, when it's their turn to stand up and sound out, they'll play all the better themselves for it.

"Take me back to Tulsa, I'm too young to marry." But Bob Wills never told how Tulsey town wasn't founded by the Sooners but by the Tallasi Locapoka town members of the Creek Nation sixty years earlier than the city of Tulsa was incorporated. Bob don't say either how that city is built upon land allotments of Muskokalkee peoples who was tricked by bankers and merchants, deliberately put into debt, with the intent of foreclosure in order to steal their land. I know this because when I was little I listened close; I was learned easy.

What I've held back, perhaps, what I want to say the most, is a right ugly sound, out of tune, off-key, a clash against the sweeter chords, a step behind the driving beat of my other tellings. This ain't no sweet-hot fiddle breakdown. You might say she's beating around the bush. Gonna put off finally telling it. Maybe I am taking the long way around the lake, but you're gonna hear it. All of it. Usually, I jump right in there, but I'm warming up on this one, stretching out, blowing a few practice notes to steady my nerves for the real thing. While I wait here for my weekly visitor Bob to show up, I'm giving it a dry run, lining it out in my head. This time I ain't gonna falter in mid-solo, give you one or two trumpet blasts and leave you waiting on the next notes.

This story begins like a stone throwed in the middle of a pond. When do the ripples begin, where do they end? What comes to mind right now is the day of Daddy's funeral. Now, if it hadda been any of the rest of us, Mama, me, or one of my little brothers and sisters, they'd have buried us regular like Indian folks. It goes without saying, naturally, that one of us would have to sit up with the body until they put him in the ground.

First off, they'd have put Daddy in his best clothes at an Indian funeral. We'd have put a jar of *sofki* in the casket so Daddy'd have something to eat as he journeyed to the next world. He was fond of his tobacco, so we'd have made sure to put a can of Bull Durham and some cigarette papers in there, too. Every one of us, all of my little brothers and sisters, we had twelve of them, some older than me, some younger, would have stepped forward and throwed one clod on the grave to "shake hands for the last time," which is what we call it. Mama might have put a coat down after the grave was full and mounded over and a few other things Daddy needed. The grave diggers and other members of the family would have to be careful and drink and wash ourselves in medicine 'cause walking on grave dirt causes arthuritis. You might ask when that dead man is ever gonna be able to eat that food or use them belongings. Well, here's your answer: the same time that white man comes up out of there and smells them flowers.

After the burial Mama would have fixed a big feast of most everything—chicken and rice, blue dumplings, hominy, beans, squash, sour corn bread, *abuske, sofki,* salt meat, and lots of iced tea for everybody. She'd of held out a little taste from each dish and put it on the grave later. It don't take too much; the dead only taste it. They would have buried Daddy with his feet toward the east. At the west end of the grave, they'd have driven a wooden stake and kindled a small fire a few feet away from where he lay. Us and Mama and the kinfolks would stay there every night for four nights until midnight. See, it takes them four days and nights to get to the next world. The men would build a little house over the gravesite, about three or four foot high, made of a wooden frame and a shingle roof. You can see through the board slats on the side, and inside Mama would put Daddy's favorite things such as his razor strap. There would have been so many kin and neighbors that after a while a person would wish she could just get off by herself for a spell.

Such as it was, though, Daddy's white people come over from Eufaula way and got him. They wouldn't even tell Mama when the funeral was. She found out by going to town and seeking out Daddy's mixed-blood cousin who he never would admit to being kin to, Betty Lou McIntosh. Even though most of her white kin didn't have much to do with her, she still knew what was going on, and told Mama the funeral whereabouts. Mama brought me, but she didn't try to drag all the little kids over there seeings how we'd be lucky to get in ourselves. We walked in that funeral parlor, and every one of them white faces turned around and stared. There was an usher there, but no one showed us a place to sit. The white Baptist preacher had been talking to Daddy's sister, but when we come in there he stopped in mid-sentence and watched our every move as Mama quietly found us a place to sit down. Mama taught me not to stare at strangers, but I looked him right back, stare for stare, locked him tight with my eyes, didn't drop my head.

That preacher had a hangdog look, like a small cur come upon a big dog twiced his size. He wasn't all that old in years, but his hair, blond as wheat straw, already showed gray, and he walked stooped over at the shoulders. He had black circles under his eyes that kind of made him ghostlike. But judging what he looked like hadn't prepared me for what happened when he opened his mouth. Daddy lay in the casket behind the front row, and they'd folded his hands over his chest. His white peoples, I reckon, put him in a brown suit 'cause I'd never seen him in anything but overalls. I looked over at Mama and wondered what she was thinking about the way they had Daddy made up, but her face, blank as a starched sheet, revealed nothing in front of these strangers. In spite of seeing the proof right in front of me—Daddy's hands that I could recollect every detail of even with my eyes shut; those big clubs, thick, stubby fingers, explosive blue veins, hands the funeral people had unfisted—I had the feeling it wasn't Daddy but some other old boy, a man in a brown suit taking a nap.

As that little preacher walked over to the pulpit on the right side of the room and climbed up there, I was a-studying whether heaven might be any better or worse than the four-day way. The preacher's first words liked to have laid me low and knocked me out of my drifting. He sounded forth like the voice of many waters; a river come pouring out of that dammed-up body. Now, I mean he didn't start low and hushed and bubbling and build up; he come into it full force:

"Though our hearts are full of sorrow at this tragic loss, to lose one of our own, a man who loved his family and was a good provider"—he never looked at me or Mama when he said that part; his eyes was over our heads at the back door like he couldn't wait to get outta there and eat—"a faithful steward, generous to his church family with both time and resources; yet, my friends, I cannot grieve! I cannot grieve because a thousand angels rejoice in glory at this homecoming. Another saint gathered in. Come home to a place of rest where earthly toil has ended. To a place where the land is no longer man's enemy, where the drought and the grasshopper do not break his heart, where wind and hail have no power to steal his labors, where he need not toil by the sweat of his brow, nor suffer the loss of those he loves."

The preacher didn't mention any womenfolks up there, so I reckoned that was the last me and Mama would ever see of Daddy. And that's what done it; I busted loose till I had to hold a handkerchief over my face to muffle my sobs. Mama looked over at me a little puzzled 'cause she and I didn't let ourselves go like that. She already felt bad enough and me showing myself that way in front of white folks. But here's the truth of it, the flat-out meanness, the part I could have never, would have never, never did tell Mama: I was crying because I was so happy that the sonofabitch was dead, and I'd never see him again.

A lot of white faces had turned again, and that made me so mad that I determined to hold it in even if it killed me. And it pert near did. Mama and me beat a path out of there when the service ended; she left some *sofki* and tobacco with Daddy for the journey, then grabbed my arm and pulled me out the door. We got up double on the farm mule we'd ridden in and started back. We had to make good time so we could stay the night at some of Mama's kinfolks on the way back. Of course, these days it don't take near as long to get from Eufaula to Weleetka, even in an Indian car.

Daddy never done but one thing nice for me. He used to keep him a Sears and Roebuck catalog on the floor next to his and Mama's bed. He never bought anything out of it and always complained 'cause the prices was too high. One day I come in all sweaty from helping Mama beat the dirt out of a rug she'd strung up over the clothesline. Mama had sent me in the house to put the rug back down while she went out to the garden to pick some greens for supper. When I walked through the door, Daddy was a-sitting there on the bed, thumbing through the catalog. He called me over and said, "Lucy, come here and sit on my lap. I want to show you something." Back then, believe it or not, I use to stutter a little; whenever I got scared I couldn't always get the words out right. That was before they started pouring out of me like the windy old woman I am now. I didn't know what to say to him; my hesitation made him angry, and he was about to blow up 'cause his face turned red as a turnip, and his jaw moved back and forth like a rusty gear while he ground his teeth. But he smiled and held back his temper and said, "Don't be afraid, sweetie," his voice dripping with molasses. "Honey, I know whether or not my little girl's too big for Daddy."

Well, I had a choice. I could say no, and a fight would break out between us, and when Mama come in Daddy'd have one of his stories about my mulish hardheaded ways when all in the world he wanted was for me to go out and hold on to the plow horse's harness while he pulled off her loose shoe. He could think up a whopper in a moment's notice if Mama walked in and saw anything puzzling. I'd stammer and hem-haw around trying to come up with the right words and get more nervous every minute with his bellering, "Don't just stand there like a mute beast, young lady! What do you have to say for yourself?" Mama'd look at me first, then over at Daddy. He had all the words, and I couldn't explain the sick feeling in my gut whenever he'd run his hands all over me, the way my tongue got thick, my head went numb, my thoughts turned muddy. It throwed me into a confusion.

I just stood there silent and ashamed, and what could Mama do but believe I was the ornery little cuss he said I was? She'd cry and wring her hands and worry Daddy was gonna run off and leave her on account of me. She'd say, "Lucy, I don't understand. You're always such a good girl and so helpful to me. How come you and your Daddy can't get along?"

Then he'd turn and glare at me, throw his huge bear paws up in the air, and tell Mama, "I'm at my wit's end. I done everthing I know to raise that girl up right. I give up. I'm plumb exhausted trying to pull what little I can out of this worthless ground ever' day, then come in and have to put up with this!" Mama'd be in such a frenzy with me bawling like a weaned calf and nothing to say for myself and Daddy hollering until the veins stood out on his neck until you'd of thought his head was fixing to come off.

So here Daddy was wanting me to sit on his lap, and I could of
run out of the house with him in hot pursuit screaming about my
behavior to Mama, or I could go over there and see what he wanted.
I sat on the edge of his knee, but he pulled me closer against him, deep
into his lap, until his face was next to mine, and I could feel his
whiskers, rough as board splinters, against my cheek. He set the Sears
catalog on the middle of my dress and started turning pages, taking his
time while he squirmed beneath me, grinding his hips and thrusting
upwards. He used his knees to hold me between his legs, and his arms
had me penned as his hands held the catalog in front of him. He
locked his feet together over the top of mine. My head went foggy as
I felt his hardness through his overalls, and I only remember feeling so
much relief that his hands was at least occupied with the catalog, turning pages through that dreamstuff none of us could afford. Finally, he
got to the toy doll section after about five minutes of commotion
beneath me and let out a groan; I felt his body go limp.

He pointed to a porcelain doll. Now, he'd seen me looking through
that catalog 'cause he often left it on the kitchen table, and I'd linger
on that one page where he now had it opened. I'd read the description
of the beautiful girl with china blue eyes, genuine leather handbag,
and handcrafted slippers. I could look at her and stare and dream,
imagine keeping her next to my pallet where I slept at night. I'd make
a special little bed for her out of a head scarf and maybe a tiny pillow
for her to rest her head on, and I'd never let anything bad happen to
her. Mama would have to tear me away from that catalog sometimes.

Daddy had it opened to that page, and the doll's eyes, deep as a
lake, was looking into mine. I wanted to dive into those eyes; I wanted
to be just like that porcelain doll, pretty and ivory-skinned and silk-
dressed and leather-handbagged and plume-hatted and on a magazine
page where folks could read about me, look at me, admire how pretty
I was but never touch me. Daddy said, "Lucy, I tell you what I'm
gonna do." His voice quivered with excitement, and his big stump of a
hand trembled as he pointed at the doll. "I'm gonna buy you that doll
if you'll do one special favor for your daddy."

Well, that done it. I jumped off his lap and kicked him in the shins 'cause I knew what he meant, and that was the one thing he hadn't dared try on me. Looking back, I now wonder where was all my brothers and sisters whenever I needed them? Usually they was so thick underfoot I was tripping over them, but Daddy always managed to find me alone. That was the nicest thing Daddy ever done for me, offered to buy me that Sears and Roebuck doll, and I was determined to never let him favor me with that kind of niceness. He must have known my seriousness 'cause I kicked him like I wanted to kill him before hightailing it out of there, and he didn't run after me.

I daydreamed of accidents happening to him: He'd get caught up in the plow lines, and a mad dog would run out of the trees and spook the mule, dragging Daddy in the traces from our house clean past the next section over to the Fixicos, his limp head thumping along those red-clay washouts. Or the plow would get stuck on an old root, and Daddy'd sit down in front of it behind the mule, slicing through the tangled mess with his Barclay pocketknife. I'd run out of the buckbrush and switch the mules with a stinging willow stick, hollering at the top of my lungs, "Hey-o-git-up-mules!" Some nights when I laid in bed I wanted to sneak out to the woods and scream, but I was afraid that if I started hollering I might not ever be able to stop.

Later that year, come wintertime, I seen something else that made me just as sick as what had happened to me. This was the year before Daddy died. Mama wanted to go over to my cousin Jennie's house 'cause her family had all taken sick with the flu. Now, Daddy had got him a car, one of the first Fords in that country, and he bragged on the way he acquired it till I'd heard the story more times than a Baptist minister preaches on sin. An old Creek man, Mr. Chawaata George, come into a bunch of oil money when he let the riggers drill on his family allotment. Many around us had already lost the family land 'cause the state and county found ways to steal it from us: special taxes we couldn't pay, or they'd declare our neighbors incompetent; other times they'd get it from elderly people who didn't have their wits about them and get them to sign a paper; maybe they'd find them an illiterate to sign over his allotment and make him think he was signing something else; or they'd put clauses in leases for an eventual sell of the land with no payment to whoever owned it.

They promised us our homelands, Alabama and Georgia forever, then stole that; they promised us Oklahoma after they marched us from Alabama and Georgia, then took that from underneath our feet; they promised our families our allotments, then found ways to cheat us out of them, too, until forty years after statehood there wasn't hardly an Indian allotment in the country in the hands of the original family it was given to. If you don't believe me, then find you an Indian these days who still has the family land. Few and far between. What do you think happened to them? They didn't disappear; the ground's still there with white men's cattle and corn, alfalfa and wheat. Oh, sure, you'll say, they was all sold off, but I'm here to tell you that just as many slipped from our hands 'cause of the dirty-dog dealings of white folks.

The whole thing from the beginning has always amounted to the same: They thought they could bring the Creek Nation down to its knees. But I'm an old woman and the Creek Nation is still here, and we still have our stomp dances, and I still see my grandkids, and even great-grandkids, there at the grounds dancing and sitting in the arbors. If you ask me, we won, even though we always got to keep on fighting. As long as we got this nation and those square grounds we'll keep right on a-going, too. This is what I'm trying to learn my grandchildrens.

Mr. Chawaata George, like I done told, still had his land back then when I was a girl and an oil well to boot. All of a sudden that old fool Indian had a bunch of money he didn't know how to spend. All he'd ever done was hunt squirrels and grow enough vegetables for his wife to can and get him through winter if he was lucky. I guess he figgered a rich man needed a fancy car, so he paid one of them mixed-blood Crane boys from over Eufaula way to drive him plumb to Oklahoma City and teach him how to spend money. Mr. George no sooner got back to Weleetka than he run that car clean out of gas. The Crane boys was off running around the jazz joints over in Deep Deuce in Oklahoma City, down there by Second Street, which would become my own well-known haunts in my horn days onced I started blowing incognito for the Oklahoma City Blue Devils, as well as my downfall from the good graces of both mens and womens alike.

I was destined to a future where half of McIntosh County said any woman who'd lower herself to play the devil's music in a beer joint shouldn't be raising children a-tall. I was banned from speech in all the proper households where it was told that the least mention of my name could 'cause the next borned kin to be a harelip. The men didn't let on none that they was in the same beer joints where I blowed, and a good deal of the commotion was over the undeniable fact that I'd seen their ways when they got out from under their wives's aprons. They held that secret knowledge ag'in me such as when I'd catch a glimpse of them out on the sidewalk in front of the club making eyes at some dolled-up high-footin' gal or maybe witnessed more than one man in my time dis-appear into the alley with a beautiful colored boy. And I'm not talking about going back there to buy corn liquor. A life of playing music in the bars opens your eyes to the real nature of folks and their truest incli-nations, that's for sure. After I knowed all that, I could never see eye-to-eye with all their outstanding holiness and high-toned judgments.

Mr. Chawaata George, the new car owner, had driving lessons but no tank-filling instruction. So he thinks the car is busted seeings how he don't know the front end of that Ford from the back end of his mule. I reckon he thought car buying was like horse trading: You might get one that looks young and spirited and chomping at the bit, but halfway home you discover she's an old nag pumped up for a couple weeks on rolled corn, soaked oats, and molasses.

Daddy happened by in the wagon on the way back from town to get a wheel mended. Mr. George, crouched on his heels, stranded, and hunkered in the shade of the car and fanning himself with his new high-dollar hat, like a danged white farmer, hollers out, "Hey, a ride, how 'bout it? I need one real good on account of this car she don't run, here. Take me yonder over to my house. If you want her you can come back and have her this car long as you make her run." Daddy thought he'd come upon the dumbest Creek ever was in this country, and he had to hold back from shouting out his good luck. He could tell they waddn't nothing wrong with that brand-new shiny black Ford.

He dropped Mr. George off at his shack back in the hills, then, on the way back to the car, stopped at a farmhouse and borrowed a gallon of kerosene, even paid for it without complaining. I tell you what's the truth; that old Ford come into our front yard sputtering and stalling and belching black smoke on account of being run on kerosene and Daddy hollering like one of them uncivilized Indians, maybe a Kiowa or a Comanche. Of course, I was to learn later from my cousin Jennie, who went off to school at Chilocco, that none of them was uncivilized like the white people had said. While Chilocco had mostly Cherokee and Creek students, they also got their share of plains and southwestern tribes, and Jennie had shown up on campus nearly scared to death that one of them wild Indians would beat the tar out of her or take her hair. Her best friend ended up being an Apache girl who she was in thick with the whole time she was there. After you been around as long as I have you wonder how come white people don't ever tell the truth about Indians, even if just by accident every now and then.

I realize my story might have parts in it that make you laugh. Go right ahead. I tell the funniness and line it up right alongside the meanness. Jimmy Rogers, the famous blue yodeler, says the blues ain't nothing but a good man feeling bad. He also says it this way, and I kind of like this one better since I ain't a man, good or otherwise: "I got the blues like midnight, moon shining bright as day." See what I'm telling you; it's both of them working together, sunshine and moon-light, water and fire. Sometimes that's all we have, a laugh.

Mama didn't want me staying alone while she was gone, so Daddy volunteered to bring my cousin Jennie over to keep me company and help out while Mama tended her sick family. Daddy really wanted an excuse to drive that Ford down the main street of Weleetka for all the white men standing around Keck's Grocery to see. So Daddy set out to take Mama over to my aunt's and bring Jennie back over here with him. I couldn't wait for Jennie to come over 'cause she's my favorite cousin and we'd talk and I'd tell her about the boys around Weleetka and she'd tell me about the boys over to Eufaula, and better yet hand-some boys she knowed from Chilocco from other tribes, and we had our games such as "Come along, Daisy" and "Who's got the secret?"

We'd play together until Daddy would storm out of the house on account of all our giggling. He had him a Bible verse that said something like "be ye sober-minded." I reckon it was the only one he knew 'cause he liked to have worn it out every time Jennie come over.

Well, I waited and waited for those two to get there. I decided to walk up the road a-piece, and maybe I'd surprise Jennie and ride back to the house in the car with them. It had been so hot and dry, so much dust in the air, that when it come a rain the first part of that afternoon red mud fell from the sky. You couldn't even look up without being blinded by dirt. I got up on the road and past the farm pond where the mules and the cows drink. Already the ground had sucked out every drop of rain, and I was kicking up dust again. My dress was streaked, and so was my hands and arms. I seen me one of those little brown-and-white killdeers feeding on a big mud flat next to the pond. As I got close to her, she cried out shrilly, "Kill-dee, Kill-dee," and ran across the flat, announcing approaching danger to all the other birds.

I knew about them killdeers 'cause I had a close call with one of them once. Those birds will nest on a plumb flat spot in the middle of an open field, and I almost stepped on one in the springtime 'cause she was so hard to see. Her underparts is crossed by two black stripes acrost her chest, and you can usually spot her pretty easily by the orange-brown spot on her rump. But she was a-sitting on her nest, so I couldn't see her markings. I liked to have stepped right on her. She never left her eggs until my foot was within a stride away, and she run off with her tail spread wide and her bright rump patch a-gleaming. She cried pitifully and drug herself along like she was crippled, falling to one side with her other wing flapping weakly. Well, I run off and hid behind the buttonbush trees so she could stop faking it and get back to her nest. See, that's how she fools people or animals. They think she's wounded, so they go after her and leave her eggs alone.

When I seen Daddy's car parked alongside of the road, I forgot about the killdeer for a while and had me a laugh. I really got to snickering because I figured he run it out of gas after telling us so many times about the dumb Creek man who didn't know a gas tank from a watering hole. I couldn't wait to get Jennie off alone and me and her could have us a good time over Daddy being dumb as an Indian. When I spotted the car, I skipped up to it, anxious to see her, and throwed open the door. I gasped and went light-headed, thinking I might get sick right there. Daddy was sitting on his side, his hands on the wheel, and Jennie on the other. Jennie had wet the seat, and they was a big puddle between them. When I threw open the door she'd giggled and put her hand over her mouth. She looked like she really wanted to cover up her face with her hands and hide from me, but she just laughed nervously. I seen right away that she was only giggling on account of she was so afraid and ashamed because I knew that feeling. But when I knowed for sure was when I looked over at Daddy because he was far too calm, too cool-headed, letting on like nothing in the world was the matter, bent over the wheel lighting a cigarette. But he couldn't look me in the eye.

Here's the part that breaks my heart. Jennie and I never said a word about it. I wanted to protect her from all the ugliness, but I couldn't ever ask her. How could I? We didn't even have words for it. If I'd have known what to call it, I might have been able to ask her if Daddy had done anything to her, but I knew he did anyway. All the stories that pour out of me now began that day I seen Daddy and Jennie in the Ford. I been saying everything I know since to throw out the right words, to set words all around me and Jennie in order to hold off the devil hovering over us in the nighttime, to explain the one thing I seen when I throwed open that door. Slowly closing the circle, moving towards the one story, the truest one of all.

I ended up with all this hateful blood until some nights I felt its darkness bubbling through my veins. Dark purple man blood that made me want to scream, rake someone's face with my nails, pound him with my fist, kick him in the groin. On the weekends I went to Oklahoma City, and I hid behind my partition and blew like a sonof-abitch, or maybe I should say I prided myself that I could blow *better* than any sonofabitchin' man around. That rage made me hit notes no man could even dream of. During the breaks, his buddies would come around and brag up the trumpet player. He was a player sure enough;

he playacted his solos. I never got any of the credit, but I'd stand right next to him and just drive him to distraction because he knew that I knew that I'd actually played the notes he was getting famous for. It might not seem like much, but I soaked up the spite of holding that high register over his head, someplace he could never go except in his dreams, and I'd remind him now and again of the true-told author of each and every line he ever lipped. I'd like to say my blood cooled down, that the foaming and frothing subsided, fed out through my veins, was absorbed into my skin and organs, sweated out through my pores until I was clean or blowed out the bell of my instrument. But instead I got madder and madder. The sins of the fathers passed down until the fourth generation they used to say in church, and I could feel the rage in me, sweeping me along in its current. Blowing hard only made me want to blow harder.

Thank God I married the sweetest man I ever knowed, my husband Glen, and he took up the slack with my babies when the darkness would cover me and pound inside my head. I don't know, some might say he drank a drop or two more than he should have, but he was the kindest white man, and he is still my best friend even though he's been gone for thirteen years. The cancer, like so many others. Here one day, gone the next, a lifetime leaves you. I would have drowned and gone under the hatred without him. He spent time with my little ones. He helped them with their schoolwork. He hunted up school clothes for them—he had an eye for a bargain and how to make a dollar stretch out where they was concerned. He was gentle, and that's why I married him.

This brings me to the part of my story that hurts me most. I ain't proud of the way I was, and I ain't even going to expect you to under-stand when I say I done the best I could. Mostly, I don't want to make excuses, and I don't want to be let off easy. But take care what you think if you ain't felt my burning, knowing every day you might explode and blow into a thousand pieces.

All these people like Bob who come and visit me at the old folks' home swear I'm the sweetest thing. I still have neighbors from long ago over Weleetka way who come to see me at the center. People I give tomatoes and vegetables to forty years ago, maybe even a bag of groceries when things was tight, and I'd give it to them letting on like it was just something extra I didn't need, not like they was having hard times. The ones that run me down as a juke-joint Jezebel, I gave the most to in order to drive them close as I could to craziness and expose to the world the underlying nature of their holiness. Such as I might have brought their younguns a pair of shoes or something that caught my eye before it got thrown out, and I suspicioned they might could use it. Bob, this one old boy, has been coming to see me at the Senior Citizens' now for five years, and I tell you what's the truth he looks rougher than an old cob. Rides him a Hardley Davidson motor-cycle right up to the front door nearly and got a red beard clean to his knees. But he's a pretty good fella. He comes and sees me 'cause of the stories his mama and daddy told him about me helping out their family. That's nice of him to remember like that, don't you think?

But none of those folks ever seen what happened in my own house. I'm going to give you a for instance because I don't know any other way to explain it. This makes me want to die, even to think about it, and some days I don't want to believe it ever happened, but I know it did. I never told nobody, not even my husband, though I've turned it over in my head a thousand times.

My little boy Keillie had turned four not too long before, and I had just got in one day from picking cotton, and I wanted nothing more than to lay down, sink back into my bed, give myself over to sleep and forgetfulness. Whenever I come in the front door, though, I knew if I even laid down for a second I'd never get back up. Dog tired. So I went straight to the kitchen and started in on my cooking, making biscuits, mixing flour, water, salt, baking powder, rolling out my dough, cutting little flour moons out with a snuff glass, slapping them down in a little bit of shortening and lining them out on the baking sheet. I had just added a log to the wood stove and had it about the right heat, and here it was already so hot in the house that I felt myself wilting, dead on my feet. I needed to get Glen to build us an arbor outside for cooking, but he was working hard as I was at the time. I leaned back for a minute there and wiped my brow, then got the paring knife 'cause I was fixing to slice up some tomatoes; I'd decided not to cook anything more, too hot out.

After checking my biscuits and seeing they was ready 'cause of the way the tops of them had turned golden brown, I put on the mitt and pulled them out, then set them over on the table. My boy Keillie come over there and got up under my feet and started in on me, "Mama this and Mama that and Mama could I have one of these here biscuits." Too hungry to wait for supper and me trying to get it finished up.

And then I got real hot in the kitchen, dizzy, my head swimming, and that shrill whine of his, just at the edge of my hearing, not letting up for a minute's rest. Keillie was towheaded, unlike all the rest of my brown- and black-haired kids, and he had just started turning real blond. I looked down at him jerking on my apron, his eyes begging, and all at once I seen my daddy's face, the smirk in the turned-down corners of his mouth, the blue eyes, the pug nose that give him a little bit of a bulldog look when he was young, and his voice, commanding, insisting on attention. I felt a white-hot hatred flame up, the heat building. I turned and begun chopping radishes, laying into them until I had gouged my cutting board. Then I stabbed my thumb. I let loose with some of my bar language, I'll admit. I had to get my eyes off Keillie for a while, but when I turned to get another bunch to chop, I seen that little white arm over by the table, snaking out, reaching toward them biscuits. I flew over there before I knew what happened; I couldn't even remember taking a step or moving, only the knife in my fingers and me pointing it in his face, screaming that if he took one of those biscuits I'd cut his hand off. He flinched from the knife and started crying, and what killed me was the look on his face.

He really believed I would do it.

All the confidence had left; he was wide-eyed and staring like he didn't know me. That's when I wondered myself if I might could have cut him. I never hurt one of my kids by laying a hand on them, but I began to wonder how much they'd suffered from fear of me. Keillie's look as he backed out of the kitchen made me think that maybe they was all so terrified of me flying into one of my rages that they'd never dared to cross me to find out what I was capable of. Even with all my wordiness, it's hard to tell you what it feels like to realize your own kids are scared to death of you. I run over to pick him up, but it was too late; he was afraid and took off out of the house.

From then on I was scared into holding back my meanness from my children, but I didn't feel any less hatred. When my girls got closer to being teenagers, they started wanting to go here and there, into town to see a picture show, or over to a friend's house for a slumber party. This was all new to me since I'd never been allowed to do nonesuch myself. Then they started to whispering and giggling about boys. I wasn't about to let them girls anywhere out of my sight, and when they asked me how come and why not and Mama what for, I screamed, "Because I said so." I guess my girls never got to do a single thing looking back on it, except when Glen took them somewheres, and even then he had to fight me over it. I was scared out of my senses to let them go anywhere I couldn't watch them, afraid that what happened to me could happen to them. I tried to push such gruesome thoughts from my head, as if thinking them could make them happen, but I kept imagining them forced into a situation beyond their control and them too young to stop it. This could happen, and I might not ever know about it, and I felt helpless. Sometimes it was terrible because I even hated Mama and wondered where she had been whenever Daddy had cornered me beneath his hot breath and wandering hands. Years later, when my kids started getting old enough to play and do things by themselves, I started having headaches during the day that would lay me low for a couple of hours, and I'd have to sleep them off, and then dreams at night about terrible things happening to them. Except for one dream that was different.

I would run through the dark woods, the trees pulsating and shimmering under a purple moon. I kept looking over my shoulder as I ran; behind me I could hear the sound of a pack of hounds on my trail, each voice distinct, one with a throaty howl leading the pack, the middle dogs in a high-pitched frenzy, and a little cur with a throttling bay bringing up the rear. Each howl darted out of the dogs' muzzles as a quicksilver thread of sound, winding along the tree trunks towards me. Even though they hadn't closed the gap between us, I could feel their hot breath rising behind me; I could smell dogs and hunger. Just before they came upon me, I reached a small scrubby cedar tree, more of a bush really, which spoke to me out of the darkness. The tree pleaded with me to climb up in its branches, and I began to cry because there was no way they could hold me. I looked all around for somewhere else to run, but I had come into a huge clearing; the edge of the woods now seemed far away, on the horizon. I cried out to the tree, "Have I become whippoorwill yet?" thinking I might fly off, above their heads. "Not yet," the tree answered back. "Climb up on my branches," she repeated. Having nowhere else to go, I grabbed a-holt of a twig and began to shinny up. I'd expected a snap and falling backwards, but instead I felt girth and strength under my fingers, and the tree began bearing me upwards, above the dogs making the slow circle around the trunk. They weren't throwing themselves against the tree, but fanning out in case I jumped.

"Can I fly yet?" I asked the tree as I looked down from a great height, the circling hounds now like red ants scurrying to and fro around a mound. "You don't need to fly off," the cedar said. "Whippoor-will lives on the woods' floor. She comes out at night and kicks up dirt and leaves, looking for seeds. Wait until darkness; return to the woods."

"But that's where the hounds are!" I screamed, afraid she would turn back to a seedling and make me get down just then. "Yes," she replied, "but I will give you a song to sing when they are around, a song to sing when you are sputtering and gasping for words, a song born out of silence, the song whippoorwill wants to teach you." I woke up then. In my nightmares I would wake up groaning and unable to speak, but this one was different; I was given words. I kept the words to that song, hid it in my heart, sang it to myself whenever I felt the need. What are the words? To tell you that, even now, might risk the power of it. Certain things are best kept to yourself. You might be thinking back to how I promised to tell the whole story, not leave any-thing out, but I aim to keep this secret for one reason: I might still need it, and I ain't just giving it away carelessly.

That song helped me pull through. I started singing it whenever I was boiling over; I sung it when I was panicked by things beyond control; I sung it beneath my breath while holding on to my kids, sung the words to the tops of their heads; I pleated it into the girls' hair, braided the words of it down their backs; I rubbed it into the boys' britches and the girls' bobby socks and blouses while my hands worked their clothes over the washboard; I kneaded and mixed and stirred it into the food they ate; I covered them up with it when I put them down to bed at night. Sometimes the headaches would still overtake me, but I had Glen to help out, and when the pounding and swirling colors left me, I'd get up and go on.

And the horn playing sure didn't hurt none either. I always had the wind and an ear, two of the most important gifts a trumpet player could ask for. And, whatever they might say about how low down I had scraped bottom, I waddn't ashamed of the money I brought home from playing the clubs when Glen would get laid off in the oil fields. I'd take that whippoorwill song and play the melody on my horn, still keeping the words to myself. Thank God for mutes, Glen useta say, 'cause I played that particular number loud enough to bring the sun up. Glen was to name it "Lucille's Morning Overture," and he made me go outside to blow it and even then with a mute in the bell end of my horn. He said otherwise half of McIntosh County would think Gabriel was announcing the last day of judgment. On the bandstand some nights I even found ways to sneak it into my solos. I figured since whippoorwill sings at night in dark places, it all made sense.

Hidden as I was behind the partition of a Friday or Saturday evening, I could still get lost inside the music I was making, blow all my troubles outta the end of that horn, and spread them around a little for my unsuspecting listeners to take up some of my load. That's what they mean by the blues, I reckon. But when Billy Strayhorn was to come along and write "Lush Life," that's when I learned the art of a ballad. That song taught me how to think and phrase my lines instead of just blow them outta my horn fast as I could get rid of them. That's when I became a jazz player, more than a body with a horn in her hand.

And it was on account of the fake trumpet player, the actor, whose solos I lipped. One night during break he comes behind the band partition huffing and puffing and says, "Lucille, I don't like those lines you're playing for me. You're making me look bad."

"Ain't you the critic for a guy who can't play to save his life," I says.

"That don't mean I can't hear," he whines. "You're playing too many notes on that new Ellington."

"Strayhorn," I corrected. See, I always was a strong believer in credit where credit's due, good or bad.

"Look," he says, "use your rests more on those ballads. Whenever you lay off for a spell, it makes it that much more interesting when you jump back in there and hit the next note."

So that's how I was learned to slow down, pick and choose, control myself.

Some of my grandkids and great-grandkids might say I'm kinda out of it, always going on, a windy old lady who never made it into the twentieth century. And they're right. Certain things *are* hard for me to understand. Kids nowadays have everything growing up; I had nothing. I remember one Christmas in particular when Mama give each one of us an orange when we woke up, and that was all we got. I was so proud of that orange; I liked just smelling the sweetness and tanginess of it, not like the wood smoke and grease smells of our kitchen. Even saved the crinkly purple tissue paper Mama had them wrapped in, folded it up in a neat little square and put it under my pallet where I slept. I was the last one of my brothers and sisters to have that orange 'cause I didn't want to eat it, just save it. My big brother, Sonny Boy, took to teasing me and trying to take it away, saying I was gonna hold on to it until it rotted. While he was wrestling me over it, I dropped it, and it fell down one of the deep cracks in the board floor, then rolled away. I cried and just hated myself because if I wouldn't have wanted to save it for so long I would have at least gotten to eat it.

So now when I hear about a grandkid getting married for the second time and spending $5,000 on some fancy wedding, I can't understand it. Don't hardly register since none of us growed up in that world. But I put on my dress like they wanted me to, the great-grandkids come and picked me up, and I kept my mouth shut afterwards during the reception when they was all eating on them little old finger foods. I could of wheeled myself over there if I wanted, but they waddn't hardly enough there to feed a pissant. I reckon I held back far too much from my own kids, but when you grow up without money, just whatever you can live off from a few vegetables and hogs and chickens and planting corn and cotton for somebody else on shares, the idea of spending money like that kind of scares you. You want to horde it up because you know some disaster's just around the corner when you'll be poor again and need it. Having it is too good to be true, too hard to believe. Even though Glen eventually got him that good job with OG&E, I had my eye on a dollar, that's for sure.

This story I began when I felt the words rising in me. Sometimes they're like that orange: I barely hold on to them long enough to know their meanings before they slip from my fingers. Other times the words come more easily, ebb and flow towards understanding. It's a lot easier telling stories about other folks than telling this one on myself, that's for sure.

Did I tell you about my rough-looking visitor, Bob, who comes to see me? The biker? Bob's the one whose grandparents I helped out a little, years ago, whenever I could. I don't reckon Bob's ugly, but I don't know on account of he's got so much hair you can't hardly see his face. I do know he has two blue eyes poking out of his red beard, which reaches halfway to his knees. He's always trying to impress me, telling about how he's part Cherokee, his great-great-grandmother a princess, the last Indian to sign a peace treaty with the U.S. government. I never have known any Indian royalty, but maybe someday I'll visit Tahlequah and go see if I can find that castle where they got all them Cherokee princesses housed up. I ain't turning any of them loose, though, since they done bred into every family in America.

Maybe Bob's got Indian blood, maybe he ain't. Bob rides a big Hardley Davidson right up to the nursing home, the thing sputtering like a machine gun, so I always know when he gets here. The nurse's aides all keep an eye on him like they think he might steal some dope or needles, I reckon. Whenever I know he's coming, I make my way over to the old hens who keep a watch from their roost near the front entrance where they wheel themselves back and forth in front of the old men playing checkers. You'd be amazed at how them old gals still has it in them, hoping one of the checker players will drop his false teeth while ogling them as they pose and preen. So, I get right up in there amongst them, see, and I tell them that Bob the biker's my date. A little lie that don't hurt them none, kinda increases their entertainment possibilities. Some of them giggle, some wave their hands in disbelief, and some of the really old nags show more disapproval, harrumphing and wheeling themselves down the hall.

What they don't know is that Bob's a right good hand with fixing cars, and he custom-builds them old ones and takes them to car shows, sometimes as far away as Tulsa or even Oklahoma City. Today Bob's coming to take me for a spin in his rebuilt Ford roadster. So I'm waiting here with the busybodies 'cause I know he's coming at three o'clock. He pulls up, and I mean to tell you that car is a tangle of shiny silver chrome pipes and brass fittings, cleaner than the plates we eat off of around here. The thing doesn't even have a roof on it. I don't know whether or not to believe him, but he told me he spent $10,000 fixing that car up. Looks like for that kind of money he'd have invested in something to keep the wind off. The engine is an open-cockpitted affair with all them chrome pipes sticking out. The front tires is no bigger than a quarter the size of the ones on my wheelchair. Bob comes in here and he couldn't of played it up better, even if he'd known of my little fib. He says to me, "Hello, sweetheart," and bends over and kisses me on the cheek, the old hens barely able to hold in their cackling. I put on my floppy fishing hat, which I haven't worn since Glen died, to keep off the wind and sun. I turn to Bob and I say, pretending to whisper a secret but making it loud enough so the hens can hear me (see, they can hear real good whenever they want to bad enough), I say, "Bob, we're gonna ride her hard and put her up wet." A couple of them old ladies turn blue, and I worry they might need resuscitation. Even the old men lose interest in checkers.

Bob wheels me right out the door and up to the roadster, and by this time the hens are fighting each other to get to the front window and look out at me in the parking lot. The thing of it is, the side doors on the dang thing don't even open, and I think he could have fixed them before picking me up, but I don't say anything. I need to climb up on the running board and step over the door panel. I know I'm fixing to have a powerful hard time getting in that car, but I hate to let it show with all the old ladies watching. Bob asks me if I need a hand, and I think about refusing. I might lose a little face in front of the old ladies if I can't get in the car myself, but they'd really gawk and chortle if I spent the next twenty minutes trying to swing my leg over, so I let Bob help me. I smile my sweetest and wave goodbye to all the faces pressed against the glass in the front window. I tell Bob to take his time, no hurry to get back. We drive down the main drag of Eufaula, and I keep one hand atop my fishing hat to keep it from blowing off, then we get on state highway number 9, puttering out toward the dam. Bob tells me he'll go slow, so as not to frighten me, but I say, open her wide up. He says, are you sure, and then roars her to life and asks me if I'm scared, but by now I got both my hands plastering my hat to my head, and the oak trees are a blur on one side, the bass boats out on the lake fly by on the other, and on the road the blacktop spins out beneath our feet. We get closer to the dam, and I think about the giant concrete wall, how it holds back so much, and all the water that has covered up places where my daddy and mama use to live, now lying at the bottom of the lake. Water and memories, memories and water.

SEVEN

Jimmy's Advertisement

JIMMY ALEXANDER, WELEETKA, OKLAHOMA, 1991

So what if I gotta advertise? Did you ever try looking for a boyfriend
in the greater Weleetka area—the famous tri-cities of Weleetka,
Wewoka, and Wetumka? That ain't nothing new, running an ad, and
at least I kept myself distracted, took advantage of my isolation and
came out of the woodworks, threw a couple fake moves on my loneliness. I must have spent a month getting my personal ad personal
enough but not too personal for the personal section of the *Gayly
Oklahoman,* our monthly hick newsletter out of Oklahoma City.

It's not easy, either, what with Clarence Albert laughing at me and
telling me it'll never work, but I don't pay him much mind anyway
since he's always looking to run off with the nearest white man he can
find, a regular Pocahontas, that one. It's no prince he's after, either; he
could be old and bald and butt-ugly and nasty with a capital N so long
as he's white.

Hell, Clarence don't need a man; he needs a porcelain gravy dish.

C.A. and I been hunting one up, though, ever since fourth grade
when we used to hide at the cemetery and clip out pictures from

magazines we kept hidden under Roy Hillabee's mother. Under her stones, I mean, piled up around her marker. I know you've probably seen those little houses they build over Creek graves in the Indian cemetery, but this was his white mother. In a shoe box was where we kept our loot, and we'd bury them again whenever we finished. Nobody ever bothered our stuff as far as I could tell because the old lady who was buried there had been too mean, dead or alive, to visit.

That went on for years before we outgrew our secret meetings, but in the last of the dying days of our graveyard gatherings, I collected about every photo I could find out of *Sports Illustrated* of Kareem Abdul-Jabbar, all goggled-up and gleaming. What I had for him back then, I don't know, but he was my man, moving in for a layup, crouched and fixing to spring around an opponent, right before he'd float over the heads of all the young shot-blockers. C.A. was tight with Shaun Cassidy; can you believe that shit? I mean, he meticulously trimmed away all the excess from around his photos out of *Teen Beat* magazines, and by excess I mean he cut out all of Shaun's girlfriends until nothing was left but the purest essence of Shaun, blond and beaming. We would put the magazine remains back in the shoe boxes, lower the lid over them, and pile the grave stones on top. The pictures we'd cut out, we took home with us. We were quite a pair, C.A. and me.

I was able to hang my basketball photos up in my room. C.A. had to give his clippings to his older sister and feign disinterest in her growing shrine to Shaun, sneaking into her bedroom to see the love of his life hanging on somebody else's wall. Sort of like going to a museum and seeing photos of your relatives, but you can't take any of them home with you. I don't guess this happens to white people.

So Clarence and I go back. A long ways. *Too* long, matter of fact. We'd just gotten in a fight inside the video store, a fight that seems to be one continuous feud with a few scene changes but the same dialogue since those fourth-grade days until now. We'd left the video store, agreed on nothing, and now we're parked out in front, still arguing.

"I'm not watching *High Noon,* ever again," I say for the millionth time. I put my hand on the steering wheel and stare ahead, determined to hold my ground. "I hate Gary Cooper. Another cowboy with attitude. And he's not even good-looking. That movie is so boring."

"Yeah, but it helps you forget how bored you are in Weleetka," C.A. says, referring to the town I moved to after I graduated from high school, one of my dad's crazy ideas, one of his many last-ditch efforts to right all wrongs between us.

And it's with C.A.'s perverse logic that I make up my mind. I need a break, and I'm not about to watch *High Noon* again, nor will I spend the next hour fighting over a 99-cent movie, and I won't even agree to the inevitable compromise of driving to Oklahoma City to spend another dreary Saturday night in the clubs on 39th Street, leaning over the balcony and watching the mob below, grimacing as C.A. slurps down his whiskey sour through a straw in between snippets of conversation about what a kick it is now that the special superstore Wal-Mart in Shawnee stays open twenty-four hours and how cute some shirtless white boy looks, swaying somewhere in the blur below us, who, even from that distance, I can tell C.A. will never snag in a million years.

I'll just stay home and work on my ad. Alone. Without C.A. But I need a decoy. I'll have to be a bitch to sound convincing. Okay, that part will be easy. But we're practically like a married couple; we've been together so long it's hard to fool each other. Or maybe we're more like warring siblings. Which*ever*. So I say, "C.A., I'm going down to Darko for the powwow at the high school gym."

Now he's almost sniffing the air like an old bird dog. Always suspicious. He knows I wanna ditch him. "By the time you get down there, the powwow will be over," he says and lights a cigarette, waiting for me to explain.

"Yeah, but they'll just be starting to 49," I answer back, maybe a little too quick.

"You'll never pitch a ringer down there," C.A. says. For some reason C.A. always equates laying his hands on a man with horseshoes. Hey, I guess we got our own language, me and him. It's a most beautiful thing, the way we made it up over the years, how no one speaks it but the two of us. The other half of the time I'm trying to hide my life from him. I'd like to take my own footsteps, a long time out from a game that has run overtime for years, let C.A. find someone else to go off on.

"Do you ever think of anything besides getting laid?" I growl.

"Gary Cooper," he smirks, then adds, "I wouldn't as much as look at one of them country Indians," which he pronounces with a droll dismissal as *cuntry*.

"You already said that. Moving to Shawnee doesn't exactly make you an expatriate yourself. You're a freakin' hillbilly, big as anyone down at Darko." Then I let him have it, full bore. "Clarence," I tell him, and I know he hates it when I call him by his full name, "why are you always chasing after anything in pants as long as he's whiter than a plucked chicken's ass?"

He rears back against the seat like a crash test dummy on the rebound and announces, "Just take me home!"

Now we're getting somewhere. I just might get an evening of peace and quiet if I don't blow it. So I back up the car, drive out of Henryetta, and get on the interstate to take C.A. to his house. C.A. has been promising for two years to get a new transmission put in his old Chevy Blazer. In the meantime, I've done endless weekend duty picking him up and driving him around and hanging out with his sorry Indian ass and putting up with him snoring on my sofa where he crashes Friday and Saturday nights. I-40 has a little ice on it, just some patches here and there, no big deal. It had drizzled rain all day, then the temperature dropped enough in the afternoon when the sun disappeared to create some sheet ice. I fishtail the first time in a low spot around the Weleetka exit but steer out of it. C.A. shoots me a dirty look, so, naturally, I gun the pickup and speed up. On both sides of the interstate, the bare skeletons of post oaks, their leaves long fallen off, begin to blur. So many skinny gray arms intertwined in the failing daylight. So stark, the hills in winter, like they've been caught with their clothes off, and you can see everything that the dense foliage of spring hides. An old sign someone forgot to remove, nailed on the trunk of a post oak just off the interstate, reads "Johnny Coweta for Principal Chief." C.A. just settles back into the seat, thinking he's punishing me with his silence.

I know he's waiting for me to say something, so he'll have an excuse to come back on the offense and start shooting from the hip again. But I just let it ride, whistle the melody to some hip-hop tune I can't even name, and turn the AM knob until I finally locate the OSU football game. C.A. is fuming, and he's picked up the newspaper off the floorboard and hidden himself behind the entertainment section, pretending to read it.

It will be impossible for him to keep quiet much longer. In seventh grade a skinny white kid by the name of Cloetus used to follow us around school and try to get me to play basketball when class let out. Everybody called him Charlie. The TV show *Charlie's Angels* is how he got his name because all the girls found him disgusting, a real hick. He'd never have a harem of beauties like Charlie's Angels. See, we knew about irony, especially as it related to meanness. Or maybe they called him Charlie for some other reason, but that's how I remember it. C.A. had the hots for this guy, and he'd run and check out a ball from gym and catch up with us out on the blacktop, wild-eyed and panting. C.A. always insisted on playing horse or shooting from the free-throw line, anything to avoid a real game. C.A. actually shot underhand, granny shots, and lifted one heel behind him after he tossed the ball, like a forties movie star who'd just got kissed. Though he launched the ball with great aplomb, just about anyone could block his underhand shots. So I told him, "Yeah, Clarence, let's play. You and Charlie against me." I could be a little mean back then, I'll admit. I had to be or I'd get trampled under.

And Charlie joins in, says, "Yeah, man, let's play." C.A. couldn't back down in front of the object of his desire, so he took the ball out and threw it to his man. Problem was when C.A. got out on the court himself, as soon as Charlie passed the ball back to him, C.A. just froze up like his tennis shoes had been cemented to the blacktop. Charlie hollered, "Move!" and when C.A. tried to take a step forward he tripped over the ball, hitting the side of his head, hard, on the black-top. I mean, his eyes teared up after that walloping, and even I felt bad when I saw him retreat to the sidelines in defeat, leaving Charlie and me to a game of one-on-one. When Charlie went home, C.A. vowed never to speak to me again.

I had on a new sports watch my dad gave me for my thirteenth birthday, so I timed C.A. He kept quiet for forty-five seconds, then he blurted out, "Next time I'm playing Charlie horse without you."

And I busted up laughing because he meant to say, "Next time, I'm playing horse against Charlie without you." Actually, that time he didn't speak to me for a week, until the next Saturday when he was over at my house, just like this Saturday, eighteen years later. So when we get to Shawnee, instead of heading through town, I pull into the outlet mall that parallels the interstate. C.A. starts to say something, then catches himself and hides behind the paper once more, keeping quiet, but clearly he's annoyed that I haven't taken him straight home. My plan is to maybe piss him off beyond reconciliation, so I'll be free of him at least until next weekend. When I park in front of the bass shop that sells factory-reject poles and gear, C.A. can't hold back any longer. "What in the hell are we doing at a fishing store in the dead middle of winter?" he says, rattling his newspaper like some kind of orchestral accompaniment to his big moment.

"Everything on sale," I answer, as I climb out of my truck. C.A. doesn't even take off his seat belt. So I amble off toward the store, still whistling the same tune. The cowbell on the door, muted against the glass, clangs dully as I walk in. The clerk, an older man in a red vest that reads "Bass Busters," is demonstrating some new lure in a trough of water set up on a bench in the middle of the aisle, pulling the long plastic worm through its simulations, the speckled, silvery tail flashing as it snakes back and forth. The man stops retrieving it when I walk in and lets it fall to the bottom of the trough, which he claims demonstrates its "dual bait action" since it dives like a "crippled minnow" when you stop reeling it in. Never mind how a minnow gets crippled, I reckon. The man watching the demonstration is holding on to an infant who keeps reaching her tiny hand out toward the rack of shiny spinners just beyond her grasp. A young woman who could have been either man's daughter stands with one hand on her hip, chewing gum.

All of them, except the baby, even the Bass Buster himself, turn away from the fishing demonstration and look at me standing there just come in the door.

I recognize the customer as Roy Hillabee, who nods in recognition and says, "Hey, Jimmy."

Even though I haven't done anything wrong, I feel like I've been caught with my pants down. I want to turn around and walk out the door, suffering as I am from extensive trash trauma upon seeing Roy. And a little embarrassment. See, it was Roy's mother's grave where C.A. and me used to hide our magazines and have our secret queer meetings even if at the time we didn't know they were queer. We knew enough not to tell anyone if we wanted to survive. We'd used the Hillabee family plot as our gathering place, and I'd always felt naked around Roy, as if he could guess our secrets.

And there was one more thing. Roy was my high school basketball coach, and besides the spectacular Kareem Abdul-Jabbar, who existed only in newspapers, magazines, and on TV sportscasts, Roy was the first guy I ever had a crush on. He was a young teacher, fresh out of school at Norman and come back home to try out his education degree on us. He had seemed like a god to me from his stance in the middle of the oval track where he used to stand and smoke cigarettes while he made us run 100-yard tagged sprints. He was a brown-haired mixed-blood, taller than most Creeks because of his German and Irish blood, more in the size range of my basketball heroes I clipped out of the magazines. And he was well known in the state as a fancy dancer, kind of unusual since not that many Creeks went in for the powwow circuit like the southern plains guys, like C.A.'s family, who almost all dance, except for C.A. himself. Roy was kind of an oddity, and in my young heart I may have hoped that this was some kind of secret sign, a kindred spirit, another lover of men, rather than merely the rare Creek who danced powwows. I'd seen him many times in action, a light-stepping blur of color and motion, and, alone in my room at night, I'd dreamed of those bustles and feathers flying off him one by one with each spin.

Roy had also become well known for marrying high school chicks soon after their graduations, always before their nineteenth birthday,

and divorcing them before they turned twenty-one. As an adult this
had soured me considerably toward Roy, who'd shrunk down from his
gigantic stature to just another lifer from around here. His latest young
white wife stopped chewing gum and smiled weakly at me, taking the
baby back from her husband.

"The Weedless Wonder is so simple even a child could use it,"
the clerk continued, pulling the lure back into its magic motion but,
instead of looking at the baby, turning to Roy's wife, easily twenty
years Roy's junior. Roy ignores the clerk, walks away, and comes over
and shakes my hand. Just then C.A. bursts in the door and says, "What
in the hell's taking so ... "when he sees Roy pumping my arm and
stops in mid-sentence.

Roy lets my hand drop. C.A. had never tried out for sports in high
school, which pretty much made him useless in Roy's book, and he'd
never done well in P.E. class, the chronic pain in the ass who needed to
know how to hold a bat or catch a grounder or when to take the ball
out of court, except Roy never had any time for coaching him since
C.A. wasn't one of the school athletes, just another lame freak to be
ignored and left to flounder around on the field until class ended.

As much as I'd like to bust C.A. upside his head most of the time,
I feel an old sadness when I see Roy glaring in his direction, and I
wish I could shed Roy's affection, defect from his group of golden-boy
successes that he'd coached to the state basketball championship some
fourteen years ago when we'd made him famous, at least as famous as
a guy gets in eastern Oklahoma.

C.A. is standing there, frozen, just like when Cloetus threw him
the ball. But this time he doesn't trip. He's been waiting a long time.
He turns to Roy's wife, ignoring Coach altogether, and says, "Looks
like you've got a handful there." He could mean Roy or the kid. The
little girl is teething on a red-and-white fishing bobber her mom has
given her in exasperation to keep her hands busy. The young mother
must sense a friendly sympathizer on account of she hands the baby
over to C.A., who takes her, and now he's got her held up, and the
little girl is laughing and waving her bobber up and down. "She's a
happy one," C.A. has just said when Roy snatches the kid away from

him. C.A.'s face falls, and he looks down, ashamed. My blood pounds in my head and I say, "Come on, C.A., let's get out of here." I turn without saying goodbye to Roy.

But C.A. has recovered all over again, and he astounds Roy by grabbing a-holt of his hand and shaking it with great relish, departing with, "Coach Hillabee, it was *such* a pleasure to meet your daughter. And you must be so proud to be a grandfather, too," all the while smiling sweetly and pumping Roy's arm more vigorously than Roy had been working mine only moments before. On the way out I notice a flyer on the For Sale board, "Wallace's Live Bait Tanks: Fewer Dead Minnows," and I imagine Roy floating faceup along the shore of Lake Eufaula, silvery as a minnow in the moonlight, bobbing from wave to wave, a victim who's fished his last winter in a drowning season, pulled in by the final call of a slippery dream. And I'd be the one who lured him into the waters for his deadly swim.

Back in the truck, C.A. acts like nothing has happened, and he seems to be his old catty self, our petty disagreement forgotten in the wake of our encounter with Roy and the missus and the baby. But I see he's been hurt, thrown back to the high school hell he'd endured as an obvious gay guy who was out by virtue of his very existence, too effeminate to pass as anything but himself. He'd endured and sur- vived those years by becoming a despised but good-for-a-laugh bitch supreme. I'd gone through some shit for hanging out with him, but, in Oklahoma, sports cover a multitude of sins. A star basketball player can be forgiven almost anything, and a star player whose team wins the state championship is incapable of committing any sins for which he need be forgiven in the first place. You even become human instead of an undifferentiated Indian, set apart from the rest of your relatives and friends at school, the greatest act of forgiveness of all. So C.A. and me might as well have been from two different planets as far as the way we were treated in high school. And I had something I reckon was kin to survivor's guilt.

C.A. seems unusually cheerful, considering, and he practically skips back to the truck. "Look," he says, seemingly beside himself with glee, and he nods toward the fishing store where Roy has just come out and is strapping the little girl into a car seat, his wife revving up their Le Mans and looking over her shoulder impatiently while Roy slowly gets their daughter settled in.

"I always hated that motherfucker," I say, and turn over the pick-up's ignition.

"Not always," C.A. says tauntingly. "I seem to remember a young batboy who showed up at every city game Roy Hillabee played, carefully dusting him off each time he came into the dugout."

"Oh, *please*. I was only there once 'cause my uncle's Indian team was playing in the same park. I was watching, and you were in the stands with me. I was never even in the same dugout with Roy. And I never was a batboy for anyone."

Although C.A. and me share so much history, we sure have radically different interpretations of the same events. I might as well steer clear of another argument that could last the rest of the night as to whether or not I was Roy's lovesick batboy and personal attendant, following him all over Oklahoma from game to game and falling down prostrate before him in parking lots after the last inning, offering to buy him a double dip in Braum's while recounting every magnificent play he'd ever made. I know how far C.A.'s stories can roam, so I just shut up. Truth is, I rarely ever been to a baseball game, a sport I despise.

Miraculously, C.A. lets it drop. "Look what I have," he says, reaching across the truck and opening his palm to reveal an old Zippo lighter, its shine long dulled. He tosses it up in the air, and I catch it, turn it over, and read the inscription:

Eufaula Chieftains
State Champions
1977
Coach Roy Hillabee

"Some people take forever to get lung cancer," I say, wondering how the hell C.A. has ended up with Roy's lighter. Of course, I don't have to wait long to find out.

"She seen me take it," C.A. grins.

"Who?"

"The wife. Young Mrs. Hillabee. She smiled when I put my hand over it. It was sitting on an unopened shipping box of spools of fishing line. Roy must have set it down there to shake your hand. My fingers closed around it just when he was giving me that dirty queer look. When it went into my pocket she winked at me."

I throw the lighter back to C.A. and congratulate him. We're almost to his house. "I guess you Comanches still know how to sneak into enemy camp undetected. Must have learned your tricks from stealing so many Mexican women."

"Mexican men," C.A. corrects.

"You were kind of hard on his wife, considering she covered for you."

"Naw," C.A. says, "she liked seeing the old man ripped off. And she liked even more not being taken for his wife, or at least someone pretending not to know she was his wife. Besides, we both know they'll be divorced in a year or two anyway. Then she'll love me."

And that's where I mess up. I'd felt bad for C.A. in the store, enraged at Roy, then gleeful with C.A.'s parting shot, and, now, glorious at the juvenile thrill of the purloined lighter. I was enjoying my clever pun and riding the crest of all that euphoria when I say to C.A., "Have you ever answered a personal ad?"

Oh, God, I think; I'm such a punk, instantly wanting to take it back. I remember all the secrets I'd let slip, more than anything just to have someone to talk to. I recollect the infamous revelation that had gotten back to C.A. about me and Lenny's "night" together and how the story had swollen up like a dead possum in a roadside ditch by the time Lenny himself had snitched all the dirty little details to C.A., and C.A. had expanded on them to make it big enough for his special mental file where he stored up just such stories to use against me in a cross-referenced drawer called LEI for Lurid, Embarrassing, and Incriminating. When I ran off to Tulsa, he used to call long distance to gather information. I couldn't even get free of him by fleeing to another city. Years later, he was still awaiting my confession, the exact details of what I'd done there. He was like a reporter on a hot lead; he'd intuited it was gonna be a big scoop once he uncovered it.

So C.A. looks surprised when I ask him if he ever has answered a personal ad because C.A. is usually sucking me dry of every tidbit,

especially boyfriend-wise—not that I ever had one to talk about once
I moved back home, but that didn't keep him from asking about who
I'd been with, what we'd done, and what I liked and didn't like, and
I was ever the recluse, hiding from C.A.'s fantasies, refusing to hand
over my private life on a silver platter. When C.A. was in his kiss-and-
tell mood, and expecting the same from me, it didn't take long before
I felt empty and exhausted and needed some space, maybe a couple of
continents, between us.

And in a small town it's hard to keep continents, much less secrets,
between you and somebody you've grown up with all your life. So it
was inevitable that C.A. would eventually learn of my night at the
Broken Pony, Muskogee's only Indian bar, the year I'd just turned old
enough to go in. Hey, I like playing pool, seeing other 'skins, hanging
out, something to do on the weekends. You know, I got my black
friends, the ones I grew up with and hung out with 'cause everybody
in Oklahoma, except Indians who know different, thinks I'm black.
And here around these rednecks that means you sure as hell can't hang
with the white dudes when you got black skin.

And I like my black friends; I mean, hell, I been around them
from day one. But I'm Indian, so I like to go places where I know
there's other Indians. I don't drink, but I go there to shoot, to talk, to
wile away the hours. That night Lenny was in the place, really working it, strutting his skinny stuff from pool table to pool table and
breaking up friendly games and egging people on to play him. So,
yeah, I took him on because he was pissing me off and starting to
bother my friends. Black *and* Indian, everybody was getting pissed.
The more he drank, the more he kept bumping into me and getting
his cue up in my face before he took a shot. I pushed it away, said,
"Man, point that thing at someone else." He'd just move in and make
sure it was in my face again by the time he got around to making his
play. And then he'd bend over like an invitation just before smacking
the ball with his stick. Yeah, you heard me, like some kind of invitation.
Or maybe a challenge. He was getting me kind of revved up. The
last game of the night, he won. He says to me, "You owe me a ride
home, dude."

I shrugged. "I didn't know we were playing for anything."

"Oh, yeah," he says. "I'm always playing for something."

So I give him a ride home since we were both headed toward Eufaula anyway. It was one of those nights: full moon, clear sky, all the stars lit up, hot and muggy as hell, both windows down, the road dipping up and down in the moonlight so the woods on both sides look like an undulating carpet being shook out in front of us, and the cicadas just going at it full force so they nearly drown out the wind and the engine. Like you just can't believe they could ever be that loud, like they're screaming to keep from dying or something. So I took my shirt off, riding around in the night breeze. Lenny soon followed suit.

Well, I think you about get the gist of it without me going into the details. It was pretty lurid, man, pulled off the side of a country road, off the blacktop, me getting Lenny off next to a shittin' feed lot, him pretending to be drunk and half passed out afterwards, which sure waddn't the state he'd been in while I was working so hard blowing him, and the loneliness afterwards when I dropped him off and watched him stagger up to his doorstep. I might border on doing some nastiness, and sometimes I have a lot of fun with it, but I ain't a dirty person. And that felt dirty. It was a defining moment that night, the proverbial last straw that broke the camel's back, and it sealed my mind that I had to get away, set my sights on the city.

I vowed C.A. would never, ever find out since Lenny was someone we'd both despised since grade school for the macho assholes he hung out with. In high school they'd walk by in their Black Sabbath shirts and tattered jeans, and C.A. would hiss and spit and make nasty jokes about their ratted-up hair, and I'd laugh at this bunch of bean pole scarecrows walking around like they could have taken on Andrew Jackson at Horseshoe Bend all by themselves, and we'd of won. I knew if C.A. found out about me and Lenny I'd never hear the end of it. C.A. hadn't been in the gang I hung out with growing up, because they wouldn't have him, but he knew about all of us. What he lacked in actual contact, he made up for in his imagination, and he had the goods on everyone. C.A. was the only person who hadn't been around when Josh almost drowned. Between me and Josh and Lenny, that must have been just about the queerest raft that ever floated on water. Sammy, far as I could tell, managed to come out of the lake straight.

The culprit, as far as leaking this sexual misadventure with Lenny goes, was Lenny himself, who couldn't resist confessing. Him and C.A. had been at the Pony, the very place of my own downfall, and after the bar closed, knowing that no liquor stores were still open at that hour, C.A. let it "slip" that he had another six-pack at his house, the oldest snagging technique in the world. And the rest is history. Except instead of feigning unconsciousness, this time Lenny told C.A. he wasn't a faggot and, in order to "prove" it, he passed on the story about me and him, telling C.A., "Now, Jimmy, *there's* a fucking queer." And how I'd lured him off into the woods and begged to blow him, and he was so drunk that he let me, and all of this to prove to C.A., somehow, that "this shit wasn't no regular thing of his, just for kicks."

Now neither one of us, C.A. or me, was about to let on that we'd done Lenny, of all people. We weren't going to just voluntarily hand over that much dirt to sling at each other. So how did I find out about Lenny and C.A.? And that C.A. knew about Lenny and me?

From C.A. himself, of course, who else? Like he could pass up such an opportunity, even when he had, well, partaken himself. It's like when I timed him with the sports watch—whether it was a matter of forty-five seconds or forty-five days, I was doomed to find out, fated to discover that even our sex lives ran downstream into the same channel. And it happened in a conversation that began, "Lenny Henneha told me something about you." After C.A. finished his sordid story, relishing all the details and smirking 'cause he now had one up on me, I just pieced it all together.

Like Lenny would go around telling that shit to anyone. No way, not that closet queen. He must have told C.A. because he was afraid that I would tell C.A. my version first. And when would C.A. have been around Lenny anyways? It's not like they ever spent time with each other; you know, Lenny showing C.A. his Metallica collection and C.A. turning Lenny on to Donna Summers. It wasn't much putting two and two together. And you should have seen C.A.'s face when I gave a Howard Cosell blow-by-blow account, so to speak, about him and Lenny, what went down, or who went down, all mere speculation on my part, but based on experienced guesswork. Sometimes it just ain't good for two people to know so much about each other.

I pull up in front of C.A.'s house in Shawnee. His Blazer is parked under the carport, where it's sat the last six months, while C.A. hem-haws around about fixing it. I stop in front of the house to let him out. C.A. lingers inside the cab and says, mysteriously, "Let me show you my collection."

"Collection of what?" I ask.

"Weren't we talking about personal ads?"

"Oh, yeah. You mean you have a whole collection of ads you placed?" I imagine a hidden drawer somewhere in C.A.'s bedroom, full of ad copy, and I envy him that he has something he's still managed to keep hidden from me. I can see stacks of ads, dated and neatly tagged, each a dusty relic, like a collection of pottery shards stored in some museum cabinet.

"No, the ones I answered," he says. He waits, standing next to the truck and holding on to the door. But I don't move. "They're in the house," he adds.

"I didn't think you were still burying things under Roy's mother," I answer sarcastically. I don't let on any that I'm a little interested, maybe, and also discouraged when I consider that guys like C.A. might be the type to answer my ad if I was to place one. That makes me think twice, believe me. On the other hand, at least if C.A. is in on my plan I'd avoid the unthinkable, meeting up with some stranger who responded and ends up being C.A. himself. There might be another reason I turn off the ignition and climb out of the truck. Maybe, just maybe, I'm a little scared, don't know what to write, and I'm not sure I want to go through with it alone. I always had confidence in myself, never at a loss for words, but I didn't know I was going to come up with this notion of writing an ad. As Roy himself often reminded me in English class, writing ain't exactly my thing. But if you just settle for what you're getting, is my newfound conclusion, that's the end of you. And I ain't getting *any,* to tell the truth, and it's gone on for about as long as I can stand it. When it comes right down to it, I need C.A.'s damn meddling to force me to follow through. I know he'll be on my ass every day, asking, "Did you send the ad yet?" all the hell buzzed up with this little vicarious thrill, after me until I do it.

C.A.'s house is something else, not like any place you ever seen in Shawnee, and definitely not like the HUD houses we both grew up in. His brother is a construction worker during the summer and a self-employed handyman in the winter, and together him and C.A. had done up the place on a grand scale. The floor plan is long and rectangular, so you walk into a stone-tiled kitchen with French doors that open into a long living room with the original maple wood floor that C.A. and his brother refinished and, behind that, more doors that open into C.A.'s bedroom. Like something that could be one of those crazy Escher prints, doors opening into more doors. The length of the house, its depth, gives it the appearance of a long grand hall. It's dramatic. It's most definitely C.A. It's not Oklahoma, something he's proud of. C.A. throws open the last set of French doors, tosses his coat down on the divan, and goes straight to his bedroom closet, urging me to follow.

I sit down on the bed. You see, C.A. has what every gay boy in rural Oklahoma needs—a post office box—where all his secret communiqués from the gay world arrive unintercepted. There he picks up his subscription to the *Advocate,* a national news magazine which keeps him up on gay rights, bashing, pending legislation, none of which will ever come to the Sooner state, except the bashing, which is an equal opportunity sport here, practiced not only in rural backwaters but on the floor of the state legislature. He also subscribes to the *Gayly Oklahoman,* which lists support groups in Oklahoma City and Tulsa, none of which C.A. attends, and advertises the drink specials and the shows on 39th Street, all of which he attends faithfully. Then there is *Genre,* his gay fashion bible and source for interviews with brain-dead gay celebrities, no less stupid than their straight counterparts featured in other slick, glossy magazines of the same caliber. C.A. has boxes of these, years of his tabloid gay life, stored in the top of his closet. I guess it's better than nothing, but I'm not really sure. He starts pulling them down and setting the boxes on the bed. "Yes, Jimmy," he says, "for you we need some special magic, something that will wake the dead, cast a spell over your suitors, overcome their will, freeze their footsteps, and keep them from running off, wailing into the night, when they first meet you."

"Sounds like you've had some prior experience," I shoot back, but I have my doubts since neither C.A. or me has had much chances in Shawnee and Weleetka. Most of our gay life consists of conversations with each other, except for C.A. and his magazines, which keep him up on the latest and the best, and the year I don't talk about where I did everything, but it felt like it added up to nothing, when I'd ran off to Tulsa to get away from my old man. I'd always had a rebellious streak, especially where Dad was concerned. We'd have our fallings-out, and, eventually, we'd always fall back in together until the next blowup. I only regretted I had to turn into a drunk whore for the sole purpose of pissing him off, especially since no one knew about any of my whoring but me. Maybe there was more to it than that; hell, I didn't know. Whatever the reason for my behavior it had amounted to a belly-ful of heartache and frustration and loneliness.

I scratch my head, what's left of my hair, anyway. I just got a buzz cut, which I usually only get before summer. But I been antsy lately and cutting my hair seemed like the thing to do. Don't ask me why.

This isn't the first time C.A. has given me "the tour," instructed me in the ways of the gay world and all I'm supposedly missing out on. Lessons I could do without. In Tulsa I'd got enough of a gay education to last a lifetime. The bars, the tricks, the white boys who came and went; I could write a book called *Jimmy's Blues*. I'd gone gay crazy, away from home for the first time. C.A. ignores all this history of mine, and I don't really know how much of it he has guessed. He's like a sorcerer, consulting his book of spells. Slick-covered magazines fly about the bed as he thumbs through them, flipping pages and conjuring up men out of them, pointing out each new Adonis smiling seductively with that "come and get me" look, reaching from the page into the room to keep you alive, give you another possession you can claim for your own, if only in your mind.

The reason these guys are all grinning is because they know you can't have them: that's sex to them, what they get off on, their power over you. When I show little interest, C.A. says, kind of whiny-like, "Oh, I see you don't like him," taking it as a personal rejection, then adding, "Here, I have just the thing for you," and more pages go flashing by, and personal photos, some very personal, are being selected and rejected beneath C.A.'s fingers, too slow for his liking, so he has another man on his way before the last one has completely disappeared, a succession of heads coming and going and trying their damnedest to show the rest of their best features before C.A. vanishes them into thin air.

"Look," I say, "vanishing white men." I'm trying to get C.A.'s attention. "I don't want to look at pictures. I want to meet someone. I want to meet an Indian guy."

"An Indian?" C.A. says, as if he's never heard of one before.

"Yeah, you know, Indians," I say, wishing I'd never come inside. "Remember? Wagon Burners? Injuns? Prairie Niggers? One little, two little? Savages? Kawliga that poor old wooden head? Redskins? Cherokee Jeeps? Cleveland Indians? Wild Comanches? Running Bear loves little White Dove? You. Me. There aren't any in your magazines."

"Why don't you just *answer* an ad?" C.A. asks. "Why do you have to write one?"

"I have to write my own because there aren't any Indian guys putting personals in the gay paper."

"That oughta tell you something," C.A. says. "Keep it quiet if you want a date." He looks lost for once, sitting in the middle of his magazines, trying to conceptualize Indian and gay all at the same time, afraid to look at another photo as if one of the blond Malibu muscle boys might turn into John Wayne himself, come riding out of the page, his horse sliding to a sharp stop and dirt clods flying into the room as he pulls out his Colt six-shooter and blasts us into oblivion for blasphemy. I can hear him now, the dust still settling as he climbs off his mount, "Well, you Ind'n boys sure ain't what you used to be," then slowly removing his lever-action 30–30 from its saddle scabbard, and before we even hear the shots go off, he's scraping two new notches in the gun barrel, a pool of blood slowly spreading over the beefcake photos, me and C.A. doubled over on the bed.

I mean, hell, we know enough Indian gay guys; they're all over the place. They work for the tribe at Okmulgee; they attend the Creek Baptist and Methodist churches; they go to the night dances; they have jobs in Oklahoma City and Tulsa; we see them in the clubs on Saturday nights. They're everywhere to see for anyone who wants to wake up and smell the fry bread. But I'm looking for one to spend the rest of my days wandering aimlessly around Weleetka with. I'm tired of C.A., of fighting with a sister; I want a boyfriend. Someone to come home to after I've been doing tuneups all day at the shop where I work in McAlester. A guy worth wiping all the grease and oil off for. Suddenly C.A. is doodling in the table of contents of the *Advocate,* drawing something with a ballpoint pen. It's a skull and crossbones.

"What are you doing now?" I ask.

"Designing your ad," he answers. Underneath the skull, in bold letters, he's written WARNING I'M POISON.

"Get serious," I say, "or I'm leaving."

"I am serious. First we have to make a list of what you like."

"You mean my hobbies?"

"No," C.A. says, "your personal characteristics and private pleasures to describe yourself in the ad. Let me show you some examples. We'll try local first; though, in your case, you might have to advertise shore to shore. Or maybe interplanetary." He picks up the *Gayly Oklahoman.*

"It's your people who are supposed to have come from the sky," I say. "Mine originated on this planet."

"From below the planet," C.A. corrects. I give him that "you don't know anything about us so shut the fuck up before I go off on you" look, but I'd just shot off about Comanches, and I didn't know anything about them, either. C.A. thumbs to the personal section of our statewide newspaper. The first ad reads:

KERRY, GWM, man to man. Cute, twenty-three-year-old, blond, blue eyes, muscular swimmer's body, 5'10," smooth, cut, for 24 hours in/out, safe and discreet escort. Reasonable.

"I'm not about to place an ad like this. I'm not looking to go into business. I already got a job."

"Well, you'd stay a lot cleaner," C.A. says. He's always pestering me about being a grease monkey.

"Not necessarily. And I want an ad that will bring them in for longer than forty-five-minute 'encounters.'"

"Well, we *would* have to change a few words. Like 'gay white male,' for example, and 'cute' and 'blond' and 'blue eyes' and ....'"

"Yeah, C.A., I get the picture. Those are your fantasies, not mine."

"But the trick, so to speak," C.A. says, "is getting by until *your* fantasy materializes. The beauty of Kerry is that while you're waiting for Mr. Right, you can get by with Mr. Right Now."

"I don't have a credit card," I say. C.A. knows all the clichés.

"Well, I see Kerry is not what you have in mind," C.A. says defensively, as if I'm challenging his abilities. He sends Kerry away and brings up another possibility. My head is kind of spinning, like standing on a canyon's edge, a huge distance between all this newsprint and what I really want, which is the end of my loneliness.

GWM, seeking same, 30, 6 ft, 175, I've got a real thing for guys in wire-rimmed glasses. Seeking hot encounters with fun-loving nebbish types 18–35 but no fems or fats. Longer hair a plus.

"I don't want a philosophy major from OU. He might make me watch German movies. They're even worse than Gary Cooper."

"Hmm," C.A. says to himself while his hands are taking off, and he forces his forefinger down the column of possibilities. "Something a little less exotic to give our Jimmy boy some ideas ...." I'm watching C.A. at work, and I'm starting to see a magic eight-ball, like the toy; you shake it and your fortune floats up to the top, a message of two or three words that surface from a small contained sea of random possibilities which wear themselves out when the ball starts to repeat itself after too many consultations. Except C.A. has floated to the top, and it's him and his messages that I'm tired of. The next ad reads:

I'm a GWM professional, 36, 5'8", 150, very nice-looking, creative, educated, generous, great sense of humor, with lots of love to give the right guy. I prefer smooth men, but a little hair is OK. I like conversation, cuddling, fireplaces, long hikes on moonlit nights, someone to share a good book with, entertaining, and gardening. Not into the bar scene. Fit bottom with varied interests, looking for a romantic, caring, taller top who enjoys passion, closeness and a healthy sex drive as much as I do for short or long term.

We're both cracking up. "Sounds like Ozzie and Harriet," C.A. says. "Except I think Ozzie may have swung both ways as far as top and bottom was concerned."

"He forgot to mention his white house and little white picket fence and the white-aproned wife he promises to be for you every night where he'll be waiting inside his white-countertop kitchen so he can pull out a bubbling white-tuna casserole from the oven the minute your white ass comes waltzing in the door."

"At least he didn't specify 'only whites need apply,'" C.A. says.

"Of course not; he didn't need to." I should have never told C.A. about my ad. It admitted a certain desperation.

"Why do you turn everything into a race riot?" C.A. asks. "You're such a cynic. It's like all those books you're always reading about Indians. You don't like any of them. They're too negative or too romantic or too academic or not written by Indians and inaccurate or written by the wrong Indians or written by Indians playing along with the stereotypes or just boring, like *High Noon*. You got to admit—you're not exactly easy to please. With all that reading, you could be a professor."

"Yeah, right. How many professors do you know who got their start tuning up cars?" I let it drop. Everyone said I talked brainy, but no one knew why. They rarely guessed I read all the time; they saw me as a dumb jock who never looked outside the pages of *Sports Illustrated*. I read, partially, to prove them wrong, if only to myself. But, mostly, my dad had gotten me started years before. C.A. responds to my silence by scrolling down to a new section of the personals. But he just has to bless me with one last bitchy remark, can't call up another ad without getting in the final word on the previous one. "Sounds to me like you're more interested in skin color than love," C.A. says under his breath. Then he adds, a little louder, "How come you can't love a white man? That's reverse racism."

"How come you can't love an Indian?" I shout. "That's self-hatred. Not to mention bad taste. Haven't you noticed how all these ads say the same thing: Desperately Seeking a White Man. They sure get to pick the race of *their* lovers. Do you ever get the feeling that history is repeating itself? Our race, or any other race besides their own, doesn't seem to be very popular with the gay boys here in the Sooner state. How come you can't see that?"

Then I say, more depressed now than mad, "C.A., you spend hours and hours on this stuff, and you get pitiful advice on what movies to see and the best books to read and the most fashionable things to wear and how to decorate your house and the latest tips on staying skinny and beautiful and scouting techniques for finding a man, then combat training for keeping him once you've found him, and, I mean, it just goes on and on forever, but what the hell good has it done you? You never been with a man for any length of time that amounts to anything, just like everybody else soaking up all the bullshit in these articles and advice columns and most likely the people writing them, too. You've been the upstanding model gay boy, followed all the rules and regulations and recommendations of the invisible little gay people who get their names in a byline, and the only thing they ever gave you was a fantasy playground that keeps you and everybody else from simply pulling the plug on them because of the ugly truth: The gay world is a totally fucked-up, racist, hateful, self-hating, boring, moronic, second-rate imitation of the straight world that despises it. They're total assimilationists, the same bunch of folks telling your great-grandparents to get a job and cut their hair and don't talk Indian."

"Well, that's a little extreme, Jimmy, even for you. But quite a performance, I have to admit. And besides, I was with Harold McKlosky a long time."

"For what, a week? That wasn't a long time; it was a long time *ago*. I'm sorry, but when I see someone slacking, I'm gonna say something about it."

"How come it's okay for you to write an ad and say you want an Indian man," C.A. asks, "but you throw a fit because white guys want to meet their own kind? What's the difference?"

"The difference is there's two hunnerd and some-odd million of them and less than two million of us. That's a big difference."

"Does this mean you won't be sending the ad?" C.A. asks, sounding disappointed. I get up to leave.

"C.A., it ain't happening," I say. "I appreciate the help, but I gotta get going."

C.A. shrugs. He doesn't look up from his magazine when I walk from the room and out the door. But he won't let me escape without a final little verbal thrust. "There's always Josh," he smirks, glancing my way and smiling sweetly.

I turn and face off with C.A. "He's not an Indian date; he's an Indian joke." Please don't ask how C.A. managed to extort that little tidbit out of me, the night of the ball game, down by the Canadian River, my last desperate act before I was mercifully graduated from high school, put out of my teenage misery so I could rapidly be absorbed by adult miseries. But he hadn't stolen away all of the secret.

Josh Henneha spooked me out, man. Yeah, we were drunk, but when I touched him that night, his face had changed, and it was more than the whiskey. He rolled on top of me, and it was someone I didn't know, someone I'd never seen before. I've never watched a face change so much, and it wasn't pleasure, this contortion. And let me tell you, it's pretty damn scary when that face is only inches away from your own.

I'd always been mouthy, a smart-aleck teenager, especially around Roy Hillabee at the height of my infatuation. If nothing else, I got him to sit up and notice me. After me and Josh had fumbled around and undressed each other in the sand, I'd gotten nervous and talked up a blue streak until the sun finally came up. But it was different than the usual blabbing I did to cover up my insecurities or to get people to pay attention. Or to sound off in the face of all that racist shit I grew up with. On the riverbank I was thinking, oh my God, I can't believe what I've just done. I'd been planning for months to get Josh down there, but I just wanted to see how he would react. It was one way of maybe finally finding out for sure where we stood with each other and ourselves.

So we were sitting there watching the sun come up, the first time I'd really had sex with anyone to that extent, and me rattling on a mile

a minute, when Josh starts talking about a swing over on Gill Creek
and the time me and him swung together out over the water, and I fell
in, and he dove in after me. I never heard of no such place as Gill
Creek, and my family has been in this country for about as long as
anyone's, and I sure don't remember taking him over to no swing. And
I said, no way, and he wouldn't back down, and it just went on until I
changed the subject and pointed out the sun coming up on the other
side of the river. And that was after he hadn't said a word all night long.
Hadn't said that much since I'd known him, matter of fact. It scared me.
I thought maybe I'd fried his brain with what all I showed him. Then
I began wondering what other stuff the guy had made up in his head.

I started to recollect the different world he was always lost in, as if
he couldn't wake up from a dream. I became a little frightened of him.
I began to wonder who had drug who down to the river, what he'd
put over me that made me tell him so much there on the riverbank
when he didn't have to say anything. And the fact that I'd gone on
later to confess all this to C.A. Josh was such a dreamer, and I didn't
know how to handle all that or what kind of influence I'd fallen under.
It was too much for me at the time, and it kept me from trying to look
him up when he went off to school. I'd relived that night on the river,
the night I'd first trusted another person with the truth about myself,
over and over again. I'd hoped for much more.

"He wasn't ready for anything," I say. So far I've thrown C.A. off
the trail on this one subject.

"No, honey, you scared him off. You don't jump on a twelfth-
grader like a dog on a bone. You're an old horny toad."

"C.A., need I remind you that *I* was in twelfth grade, too? If
you're gonna go there, you better be ready. He came with me of his
own free will. I was ready. He wasn't. I didn't show him anything he
didn't wanna see."

"There you go bragging again," C.A. says.

"I was referring to the river," I add slyly. "Why are we talking
about something that happened when we were kids?" Since then, Josh
was the one who made good, went off to college, moved away, became
a professional. Not likely interested in his old skinjun buddies. On to

bigger and better things, graduated from the local yokels. The last we heard he was in Oklahoma City. C.A. claims he seen him in the stands at one of my Indian league ball games, but C.A. is always feeding me this kind of bullshit. But it sounded about right, Josh appearing out of nowhere like a ghost.

"Let me get this right," C.A. says. "Player sustains injury while running ball at the corner of Wheeler Park and the Canadian River. At point game, he checked man. After every basket, chests bumping; after every dunk, mayhem. Josh, unconcerned with playing D and trying to make some time, becomes distracted. His man took advantage of the situation, came off the wing, faked left, went right, and broke Josh off at the ankles. Due to this injury, Jimmy complains of a chronic inability to get it on in the larger game due to extensive postgame trauma. How's that?"

"Pretty good for a non-baller," I say.

"A lounge-chair baller. I watch the game," C.A. replies. Sometimes we get in this groove where we just jam off of each other.

"Watch the game, maybe. From behind your magazines. You never could play it. You were one of the dribbling impaired."

"A divine baller, any time, any place," C.A. says, throwing up his arm like a disco diva to underscore the last part of the statement.

"Now you're dreaming. Time to go before the shit gets too deep."

On the drive home I think about C.A.'s family. They're outsiders here in Creek country. I mean, it would be one thing if one of C.A.'s parents was Creek, but everybody kind of wonders why his family moved up here from southern Oklahoma in the first place. I think that's a good deal of the reason C.A. left, moved to Shawnee. Though I expected him to get a little farther away, or move all the way back home to Comanche County. Oh, on the few occasions his folks show up at Creek doings, at the community house for a feed, everybody is nice enough to them, but C.A.'s family has no relatives amongst us. Us younger ones know C.A.'s kin from going to school with his brothers and sisters, and we've seen them dancing at powwows, but the old folks only know C.A.'s parents, who'd moved in inexplicably years ago, and such southern plains doings as what C.A.'s siblings participate in don't mean a whole lot to our elderlies. Around here you're either Indian Baptist church or Indian Methodist church, or stomp grounds. Or the bunch that just don't participate in neither, but that's not regarded too highly in my family. That's how we know you in these parts. Every summer C.A.'s family has their own stuff to attend to in Comanche County, and we have church camping-ins and the stomps.

That makes summertime a vacation for me, even though I been a long time out of school, because it means I see C.A. much less frequently since we're both busy with our relatives' summer activities. It's these winter months that are the problem, when it seems we're cooped up together forever with no reprieve and little to do besides make each other crazy.

I drive around the curve and pass the black cemetery. A couple non-Indian relatives are buried there. I stop on a wooden bridge and there, under the full moon, look at the washed-out road where the bridge had been before erosion created its new location. I pull open my glove box and take out the envelope, unfolding its single sheet of paper, reading it yet once again. The ad I'd written before I'd asked for C.A.'s help. I'd been stumped for three weeks with the same eleven words. "I'm Indian. I hope you are too. Give me a call." Sure, there's other things I dream of, but I don't know how to turn a dream into a classified ad for the personals section of the *Gayly Oklahoman*. I turn my truck off and get out. The boards creak and sag as I walk to the railless edge and sit down. It's dead winter—no fish rising up to swallow insects on the water's surface, no raccoons coming down to the creek edge; even the cicadas have stopped their grinding hymn, thousands of voices fallen into silence. Just the bare black creek banks and swirling muddy water beneath my feet, stirred up from the earlier rain. I go back to the truck and return with a pen, sit back down, stare at the paper some more. As if the message might be written for me in its cratered surface, I look up at the moon, but there's nothing there to copy onto my single sheet. The only thing I can think to add is my post office box. So I write that down and get back in the truck, easing it over the bridge and onto the dirt road.

Then I stop again, get the envelope out, and remember to address it. I use the steering wheel for a writing pad. I've almost sent it so many times by now I know the address in Oklahoma City by heart. I let the letter lay next to me and start back down the road. I pass by my neighbor's farrowing barn where he houses his breeding sows, who are nursing their winter broods inside, then I go by the unbred younger gilts grazing in the last dim light of an alfalfa pasture; tawny, dirt-red, bristly shadows look up when the truck passes by, and, finally, I reach the feed lot where the market hogs are being finished out for slaughter. I turn into my driveway. It doesn't smell as bad as you might think; I've grown accustomed to alfalfa and pig shit; it means I'm home.

I pull the truck alongside my mailbox, roll down the window, and pry open the metal door. The squeaky door hits the wooden post, and when the market hogs hear the loud metallic clank, they jump up together, snorting and rushing toward a dark corner of the three-sided pole barn. The back of the structure faces the road, and it has an ad painted on the whitewashed background. "Buddy's Country Sausage," it says, and beneath the logo a spotted Poland China boar stands in front of a red barn alongside a white Yorkshire sow, each bearing its personalized name blazoned on a knit sweater that each of the hogs is wearing, old-fashioned cursive that spells out "Chet" and "Big Suzy." Big Suzy has a cartoon bubble over her head that reads, "Chester, I couldn't have done it without you."

"Now, that's love," Chet's bubble says, and Chet is all moon-eyed, but what he doesn't see is that parked behind Suzy is a truck pulling a trailer which is backed up to a loading chute where hogs are being led up the ramp inside, and the trailer has the same logo painted on it as the barn sign itself, "Buddy's Country Sausage." And Suzy's cute little pig tail is curled around a pennant flying in the breeze that reads, "Don't forget Chester. He's over here."

"Thanks a lot, C.A.," I mutter to myself, then place the envelope inside, clang the mailbox door shut, and raise the red flag.

EIGHT

Visiting Lucy at the Senior Citizen's Center

Josh Henneha, Eufaula, Oklahoma, 1991

I drove my car down Main Street Eufaula, past the old hewn-stone front of the state bank, past the drugstore, past Dr. Shelby's office which I had visited once after having stepped barefooted on a rusty fishhook, the result of having taken up Sammy's adolescent dare to see who could walk the farthest on hot lakeshore rocks in August. I lost, though the trail of blood I left from the lake to the Main Street doctor's office, and Sammy's loud announcement to all those we encountered that I'd hooked myself, certainly livened up that dull summer day. I hadn't thought about Sammy since I graduated from Oklahoma State University, the year I started working for the state Department of Agriculture and ran into him selling tires at the auto shop in Wal-Mart, down by the stockyards in Oklahoma City. I remembered because I'd gone to the trouble of driving to another Wal-Mart rather than speaking to him.

From the four-way intersection just on the other side of the lake, Grandpa lived seven miles east of town. He was standing in the doorway of the brick house he lived in when I pulled up. I parked next to the barbwire fence, under the catalpa tree, just behind a haystack covered with a blue plastic tarp to keep the rain off.

"Lester, you're letting the cold in," Grandma said. "Come on in. You'd think he hadn't seen you in a month," she said.

It had been a while. I tried to get by there as often as I could, but every weekend I managed to make the trip, they sure let me know they were keeping track.

"B'lieve I'll just sit in here with the boy," Grandpa said, settling in at the kitchen table. He rarely ventured into the living room, my grandmother's kingdom. He'd even rigged up a portable TV on a kitchen cart, and he always had one of his ball games on, even though there was another TV in the living room. That was Grandma's; this was his. *"Lekibus,"* he said, pointing to a kitchen chair. "Miami's playing." Grandma came in the kitchen and poured us some coffee. I put my hands around the cup and let it steam awhile.

"What's the score?" I asked, not much interested.

"Don't know. It was 6–0 at halftime. Not much of a game." My grandpa went over to his kitchen cart where he kept his stacks of *National Geographic* and brought a pile of them back to the table, thumbing through the issues. "Looky, here," he says, pointing to a picture of a bald eagle perched in a huge aspen next to some Yukon lake. "You know we got birds just like those in Eufaula?"

I didn't remember seeing eagles when I was young. "They come down and overwinter in Oklahoma," he said. "Last year state Fish and Game found one of them nesting here. They says more gonna stay the next few years." My grandpa's only indulgence for book learning was *Field & Stream,* where he picked up hot bass tips, and *National Geographic* that he could study while watching slow ball games. "Let's take a drive to the east end of the lake," he said, yawning.

"You wanna go, Grandma?" I asked.

"Naw, she don't wanna go," Grandpa answered.

"I can speak for myself," she said testily. "I got work to do." She was folding clothes in the living room. It seems the years had firmly established their separate domains.

I drove past the dam, and before we even parked, we saw a bald eagle lifting off a stark oak branch across the water. I had expected to see maybe one or two eagles, and within five minutes I had counted a dozen. Steam was rising from the black stumps at the water's edge, and the winter sun hung like a swollen orange, blood-red and burning in the mid-morning sky. An old patriarch, whose white head and snow-plumed tail feathers were floating through light, sailed into the yellow rays, patiently abiding the playfulness of a younger, pesky companion, still immature and gray in coloring. The younger bird was playing tag—sweeping above us in long, ever-expanding circles, then diving after the older one and pulling up just above the water, taxiing across the surface. The wings of the eagles dusted the sky, and, when they banked over the shoreline, they cast shadows on the shimmering sand. I shivered and blew on my hands, remembering the coffee.

"That ball game sure was a bust," Grandpa said. His understatement was not lost on me, the magnificence of these great birds within miles of our house, compared to sitting around watching TV, even if it was Miami, not to mention a chance for him to get out and leave Grandma to her own devices. I finally said that maybe we should get going. Grandpa nodded but didn't move or get up to leave. "You oughta visit Lucy before you head back," he said, a request he made every time I came home, which I had managed to dodge. Lucy had Alzheimer's. Bad. She had deteriorated fast, just within the last year. I'd put off going by, not ready to see her in such a state. Everybody always thought of her as a kind of local encyclopedia. She knew the history of families in Weleetka and Eufaula, all the way back to who settled where after Indian Removal in the 1830s and then all the white families and when they had come to the area, as well as when the illegal ones had snuck into Indian Territory.

I'd always thought of her as kind of loopy, the way all this stuff poured out of her all the time, yet it was a tremendous body of knowledge, if only in terms of its volume. To see somebody like that who doesn't even remember her own name some days was just too much. Around Lucy, at least, I never had to worry about coming up with something to say, unlike others always trying to get the shy kid to speak. For this same reason, the fact that she never shut up, she drove a lot of people crazy.

"She ain't got all her wits," Grandpa said, "but she gets round real good. Just last week your grandma took her over to McAlester, and they sat in the Italian restaurant and drank Choc beer. Your grandma didn't drink none, but Lucy still has a taste for it, and she likes to get out. 'Sally,' she says, meaning your grandma who she mistaked for her cousin, 'you sure have gotten fat.'" Grandpa slapped his knee and repeated the line a couple more times for amusement's sake, "'Yeah, you sure have gotten fat,' she says. She told your grandma that she must be pregnant with triplets."

I fished out my car keys, ready to leave, but I didn't make any promises. "I'll go over there with you," Grandpa said. "It might help her recognize you." If I was going to go, this was the time. Having the old man with me would be better than facing Lucy alone. He had seemed so insistent, implying with the power of the old to inculcate guilt that Lucy's happiness in her declining years hinged on me stopping by to visit.

We got in the car and I drove up the hill and pulled onto the blacktop. Off of one of the residential streets in town, Grandpa pointed out the white signboard that read "Eufaula Manor," the *M* leaning over and resting on the lowercase *a* like a statement about the tired occupants of the home.

After the first couple of minutes wandering the halls, I adjusted to the sterile smell of ammonia and watched the people in wheelchairs spilling out the doors of their rooms, filling the halls, some immobile and sagging like decrepit barns, others chattering incoherently, as lively as fireflies, their hands flitting here and there before their faces, a contrast to their blank eyes and uninhabited bodies. When Aunt Lucy looked up and saw us standing at her door, she smiled and settled back in her wheelchair.

"Did you bring my snuff?" Lucy asked huffily, pinching the last dip from a Copenhagen can and putting it in her mouth.

But there was nothing in it.

"You know you ain't dipped in a hunnerd years, Luce," Grandpa teased. "You know who this is, doncha?" he asked. "This here's my grandson. Clem and Nita's boy," Grandpa added hopefully, giving Lucy another clue. "Nita's your niece."

"Yeah, that's Crazy Horse," Lucy said, with gusto. I waited for an explanation. None came. I was Crazy Horse, and that was that. Maybe she was kidding. Maybe she wasn't.

Grandpa laughed. "Well, there's worse a person could be than Crazy Horse."

"You sure look nice, Aunt Lucy," I said. "It looks like you got a new permanent."

"Yeah, me and your grandma pays a little extry for her to get done up like that," Grandpa said.

Lucy was fussing with her hair. "They done all right," she says, "but you know they're all jealous of me in here. My bowels," she whispered, indicating some profound suffering. "They been kindy loose lately. Nothing lays on my stomach right." Lucy wheeled herself toward the door, and we had no choice but get out of her way. She turned into the hallway and kept going without looking back, no warning or goodbye.

"Did you make her mad?" I asked.

"She just takes off to go visit her friends," Grandpa said. "Don't take it personal. They wander in and out of each other's rooms all the time. They trade clothes amongst one another or just give them away. Every time your grandma comes here she sees someone going down the hall with something on we just bought for Luce. We pull open her drawers and find shoes and I don't know what all we ain't never seen before. They all share, including each other's beds; they'll just crawl right in with one another. We got pictures of you grandkids we hung on the wall in here, and if you walk up and down the halls you can see all of you in other people's rooms."

What surprised me the most was in all the years I'd known Lucy, I'd never seen her wander off in the middle of one of her own stories. I'd heard her stories wander all over the place, but she always stayed put. She had an intense focus that demanded attention, and she saw her stories through to the end. The world around her stopped until she finished, but now she had succumbed to her surroundings; they had become larger than her words.

Me and Grandpa went into the hallway, looking for her. A nurse's aide passed. "She's in the dining room," the nurse smiled, "eating lunch." As we got closer to the cafeteria, I heard someone bellowing like a cow coming in at feeding time. Lucy, seated at the same table with this unhappy old man, ate her lunch while nurses fluttered around his chair, readjusting the belt that kept him from falling out and admonishing him against screaming. The nurses had regressed to infantile behavior as much as their patient: They had put a bib around the man's neck to feed him and, having dressed him like a baby, began cooing in baby talk, trying to get him to take a bite, tasting the food themselves first, commenting in saccharine voices on how delicious it tasted. I wanted to come to his aid, throw off the nurses, goad the old bastard on as he pounded his fists on the food tray in front of him.

Lucy ignored us and started speaking Creek to him when the nurses gave up and went away. I looked over at Grandpa. I thought her friend was a white guy. Most language speakers, though not all, look Indian, have a pretty high blood quantum. I didn't ask because I didn't want to be rude.

"He's white and deaf to boot," Grandpa said. "Lucy's convinced that he's Seborn Bigpond, somebody she knew years ago. You can't tell her any different." Lucy was enjoying her mashed potatoes and talking up a storm in Indian between bites. The old man seemed to be listening intently, and he had calmed down to a low whimper.

"What's she telling him?" I asked.

"She wants to know if him and Tarbie is gonna sell their house now that they've moved in here with her. Seborn and Tarbie farmed together for years around there where we grew up. She's telling him she didn't start the fire. She says Dave set the home place on fire, not her. She made Dave promise not to start anymore fires or she was gonna take a hickory switch after him."

"What's she talking about?" I whispered. I felt guilty, me and Grandpa having this conversation right in front of Lucy, dismissing the world she saw in her head. Grandpa seemed used to it.

"Dave was a ward of the court Lucy's dad raised up. He was related to either Tarbie or Seborn; I can't remember just which."

"Tarbie," Lucy spoke up.

"Tarbie, then," Grandpa said. "They was a long time ago. Just last summer Lucy had to go into the retirement home here because she liked to have burned her house down. Me and your grandma took a notion she could go home and take care of herself if we checked on her every day. So we got her out of the old people's. That lasted two weeks. She left the oven on broil and set a loaf of bread on fire, plastic wrapper and all. The smoke detector went off, and she called over to our place while the fire trucks was on their way. She told us, 'I've burned the place down, and Daddy's still inside.' There was a lot of smoke by the time the firemen got there but not a whole lotta damage. That's when we started worrying over her. She wouldn't move in with us. Absolutely not. She loves the retirement center; you just wouldn't b'lieve it. She's surrounded by friends and thinks she's kin to ever' one of them. Every day's a family reunion for Lucy. Refuses to leave them.

"Ain't that right, Lucille?" Grandpa asked.

Lucy looked up from her tray and announced defiantly, "God is Creek," as if she was daring one of us to prove her different.

Grandpa was amused by this non sequitur. "See, your auntie's become a real radical in here," he said.

"You know that head nurse?" Lucy said, pushing her tray away.

"The one out in the hallway? Yeah, we seen her." Grandpa passed Lucy's tray to the empty table behind us. "She told us you was eating lunch."

"That's her," said Aunt Lucille, dropping down to a whisper. "Margaret Hoolihan."

Grandpa nodded toward the TV mounted in the lounge area on the other side of the cafeteria. "Your aunt watches all those MASH reruns every night."

"That head nurse wants to kick me outta here." Lucy slid the deaf man's tray in front of her and was eating his green beans. She hadn't touched hers on her own tray.

"How come she'd wanna do that, Luce?" Grandpa said. "A nice

lady like you. I might have to have a talk with her." Lucy pursed her lips. She had to think about that for a while. Her brown eyes narrowed to slits until you could barely see her pupils. Lucy's left eyelid would raise independently of the other one on the rare occasions she fell silent, giving her a slightly skewed, comic look. Old age had left her with dark-stained blotches of skin, red as earth in places, especially over the mounds of her cheeks. From too much sun, picking cotton, hard Oklahoma work, a tougher life than anything I could even imagine. Her mottled skin looked like a topography map with different colors for changes of terrain. Lucy's hands rested on her lap in front of her until she finally came up with the answer.

"I stole all her sheet music," Lucy said. "Here, I'll show you." She picked up a copy of the *Eufaula Indian Journal* from across the table. "See this third measure?" Lucy was pointing to a front-page article about the city council debating the zoning codes and whether or not modern classrooms could be added to the old stone building of Jefferson Davis Elementary. "I told her when you get to the third measure of 'A Train' you gotta play a flat five chord. When she looked down at her fingers, I grabbed the music off the piano board and hid behind the bandstand."

Then Lucy turned to me and said, "Leon, are you still playing pedal steel for Bob Wills? I heard you yesterday on KVOO at noon. 'Take it away, Leon, take it away.' Lester and me is going to Cain's this Saturday night to dance. Don't tell your grandma."

She seemed to have pinned me down to the right relative, if not the right name. So I refreshed her memory. "Me? You know, Aunt Lucille, I went to school at Oklahoma State University. Remember, when you and Mom come up to Stillwater to visit? I got a degree in agricultural economics. I took a job with the state Department of Agriculture. Been there for quite a while."

I worked for the USDA as a statistician in one of the most conservative agencies in all of civil service. Even to be single among all my married male co-workers who hailed from Iowa and Indiana and Minnesota and Georgia, all rural farmboys, made me suspect. These guys weren't known for liking Indians, either. But it had reached a point where the agency could no longer justify its whites-only policy. They had hired a few blacks, but many of the policy-makers stationed in D.C. were from the Deep South. An Indian was a great coup; they got a person who wasn't white and buoyed up the minority pool without having to hire a black. That was their version of equal employment.

I sat in front of a computer screen all day crunching numbers. I never used any of the stuff I learned in college—the high-powered math and statistical models I'd struggled to get under my belt—and it seemed like such a waste now. I compiled crop-yield reports where all the words stayed the same and just the numbers changed. The only words I ever replaced in the ag publications we printed were "up" or "down," depending on whether the crop year was good or bad. The rest consisted of charts, graphs, columns of figures: yield per acre, total yield, county breakdowns, statewide totals, every variation possible on the same theme. All the real analysis and interpretation of the data, which I did have some interest in, was done outside the state office in D.C. by people I only met at meetings the government sent me to, consolation trips for my dreary work.

I shared none of my male colleagues' interest in the agency's philosophy, the latest promotions, or the newest directives from D.C. This last year things had gotten especially unbearable. The men in the state office, and the majority were in fact men, and all their bosses in D.C. were married, or making it obvious about the women they were seeing, and staying in good favor with the bosses depended on presenting the right image. If they didn't like something about you, they could manage to find things about your work that were "unsatisfactory" and hassle you during evaluations, pass you up for promotions, eventually make it miserable enough to force you to leave. I had chosen ag economics in college because I knew statisticians were getting hired easily at the time. None of this translated very well into Lucy's world, and she hadn't understood it any better back in the days when she was lucid. Following a plow in her day didn't have much to do with predicting yield by means of random sampling. Well, it did, actually, but people stood around and talked about such things on porch stoops, telling stories and giving their opinions about crop conditions and weather, rather than reading government reports and plugging the data from them into regression equations. I tried explaining it once more, though, as if Lucy hadn't heard it before.

There *was* part of the job I loved. I had to set out plots in corn- and wheatfields to make actual crop measurements and interview farmers about their own projections in order to get as many indicators as possible rather than relying on just one set of data. This meant traveling all over Oklahoma, from the arid panhandle out west to the wheat belt in the central part of the state to the rolling Oklahoma hills of my eastern upbringing to the swampy country in the southeast to the pine woods in the far east near Arkansas. I had come to know Oklahoma from one end to the other.

"He sure has done good, hasn't he, Luce?" Grandpa said. My parents hadn't graduated from high school, and my grandparents didn't make it past first grade. I had lots of cousins who never finished secondary school. It was considered a success in my family to get a GED.

"You never said that about his fishing," Lucy said.

"Let me go see that nurse," Grandpa replied, changing the subject. "You point her out to me, and I'll take care of her. I don't let no one treat my kin like that." Grandpa got up and wheeled Lucy into the hall. "Come on," he said to me, "in case she gives us any trouble. I may need you for backup assistance. Beings how you went to college and all. Now, where is she? Hoolie," he called out into the hallway.

We found "Hoolihan" at the nurse's station, paging the visiting physician. Grandpa waited patiently until she got off the phone. "Mr. Henneha," she said, hanging up the phone, "how are you today?"

"Don't 'Mr. Henneha' me," Grandpa said. "Lucille told me what's going on around here."

"I see," said Hoolihan. "Sounds serious."

"Now, nurse, I know you might think we're a bunch of hillbilly Indians," Grandpa began, clearing his throat. She started to protest, but Grandpa cut her off. "But my grandson here got a degree in agriculture from Oklahoma State University. As for me, when I see something that don't sit right, I gotta speak out."

A couple of nurses had poked their heads out of doorways at the commotion. One of them approached the nurse's station. "Is everything all right, Nurse Hoolihan?" she asked. Grandpa looked over at me and winked. They were all in on it, this game, like they had been onstage together many times.

"Now the situation wherein," Grandpa continued, in a voice like the Wizard of Oz, "you was to ask Lucille to leave Eufaula Manor. Me and my wife pay good money to keep her here. And we worked hard all our lives for it. Hill Indians or not, our money is as good as anyone else's. So, Nurse Hoolihan, from this moment forward, you will lay off of Lucille. You will cease and desist all torments and unusual cruel punishments. Now, this boy here has something to say about his aunt."

I felt my feet lift off the tile floor about three or four inches, just enough to make me taller than anyone near the nurse's desk. Not full flight, but I could almost believe I'd once taken to the air. They all stood there, waiting. Speak or spell; it was now or never. The words hung just above me in the treetops, but I'd have to fly up there and bring them back down to this world. It was the opposite of diving. Time was of the essence; if enough words bunched together they might fly off in clumps of silence forever. I was a child standing in a grassy park, who, in one brief moment of forgetfulness, had let my fingers uncurl from the string of a helium balloon, which mounted higher and higher in the sky, first a spiraling *S*, then a circle, then a dot, then a speck, than an indistinguishable blur. It was time to look up.

Lucy interrupted my thoughts, covering for me as usual. "If his friend Jimmy was here, he could get us out of this mess."

Jimmy. I'd lost track of him after I moved off to go to college.

"He works over at that Oklahoma Auto in McAlester," Grandpa said. "He does good tuneups. You want me to bring him by here to straighten this out, Luce?"

"You boys never took me to the music store," Lucy said, accusingly. "Where'd you run off to?" I felt myself rise a little higher; maybe I would float away. I had tried many times to understand that evening.

Lucy seemed to have her own crazy answer. "Jimmy disappeared down a snake hole," she said. To this she added, "Do you still miss him?"

"I haven't thought about him in years," I lied.

"I see him sometimes at Indian ball games," Grandpa said. "We better get going. Thank you, Nurse Hoolihan. You lay off Lucille, now, you hear?"

Lucy was beaming with pride at the way Grandpa had come so strongly to her defense. Nurse Hoolihan feigned humility after her fake talking down, looking at her shoes as she told us goodbye. She was really trying not to laugh. It seemed she liked Grandpa and Lucille a good deal.

Out in the car I asked Grandpa, "What was that all about?"

He put down the *Indian Journal* he'd stolen from the retirement center. "Your grandma told me, 'Just make her happy, whatever world she's in.' Last week she thought I was your daddy. It don't hurt me none to be your daddy for one day. If your grandma comes in here and Lucy thinks it's her cousin Sally, then Sally it is, and old fat Sally and Lucy goes over to McAlester and eats together. I tried to straighten her out at first on all her facts, then I give up. It was a bigger job than I got time for what with all the hours we spent trying to put her straight and get her on to the right names and tell who all's related to this one and the other and bring her up on her decades since the turn of the century. It liked to have wore your grandma and me out. Maybe we're all supposed to be more like her anyhow, sharing clothes and taking care of each other.

"And crawling into bed together," he added, laughing. "I might see about getting me a room over there. That Margaret Hoolihan could take pretty good care of a feller. You wanna check in next to me?"

How could I tell him I didn't have any interest in Margaret Hoolihan? He had asked, but could he understand the answer? Could I give him one? Could anyone explain desire?

I could have driven back to the city that night for work the following morning, but lately I'd been staying as far away as possible until I just had to go in. On flex time we could show up anytime between seven and eight-thirty in the morning, as long as we put in eight and a half hours afterwards. I'd just get up early.

I stayed in the spare bedroom. Neither my dad nor any of his siblings had been raised there; Dad was born in a dirt-floor share-cropper's cabin on land where Grandpa grew other people's crops. A nation, the Creek Nation, that had donated money to Ireland during the potato famine, developed its own formal education and social welfare system, and sent its successful students to universities in foreign countries, such as the United States and Britain, had been reduced to paupers shortly after statehood when the United States dissolved one of the most self-sufficient governments within its borders. Dad, and Grandpa before him, had been born about as poor as anyone could possibly be, back before tribal housing, which was a relative newcomer out of the war on poverty programs of the Johnson administration in the early sixties. So the spare bedroom showed no signs of dad or his siblings having lived there since they never had, located as it was in one of the more recent "Indian houses."

The walls were hung with lots of photos, overflow from the living room where the kids' wedding pictures were enshrined and the grandkids were captured doing things their parents never could, like running track and graduating from high school and college, proclaiming a life beyond getting married and having babies and toiling daily at physical labor, which was the real subject of their parents' photos. Even though their 1950s parents seemed to be cutting wedding cake with big grins and holding bridal bouquets anticipating their lives together, this was simply a brief respite from the exhaustion they would return to the day after the photo. The camera's tricks couldn't erase the weariness around their eyes.

The spare bedroom had the older pictures. I thought of it as the Indian room. The photos of the previous generations hung on its walls. The two that seemed out of place, like they belonged out in the living room with the younger ones, were Grandpa's and Lucy's, as if they'd conspired to disturb the equilibrium of their respective eras. One I liked showed Grandpa posed as an effete figure skater, a handsome young hunk at the roller rink in Muskogee. His arms spread wide, inviting the whole world to behold him, he had crossed one leg gaily in front of the other, the front brake of his skate touching down lightly on the floor. He was decked all out in a white costume which accentuated his handsome dark features, and he stood behind a

painted sign that read "Oklahoma and Texas Regional Champion-
ships." He'd been quite a skater, they said. His blond skating partner
held the championship cup, flashing pearly whites and beaming
behind curls and red lipstick. It was all so unlikely, a young Indian
farmer working in the fields and odd jobs and competing as a championship figure skater on the weekends. Lucy told me he never had
time to practice; his girlfriend would pick him up in a busted-down
roadster she drove, and they'd rehearse by competing. He was known
as "the Indian skater," and few locals looked kindly on his winnings,
though he attracted quite a crowd as a "novelty act."

He met up with trouble at the Muskogee event. The same open
arms that proclaimed his triumph would soon be pinned behind his
back that very evening out in the parking lot. The judges had set
their own record in coming up with a decision. They couldn't deny
Grandpa had outskated everybody on the floor. He got the cup, but
he also got two broken ribs and a punctured lung as his girlfriend's
cousins held him down and nearly kicked him to death behind the
roadster, while one of the judges held her back as she screamed hyster-
ically for them to stop, and the other two judges helped hold Grandpa
down on the pavement. The girlfriend's parents forbade her from
seeing Grandpa after that under pressure from their own relatives. Lucy
had hinted that my grandmother was Grandpa's second choice after
losing his girlfriend and that over the years they had managed a long-
suffering, if not entirely amicable, truce by mostly ignoring each other.

Lucy's photo seemed like it wanted to jump ship as much as
Grandpa's. All around the room her sisters stood stiffly in long dresses
and shawls and plain hats next to their men. Attired just as oppressively
in suit vests and coats and thick dungarees and leather boots, the men's
watch chains seemed a heavy-handed symbol. It wasn't easy to smile in
such a photo; the clothes wouldn't let them, and they probably had a
long, hot wagon ride ahead of them from the studio back to the farm.

Lucy had somehow escaped the photographer's studio. Posed on
a wooden bridge somewhere around Eufaula or Weleetka, leaning
casually against its wooden rail, she looks like somebody came along
and snapped a photo of her with an automatic camera, an impossible

illusion, given the time period. You can see the dirt washout that
the bridge spans and the cracks between the boards, also dirt, leaves,
and debris around Lucy's feet left behind from the wake of wagons,
surprising realistic details nowhere to be seen in the posed photos
elsewhere in the room.

It's summer, that's for sure; there's no water in the washout, and
the cut bank frames Lucy's lower body, while a large oak behind the
creek looms over the rest of her. She has on a simple dress, open-
armed, that reaches to the top of her knees. It could be white, or it
could be checked or print; it's hard to tell in the black-and-white
photo. She has her legs crossed, like a conspiracy with Grandpa, with
the next generation. But she boasts of no championship, of little but
the fact that she's there on the bridge being photographed. She doesn't
give away much. She has the narrowest eye slits, but she's not squinting
into the sun, and she is wearing the most tenuous of smiles, a half-grin
that refuses to quite acknowledge itself. She is dark and beautiful, like
Grandpa, but she'll be goddamned if she lets on as such. Her hair is in
a short bob, beautiful, black, and thick, cut in the shape of a helmet
that just covers her ears. She looks a little like a 1920s flapper, though
she precedes even that generation. If you put overalls on her, she'd be a
dead ringer for a young, handsome Indian boy of seventeen.

But your eyes are drawn to her arms before you look at her face,
the bridge, the landscape, or anything else in the photo. They are thin
and dark but knotted with natural muscle from hard work. Her right
arm is crossed over her waist like a protective shield; her hand rests on
her left hip, locked into place. A support is formed here for her opposite elbow. She uses this hand to prop up her chin and at the same time
hold on to a large, flat beret which she lets lay over her shoulder and
upper arm, a mark of control, an insistence that she chooses how much
of herself to reveal, not the photographer or anyone else. No doubt
about it; there is an attention to style in her pose, her attitude, though
not a self-conscious one. Judging by her sternly attired siblings, the
photo may have been something of a scandal.

Outside the room a night bird calls from the tree line, the saddest
sound, its voice muted inside the house. Though surrounded by so

many in the room, watching from their places on the wall, I am by myself in bed, and I become aware of my own solitude. A wave of loneliness sweeps over me. I close my eyes and think of Lucy on the bridge, standing there, one arm wrapped around herself, the tree looming large behind her. Just above the treetops, I watch her, the shadows that fall on her shoulders, slowly spreading out over the wood planks at her feet. She knows I am watching her; she has always known. I leave the treetops and pass over the lake. The moonlight shines on the tops of whitecaps, blown by a wintry wind, and the waves beat against the dam. Lucy stands on the dam road, holding down her cotton dress. She points me in the direction I must go, toward the Honeycomb Bluffs, then walks back toward town.

Since Lucy has sent me out into the woods looking for him, I touch down in this world and start walking. I hurry out past the pasture to where the dogwood trees grow along the fence rows. Their flowers have just turned from white to pink clusters, and I stop for a minute when I get a sniff of their perfume. I cross the barbed wire and go out into the post oaks, clambering up banks and through the woolly buckbrush, the soft rust-colored hairs of their leaves itching my arms and sometimes prickling me. I traipse through the grass and chiggers while the insects hum and buzz in my ears. Sweat keeps dripping in my eyes, and my clothes stick to me. I'd left in the dead of winter, and the heat is a surprise. Stopping to rest, I look up into a white ash tree, trying to see the highest branches, but it must be a hundred feet tall, and I get dizzy since that's higher than I've ever flown. In the air I usually skirt around those big trees. Walking has its advantages. Especially if you want to watch unobserved yet still be a part of what you see. Flying is perfect for hiding, and escaping danger, but it takes you so far away.

I get to thinking, well, where would *I* go if I wanted to get away from all the little ones, the whole screaming brood, all twelve of them, escape the older ones hollering and the younger ones crying and their mother busy diapering them and wiping their noses, their mouths always open waiting to be fed like baby birds in a nest. Considering the cost of turning back, the possibility of my feet never leaving earth or leaving earth forever, I head for a peaceful spot over by the spring, a place to get water, a shady rest a person can escape to. I feel good just thinking about being there.

When I finally make it over to the spring, just before I think I'll smother from the dank air, I can see Dave in the distance, sitting in a little flat clearing behind the pool of water, just across from the button willows that grow close to the bank. I've seen his picture, hung in the room across the wall from Lucy's, but this is the first I have seen of him as a child. Dave is working; he clears out all the brush and rocks from about a twenty-foot spot, and then he uses a willow branch to sweep away the smaller leaves and twigs. He finishes and starts tamping down the earth with the back of a shovel. Behind Dave is a little house, a miniature replica, a dead ringer for a farmstead. His cleaning is the final touch for the home he has built himself. My yearning returns, my loneliness, a keen awareness of my solitude as I watch from my hiding place. Or is it Dave's loneliness I feel? I want to speak to him, find out what he knows.

His farm is a little two-room log house. One thing stands out that sets it apart, for sure: It's about four foot high, and if you were to crawl inside, you couldn't even stretch your legs all the way out in any direction. He has tools all around the place that he's put together; the blades must have been salvaged from people's junk piles, the handles from strong hickory limbs. He might have started his little farmstead by sharpening a pole ax and cutting down scrub oak, trimming off all the smaller branches and twigs and cutting the bark off on all four sides to fashion square ends. The square ends make double-locked corners, the logs notched so that once set in place they can't be pushed free in any direction. A strong house, well made.

He has a hall between the two rooms, and he's walled it with cut timber; he must have sawed off the good parts of thrown-away lumber that he'd drug into the woods and there pieced it all together. A froe is lying around, a heavy knife with a blade used to split shingles from a block of wood, and a wood hammer, the handles of both of these made out of hickory, too, tools he'd fashioned for himself just as if he was a grown-up.

The beauty of it all is the layout of the place, everything arranged in relation to everything else just like you might see in this country a long time ago, riding up to any one of your neighbors, and it seems so real I can almost hear wood being chopped, hogs snorting in pens, and folks talking Indian inside. Dave has his little patch of cleared-out woods surrounded by a split-rail fence, a gate, and a garden walled by wooden pickets to keep the chickens out.

His house has a stick-and-mud chimney. Some of the houses around here had dirt floors back then, but Dave has took care to build his floor out of split logs. The cracks in the sides of the walls are filled with chinking, and the house doesn't have any windows, just the one door. Out front of the house is a well, the old-time dug kind he has earthed out with a pick and shovel, and he's walled it with rocks from his clearing. He has a homemade windlass above it to hoist his bucket.

Dave walks up to the little house, pulls open the front door, sticks his head inside, and says, "Seborn, I'm home." Then he gets down on all fours and goes in, and he says in another voice, "Tarbie, what is it you want for supper this evening?" Dave has built a replica of the two men's farm.

Dave comes out of his little house after a while and sits down in the front yard where a porch should have been. I can see he has a little more work to do on the place. He has a pile of raw cotton before him, and he begins picking seed out of the white fibers like women might do before they card it, reel it, then weave it. "Tarbie," Dave asks, "how come it took so long for us to meet at Bacone? We'd had classes together, went to dances, seen each other around campus."

So here I am listening to Seborn and Tarbie, thanks to Dave. I have to admit I was having a good time, and that farmyard started to come more alive than anything I'd seen from the treetops in all my years of flying.

Tarbie answers, "Too many girls sparking me, I reckon." Seborn frowns, and Tarbie quickly adds, "But once we was together we sure took to each other right away."

Seborn smiles. "Yeah, you couldn't hardly pry us apart."

"Still can't," Tarbie says playfully.

"But you didn't even notice me a little bit before that?" Seborn asks. Dave has pulled the seeds and debris out of one little pile of cotton, and he scoops up another pile toward his lap.

"Well, there was one time," Tarbie says, "when you come to class late, and I felt sorry for you."

"Felt sorry for me? How come you was to feel sorry for me?"

"Everybody turned around to look when you come in the door. The teacher stopped in the middle of her reading. You was late and had interrupted her. But the students took to laughing because you had on a homemade Indian shirt, one colored red with boiled-down sycamore bark. Everybody else had on their starched-white shirts— pr'y the only one they owned—that they parents had bought them in town. I remember thinking you was beautiful in that red shirt, but I laughed, too, because everbody else had taken to giggling. When I got home I felt bad because that's what I wore, too; that's what we all wore out in the country. Then I couldn't sleep that night in the dormitory— I felt different than I ever had before. I couldn't get over how handsome you was standing there in the doorway of the classroom—first you come in proud as could be, late, Indian shirt and all, and then, when you was embarrassed and looking down at your feet, you sparked my mind even more. I imagined what it would have been like to take you by the hand, and lead you to your seat. I seen myself giving the evil eye to anybody who laughed at us."

"Ah, Gawd," Seborn says, a little embarrassed. "I'd forgot about that." But that seems to be the answer that Seborn had been looking for. In fact, it seems to make him feel so good, he perks right up and says, "Tarbie, I got an idea."

"Oh, Lord," Tarbie says, "What is it?"

"Let's take us a long trip to Tulsa, and let's bring your nephew Dave along with us. We could have all kind of fun like go downtown to the ice cream parlor, for instance. I bet the boy never seen tall buildings before."

"You wanna bring Lucille, too, Rachel's girl?"

"No, just us and Dave," Seborn says. "We'll buy him a kite and make a long tail and go to the park and teach him how to fly it, have us a picnic. He can fly that kite around the park, and we'll fix us something to eat."

"Yeah, I think we're gonna do that," said Tarbie. "He's a good boy."

And then, crouched down in the cattails by the spring, listening to all that, something just broke in my mind and came flooding in on me. Those two men loved each other. They loved me. I knew if I ran fast enough, I could tell my story before I floated away, share the good news before I lost it. There was no time to lose, not a moment to spare by staying there and thinking until I got scared and changed my mind. I ran from the spring, I mean just a-hooking it, all the way to Lucy's house without stopping. I burst in the front door, and Lucy's mother looked up, surprised, and dropped the wild onions she'd been washing. "Am I dreaming?" she asked.

"No," I tell her, "Lucy is dreaming *us.*" I didn't give her any time to argue. I just sputtered out, "Ma'am, you have to come see what Dave is up to out in the woods." I said it fast, without thinking, before the words could go away. I couldn't risk losing the only person who might understand. And even then it was a gamble.

"This isn't the first time he's run off with the *'Stiloputchkogee,'* " she said. I knew about the Little People, like any other Creek. They are invisible most of the time, but sometimes children or a medicine maker can see them. They look like Indians and speak Muskogee. They wear the old-time Indian clothes, like deerskin and leggings and colorful turbans wound up on top of their heads. They live in the tree-tops and use raccoons for dogs. They like to play tricks on people, but they are not mean if you treat them right. They need help crossing creeks, streams, and watering holes, so mostly they're nice to folks. They'll take in small children who are lost or who have wandered away from home and feed and care for them and teach them medicine. Medicine makers often receive their training from the Little People. A little boy or girl might end up wandering back home in a day or two, in the parents' yard, unharmed. Little People also have children of their own that live in the trees with them.

"No, ma'am," I say, trying to catch my breath. "He's talking to Seborn and Tarbie."

"What?" I could tell this had her rattled. "Seborn and Tarbie," she repeated to herself. "Josh," she says, "I think you should go visit the *hilis heyya,* the medicine woman, Becky Katcha. She might have some notion about what to do with Dave. And," she said, looking at me sternly, "no flying."

I wasn't crazy about the idea. Lucy had told me stories about the medicine woman, like maybe she could turn herself into an owl and fly off. From the way Lucy told it, though, it seemed like enough people relied on her, no matter the rumors. I didn't like promising to stay on the ground if I got in a tight spot.

I tried not to let on like I was scared. "I don't know if I can find my way over there," I said. "It's bound to look a lot different than the way it does in my mind. This is, what, seventy-five, eighty years ago? And I've only heard about it in the stories."

"Yes, but the Fixicos is going over thataway to sell some eggs in town," Lucy's mom said. "You worry too much. Just go. You can hitch a ride with them in the morning," she said, then went back to work, scrambling the wild onions into some eggs.

The next morning we head off to town in the wagon, dust parting before us like the Red Sea rolling back for the Israelites. It is dirty—I feel the grit in my hair and eyes—but grand. Mr. and Mrs. Fixico sit up on the front seat, planning what to buy with their egg money, and I sit in the back of the wagon, my feet hanging over the end, my butt bouncing as we bump over the potholes, and me whooping as I grab for the sideboards and watch the road spool out beneath our wheels. I wish we had a load of cotton. Lucy has told me so often about her daddy parking at the gin underneath the chute that sucks up a whole bed full of bolls with a *whoosh!* while she sits turned around in the wagon seat watching that sea of wavy white and brown stems stirring and flying up all over the place, slowly draining out of the wagon bed and finally disappearing altogether.

The Fixicos let me out just on the edge of town, on the curve at the black cemetery. Now that's a landmark I know—it's still there today. I see Becky Katcha's shack next to the barn with the slanted roof. I walk up to the door, and the old sagging porch boards creak.

My knees knock together, and I feel my stomach churning. I have to
grab on to the railing to steady myself. I'd heard it all from Lucy:
Church folks say she's a witch; Lucy's daddy claims she's a harmless
old woman; Lucy's mom says she's a powerful medicine person. I don't
hear any signs of anyone stirring inside or out back, and I knock pretty
quiet, half hoping she won't answer but curious all at the same time
and wanting to see her for myself. I stand there on the front porch,
shifting from foot to foot. I lean over the porch rail and peek around
the side of the house. After a while I give up and decide to walk the
short distance into town and meet up with the Fixicos and come back
later and see the medicine maker.

I am walking past the black cemetery when I look over my shoulder one last time toward the house. The slant-roofed barn comes into
view; the thing looks like it's ready to lay over, more leaning than
standing. Maybe she's out there milking or something, I think, and
I know I'll have to give a good account for myself when I report back
to Lucy's mom. She would most likely know if I left the thing half
undone. So I head toward the barn for one last try. When I get close,
I can see sunlight shooting down through the gaps in the roof and
wall, streams of hay dust floating and shifting in the light from the
door. I put one foot inside and step through. Just as I pull myself in,
someone taps me on the shoulder, and I jump up and holler so loud
my throat hurts afterwards. This scares the old woman right out of her
wits. She drops a handful of cedar sprigs she's gathered and jumps
back wide-eyed and staring. Then she sees me backing up to the door
just as scared as her, and she picks up the cedar and sits down on a hay
bale and starts laughing so hard tears are running down her cheeks. I
don't know what to say at first, but pretty soon I'm laughing, too, and
she gets up and shakes my hand.

"You Rachel's boy from over by the river?" she asks. "Dave, ain't it?"

"Yes, ma'am, they live pretty close to the Canadian, right by the
sand hills. But, I'm afraid you've mistaken me. My grandmother on
my mom's side is Lucy's sister. Rachel's daughter."

"That's quite a trick," she says, "since none of Rachel's kids has
childrens yet. Are you sure you're not Dave?"

"No," I answer honestly.

"Whoever you are you liked to scared all the meanness outta me, boy," she laughed, "sneaking up on me like that." She was pulling willow roots out of her apron and setting them in front of her. She catches me in her bright gaze, smiles, and nods. Right away I forget about being afraid.

"Lucy's mother sent me over here," I say. "I figured you'd be up at the house," I stammer, a little embarrassed but surprised to find myself speaking at all, the words coming out much easier now that I might be somebody else.

"Oh, yeah, me and Rachel been friends since long time ago," Mrs. Katcha says. "We was sent off to boarding school together, over to Chilocco Ind'n School: I got one to tell on your great-great-aunt. Rachel and some of her schoolgirl friends and me was back home for the summer from that white man's school for Indians. The Sandlanes, W. W. Sandlanes, wealthy white folks, was real good friends of Clayton Longcoach, them ones was. And so this ole man, W. W. Sandlane, he got to be pretty well off, and they was big farmers and everything, and they had them a watermelon stand on the highway there out of Weleetka. The boys, the Sandlane boys, always wanted Clayton to come and stay with them. One night Clayton stayed there all night with them Sandlane boys because they had a tent spread and a place to sleep; watermelon stand open all night, they had it. That night they was sleeping in the wagon bed on account of it was so hot. So, 'bout two o'clock of a morning, here come me and Rachel and a whole carload of Ind'n girls, and we was just laying up and a-carrying on talking like we was gonna get out and go to bed with them Sandlane boys. Rachel told me, 'Bob,' she always called me 'Bob,' says, 'Bob, I'm gonna sleep with them Sandlane boys and stay all night with them tonight.' Around them white boys talking big in Creek. Us just among each others, you know, talking to have a laugh. What we didn't know was Clayton was right there in the wagon bed amongst them. 'Course, him being Ind'n, he understood ever' word. Ole Clayton raised up out of that bed like a ghost and says back in Ind'n, 'Girls, all y'all come on.'"

Mrs. Katcha keeps saying the last line of her story over again, "Come on," then laughing uproariously as if the boys are out in the wagon right now. "Yeah, Rachel and me was having a lot of fun," Mrs. Katcha says, "until Clayton raised up out of the wagon like that." I like Mrs. Katcha right away. She is easy to talk to. She asks what brings me over Weleetka way.

"Well, the Fixicos have gone into town to sell some eggs, but I'm here because of Dave, the boy Lucy's family is raising. Lucy's mom thinks maybe he's not acting right, and she's getting worried."

"What's he doing?" Mrs. Katcha asks.

I tell her about Dave talking to Tarbie and Seborn out in the woods.

Mrs. Katcha listens to my story about Dave, then she doesn't say anything for a long while. I thought she would have seemed more surprised. I sure wish she'd say something instead of leaving me standing there fidgeting around. But her silence is different than mine, a careful consideration.

Finally, she says, "There's nothing I can do for Dave."

"What?" I ask with a start, thinking, oh God, there's something really terrible that even the medicine woman can't fix.

"I can't help him," she tells me, "because there's nothing wrong with him. He talks to Tarbie and Seborn because they understand him. Who do you talk to?" she says, looking at me and waiting for an answer.

"I'm looking for someone," I tell her.

"Well, hurry up and find him," she says. "What's stopping you?" I have to think about that one for a while. I'd never considered the possibility that the world might be crooked, and I might be okay. That might have been the reason I had to leave it so often, the meaning of my flights. I had to dream a little to get a proper perspective on things, from my place just above the earth.

"Go back and tell Rachel she should trust what she knows already. Dave's a good boy. Not a thing in the world wrong with him."

I gave Mrs. Katcha the tobacco plug and a sackful of salt meat Lucy's mom had sent over with me. Mrs. Katcha gave me a big ole wide-tooth grin and shakes hands again. She walks with me back up to the road, all the while shooing chickens out of our path, and the old hens and guineas hightail it off toward the thickets of buckbrush.

I get up on the roadway and make my way into town to meet up with the Fixicos. It's not that much different than today, other than the lack of pavement anywhere, and I can figure my way back once I find the black cemetery. I feel relieved, to tell you the truth, to find out about Dave because I started to like him, watching him out in the woods—the house he'd built, the voices of Tarbie and Seborn. I knew Rachel put a lot of stock in Mrs. Katcha's word, and this would put her mind at ease.

So I feel pretty lighthearted, half skipping, kicking up dust, singing right along with the katydids. Then I hear her. The night bird who'd sent her song in the dusky evening when the shadows started to fall outside my window, singing while I looked at Grandpa's and Lucy's pictures. Whippoorwill. I hear her say things, the first time I've known her to speak in broad daylight; mostly she feeds around on the ground in the dark. I listen to her call, break the notes apart into words and meaning. *Whip-poor-will,* laugh, Lucille; I keep playing with the sound, the notes, the meanings, the idea of speaking in the light. Then I stand there quiet, my ears open, soaking it all in. I just let that sound, those three notes, fill me. Some say she sounds lonely, that she's the saddest bird, but not me. Not anymore.

I haven't even heard the preacher's voice once. He never ventures out into the woods. I decide I can pick and choose who I want to listen to anyway, so, just to piss him off, I sing one of his own hymns and change the meanings all around, just like a whippoorwill's song. I mess around with the drone I could never get out of my head, or my heart, adjust the pitch, turn down the volume, change *Jesus* into *Jimmy,* and laugh about all that hunger and yearning I'd been raised on until I could feel it hanging in the hot August air of Sunday morning services:

> He touched me, oh, he touched me
> and, oh, the joy that fills my soul
> something happened, and now I know
> he touched me and made me whole

Grandma wakes me early, before dawn, comes padding into my room in housecoat and slippers. "You better get up," she says.

In the kitchen she pours me some coffee. "I don't have much fixed this early. Is biscuits and gravy okay?" she asks.

"Great," I reply. "I'm starved."

"The old man's still sleeping," she says.

"Don't bother to get him up," I tell her. It's starting to get light out, and the farmyard is coming into view. Grandpa had told me many times that the countryside around the lake no longer looked the same. In his day the land, now covered with water, once grew rows of cotton and corn in every little flat spot between hills and creeks. Since the days of small-scale cotton farming had ended, and the crop economy had moved to the wheat belt in central Oklahoma, eastern Oklahoma land had reverted from farmland back to woods and grasslands where white ranchers now ran cattle.

In the old days, Grandpa told me, when the Muskogees were forced out of their homes in Alabama and marched to Oklahoma by federal troops, the first Creeks, after arrival in the new territory, let their newly acquired cows and hogs run wild in the woods where they ate grass and acorns, which lay on the ground knee-deep among the oak trees, only rounding up the livestock periodically to sell or slaughter. The Creeks had Indianized farming, never turning into the agriculturalists that the government hoped for, the kind of farmers whose acres of wheat and corn I now took measurements in. Even in their farming the Creeks had resisted, and the land itself had resisted even more. Grandpa got a big kick out of the fact that the land had covered up the corn and cotton and returned to itself, to trees and grass as it had been when the Creeks first arrived.

What's it like to live long enough to have seen the change from farmland to woods, the hills and flat places reclaimed by grass, brush, and trees? I wondered. A more natural state.

"Thanks for breakfast, Grandma," I say.

"You're welcome. You better get on the road," she tells me, picking up my plate. "You don't want to be late for work."

Yes, I do, I think, and say goodbye. She pats me and says, "Come back soon as you can." On the way toward Eufaula, feeling defiant, I decide the government can wait. I can always work a little later if I don't get there quite on time. I pull off the road where me and Grandpa had seen the eagles that previous morning, remembering their circles of grace against the cold, wintry light when mist covered the water like a fog. It was the first time I'd seen an eagle outside the zoo. The wind currents under their wing tips had lifted them as they effortlessly rose up on columns of air, and I knew by their movement that I had seen other worlds beyond words, other languages inside circles of motion. I wanted to learn that language.

NINE

Aunt Lucy's Funeral

Josh Henneha, Eufaula, 1993

"Do you hear somebody knocking?" Grandma called, just as I walked out over the silence, stepping carefully, afraid of falling back through. The knock on the door came as my Aunt Lucy's unadorned coffin was lowered into darkness. Somebody's knocking reached me as my grandpa walked toward the grave's edge and threw a black clod, which thumped and shattered on the casket's lid. The knocking stilled the crickets at the edge of the graveyard, hushed the gray voices just within hearing, brought me out of my daydream and back to the tattered sofa and yellowing curtains of my grandparents' home, east of the lake.

It was only my grandfather and his funny habit of knocking on the front door of his own home, and, in a sense, I guess, since everything the BIA gives Indians has strings attached, he might have felt himself an intruder there. And then there was his and Grandma's weird separate kingdoms, the wide berth they gave each other. On the way home from the funeral he'd gotten out at the gate to check the float on the automatic waterer in the cow trough. Before he came in and interrupted my thoughts, I'd planned to shake hands, say goodbye.

Instead he asked me, grinning like a little kid, just to stay a little
longer. Wanna go down to the river like how I useta take you, how
'bout it? he'd asked. I knew this game, maybe I even liked it, so we got
in the truck and drove out to the Canadian.

We cross fences and make our way down to the river and stand
next to the slow-flowing water in the center of sound, the metallic
hum of cicadas in our ears, the Oktahutche parting at a sandbar out in
the middle, the systolic pulse all around us, ebb and flow, surge then
cease. You still remember their names? he quizzes, and I ask if I have
to say them in Creek or English. Stupid question, no response. I look
for signs. I pick out the tallest tree, easy, a sycamore. I say its name,
Akhatka. Farther up the bank, *Achena,* a cedar, red trunk and dark
blue-green funnel top against the hillside. Almost as tall as the
sycamore, its rounded crown helps me to recognize a black walnut,
Uhah mape. Blackjacks, *Secha.* The more trees I name, the more comes
back to me until I start to recall the names of catbirds and woodpeckers,
flickers and cardinals, crows and buzzards, water moccasins and
tarantulas, deers and hawks, even though I do not see all these animals
here. Quite a few names, more than I knew I remembered, the sum of
many days he and I'd walked the river. Wherever you go, and there's a
Creek town, it seems like the river's not too far away. I guess that's
why the whites called us Creeks, our attraction to water.

"She went so quick," Grandpa sighed, "soon as she got the pneu-
monia. It just waddn't no good for her after that. She had to leave the
old people's and go into the hospital. So her friends waddn't around
her no more. Then she couldn't talk while they was trying to drain her
lungs. You know your aunt could take most anything, but she gotta be
able to tell someone about it. We'd come in and visit, but she had to lay
there and just listen. She'd cry whenever we was to get up to go and
hold on to us, not wanna let us out of the room. Lord, that was a sight,
her holding on to us after dark and us having to go."

I give Grandpa a smile, not much else I can do. He's crying. I think
of the story he told me once after taking me to this spot. Posey's hole,
now under Lake Eufaula, once part of this very river. It was haunted,
the place where Alex Posey, the famous Creek poet, had drowned, taken

under the waters, they said, by a tie-snake. My grandfather said this was
due to Posey turning away from the Creek Nation after statehood and
becoming involved in the selling of Creek allotments. The very river
he loved so much had pulled him in, taken him under, the result of
forgetting one's nation, giving in to white interests. After Alex's death,
there were ten other drownings in the same spot in the next few years.
Posey had written a poem before his death about the trees along the
river, whose branches leaned out far to provide clutches for drowning
men. Grandpa knows the words, and I ask him to say it, to get his
mind off of Lucy. He wipes his tears on his sleeve and looks grateful:

> Why do trees along the river
>   lean so far out o'er the tide?
> Cold reason tells me why but
>   I am never satisfied
>
> And so I keep my fancy still
>   That trees lean out to save
> The drowning from the clutches of
>   The cold, remorseless wave.

Tie-snake's real name, which the old people don't say for fear of evoking
his presence, means coiled-up person. His spoken name, the one safe to
use without repercussions, is *owapochasii*, which Grandpa told me
means something like owner of a swimming hole or patch of water.

My cousin Lenny came by Grandpa's that evening and wanted me
to go out partying. Lenny was still, as always, a cheap punk of a not
altogether unlikable sort. Lenny and I had old scars between us which
we'd superficially smoothed over, at least when Lenny wanted someone to go in on some beer with him. I saw him only once a year or so,
on special family occasions, so why take up the old battles? At first
Lenny wanted to go to the Broken Pony, the good old, bad old Indian
bar in Muskogee. It was good because Lenny knew everyone there. It
was bad because everybody Lenny knew there was a drunk. We ended
up going to Weleetka, where the same two rules applied. We came

around the curve and past the sign that says "Weleetka FFA Welcomes You." Not nearly the cosmopolitan center that Eufaula is, Weleetka has one main street, and on a Saturday night the county sheriff stakes out his ground in front of the Weleetka State Bank, and the Creek Nation tribal policeman faces off in front of the old Royal Crown Cola sign at Keck's Grocery. An old, unsatisfactory truce, mediated by a mere city block.

I felt like I could use some diversion after Lucy's funeral, which left me depressed when I realized what all the old woman had taken with her. The stories I wouldn't hear. I wondered how many she had never told me. I knew I couldn't explain this to Lenny.

We never made it as far as Muskogee. Lenny sniffed around and flushed out the nearest party, and we ended up down at the river outside of Weleetka, passing a joint and sitting on a log next to the fire. Big Ed, the town comedian, was telling a crazy story about getting arrested by a white trooper who thought Big Ed was drunk, which, of course, he was, according to Big Ed.

"Pull up a log," Big Ed says, motioning from across the fire. Firelight falls on brown faces moving in and out of shadows cast by the flames, and, as I recognize people I know, it feels good to be home tonight. Lenny sits down next to Big Ed's wife, closest to the weed going around. I choose a log far away from Lenny, and because it's pulled up against a scrub oak I can lean back against it. It isn't five minutes before I feel a tick trying to burrow in behind my ear. I pull him out and cast him into the fire. The log is mostly unoccupied except for someone carrying stones and setting them down in front of it to make a wall to contain the flames.

"You're supposed to do this *before* you get the fire going," he says to Big Ed. "It's a wonder you didn't blow us all up with that gasoline. It's good there's no wind."

"I believe in the Big Bang theory," Ed laughs.

He sits down to rest, taking his time before building his fire wall. He looks over at me. There's no mistaking him. It's not the skinny little kid jigging for crappie from the shores of Lake Eufaula, nor is it the gangly-armed adolescent discovering he could outmaneuver any challenger who'd meet him out under the single hoop of our junior high playground, and not even the soon-to-graduate senior, the last time I'd seen him, walking out of the locker room showered up after a game, surrounded by his buddies. But it's Jimmy, nonetheless, no doubt about that. He looks at Lenny, busy smoking up. Then over at me. If he's startled, he doesn't let on. He gets up and starts placing the rocks at the edge of the flames.

It was bound to happen; around Indians in Weleetka and Eufaula I'd have to run into him sooner or later. I'd told myself I had come home once or twice a month to give a report to my parents about the job and life in the city, to help my grandparents with chores at the farm at busy times like calving and cutting hay, to relieve good old-fashioned Indian boy homesickness for hills and heat and beans and corn bread and soft voices on porches in the evening dusk. Truth is, I'd looked for Jimmy every time I came back, everywhere I went, and I'd visited each spot I might have a chance of running into him short of simply asking around, finding out where he lived, and going over there.

"Ball boy," Lenny says contemptuously, "my man Ed here knows how to build a fire already."

"Just didn't want you getting too hot," Jimmy says. "I know how you get when you're overheated," he adds, then elegantly turns away from Lenny as if he simply doesn't exist. This seems to shut Lenny up somehow, like Jimmy hit a nerve. Jimmy didn't look a whole lot different than the school athlete I'd known. He'd filled out a few pounds heavier, but he still looked like he could hold his own on a court, not one of the locals with a beer gut who played after graduation on the Indian league for whom every game was a near death experience. That wasn't it. He was stockier rather than a skinny mess of arms and legs. His face was mature, rougher, more beard stubble instead of the peach fuzz he never shaved off all through high school. It wasn't the broad shoulders or muscled arms that had rounded out, replacing the stringy, elongated body of his youth. It was his eyes. His eyes had changed everything; dark, deep-set eyes that seemed to take everything in, to measure and control his response before speaking, to gauge what poured out of him.

"Josh," he said, after some consideration, "I see you brought your cousin along," speaking of Lenny in the third person as if he barely knew him. Well, a lot of people wished they didn't know Lenny; I guess that wasn't so strange. When you went out with him you kind of hoped nobody saw you together; that was the kind of cousin Lenny was.

Given years to daydream, I'd carried on a lot of conversations with Jimmy inside my head. Now I realized that me and him had always been alone in my imagination, not surrounded by people we'd grown up around. I found all the words floating away, and the years had immediately disappeared; the boy on the edge of the playground, I watched across a great chasm, the distance of which couldn't be measured solely in feet and inches. And that's what happened next. The night just went on without me.

Big Ed proceeded to tell how the cop had thought he had something in the back of his car like dope or stolen goods, and when he had him pop the trunk, the policeman jumped back and pulled his .38 out of the holster. The old boy was really pissed and embarrassed because he'd drawn his gun on a trunk full of turtles crawling over each other. The cop put his gun back, mumbling, "Fucking Indians." Big Ed had been puttering all over the countryside for hours in low gear since early morning, slamming his car into "park" in the middle of the road and jumping out to catch turtles making their way across the warming pavement. He was collecting them for his aunt who made turtle-shell leggings for the women shell-shakers at the stomp grounds. This better than their usual fate crossing the asphalt. The cop had only seen Ed lumbering up to his car parked in the middle of the country road, not his pursuit of the turtle.

But wait a minute, I think. Jimmy said, "Josh, I see *you* brought your cousin along"—not, "Hey, Lenny, I see you brought Josh along." The whole world had changed, not just Jimmy adding a few pounds or going to work in McAlester or me moving off to Oklahoma City. *I* was the one, when we were kids, that Jimmy would beg to include because no one wanted me hanging out with them. Now, he's saying, "I see you brought your cousin, Josh," like it's me who has a place around the fire, and Lenny is the intruder. I see there's more than one way to look at it. I wasn't about to go under or float off like smoke; the words could be reconsidered, and you could even bring them back after they'd disappeared, as long as you knew more than one way to look at a thing. What would Lucy have to say about all this, I wondered?

So I piped up and said, "Ed, how come you didn't just pull into the ditch whenever you saw a turtle crossing the road?" It wasn't like the world stopped when I spoke. They didn't all turn around and glare at me because of my stupidity or stare in astonishment at the profundity of my question. Jimmy kept carrying rocks over, and Ed went right on talking. He told how it was on account of his being so drunk he didn't like parking on an incline because it made him dizzy, and he had a hard time crawling out of the car as fat as he is. I knew, however, that Ed was bullshitting because those guys fast and pray whenever they do anything important like go after turtles or medicine. They don't drink then, but Ed had his reputation to keep up. Part of the reason the story was so funny, in fact, was because we all guessed, without Ed saying it, that he had been up since early morning, fasting, and really looking forward to getting the last turtle collected so he could go home to breakfast, when the trooper detained him. Like I said, I could see there was more than one way of looking at it.

Big Ed stood up and nudged his wife. "Let's go," he said. He nodded over my direction, "Bring the party over to my place," like it was up to me to keep the evening's festivities alive. "I'm barbecuing," he added. I wondered if Jimmy would come along, especially with Lenny in tow.

"Yeah, I'll do a three-sixty, man," Lenny says, as if Big Ed was speaking to him, "and leave ball boy here to tend his fire."

"Maybe you'll stop and play some pool on the way," Jimmy said. "For small stakes."

"Don't hate on my game, champ. It's called being a sore loser."

"No, it's called, my name is Jimmy. Not 'ball boy' or 'champ.' It's called, wouldn't it be nice if you shut up every once in a while."

"*Girlfriends,*" Big Ed interrupts, "mind your manners." Even though it was already late and way past suppertime, free food around Indians had the usual response, so we started to get up and wander off toward whatever cars were still running and head for Ed's. Lenny and his buddies made it up to the top of the road first and took off. Jimmy was bringing up the rear, you might say, with Big Ed, who was slowly lumbering up the hill.

"Josh," he says, calling to me, "your cousin seems to have driven off without you." I hear this as an accusation. Just like the old days; I get ditched, and Jimmy has to take up for me. Or maybe he was just pointing out the obvious, that Lenny was an asshole. "You need a ride?" he asks.

"Oh, please say yes," Ed begs facetiously. I grin at the teasing.

I climb in on the passenger side. Jimmy just shook his head while he started the car. "What a night," he said. I offered him a cigarette. "Don't smoke much," he said, "but what the hell."

Big Ed hasn't loaded himself in the car yet, and his wife is pulling on him from the back seat, trying to get him inside. "Unhand me, suh," he tells her in a kind of Scarlett O'Hara voice, "I'm quite capable of seating myself."

Jimmy, practically bent in half, is smashed against the wheel with his seat pulled forward as far as possible so Ed can get in. "So what is it you do again?" he asks me, while we listen to Ed huffing and puffing. It seems to me he might be a little nervous like he used to get before a game. But Jimmy had always been the master of covering his fear with a truckload of chatter, so I don't know.

"It's kind of hard to explain," I said. "I work on crop surveys." I watched Jimmy, his eyebrows raised skeptically, like everyone I tell about my job, who wonder what the hell good crop surveys do anyone. And in the eastern part of the state, where everything is woods and hills with some cows running on them, there are few crops, except for small-time hay fields, sorghum, and other row crops planted in little valleys, not like the expansive wheat acreages in central Oklahoma. I thought nobody understood, but maybe I was the one who didn't know what I did or why I was doing it.

"My job isn't hard to explain," Jimmy said. "I tune up cars. Doing it is a lot harder than explaining it with all these computerized engine systems and just finding a damn distributor cap buried underneath a ton of metal and wires in the new ones. Around here you still get a lot of the old heaps that are easy to work on. But, yeah, it's pretty easy to say, 'I do tuneups' if someone asks where I work."

"That's one advantage you have over me," I said. Jimmy laughed.

"Could be it's more complicated than you make it out to be," Jimmy said. "Maybe even a country boy like me could latch on to it quicker than you think."

"Enough of this banter," Big Ed says with a flourish. "Where are my driving gloves?"

"You're not driving," his wife reminds him.

"Right," Big Ed says. "Onward, driver!"

"See what happens when you skip college?" Jimmy says. "You talk like Ed."

Jimmy and I hadn't been at Big Ed's five minutes—we'd just settled down in the living room with our beers—when we heard the sound of shattering glass hit the picnic table in the backyard. We both got up to look. Jimmy turned down the music, and we peered out the window through the moth cloud buzzing around the yellow porch light. "Who's fucking up out there?" Jimmy shouted. Out at the picnic table Big Ed readjusted his girth and wobbled to his feet. His old lady had kicked him off the end of the bench. He laid there for about five minutes muttering "white bitch," but not loud enough for her to hear from where she'd traipsed off in the backyard and was crouched down pissing behind a tree. Jimmy turned away, and I followed, not interested in the drunken argument. He wandered off, and I wondered if he was avoiding me.

Over on the couch, Jimmy's cousin from Okmulgee was telling navy stories. He had on a University of Maine sweatshirt, though I doubted he'd ever attended a university anywhere, and he was going on about how he'd almost made it to Desert Storm, but his ship got tied up offshore in Chile doing drills. Jimmy's other cousin, Darren, snickered and leaned over toward me. "You wanna know the real reason he ain't in the navy?" He looked at me slyly. "Discharged, ennit cuz?" He leaned closer as if revealing a deep secret: "He's a faggot." As usual I laughed like everyone else.

Everybody had eaten; Ed must have spent a fortune on hamburgers, chops, chicken that he'd grilled, not to mention enough beer for a bunch of Indians, the biggest expense of all. Darren had gone out on the porch to fire up a joint, not wanting to have to share it with everybody inside, but it didn't last long between the half dozen people who soon gathered around the burning weed. "I sure wish I had some more," Darren complained from the center of the smoke haze.

I started to get bored and tired. We'd been there for several hours, and it had to be at least mid-morning. I wandered back into the kitchen where Jimmy was getting another Budweiser.

"Could you hand me one of those, too?" I ask.

"Yeah," he says, but instead of handing it to me, he puts his arm around my shoulder, so the Bud can is right in front of my face, and at the same time he pops open the top of his can with his other hand and takes a swig. This happens fast, like one of those fifties jitterbug moves where people wrap in and out of each other in complicated ways, but Jimmy doesn't let on like it's any big deal. I think, Christ, does he practice this shit or what, the way he's wrapped himself around me like a snake here. Everybody else was in the living room.

"You like that?" Jimmy says, taking another swig.

"Uh, yeah, it's cold," I manage to stammer even though I haven't even got the can open yet. I just stand there awkwardly, wondering what to do. The most natural thing would be to throw my left arm around his waist, and we'd look just like two good old boy drunks and nobody would know the difference, but I let my arm dangle at my side. It feels like a dislocated limb, swinging there. I remember a picture I've seen hanging at my grandpa's house of him and his brother Zeke, teenagers in overalls, their arms around each other, grinning to beat the band. Jimmy had guzzled his beer and set the can on the table, and he started jostling me around a bit, punching me playfully with his other hand on my right shoulder. We'd been standing there long enough, nothing had happened, so it almost started to feel normal, but I kept a lookout anyway, ready to pull away at the first sign of anyone getting up in the living room, headed for the kitchen. We were both a little buzzed up, but when we were wrestling around, he let his eyes pass over me, luxuriously, taking everything in. It was at that moment that we were no longer two country Indian boys helping to keep each other propped up at a party. He followed this by looking straight into my eyes, like right before you're fixing to kiss someone. I knew he was buzzed up for sure, then.

"You wanna go for a walk?" Jimmy said.

"Yeah, it's nice out," I replied.

"You're not afraid of the dark?" he asked, but he didn't laugh.

"No," I say, "are you?"

"Spooks don't scare me none," he answered, as if challenged, like I'd dared him or called him chicken, but he didn't sound all that convinced.

We went outside into the night, still humid, and started walking the dirt backstreets of Weleetka, past the bend in the road at the old black cemetery. There used to be a shack on that corner where my dad was born. Not anymore. I was walking with Jimmy, his arm slung around my shoulder, two invisible Indians, the soft glow of our eyes like animals peering out of the darkness. My granddad had told me a story about walking home past the old cemetery at night and having a scary feeling of being followed.

So much time had passed. Me and Jimmy's lives had gone on apart from each other, but my mind had drifted past every betrayal, recalled each touch, haunted all the places we'd been together. Did I need to say something to make sense of it all? Offer him an explanation? An apology? Demand one from him?

"Do you want anything?" Jimmy asked. A strange question that sounded like, "I'm going to the store, do you want me to bring you something back?" Clearly this night I had to choose my own meanings.

"I could use another beer," I said.

"Me, too," Jimmy laughed nervously. "But I mean, do you ever want anything besides working on crop surveys? Do I ever want any-thing besides bending over a hood all day? That kind of thing." He'd stopped at the curve. We were standing in the middle of the road. Jimmy kissed me. All I could think of was a big truck coming around

the corner, no time to put on his brakes, our kiss framed in the headlights right before we were sent flying off over the moon.

Jimmy led me the rest of the way to his house. He didn't keep his
door locked, so we just walked right in. It was another cookie-cutter
Indian house and minimally furnished, not much but a barbell set in
the corner of the sparse living room. He led me by the hand to his bedroom. My head was spinning. I sat down on the floor because I didn't
know if I could stand up, and it wasn't from the alcohol. He didn't
even have a bed, just a mattress. Some NBA posters hung on the wall.
We undressed quietly.

As Jimmy approached, I felt my hackles raising, the hair on the
back of my neck bristling. He placed his brown hands on my shoulders,
and I felt my body lowering even though I growled, "Not yet. I'm not
ready." He nuzzled his cheek against mine and kissed me, and I rolled
over on my back while he remained standing over me, straddling my
body, half erect. He got down on all fours then, crouched over me. I
placed my hands on his ankles, drummed my fingers on the bony car-
tilage, reached up and rubbed his thighs, felt the cordoned muscles
elongating and tightening while he squatted down further. He wrinkled
his forehead and just squinted. He stayed in that position, still and
erect, staring. I turned slightly away from him on my side; I could feel
my lips pulling back, revealing my teeth, and I twisted my head so I
was staring back at him over my shoulder. Then I was up and on my
feet, knocking him over. As he fell back in surprise, I lunged forward,
taking advantage of his loss of balance and pinning his arms at his sides.

He whined, out of shock and pleasure, and I arched my back to
hold my weight over him while I held down his arms. I began licking
the space behind his ears, up and down his neck, nibbling at his lobes,
kissing his warm eyebrows. Then, clamping my mouth over his, we
bared our teeth and locked jaws. We both started when we heard
something pawing the door outside. Whatever was out there, it
seemed to be scratching around the house. This was not unusual with
all the opossums and raccoons that came out from the line of post oaks
not twenty yards from the house to grub up some food from the

garbage cans. Out in the country, raccoons rustling around outside
sound just like human footsteps. After a couple minutes the scratching
subsided. I placed my hands on Jimmy's neck, felt the ridges of his
windpipe beneath my fingers. I moved my hands down to his shoulders,
a curious imbalance there, and I wondered what had happened to him
that caused his right side, the one side of his chest, to be atrophied and
underdeveloped, like a child's.

I had to resist the urge to laugh because I thought, of all things, of
my Aunt Lucy's right hand with her large malformed finger twisted
like a bent tree stump. She'd told me her brother had mashed it with
a rock. As a kid I'd always had to fight the temptation to stare at it,
which was exactly what I was doing with Jimmy. I kissed the small
nipple, a tiny bud, barely felt its tip at the end of my tongue. For a
moment I was unnerved, hoping I didn't embarrass him by concentrat-
ing on this imperfection, but he was rolling beneath me, arching his
crotch up toward mine.

But he'd turned his face away, staring at something in the room,
creating a tension that made me look at the place he had fixed in his
gaze. There were snakes everywhere, shimmering rainbows of color
and motion, circles inside circles. My dad had told me that in the dirt-
floor tenant shacks he grew up in, they'd find snakes under the blankets
where they slept. Dad had made it a nightly habit to pull back the covers
before crawling into bed. A copperhead was dancing around one of
Jimmy's Air Jordans lying on the floor. A giant rattlesnake sat coiled
around the copperhead and the tennis shoes, shaking his tail like an
accompaniment to the swaying dance inside the circles they had made,
the snakes within snakes. Around and around the rattlesnake crawled
a water moccasin, leaving a wet trail across the floor as if he'd just
climbed out of the lake. A whip snake was writhing up Jimmy's lamp
stand, a sentry going up to his lookout. Swirls of rust ran through their
skin; their tongues, darting in and out, shone blue; the tips of their tails
were green; purple streaks ran along their noses and foreheads. On
their sides the colors blended together like a palette. The many colors
increased their motion the way the colors of a kaleidoscope move in
and out of each other when you turn it. The whip snake came down

from the lamp, crawled over our way, placed his head on the edge of the sparse white sheet, and flicked his tongue at us. Jimmy turned back toward me and said, "The secret is, don't act like you're afraid. And then you won't be."

And somehow I wasn't. My grandpa used to take me out at night to check the cows, and he would tell me if we were to see anything, not to show fear, just go about our business. I knew what he meant by "anything" since the old people always talked about witches, ghosts, and the Little People. I felt safe with Grandpa, though, out in the fields under the moonlight, as if he could confront the night with the strength of his spirit. I had this same feeling lying there with Jimmy.

Stretched out beneath me on the bed, drops of sweat on his forehead and upper lip, Jimmy's long brown body against mine, I had panicked, at first. I had always been lousy at sports, uncomfortable around athletic boys who had laughed when I missed balls that sailed out over my uplifted glove, ran forty yards up into the infield when my turn came up to bat, hissed when I invariably struck out. Now I had one of them beneath me wanting everything I could give him, rising up to meet me.

I put my hands on his face and pulled him closer. A fan on a stand blew air down my back, and the snakes on the floor would rise up and sway in its current whenever the oscillating blades blew air across their path. I ran my hand across Jimmy's belly, tracing circles on his skin. I reached down farther, and it was only the beginning.

We had lain side by side in the silence for at least an hour after dawn without saying a word, the only sound the hum of the electric fan turning back and forth. I sat up, and Jimmy laid back and rested his head on my lap, closing his eyes. I put one hand on his collarbone, then smoothed back his wet hair.

"You remember when you used to walk all over Eufaula, knocking on our doors, trying to get us to come out and play ball?" I asked.

He looks up and smiles, stretches out. "I was like the door-to-door missionary of basketball or something. Everyone used to hide from me. I'd stand out there trying to stare through the screen and catch them scrambling to their rooms. 'Tell him I'm not here.' I don't know how many times I've heard that, like I was deaf or something. Not you, though. You were already up in your room reading. Your mom was always nice to me, didn't leave me standing on the porch or shoo me off. She'd invite me in and give me some iced tea, then go fetch you. You'd come down the stairs, book in hand, in another world. I felt bad dragging you away. But, hey, I needed players."

"I could never escape you; that's for sure. Thanks, Mom," I laugh, but maybe I mean it. "Why'd you want me in the game?"

"What do you mean?" Jimmy asked, holding my arm against his chest.

"Well, I couldn't play for shit," I say.

"Oh, that. It's just kids playing, you know. Out on the street. What were you so uptight about?"

"I always thought my lousy ball playing was like a billboard-sized announcement that I was queer or something. Every time I had the ball I thought I gave it away, that the whole world knew." Jimmy wraps his fingers around mine.

"If that's the case, there's more queers than any of us ever dreamed of," he laughed.

"Yeah, but I mean, I wasn't just bad; I was unusually bad. Ball games were what we did, what we were supposed to be good at and the girls lousy at. Someone like me screws all that up."

"Naw, man, you made it *interesting*. Remember, they always made me play with you, like a handicap? If I threw the ball to you, they thought, okay, easy steal. Right away Sammy would run up and try to take it off you. Or if you were gonna shoot, they assume you're gonna miss, and run up for a rebound. One-track minds, only one way of seeing everything, like it's a scientific law that you're gonna fuck up every time. I loved that because of the fact that you were standing there panic-stricken, and falling all over yourself, proved that you thought someday your feet would leave the earth and you'd put your arm through the rim. Otherwise, you wouldn't be out there, putting up with all that shit. You wouldn't even have come out on the court. You were like a perpetual *possibility*. I gotta admit, it let me play a lot too, since you were most grateful not to get the ball."

"That sounds pretty good the way you tell it. But promise me. I don't have to play ball no more, okay?"

"Just trying to boost your game, man. I mean, to me, those were the best games of my life. There's nothing better than kicking your best friends' asses, putting one over on the guys you gotta live with every day, running them all around and making fools of them, for all the nasty shit they say about you. And if I lost, it took like two or three of them against me. Four, if you were with them. Playing strangers means something totally different. Anyway, what difference does it make now?" Jimmy asked, pulling my head down and kissing me.

None, I thought, when I felt his lips against mine.

I wished I could have stayed over another night and gotten up early Monday morning for work. But Jimmy had to go to church that morning with his family. He'd gotten out of camping-in for the full weekend by promising to at least show up for Sunday services and eat with them at the church grounds afterwards. He fixed me eggs and potatoes, and we sat around and drank coffee for as long as we could before he had to go. He walked me out to the truck, and pleaded, "Promise me you'll come back."

I promised.

It ended up I needed to get back as well. At Grandpa's house where I stopped to pick up my stuff, Grandpa tricked me into stopping and seeing his brother Zeke in Newcastle on my way home.

"Where'd you stay last night?" Grandpa asked.

"I ran into Jimmy," I replied casually. "I stayed over at his place."

"How's he doing?" Grandpa asked.

"Good. He asked about you and Grandma. Said he was sorry to hear about Lucille."

"Can you drop off something at Zeke's for me?"

"Oh, man," I groaned. "Do I have to?"

Zeke was always sending Grandpa Kenneth Haigland videos. Haigland, a white Tulsa Pentecostal preacher, taught that faith, and mailing money to Kenneth Haigland Ministries, would make you rich. Grandpa had boxed up the tapes and left a note on top that said, "Thanks, I'm rich now."

"You'll pass right by there," he argued. I knew he didn't want to go there himself, and he wanted Zeke to get the message he wasn't interested in his religion. "How long's it been since you seen them?"

"How long's it been since *you* seen them?" I answered back. He gave me that "I'm your elder" look but didn't say anything since I had a pretty good point.

"It's Sunday," he said. "If you was to get going right away, you'd beat them before they get back from church, and you could just set the box on their porch. How much trouble is that?" I looked at my watch. It wasn't quite 10 A.M. I could do it if I left right away. Grandpa threw the box in the back of the truck; I poked my head inside and said goodbye to Grandma, and I hurried out of there. They're just across the river from Norman, I thought, as long as I get a move on.

It was fitting that Uncle Ezequiel Elmer Henneha should be named after an Old Testament prophet since in his early years he'd stopped going to stomp dances and become a Christian. Not only had Uncle Zequiel converted, but he'd quit the Indian Baptist church, and when he moved from Eufaula he'd joined the Newcastle Pentecostal Holiness Tabernacle.

The family called him "Zequiel" in that Creek way of dropping off initial vowels; they'd also nicknamed him *Chawaata,* meaning goat, because he raised them, and one time he'd invited everybody over for a family reunion, and, much to all the kinfolks' horror, set out goat meat under their noses when they expected the usual—salt meat, chicken and rice, sour corn bread, blue dumplings, maybe some *sofki* if they were lucky. They'd suspected that Uncle Zeke's herd sounded a little thinned out, imagined one less bleat, noticed the unusually moderate smell from the barn, and recalled that the old billy goat, who usually butted his head against their fenders when they drove up, was notice- ably missing. When Zeke came out and set a platter of chops on the porch table, everyone looked from face to face, noticing how small they were, but no one wanting to ask.

When I pulled in Zeke's driveway, the screen door opened up, and they all poured out onto the porch to greet me: Zeke; his wife, Arlene; and their identical twin daughters, Docia Mae and Zadie Fay. They saw me long before I could back out of the driveway; they were already waving. Docia and Zadie bounded down the gravel road toward the truck. They had on their baseball uniforms and fielder's mitts. Docia reached out her glove as I came up the drive as if she was going to scoop up my pickup like a fast grounder. Zadie was on the passenger side, opening my door before I got the ignition turned off. "That Docia is a cutup, ain't she?" she said. "I guess I was always the shy one."

I climbed out slowly, instinctually looking around for possible escape routes amid the collection of busted-down cars up on blocks, washers and dryers, and old rusted plows in the front yard. "You're just in time, son," Zeke said from the porch, motioning me inside. "Arlene just got lunch cooked up." Zeke and my grandfather didn't share much in common that I could ever see other than their walk— bears swaying from side to side as they ambled toward wherever they aimed to go. Zeke had the body and looks to match the gait—short and stocky, his hair always tousled like he'd just risen, the same plaid flannel shirt with the collar sticking up in back like he'd thrown it on half awake, a pair of overalls that he'd worn every time I'd seen him, like he was born in them. My granddad, though he walked like his brother, was thin and wiry and fastidious in his appearance. Grandma made him wear new clothes now and again, and he reluctantly complied, acting put out, though I think he actually liked dressing up. Uncle Zeke's eyes were slightly clouded with cataracts, and he had the look of a holy madman, a little frightening to me as a child.

"I figured you all would still be in church," I said.

"Why'd you stop by, then?" Docia gawked, slapping me hard on the back.

"I was just going to wait," I lied, "until you got back."

"Come on in now," Zeke said insistently. "Food's a-getting cold. Plenty of time for visiting inside."

"Really, Uncle Zequiel, a cup of coffee's fine," I said, hoping to come in for a minute and think up an excuse for leaving. We went in where Aunt Arlene had fixed a big platter full of over-easy eggs, the whites running toward the center of the plate, and a baking sheet full of biscuits to sop them up with. I immediately began improvising excuses—Aunt Arlene, I'm not a lunch-type person; my stomach doesn't agree with big meals before nightfall; I've got a problem with high cholesterol and blood pressure; I had a big breakfast in Weleetka; I can only stay a minute—but Zeke had already shuffled up to the chair next to where they wanted me to sit and tipped the plate so one of the eggs had oozed to life and started moving itself like a slow yellow-eyed snail, leaving a trail. It lipped its way over the edge of the plate, riding out over a crest of bacon grease. Zeke didn't pay any attention to me; to him, eating was mandatory, something everyone did, not discussed, and clearly he expected me to sit and partake. The way we all grew up, you had to take a little food, if only a bite or two, when you visited someone.

"Sit down," he said, nodding toward the chair. "We sure are proud to see you."

Attention was diverted temporarily from the meal when the twins Docia Mae and Zadie Fay came thumping in off the porch. Docia and Zadie, in their early fifties, still lived at home. Soon the twins were bent over side by side in the kitchen, arms extended toward the floor, fielding imaginary grounders into their baseball gloves, which they held out over the cracked linoleum. Docia would throw the ball over to Zadie, and she'd tag the runner that only the two of them could see.

"Just working some plays," Docia said.

"Keeps us mentally alert," Zadie added. "'Course we don't play no real ball on Sunday since it's the Lord's day and all." The twins kept getting under Arlene's feet while she made coffee; her white hair was still down instead of up in her customary Holy Roller beehive, which she usually had piled on top of her head in a precariously leaning tower by early Sunday morning for church. She still had on a torn night robe, and she looked like she had swaddled herself in a checkered tablecloth from a fifties diner. Definitely a blue-light special which had seen better days. She kept trying to swoosh the twins away like flies. "Girls, take off them gloves and sit down to eat," she said. The "girls," as Zeke and Arlene called them, were on an over-fifty women's softball team. Neither was married, and they took Arlene to all their games.

The most obvious question about Docia Mae and Zadie Fay, the stereotype associated with women softball players, had never occurred to Arlene and Zeke, who were always claiming "the girls" were shy around men, and Docia and Zadie, confirming this assessment, would gawk and blush. Actually, I'd never seen two people less inhibited. The twins had no filters between thought and speech; they'd just bust loose with whatever occurred to them at the moment, often both speaking at once, a profusion of speech equaling or exceeding the confusion of tongues at Babel. Around the twins, my painful shyness seemed like a gift.

I had gone to one of their ball games years ago when I was a kid. A strange thing happened *every* time you were with the twins in public. They ran into people they had known from years ago—old elementary and high school classmates, people they'd worked with over the years. The twins would approach their unsuspecting victims grinning, planting themselves, feet spread, in a masculine stance and simultaneously extending arms for a hearty handshake, carrying on as if no years had elapsed and they had found their long-lost best friend. These people always remembered the twins and were frightened at seeing them again. At the baseball game my Aunt Arlene took me to, one of the twins thought she saw someone she knew. The game had ended, and the familiar-looking person had played third base for the opposing team. Sure enough, it was a doctor who had operated on her the year before. Docia Mae sauntered up to where the woman was standing in a circle with her teammates, rehearsing what had gone wrong in the last inning. Docia Mae, grinning and looking like she might hug the doctor, stuck out her hand to the confused woman and announced, "Hi, I'm Docia, and you worked on my ovaries!" I had hid behind a Dodge van, hoping nobody had noticed I had come to the game with them.

I doped up my coffee with cream and sugar and asked for a "to go" cup, a not-so-subtle transition for leaving, and since Docia Mae had now stepped up to the imaginary pitching mound and was winding up to pitch to Zadie, who was up to bat, a fastball, I thought maybe I could sneak out by just saying goodbye to Zeke and Arlene before the twins noticed and begged me to stay.

"Foul ball," Arlene cried out. "Now you girls sit yourself down and eat." That ended the pitching, and without any runners to create a smokescreen for my departure, I had to stay.

"One last pitch, and she'll be out," Docia pleaded, but Aunt Arlene had started herding them toward the table with a greasy spatula, whining "you girls" in exasperation.

The twins giggled and left off the softball game, seating themselves next to me. At least the invisible ball game had diverted attention for a while and allowed me to escape our usual opening round of the "When you getting married?" game. I might well have queried back, "What about Docia Mae and Zadie Fay? Who's gonna marry those dysfunctional inbreeds?" Yeah, I wish. I remembered Arlene's story—she and Zeke had the habit of repeating the same thing every time you saw them—of how the twins had been born a month premature, and since they were sickly and no one knew if they'd make it, the midwife had put them in the stove in order to keep them warm, but they were both healthy as horses now. She always told this at supper; I guess cooking reminded her of their birth. Docia Mae always came in right on cue, bragging about being the first one born as well as the first out of the oven.

Uncle Zeke blessed the food, and since I had my eyes open I watched him fiddling around with his overall flap, which had come unbuttoned over the frayed bib as he prayed. Fortunately, this afternoon the Holy Ghost hadn't descended like He had one time in years past when the Lord had spoken to Zeke at the breakfast table and told him to anoint Arlene with Wesson oil on account of her rheumatism, an event which ended up with Zeke prophesying in tongues, the twins interpreting, and Arlene slain in the spirit on the cold linoleum. "And, Lord," he said, after expressing appreciation for his family's good health, "we thank you for bringing this boy by here and protecting him from the ways of the world." Not exactly a prophet, that Zeke, I thought, considering just how deep I'd dipped into the world the last couple of days. After the prayer he started mashing up his eggs with his fork and salting them at the same time. I tried to push various thoughts from my mind; these eggs were so undercooked they looked like aborted chicken fetuses, which, basically, is what eggs are.

I'd eaten a biscuit and avoided the runny eggs, but I could put off eating them only so long. I stood up and announced, "I gotta go."

"You hardly touched your food," Arlene said. "We ain't seen you in quite a while," she added.

"I've got to do laundry, so I'll have something to wear to work tomorrow," I answered. "The Laundromat closes early on Sunday." I sure had been coming up with some stretchers lately.

"What's wrong with what you got on?" Zeke asked.

"They make us get dressed up," I said. "Don't bother to get up. I don't want to interrupt your lunch. I've got something Grandpa wanted me to leave off," I added, remembering the videotapes. I got up and fetched the box from the back of the pickup and brought it in and set it on the sofa in the living room. I didn't want to be there when Zeke read the note; it could turn into a prayer session for Grandpa. On the refrigerator was a magnetized kitchen doily from the Haigland Ministries that read "Monthly Prayer Warriors: Zeke and Arlene Henneha." It held down a letter which listed the heathens in the family, and they'd "covenanted" with "Brother Copeland" that they'd "intercede" on the home front while he "spoke faith" every morning from the personal confines of his own private prayer study for their loved ones' personal salvation. I looked for my name, but they'd reserved their prayers for immediate family, thank God. I'd read it at the table to keep from looking at the eggs.

The twins couldn't contain their excitement. "What's that you got in the box?" Zadie asked, but Arlene wouldn't let them up to look until they finished their lunch. I said I didn't know.

Zeke knew. He was on to Grandpa's tricks. In the process of salting and mashing his eggs, Zeke decided to see if Grandpa's moral turpitude had rubbed off on me. "You spend a lot of time with your grandpa, don't you, son?"

"I try to make it out there often as I can. At least once or twice a month. We're looking into buying a new aluminum boat to fish out of around the lake. A small outboard motor don't cost that much," I said, hoping to keep the conversation away from where I thought it might be headed.

Docia came to my rescue. "I got a 35-horsepower up on a sawhorse out here in the barn," she said. "Don't need no more than the carburetor flushed out. You're sure welcome to it."

But before I could inquire about the motor, Zeke says, "Josh, do you know Jesus as your personal savior?" I was at a loss for words because I'd been a victim of salvation all my life, and I didn't know how *not* to know Jesus as lord and master.

A long silence ensued when I didn't answer Zeke's question. Arlene got up and poured more coffee. Zeke quit messing with his eggs and leaned back in his chair, waiting for my response. The twins exchanged looks, until one of them said, "Now, Daddy, you know our cousin is a good boy."

"I know he *is*, Docia, but all have sinned and come short of the glory of God. I just don't want the boy to slip off into eternity unprepared," Zeke said, frustrated at her inability to comprehend the great danger at hand. "You know not the time, nor the hour." My silence felt good for once; it actually meant something to me, a demand for my own spiritual terms and insistence on who to share them with. I felt happy about having nothing to say. I wondered, since being a fag automatically canceled out salvation, when did God strike one's name out of the Book of Life? At birth? That would tend to lend support to the genetic argument of the nature versus nurture theory. Or was it that night long ago at Jimmy's house, when I'd sat on the opposite edge of his bed and imagined him peeling off his underwear, only to wake up and find him touching me in the night? What about all those encounters as an adult with faces I didn't even remember the next morning? Maybe that was the real sin, forgetting. Did God know their names? Perhaps I had been stricken from the rolls of the godly that very previous evening with Jimmy, having not only done "it" but having committed the much more serious sin of liking "it" and deciding I was going to do my damnedest to do "it" as many times as I could in the near future, whatever the consequences.

So, in answer to Zeke's question, I looked at all of them, and I said, ever so innocently, "It's a shame none of you all could make it for Lucy's funeral. It sure was a nice memorial." It was a sucker punch, but it would let me get out of the house while they stewed in their guilt for a couple of minutes. I knew they didn't much care for Lucy, given her reputation as a wild woman who'd played music in bars and run around in her day. Yet they were obligated to love and pray for her.

"It's so far over there," Arlene sighed, "and my rheumatism don't allow me to get around much anymores."

"Ah, like the Ellington tune," I quipped. I knew only Willie Nelson's version, and I'd seen the composer named on the back of Willie's *Stardust* album. It was a bitchy, superior remark, and I felt bad right away, whether or not they got it. I thanked them for lunch. Arlene told me they'd be praying for me. I didn't respond. I walked out on the porch and took a deep breath, taking in the cow pond across the road where a scissortail perched on the barbwire fence, and I thought, don't look back, get out to the car, quick as you can.

I climbed in and turned the key, already anticipating hitting the interstate, plugging in a Hank Williams tape, and letting some loud honky-tonk music wash away Zeke and Arlene's terminal righteousness, but the ignition made a series of clicks, and the engine didn't turn over. "Oh, fuck," I said, punching the steering wheel. My arm had bumped the horn by accident, and Zeke, Arlene, Docia, and Zadie all came out on the porch again. Well, the horn works fine, I thought, bitterly. Docia was approaching fast. I turned the ignition again in desperation, only to hear the same sick rattling clicks. I looked up when I heard Docia rapping on my window. I opened it a crack.

"Pop the hood," she said, grinning. "Zadie," she directed, tossing her a set of keys, "go get the toolbox out of the shed." Now Zeke was standing on the other side of the car, too.

"Don't worry, son, these girls is first-class mechanics," he said, opening the passenger door and sitting next to me, as if to provide reassurance, while Docia raised the hood. "And if they don't get her fixed tonight, why, we'll give you a ride on into the city in the morn-ing." My mind raced over possibilities of who I might call for a ride.

The guys I worked with at USDA scared me even worse than Zeke and Arlene. I climbed out of the truck in defeat and smiled weakly at Zeke. "Like I said," Zeke told me, "we'll get you to work in the morning. We just thank the Lord you got a job. They's so many these days that's too lazy to work. Me and you will sit out here on the porch while these girls troubleshoot and your aunt finishes up in the kitchen."

Zeke brought out his guitar case from the hallway and set it outside. He had another guitar somewhere around the house, and he invited me to play along since I knew a few chords, but I politely refused, my patience worn dangerously thin. Anyway, I'd given up trying to play music with him years ago because he was impossible to follow, anticipating the chord changes way too soon, one or two beats early. For a while I'd tried to get him to play old Jimmy Rogers country blues like "Hobo Bill," "Waiting for a Train," "Blue Yodel Number 9," and "Mule Skinner Blues," but, though he knew all of them, he resisted singing these carnal words of the devil after he'd become a Christian, having put aside the things of this world.

Zeke started thumbing the bass notes and fingering the chords, belting out "Are You Washed in the Blood of the Lamb" in a loud basso profundo. He had his fingers on a G-chord, but what issued forth from his lungs was in some other key, and he was completely oblivious to the disparity between song and accompaniment, propelled over the dissonance by the words of salvation, making "a joyful noise unto the Lord" as the psalmist had said, who, obviously, had my uncle in mind.

Uncle Zeke was the weekly soloist at the Newcastle Holiness Tabernacle, in spite of not being invited to sing, but it was one of those spirit-led churches where things just happened as people got the feeling. And Zeke had the feeling most all the time, in fact a little too frequently for his fellow churchgoers. I felt guilty about my shitty attitude toward Zeke and Arlene, yet even my granddad, who usually didn't say anything bad about anybody, stared at the floor and shook his head whenever anyone mentioned their names. They provided the family, nonetheless, with endless gossip and storytelling material. The relatives all knew the truth that somehow Zeke remained oblivious to: He wasn't welcome in the least at the Newcastle Pentecostal Holiness Tabernacle.

It didn't take a rocket scientist to figure it out, and all the kinfolks had sense enough to know that when you're the only brown face sitting in an all-white congregation, you'll be tolerated at very best. It was a country church. Black folks knew there was no way in hell they could go in there. And from little things Zeke had let slip, we could tell that his brothers and sisters in Christ were subtly trying to tell Zeke he was in the wrong place. But subtle doesn't work on Zeke, and good Christians don't like coming right out and saying, "No Indians and niggers allowed." They were at a standoff, but one of the parties didn't even know a battle was on.

After the last chorus of "Are You Washed in the Blood," I asked Zeke, "How come you all weren't in church this morning?"

"They got me driving bus for them now," Zeke said. "By the time I pick up all the Sunday school kids, then go get the elderlies for the main service, fill out my sheets for attendance and who all I picked up, then go fill the bus up with gas and check the oil and fluids and all, the service has already started up. The pastor explained it to me that it would be better if I was just to stay out of meeting so as not to interrupt the Lord's work coming in late and that driving the bus would be full of its own spiritual blessings that would make up for it. He gives me copies of the Sunday service tapes they record for the radio show." I know the kind of pain you have to listen for underneath the words, the meanings of things unsaid, and I can hear it in Zeke's voice.

Before Zeke had become a Christian, he'd drunk and fought, as the stories went. My grandpa told me that even as an old man, Zeke had retained some of the toughness; only the year before he'd knocked out some trashy white guy in downtown Oklahoma City, hitting him square upside the head with a hard iron fist when the guy had held a blade against his chest and tried to rob him. After the old boy was already knocked out cold, Zeke continued rebuking him in the name of Jesus and pleading the blood until a cop happened by and rescued the downed hoodlum. As crazy as Zeke was, I had to admit he was also the most generous person I'd ever met; always concerned if I had enough money, willing to help, he'd give his last dollar to me if I ever were to ask.

Yet I couldn't help but wonder about the limits of his generosity—
what if he knew of my sexual activities? I found it more than a little
discomforting that I could sit there in their house and eat while carrying
this big secret, the revelation of which could cause them not only to
hate me but to associate me with the very embodiment of evil, a
demoniac. A sick conditional love which rewarded me as long as I
continued to lie. Since I was family, maybe they'd think I was just
pathetic and fallen in with the wrong crowd and in need of prayer,
rather than evil down to my bone marrow, who knows?

Possessions, nonetheless, were completely meaningless to Zeke,
only of value to give away, and though he lived in a shack behind a
sagging fence, all the paint peeling off its walls and surrounded by
junk, his detachment seemed somewhat appealing, his ability to dismiss
this world completely and see through to some other reality. At the
same time, the way he and Arlene and the twins lived horrified me,
and I always left their house feeling like I needed a three-day hot
shower with some of that Lava soap, the caustic kind that scrapes the
grit off like sandpaper.

Zadie walked up on the porch. She had Zeke's coon-hunting light
strapped on her head. She was holding an amp meter like electricians
use to check voltage. "Your battery's good," she said. "It's the alternator.
If the parts store was open on Sunday, me and Docey could get right
on it. But we'll have to wait until the morning."

"What about Wal-Mart?" I said, gritting my teeth.

"For an alternator?" Zadie laughed. "We can get you a rebuilt
one in the morning. You got your owner's manual? I wanna check
something."

"It's in the glove box," I said.

"Don't worry," Zeke says, "I got a built-in alarm clock," pointing
to his forehead. "I'll get you up in the morning and take you to work."

The rest of the afternoon was torture, but at least I didn't have to
eat anything. Zeke played guitar and sang some more, and the girls
showed me videotapes of their ball games. At night I volunteered to
buy everyone hamburgers at the Braum's in Newcastle, just to get out
of the house. I tried to talk them into going out, but they insisted that

I bring the hamburgers back, so I didn't have to pay for Cokes. We ate, and when they told me before bedtime I was sleeping in the card room, I was instantly confused because I knew they believed that card games were sinful. After Arlene showed me upstairs and opened the door, however, I immediately saw the reason for the name.

They had saved all the Christmas cards anyone had ever sent them, cut them in half so they could display the colorful nativity scenes *and* the loving inscriptions they contained, and used both halves to completely wallpaper the room from floor to roof à la joyeux noel. Before going to bed I had run my finger all along a wall, tracing my way through a living family tree that spanned the last forty years. I found one of Aunt Lucy's cards, signed simply "Love, Lucille," and I was taken with her beautifully controlled slanting script, exactly the opposite of what I expected because of her storytelling, which ranged far and wide.

I went to bed thinking of Jimmy. He had seemed so bold with his body, approaching me the night before without trying to hide, cover up, or turn off the lights. And I couldn't believe how I'd responded in kind. Most of the sex I'd known had been quick and anonymous and without speaking. With Jimmy, though, I'd instigated much of the encounter myself, poured fuel on the fire, fanned the flames. I longed to love Jimmy, even from here, his brown body, his wide-eyed gaze, his bold stride. I wanted him to touch me again. I wanted to lie in the dark and listen to his breathing. I wanted back inside his room within the bare walls of his house. When I go back home, I told myself, I will have forgotten nothing. I said this to myself, over and over, I will *remember,* until I eventually fell asleep.

The next thing I knew, I heard Zeke's knock on the card room door. I felt like I'd just gone to bed, and Zeke had roused me soon after my eyes had shut. I looked out the card room window, the porch bathed in dim light from the kitchen, the yard still dark.

I came downstairs. Everybody was already up, and Arlene was cutting out more biscuits. "We got no time for breakfast, Mama," Zeke said. "We got to get this boy to work like we promised."

"I got a clean white shirt he can wear," Arlene said. "Just let me get it ironed right quick." Arlene brought a shirt into the kitchen where she had the ironing board set up and passed a few deft strokes over the cotton button-down oxford and handed it to me. "Zeke's Sunday meeting shirt," she said. "He don't need it no more since he's driving bus." She handed it to me. "If he needs another one, we'll get him one." If only I had the overalls to match, I thought, then checked myself. They could be really sweet when they weren't trying to save you.

I walked out on the porch and threw it on. Docia and Zadie came out. "What cars you girls got running today?" I joked, glad my ordeal was nearly over.

"That little Toyota," Docia said proudly. "Zadie rebuilt the engine, and I designed the camper shell." I looked at the homemade wooden A-frame in the bed of the truck. They had shingled it and plastered bumper stickers on both sides of the roof; a few special ones, which Zeke proudly pointed out to me, were fluorescent and flickered their messages in neon glow-in-the-dark green: "See You in the Rapture," "Abortion Is the Ultimate Form of Child Abuse," and "Don't Be Caught Dead without Jesus." I have a light stomach in the morning, and I wasn't prepared for the salvific onslaught. After my weekend partying with Jimmy, these reminders made me nervous. What if by some fluke people like Zeke were right? While my cousins who drank too much beer and smoked too much dope might or might not go up in the rapture, depending on whether or not they had an opportunity to repent from their backslidden condition just before it took place, I didn't stand a chance. Even if I hadn't done what I just did with Jimmy, and a slew of other men I had forgotten, I was written out of the kingdom of heaven for simply existing. Truth was, I no longer believed that God was this hateful, but sometimes the old stories I grew up on, of his wrath and terrible holiness, played through my head without ceasing. Whatever the case, I couldn't imagine giving up what Jimmy and I had done, sacrificing the flesh in hopes of gaining the spirit.

We loaded up the twins and Aunt Arlene stayed behind, the cab of the pickup already overcrowded. I quickly volunteered to ride in back, but they were all aghast at the notion of a guest not sitting in the cab, so Zadie climbed out of the front and went around and swung open the door of the wooden camper and cleared a place among the bundles of old newspapers they had been saving.

"Open the windows up, Docey, and give her some air," Zeke said. Docia climbed out of the truck and pried open a sliding window while Zadie pushed on it from the inside. I was anxious to get away and be done with them. It seemed like I'd been with them for a year. A good deal of time had passed since Zeke got me up, yet it was still pitch-black out. I hadn't seen a clock anywhere, nor had I heard the rooster crowing who roosted on top of the busted-down washer in the front yard. Zeke said we were going to beat the morning traffic to Oklahoma City, mentioning his internal alarm clock again. Docia Mae asked if on the way back home they could stop and get a McWhopper at the Burger Dream. They had the most curious way of inverting and combining the names of fast foods and the places that served them: McBurgers, Big Whoppers, Quarter Whoppers with cheese. Uncle Zeke, unlike the twins, had one generic name for all these establishments as well as for their food—the Frosty Dog.

Before getting on I-44 we passed through Newcastle, and I saw the temperature and the time blinking from the digital sign of the state bank. It was sixty-eight degrees and two-thirty in the morning. It seems that Zeke's built-in alarm clock was running fast, and I prayed that he wouldn't see the sign, not because of the shame it might cause him, but for fear he might turn back for the house. We made it to the freeway entrance without incident except for I'm sure Zadie saw the sign because I could hear her banging on the wooden frame of the home-made camper, but Zeke was oblivious to the noise in back, exhorting me about the ways that faith and prosperity went hand in hand.

My mind drifted off and I thought of Jimmy, bare-chested, lifting up his hips so I could pull off his pants, giving me his sweet gaze and the flash of his teeth as we moved in and out of the shimmering silence at will. Now that's prosperity. In junior high and high school I had watched and burned and faked disinterest while my friends had lain half-dressed in front of their TV sets. All off-limits forever, buried under an eternal silence. Only in the dark or half-lit places had I allowed myself to be seen by another. Jimmy's body became all those

I could never have. We had emerged into broad daylight and not turned into ghosts. We had whispered the sounds of our names to each other.

When I realized what I was thinking I became self-conscious, as if Zeke, with his mad prophetic anointing, might be able to discern my thoughts. When he pulled up in front of the state office building downtown, I told him he didn't have to wait, and before the twins, who wanted to come in and see where I worked, rushed the building, I ventured that the Burger Dream would probably be opening up any time soon, and that shut them up.

At work I sat in the dark behind my partition, trying to concentrate on a computer graph that showed yield projections. I realized that visiting Grandpa, spending the night with Jimmy, and enduring Arlene, Zeke, and the twins had made me forget why I'd ventured out of Oklahoma City in the first place, to attend Aunt Lucy's funeral. I felt like I had left something undone. I wished I'd had the chance to ask her so many questions before she died, though I probably never would have, even if given the opportunity. I mean, how do you ask someone if they've been trying to tell you something? If you have to ask, doesn't it cancel out whatever they've been trying to say? She had interrupted my years of silence with three long and piercing notes: smoke blown in my ears, stories breathed into me, words held up like mirrors.

TEN

The Colors of Fire

Josh Henneha, Oklahoma City, 1993

I had tossed memory and dream together, a dizzy tumble like clothes in a dryer, the feeling of flight itself when I would grab handfuls of air, reach for support and pull back nothing, and struggle to place a foot on something solid until my body grew accustomed to floating, relaxing and riding on wind current alone. Lately, I had started flying to new places, gave up my childhood hovering for touching down on arrival. The flights had become mere transportation, to and from, though I now chose to believe the reality of the earlier days, when my feet could actually leave the earth; the weightlessness, wind in my hair, places I'd known passing beneath me, the burning weight that pressed me down left far below. I knew, full well, what I had felt, what I had seen, the importance of remembering, of believing.

So Dave and me were going to be all right, near as I could tell, judging by Becky Katcha's explanation. The last time I'd found my way in through a photo, but I began to wonder if I needed anything other than time to think and speculate. Why rely on stuff you might not always have around? There was a lot of medicine in a person's brain, I figured, if he could collect his thoughts, consider the things he'd heard, make up stories to suit himself. Lucy told them, why couldn't I? I'd always been my own best listener.

So I put my mind to work, recollecting as best I could. Thought about Tarbie. About Seborn. Dave and Lucille. Family and friends to each other, just like I'd known. I didn't have all the facts, so I did the most sensible thing and proceeded without them.

Lucy seen them. She ran right into the middle of Tarbie and Seborn's camp. That's the way I began my story, no longer content to just watch from above. It's funny that after having lived with a man all his life, sometimes Seborn forgot Tarbie's face, yet he remembered the gaze of that little girl, the memory of her standing perfectly still and staring, like a photo that captured him and Tarbie together and held it forever, more real than the picture he would sometimes stare at from the Bacone annual, the handsome boy in a football uniform. That little girl seemed to be everywhere back then, always pretending she wasn't looking when she was. The harder she tried to ignore you, the more she was taking in. This is something Seborn had always noticed, those Saturdays, when they came into town to sell eggs or pick up supplies. The higher she loaded her arms up with flour and sugar sacks, the busier she got hauling stuff from the aisles to the counter, the more distracted she seemed carrying things and then begging for a piece of horehound candy while her mother settled up the bill, the more she'd have learned of him and Tarbie. Mind like a cyclone, pure forward motion and busting through ideas nobody else would even consider, and he suspected she remembered everything she saw, even if she was too young to understand its full implications. He wasn't so worried about her knowing, but that white man daddy of hers was another story.

Out at the grounds, they called Seborn "history book," and covered their ears when they saw him coming, always teasing. "Some things need telling," he'd say. So much was going on at Hickory Grounds those early days in 1901, the year after Tarbie and he had graduated from Bacone College at Muskogee, the place where they met. Even before the others came riding into the Square Grounds, you could see a cloud of dust rolling down the road as the Lighthorsemen, recently instated with the election of the new tribal government, rode up the road toward camp. He heard the approaching horses' hooves drumming into the dirt their oath of loyalty to the Creek Nation, their refusal to recognize this new state the *'stihuktis* wanted to call Oklahoma. He was dreaming of taking back Indian land, land many claimed was already lost.

Tarbie, his face streaked with dust from the twenty-eight-mile ride to Lenna and back, rode over to the camp they kept on the east end of the grounds, where, unseen behind the campsite, Seborn hugged him when he got down from his horse. Seborn couldn't help it; he was glad to see him, and even if he didn't let on like it, he knew Tarbie was glad to see him, too. If the other men noticed the two of them, it would only amount to some rough teasing anyway, and Seborn knew how to dole it out every bit as mean as they could. They had wives who kept them hopping, and he could expertly mimic the voices of their women giving them "advice."

Naturally, both Seborn and Tarbie had family in their camp. They had women relatives who cooked and cleaned around their fire while Tarbie and Seborn worked apart from them with the men. Seborn's mama was across the way that very moment at the Stillicoes' camp, where she'd hobbled over in her apron with a pot of beans 'cause their fire was going stronger. That's how Tarbie and Seborn, two men together, fit in; it was through the women with them. They didn't need wives, but nothing at the grounds could work without the women doing their part. To anybody passing their camp, theirs looked like all the others, women cooking under the willow arbors, Tarbie and Seborn working away from the women, following the instructions of the *micco*. Tarbie's mother was off at the Creek Baptists' monthly camping-in, but everybody at the grounds knew her, and some of Tarbie's nieces cooked right alongside of Seborn's mama. What was said when Tarbie and Seborn left together, when the doings ended and they returned to their farm without any women, neither could say. But there were plenty more important things for the two of them to worry about than idle chatter whispered behind hands.

This tolerance and teasing was not the case with some of their more "progressive" citizens outside of Hickory Grounds, those who'd accepted the ways of the whites, gone along with the allotment of land. But he was here among the full-bloods, some of whom, like Chitto Harjo, a great spokesperson and intellectual among them, remembered the homelands in Alabama, and here Seborn and Tarbie were pretty safe. At least safer than with the white Indians—in spite of the trouble they were all about to get into. The conservatives, those guarding Creek land and traditions, had been branded as "Snakes" throughout Oklahoma because Chitto Harjo's first name meant snake in Creek. In a bout of mischief Seborn commenced to beating Tarbie with the broom.

"Damn you, Seborn!" he hollered. "If you had a brain you'd be dangerous."

"I'm just trying to knock some of the dirt off of you," he said, when Tarbie grabbed the broom handle and busted him a good lick across the ass.

He loved it.

And Tarbie loved *him*.

And those men loved me, I thought, once more, from outside the story.

Lucy. She came bounding through their camp, a shortcut to the stickball field. Never mind the bad manners of this, some boys had started up a ball game, and she wasn't about to miss anything that was astir. Seborn had felt safe by their fire, and, thinking the other men were in council and the Lighthorsemen were all just pulling into their own places, he had laid a pretty substantial kiss on his man, who was as surprised as Seborn had been bold. Tarbie, wide-eyed at this play-fulness, had seen Lucy and pulled away. He said, "Seborn, not now!" but Seborn thought he was being shy as usual, so he grabbed Tarbie's big old Indian ears and pulled his face toward his own. He still didn't know what all the fuss was and pecked him again. His back was toward the open side of the camp. Tarbie nodded toward the direction of the ball field, and Seborn looked over his shoulder.

Lucille had stopped dead in her tracks. She waved at me and smiled, from inside the words I had created. I waved back. I hoped she could see me, but I had work to do, so I turned her back toward Seborn, who was holding Tarbie's horse while Tarbie pulled the stirrup up and loosened the saddle girth.

Lucy didn't look shocked at Tarbie and Seborn's affectionate embrace, more like a sudden realization that her manners had just up and left her, running through their place and all. She walked back toward where Tarbie and him were standing and smiled at the two of them together. She stopped at a distance, about ten yards away. She looked as if she might bound away on the slightest impulse, yet it seemed certain that she wanted to say something. Without further warning she ran off, forgetting, evidently, about the ball field, and headed toward the creek. Tarbie looked over in her direction—by now she was a hopping blur along the bank—and he said, "She runs like her tracks are on fire.

"You reckon she'll tell her daddy?" Tarbie said, sounding a little worried. Lucille was at the grounds with her cousins and their parents; it was doubtful her father knew her Indian kin had taken her out here.

"That girl's too smart to tell that man anything," Seborn reassured him. "I imagine this will give her something to think about, though. No bigger than she is, she don't miss much." He didn't want Tarbie to worry, though he wasn't too sure himself.

Well, white folks were one thing, Indians another. Sometimes he thought about Tarbie and him, what people thought of the two of them together. He didn't have an explanation for it, never heard of such a thing in English and didn't have to explain it in Muskogee. Could be nobody at Hickory Grounds thought much about it at all, since he never heard anyone say a whole lot one way or the other. Those whites in Weleetka was another story; two men, long unmarried, coming into town together from a farm and home they shared. It would be different if they were bachelor brothers or had lost their wives or some such. White people stared hard; he had white relatives and knew how rude they could be. They would never say right out what it was that bothered them about him and Tarbie, but they had other ways of talking about it, plenty of strategies for hating them, even when they didn't know what to call their hatred. The whites seemed capable of hating even those things they couldn't name. He'd never understand white folks for the life of him. Him and Tarbie themselves didn't even try to figure out the meaning of their lives together; they just worked, farmed, knocked together whatever little coin they could from taking some cotton to the gin, a few eggs into town. Between growing corn to raise up a few hogs they'd kill in the fall and running a couple steers wild in the woods and rounding them up when they ran out of meat, they got by.

Tarbie sat down on a plank bench under the open shelter they'd built. Seborn had finished the table while Tarbie had been riding the countryside with the Lighthorsemen, looking for those who'd committed treason against the nation by signing up for allotments, leasing lands to the 'stihuḳtis, or hiring whites as laborers. Tarbie looked down, shy and sweet, glad to be back in their camp. He watched a line of red ants making their way to a garbage heap twenty yards away that he needed to burn that afternoon. Lucy had nearly run into it before she stopped in her tracks. Tarbie was about ready to burst with something he wanted to tell Seborn.

Tarbie looked up and smiled. "The council put Alex and me up to lieutenants in the Lighthorse," he grinned. Alex Thlopthlocco was one of their best friends. Seborn and Tarbie had missed the council meeting that morning; in fact, it was still going on. The meetinghouse at Hickory had become the capitol for the "pull-backs" to vent their political frustrations.

The soft rush of wind in the oak trees carried the voices through the camp that day. Seborn was glad he'd missed the council; the complaints weren't new, and the strategies hadn't changed: Hold on and salvage whatever was left. Don't give up anything else. Sell no more land. Uphold the Treaty of 1832, its promise of unbroken land tenure and Creek national government in Indian Territory into perpetuity. Keep the faith that what had been lost would someday come back. Purge yourself from bad white influences. Stick with the grounds and the medicine and the dances. This had been the full-blood position now and always. He walked over to the wooden shelf they'd built and got down the black ceramic coffeepot. He heard George Talosi's voice and imagined George filling his clay pipe, sitting on the bench, legs crossed, speaking between puffs, as always. "We're the real Creek government," George said. "We wasn't give permission for the Okmulgee government to agree to disband and allot."

Seborn loved sitting with Tarbie mid-morning like this, the luxury of just being outside and talking, staring out into the ceremonial grounds. He liked the emptiness and the silence in the center of the square grounds and between the arbors. The dead willow boughs of the arbors, the sound they made as their dried leaves rattled in the breeze, made him a little lonesome for the time they'd rebuild the roofs with the new green branches and have a dance. The empty plank benches, the quiet; such a difference from the night dances, the shell-shakers, the men echoing one another in song, the fire, the circles of dancers, the seating of clan relatives. The dancing seemed all the more beautiful for its absence this morning.

Seborn got some grounds scooped into the pot and filled it up with water from the bucket, then set it on the metal grate over the fire. They held on to their empty cups, waiting, listening to the Speaker's voice, from his appointed place, in the center of the council house. "The Okmulgee government says that since the Curtis Act was passed they can't do anything to stop allotment anyway."

Washington Tookpafka, a Creek Baptist preacher, spoke next, and Seborn and Tarbie looked at each other, grinning. They knew his church ways, how he'd stand up slow and look around, clear his throat, and maybe spit once or twice before he worked his way into his speech, then look down at the ground, and, occasionally, out at his audience. No mistaking a preacher, even if they couldn't see him. He wasn't very comfortable, out at Hickory with all the stomp-dance people, but he was as opposed to statehood as anyone. "We got the Treaty of 1832," Washington said. "It is *inviolable,*" this last word spoken in English to show that the treaty stood on both Creek sacred principles and the legal terms of the whites, and it was quite a word out there at the grounds among all the non–English speakers listening, Washington included. It hung in the air, this *inviolable.*

Grabbing a rag hanging on a post, Seborn went over to the fire and picked up the coffeepot. He poured Tarbie a cup, then himself some, sipped, and listened to the cicadas singing about the heat. It would get so hot and muggy, and they'd just get happier and sing louder. Maybe because they didn't have to cook, like the women.

"We even sent that warning to the Great White Father, William McKinley," the Speaker said. "We told him we would forbid our citizenry to accept the allotments and those taking the certificates would be punished. Did you men get the warnings posted around here?"

"We forgot to post one on the Big White House of the Great White Bother," Washington said. "You told us to be back before noon." The men laughed.

"Now the warnings are up," the Speaker said. "Next, we'll go out and confiscate allotment certificates. Soon we'll be the only Creek government left since the Okmulgee government has decided to give up. Since we elected our principal chief and the legislature and the court system, we can enforce these decisions."

"Trouble is," George Talosi said thoughtfully, "neither the Okmulgee elected government that's going out when the new state comes in, nor the new state, nor the U.S. government recognizes us. Nobody but us recognizes us."

"Then that's who we'll keep it going for," the Speaker said, "for ourselves. It won't be the first time we had to fend for ourselves. We'll just hold on." Seborn listened to the murmurs of assent among the men. He blew on his coffee, thought about how nice a little cream would be if they were back at the farm.

"There's more," Tarbie said, studying the rough plank tabletop Seborn had fashioned for the makeshift camp, not one of his better jobs, but good enough away from home. Tarbie might have been stronger and more athletic than Seborn—he could bear down on a plow like nobody's business—but Seborn was a good hand at carpentry and repairs around the house and barn. Seborn sensed Tarbie's hesitancy. They both knew, everybody at the camp knew, that what they were doing would lead to trouble. "Alex just got back from Okmulgee where members of our newly elected government warned the Indian agent that the Creek Nation would continue at Hickory Grounds no matter what happened at Okmulgee or with statehood. There's rumors that the white people have asked that their federal government send out cavalry troops. They say these cavalries is fixing to leave from Muskogee."

Seborn reached up and touched the back of Tarbie's neck. There was nothing to be said. Seborn went over to the fire and fixed Tarbie a plate of beans and sour corn bread. "Ain't you eating?" Tarbie asked him. Seborn didn't have much of an appetite, disturbed at finally hearing what he'd known was coming all along.

Tarbie had a serious streak, didn't need any small talk to get right down to business, though Seborn had seen him a time or two, given enough corn liquor, tell hilarious stories about the crazy ways of the whites flooding the territory. Tarbie continued, "These white people are spreading like a disease. They're overrunning our country. Setting up a Federal District Court and telling us what to do in our own nation."

"Did I tell you about Lucille?" Seborn said, changing the subject. "The sheriff rode out to her house asking questions. He'd been all through that country, nosing around full-bloods, trying to get them to talk about what's going on here at Hickory. He found out Lucy was kin to some of our members. Sheriff knocked on the door, and Lucy opened it up. Her mama and her daddy, that white man, was out in the field, picking, and Lucy was up at the house. She'd just gotten a bucket and a dipper, was headed for the well to get some water and give her folks a cool drink at the end of the cotton rows. Lucy stood in the doorway with her bucket in one hand and wouldn't tell the sheriff a durn thing until she finally got tired of him and said, 'We're doing the same thing out there we always been doing.' Then she walked off toward the well and let the bucket down, left the sheriff standing on the porch, and she went out to the field to give her parents a drink. Just let him stand there until he had sense enough to ride off."

Seborn fell silent, finished most of his coffee, and threw the grounds outside the camp.

HICKORY GROUNDS, CREEK NATION, INDIAN TERRITORY, 1902

Should I call him or wait for him to call me? I looked at the slip of paper with Jimmy's number on it and reached for the phone, then put it back. It had only been a couple days; still, he might wonder if I'd be back in Eufaula for the weekend soon as I got off work in Oklahoma City Friday night. Maybe I had set myself up for another betrayal, pitifully clutched for the hand that reaches out, then falls away, relinquishing the drowning to the cold, remorseless waves. I could go on torturing myself or cut my losses. I tried to keep my mind sidetracked, but at work I couldn't concentrate. My boss called me into his office and gave me a speech about the image of the agency, a helluva long prelude for a simple request: Get a haircut. I'd been growing it out. I said I'd think about it, but what I meant was I was thinking about some other line of work, and Jimmy had made it worse; opening up one world made me consider the possibility of others. Yet I didn't have any idea where else I could get a job. My apartment now seemed abandoned, waiting for me to move out or for him to move in with me. Ridiculous, I thought, one weekend and I'm making plans that include the two of us. Still there was his own plea before I left: "Promise me you'll come back." It could be he meant it; all I had to do was return.

They had sat behind bars a long time: Seborn, Tarbie, and Chitto Harjo and a hundred of his men in the federal jail, or inside the story exactly where I'd put them, depending on how you looked at it. Either way, they had no charges against them and no trial. They sang stomp-dance songs during the day and told jokes and funny stories. The sheriff put Chitto alone in a cell, to isolate him from his followers, but he would sing, and the men would echo their responses back and forth, even though they couldn't see him. Tarbie was in a cell next to Chitto; Seborn was farther down the cell block. The men joked about their free haircuts; they'd been shorn in order to humiliate and civilize them, so when Tarbie came down the walkway, one of the last to lose his hair, his ears now bigger than ever, Seborn reached out between the bars and said, "Let me feel that ugly head." But that was the beginning

of him and Tarbie's luck in jail. Instead of taking him down to the end
of the cell block, the jailer stopped at Seborn's cell and stuck the key in
the door. "This will keep you from whispering messages to Harjo," he
said gruffly, and shoved Tarbie in the cell with Seborn.

"That'll teach me," Tarbie said, shaking his head and laughing.

"What all were you two whispering about?" Seborn asked.

"Oh, our corn crop, how bad it was this year, what to do to help
our grounds members who don't harvest much. Secret stuff like that."

"I got a secret," Seborn said, "but come here; I gotta whisper."

"What is it?" Tarbie asked.

Seborn cupped his hand over Tarbie's ear. "This may be the only
honeymoon we ever get, so we better take full advantage of it. We'll
never have our own private suite like this again."

Seborn and Tarbie's honeymoon was cut short compared to Chitto
Harjo and some of his followers, who were sent from there to
Leavenworth. They were released at the same time some of the others
were sent off. Leavenworth was not an unfamiliar place to Chitto. In
1861, he had volunteered to fight for the United States Army during
the Civil War. He reported to Leavenworth. He did this out of respect
for the Treaty of 1832, the agreement between his nation and the
United States government. Now he was returning as a prisoner, over
the same treaty and his insistence on its validity.

Next to the sheriff's desk, Seborn and Tarbie stood, still manacled,
while the sheriff finished up some paperwork. So close to the front
door. Seborn could even see light coming in. He wasn't going without
what was due him, though. "Sheriff," he said.

"I'm busy," the sheriff replied, not looking up from his papers.

"I want that pocket watch and the dollar I had when you arrested
me." The sheriff grunted. Seborn didn't care about the money, as much
as it was, but Tarbie had given him the watch the first Christmas they
were together after secretly skimming off the egg money for months
and hiding the change in a jar in a tree fork whenever he went
squirrel hunting.

The sheriff got them uncuffed and escorted them outside. "Seborn
asked you for something," Tarbie said to the sheriff.

"Get the hell out of here," the sheriff replied. "Before I send you off to Leavenworth with the rest of them." Tarbie, never long suffering or patient, stared the bastard down, the way no Indian is supposed to look at a white man. "I got no record of any possessions," the sheriff said, daring Tarbie to push it a step further. Seborn knew it was time to get him out of there.

They were just bringing Chitto out as well, putting him on a wagon. The sheriff took him across the street to where the wagon was parked right up against where a patch of woods started up, and Chitto was trying, with some difficulty because of the hand and leg cuffs, to hoist himself up. He was on the running board, fixing to kind of lay over onto the seat, when Tarbie and Seborn heard sharp, squeaking noises and saw Chitto bending at the waist and ducking every which way, trying to raise his manacled hands to cover his face. It ended up being a hummingbird, a little ruby-throated female, most likely with a nest nearby, diving and attacking. The sight of the big manacled Creek man, shorn bald, jumping up and down, the wagon rocking on its wheels, and the sheriff trying to push Chitto up in it and hurry things along, made for quite a show, the first thing Tarbie and Seborn saw when they emerged into the sunlight and the most action they'd witnessed since their time in jail.

After Chitto got seated he posed much less of a threat, and the bird went on her way. Chitto saw Tarbie and Seborn standing outside the jail. Chitto, looking serious as could be in front of the sheriff, said in Indian, "That bird liked to have killed me, Seborn."

Seborn and Tarbie laughed until they cried at Chitto headed to Leavenworth and joking about a hummingbird not much bigger than a mosquito posing a serious threat to his life. The sheriff thought they were laughing at his difficulties getting Chitto loaded, and he stormed back into the jail, beet red and cursing.

Seborn and Tarbie had made promises to their friend Alex to help his family while he was in Leavenworth with Chitto and the others. Just before all the trouble at Hickory Grounds, Tarbie's sister had married a man from Wetumka, but she had died after giving birth to a baby boy, whom the family named Dave. Tarbie's mother raised Dave until Dave was made a ward of the court under the new white people laws for orphans. This meant children were given over to white people, who then gained control over their land allotments. So, instead of letting Dave's mother's family raise him, he was taken from Tarbie's family. Lucille's father got Dave, and he was pretty glad about it because he needed another hand to work on the farm, not to mention Dave had been allotted a nice stretch of flat bottomland between Wetumka and Wewoka, land the field commission assigned to him since his family refused to enroll or sign up. Lucille's father had seen an opportunity, petitioned the white man's federal court, and gotten custody of the little boy.

Alex was brother to the man from Wetumka who had married Tarbie's sister. Dave was Alex's nephew. Tarbie's, too, naturally. Alex started coming around with his brother, around Tarbie and his family, and they started making plans, with Alex's help, to get Dave back. Tarbie and Seborn liked Alex, and they wanted to help him keep his family together. Alex was a good man. He wasn't trying to get the boy for himself, but he had a plan to return the youngster to Tarbie's mother.

Alex, his brother, and Tarbie had nearly burned the road up from Weleetka to Muskogee, filling out papers and talking with white officials, all just to get their own nephew sent back to his mother's family. Seborn had helped them every way he knew how and tried to run the farm when they were all away at Muskogee. After about six months of trying to get the boy back, however, Seborn knew what they were up against. So one day, when they had just got back from Muskogee, he sat Tarbie down and told him, "You all been doing it their way; now it's time to try something new. Indians hanging out in the white man's buildings in Muskogee don't amount to no more than a nuisance, like a few pissants that crawled in under the door. They ain't nobody reading those reports you all been filling out, and white peoples make a profession out of writing down words that don't mean anything." Seborn had learned about words at Bacone, how to write and make sense in English, but they never showed him how to give the words back the force they lost on paper.

Tarbie knew fully well what Seborn meant. They had their own ways of dealing with these kind of problems.

In the meantime, Tarbie and Seborn had agreed to help keep an eye on Alex's little nephew Dave, since they lived outside Weleetka, same as Lucille's family. Watching from a distance, waiting.

TULSA, CREEK NATION, INDIAN TERRITORY, 1906

When the delegation of Snakes passed through Okmulgee on the way to Tulsa to voice their concerns at the Senate Investigating Committee, they were sad when they rode past the Creek Council House, the seat of national government, built in the late 1870s, knowing that it looked like the whites were going to shut it down. The square was such a beautiful shady spot, surrounded by stores on each corner, a nice place for Indians to stop and rest and talk and catch up on the affairs of the nation before heading for their homes in the countryside. Seborn looked at the two-story stone building, its shuttered windows and cupolaed roof. It had once made him proud just to ride by; his own father, a stone mason, had leveled the ground and helped raise the walls, and the building represented, more than anything else, hope, a belief that the whites would leave them alone if they proved their ability to run a sound constitutional government. Hell, they hadn't much more than got the thing built, and the whites were proclaiming the end of their tribe.

The Creek government hadn't always represented the full-blood point of view well, since the Creek progressives dominated the political leadership, but they had maintained enough full-blood representation that it made a difference: The national government held on to the land for about as long as they could. Not long enough to Seborn's way of thinking, but the constitutional government seemed to believe in getting out with what they could salvage, whereas the Snakes believed in holding out for all that was rightfully theirs no matter the consequences. What seemed most depressing was that neither position seemed to show much promise anymore. There was one thing Seborn, the Snakes, and every member of the Creek Nation now shared in common: fear. Fear of their imminent demise. Nobody knew what it meant, the end of their nation, the allotment of land, what would happen to their families, their children, nor how long it would be before the whites wanted something else from them, if there was anything left to take. In order to keep their minds off their sore asses, and probably to help lift their spirits, Chitto started telling stories.

He had a jar of corn liquor that he uncapped and passed around. Everything had slowed down. It was god-awful hot and muggy for the fall. The breeze had died, the horses were hot and clomping along with their heads low to the ground, and the men had given into this rhythm, too, sunk low in their saddles. Chitto started in quiet with his story, almost as if speaking to himself; he was sometimes so unassuming, but it was a ploy—that was how he fooled people. While he talked he acted like he was really looking at the field of fire wheels they were passing, their red and purple rays, yellow at the tips, motionless in the still air. They were on their last legs this late in the year.

"One time I was gone to Washington," he started in, "and I had a meeting with Senator Dawes. So I gone to his office and told his secretary I was there.

"She said, 'I'm sorry, Chief Harjo, but Senator Dawes isn't in.'

"I didn't tell her I was never a chief, but I said, 'The Speaker of the House and me was supposed to meet with him, what you think?' She give me promotion to chief, so I give our meeting promotion to talking with the Speaker of the House. I might as well pretend like I was meeting with the most important people was how it lined out to me. I could tell Dawes had made her lie. I wished her a good day and left. Down one of the hallways, I seen Senator Dawes sneaking into the bathroom. Most likely hiding from me."

Chitto clucked to his horse and turned his heels in, tried to break him out of his slumber. The bay picked up the tempo for a little while but soon dropped back into his drag-ass crawl after Chitto started back up with the story.

"I'd had so much good laugh with the secretary, I decided to follow Senator Dawes into the bathroom and look for more jokes. We Indians weren't supposed to use the white man's restroom, so I peeked in first. Nobody in there. Not even an echo or anyone breaking wind.

I come on in. I looked under all the stalls until I seen a pair of feets. It was the fanciest gilded and marble-topped place I'd ever seen. I knocked on the stall door and said, 'Senator Dawes, are you in there?'

"Dawes knew something wasn't right; I could hear his brain fogging up. Here I was speaking bad English in the stalls of Congress, but he didn't know who I was. He couldn't see no Indian on the other side of the door. Dawes just lost a-holt of his thinking, only heard bad English. He cleared his throat. He said, 'Sorry, Mister Ambassador, about missing the meeting at the French embassy. My secretary forgot to write it into my schedule. We've been very busy lately with the Indian problem.'

"I said, 'Senator Dawes, maybe if you was to found a better place than a shithouse to study Indians, they wouldn't be such a problem.'

"They was no sound from the stall, and I left him sitting there."

Chitto went on to tell how he had once even seen the president, handed him the Treaty of 1832, and told him that if he could explain how the treaty allowed for allotments he would believe it was so. Chitto ended the story by saying, "He just shook hands with me and that was all." They had gotten all the way to Preston on Chitto's stories before they gave in to the heat and their asses started hurting again. They pulled under a pecan tree and rested, then gathered up a bunch of nuts. This gave them something to do, shelling in the saddle, and Seborn and Tarbie throwing the hulls at each other.

It took a lot of rousing for Chitto to get them out of the shade and back on the road. Seborn rode next to Chitto, and he felt a little bit overwhelmed by the old warrior. The more he wanted to speak to him, the less he could think to say. Chitto rode straight-backed in the saddle in his black suit and hat, the same way Seborn had seen him sit in countless territorial meetings. Seborn didn't know if Chitto was really so solemn or if this was part of his political persona. Sometimes Chitto seemed to know he intimidated people, and he'd try to put them more at ease around him. He started goofing off, letting go of his reins and throwing his knee over the saddle horn. Seborn's horse was carrying the saddlebags with the salt meat their kin had sent them off with, and when they stopped to eat under some willow trees, Chitto turned to Seborn after he'd finished eating. He looked over at Seborn and said, "Do you know what you call a city full of Cherokees?"

"No," Seborn said, the first time he'd spoken to Chitto that day.

"A full-blood," Chitto replied, and then Seborn knew he was being teased, relieved of the tension he felt in Chitto's presence. Chitto knew Seborn's mother's side of the family was Cherokee and part white, and he knew Seborn would understand the joke since it dealt with a popular false notion concerning the tribe that didn't really hold true since the Cherokees had also formed their own resistance factions, fiercely nationalistic groups like the Nighthawks and Ketoowahs, and many of these traditionalist full-bloods didn't even speak English, like many of theirs. Chitto had met with them many times, and they were welcome at Hickory.

Chitto ran out of stories and settled into the saddle again. Seborn recollected the day he met Tarbie at Bacone. He had seen Tarbie in classes, but he was always surrounded by girls, and Seborn couldn't get anywhere near him. Tarbie was the damnedest boy at school—in spite of his shyness, his disinterest in his female admirers, and his all-out dedication to nothing besides football, he was, nonetheless, worshiped. Unlike most students, he returned home more often, where he lived with his grandparents. His grandfather was a well-known *hilis heyya,* a medicine maker in the tribe, and Tarbie was quiet and shy in school, more like his traditionalist grandparents than the pretty young breeds who flocked around him.

At the end-of-the-year school dance, Seborn had come alone. Seborn had seen Tarbie dancing a waltz, with a young freshman girl he'd been sparking, or maybe he should say she'd been sparking him. Betty Lou McIntosh. She was a pretty young mixed-blood with brown hair and blue eyes whose daddy owned a store in Holdenville, and she had a thing for football players; she'd dated three or four in her first year at Bacone. Seborn wanted to talk to Tarbie, but he didn't know what to say. The girls, as usual, were gathered in clumps, and they were talking about Tarbie and Betty. The usual gossipy small talk— how long they'd been going out and all of that. Seborn felt a grip in his stomach, jealousy rising. He tried to put it out of his head; it didn't make any sense at the time. He wanted to ask these girls about Tarbie, but, of course, he had to hide his interest. He didn't know exactly what he wanted to say anyway.

The fiddle player hit his last note, and Tarbie and Betty walked off the floor. They were walking straight toward Seborn, and he could feel the blood in his temples, his face reddening. Then they were standing next to Seborn, and they all watched the dancers beginning to filter back out for the opening strains of the next song. Tarbie's admirers were approaching just when fortune turned in Seborn's favor. Betty Lou's corsage fell off her dress. Tarbie, embarrassed, picked it up, clumsily trying to put it back on. He couldn't get it pinned. At that moment he looked like exactly what he was: an Indian in a coat and a tie, sweating, out of place, and wanting to be just about anywhere else. More than anything, perhaps, this is what Seborn loved him for through the years—who he was always came forth, no matter the circumstances.

Seborn had cautiously offered to help Betty, and Tarbie handed over the corsage. Seborn knew he was on dangerous turf. Tarbie might think Seborn wanted to steal his girl, he might think Seborn was making fun of his discomfort, or he might just think Seborn was really strange, overeager.

It was a miracle: Seborn stumbled on exactly the right thing to say. After pinning Betty Lou's gardenia back to her dress, he managed to stutter, "These things are really embarrassing, aren't they?" He had directed his question at Tarbie rather than Betty, who looked puzzled since she should be the one embarrassed, having her corsage fall off and all. Knowledge passed between Tarbie and Seborn in that very moment, a code Betty could not crack, an unspoken understanding of how truly embarrassing all this *really* was. Betty had a lot more to be puzzled about when it was time for Tarbie to walk her back to the girls' dorms at the end of the evening. Tarbie said, "Seborn, you've been so nice to Betty, why don't you walk back with us?" Now Tarbie and Seborn were talking a language they both understood, and it was that very speech that would draw them together, words whose real life was fueled by things unsaid, the drifting smoke rather than the flame itself. The colors of fire, the crinkled edges of burned words.

That summer, and for all their senior year, Tarbie and Seborn ended up best friends, and Betty managed to find another football player more interested in giving her his full attention. Betty's loss was Seborn's gain, and Tarbie finally learned about something more fun than football.

The years after Bacone, Tarbie and Seborn faded back into the quiet life they had enjoyed during their childhoods, at least in terms of living among their own people and having minimal contact with whites. For the most part, white Oklahomans didn't know anything about any of them except as a roadblock to their plans for statehood. About the most Seborn and Tarbie and the Snakes had to do with them was trading at their stores, ginning at their mills, and spending time in their jails.

They got to Tulsa, and the next day they headed over to the old Elk's Lodge Hall in the Seaman Building on West Third Street. The meeting was a special Senate Investigating Committee reporting on the state of affairs in Indian Territory now that statehood was coming. Seborn walked up to the big wooden doors and just stood there, looking up. Chitto was behind him. "This is the place they lock up rich white criminals," Chitto said. "Open up," he hollered, pounding on the door. "Seborn wants in out of the heat."

An usher came out and looked Chitto over from head to toe. "Can I help you?" he said, but he didn't motion them inside.

"No," Chitto replied and walked in. "Come on," he said in Indian to the rest of them, "what are you waiting for, an invitation from the president?" The secretary of the Interior was there, along with senators from Colorado, Montana, Connecticut, and Kansas. The Snakes knew they had to address these people in a deferential manner, yet they were also smart enough to know who they were dealing with: a bunch of the worst kind of criminals with no regard for their own Constitution, international agreements, or justice. Nearly all of them had deals going with real estate companies and the railroads, and they had

cashed in from the opening up of Indian lands for white settlement.
They had become rich off of Indians. Seborn and the Snakes walked
down the aisle toward the front of the hall, looking for places to sit.

A large block of seats had been cordoned off in the two front
rows. Chitto unhooked the cord, and held the rope while he ushered
them all in. The usher came prancing down the aisle. "Those seats
are reserved, sir," he said nervously.

"Awfully kind of you," Chitto said, "holding them for us like that
until we got here." Everybody had been leaning over and talking and
fanning themselves and waving at acquaintances as they came in, but
everything got really still and quiet. They'd been too busy up until
then to notice a bunch of Indians had come inside and taken over the
front seats. It was the first time Seborn had ever witnessed an entire
building of people quit talking on his account.

"I'll go get the senator," the usher said, hurrying off. When he
came back, accompanied by a stern-looking bearded gentleman in a
black suit with long tails, Chitto reached out his hand and said,
"Good to see you again, Mr. Chairman."

"Chitto," the chairman said, "my wife has driven me to distraction
making me promise to give you this." The senator handed Chitto a
gold-framed photo of Chitto himself, standing next to the senator and
his wife. "She was so charmed when you joined us for dinner. She
placed the turtle shells you gave her, and the hickory ball sticks you
gave me, up on the mantel. She tells all her acquaintances of the
friend she made from Indian Territory.

"I hope the seats are satisfactory," the chairman said, giving the
usher a knowing look. "I must now mount the podium. Go easy on
me, Chitto. Remember, I'm just a humble public servant." He clapped
Chitto on the back and headed for the stage. The other senators had
already come up to be seated behind the podium, and they had spotted
Chitto the minute he started down the aisle. Unlike the rest of the
public in attendance, the senators knew exactly who he was, an old
familiar face who'd stood before them in their Washington offices with
the Treaty of 1832 spread out on their desks, explaining to them that

their own agreement was the law of the land. They didn't dare ask him to leave, then or now. He'd always be back anyway.

The proceedings started. First the minutes of the last meeting. Then seconding the minutes and approving the minutes. Then a report that updated the committee on what had happened since they met last. Seborn wondered how these whites had ever taken over anything, much less five of the most powerful Indian nations on earth, by reading reports to each other. It was more than he could possibly comprehend, trying to put his mind on when the Creeks had first began to lose control of their territory. Seborn nodded off, and Tarbie poked him with his elbow. Seborn grabbed Tarbie by the back of the calf and squeezed as hard as he could through Tarbie's black riding boots, trying to give him a charley horse. Tarbie slapped Seborn's hand away and rolled his eyes.

Then the senators themselves started their speeches, and they all emphasized conditions of overcrowding in their own states, farm- and range-land that had given out, and all the surplus land in Indian Territory going to waste. One or two threw in speeches about conditions of lawlessness in Indian Territory and the inability of Indian governments to control their populations, forgetting to mention that the criminal element was the whites who had poured into the territory illegally.

Chitto had so much presence in D.C. that the senators felt obliged to let him address the meeting when they had finished, knowing that they could question him after his speech, thus giving themselves some room to try to correct things before the crowd if Chitto talked about the Creek Nation's current legal status, which he was sure to do. At least there on their own turf they had some control over him, which wasn't the case when he was out among his people. Chitto got up from his seat and walked toward the stage, taking his time, forcing the audience to watch him make his way through the hall, to confront them with the lingering presence of the Indian troublemaker who was now being called upon to address the crowd. But when he reached the stairs he mounted them in quick little bounds like he owned the place, like he had been called up to receive an award.

He stood at the podium and looked at his audience, letting his eyes pass over the crowd, showing them he wasn't afraid, and, at the same time, that he knew they were out there, and he would consider them while he spoke. He looked at Seborn and nodded. Seborn imagined that he could send Chitto messages, and Chitto would speak Seborn's thoughts, say the things Seborn couldn't say himself.

"I'm Chitto Harjo," he began, in Indian. "I don't have a seat in the U.S. Senate, but I have a seat at Hickory Square Grounds, out under the arbors." He paused, giving David Hodge a chance to interpret. His eyes swept over the audience, taking everything in. They had been listening to the senators reading from prepared scripts, and Chitto had captured their imagination with his first words, the authority of his voice that came from somewhere inside himself rather than from a piece of paper held out in front of his face. "My seat at Hickory Grounds is determined by my clan. My clan is part of a town. My town is part of a fire. My fire is part of the red and white divisions of war and peace in our confederacy. My seat, my clan, my town, my fire, my nation, the Muskogee Nation, was in existence long before the Senate was an idea in the minds of the founders of this great nation, the United States. In fact, my nation reaches back before that first great senate, the Roman Senate, that some of you may have heard of. So, I welcome you, senators, and I am prepared to advise you, should you need any help running this new nation you have most recently founded." There was laughter and applause in the hall.

"And I do, in fact, have some suggestions," he said. Less applause this time, but everyone leaned forward in their seats, waiting to hear what the Indian would say about improving the U.S. government. "But first," he continued, "you all need a little history lesson. I promise to be brief."

Chitto, of course, was anything but brief. It was not likely he would ever again have the floor in front of the most powerful senators controlling events in Indian Territory, soon to be Oklahoma. This was his last chance to make a difference before the new state came in, and the fated statehood was like hearing a doctor pronounce a loved one will not recover: The Snakes had kept hoping until the last breath it might not be true.

His speech covered contact with the first European explorers, their promises to respect Indian landholdings and governments, the Treaty of 1832 and the fact that his nation had "carried out these agreements and treaties in all points and violated none," the Civil War and his own participation on the side of the Union out of respect for the treaty, and the allotment process which flew in the face of everything sacred the Creek Nation and the United States had ever agreed on.

The amazing thing about Chitto's speech was not only the way he covered four hundred years of history and still stayed focused on the issue of holding the Creek Nation together, but his understanding of what all this meant.

"I am now near the end of my big talk," Chitto said. He turned to the senators seated behind him. "Before I close, I would like to hear from each of the senators what they think about all that I have said." There was a lot of squirming behind the podium. The chairman adjusted his starched collar. He stepped up, and Chitto shook his hand and stepped aside.

"I can speak on behalf of the other senators," he said. The chairman looked down at the lectern. No prepared speech to guide him this time. Then he saw the audience, expecting him to answer the serious allegations Harjo had made, and he looked down quickly again. He cleared his throat. "The times have changed," the senator began. "The treaty no longer holds because it was modified by later agreements, signed by the Creeks themselves. These are legal processes that must be honored. I'll be glad to try to explain them to Mr. Harjo after the meeting. Resisting the law is futile."

Chitto needed no time to prepare his rebuttal. He stepped right up and said, "I think I have the privilege of appealing to the other tribes and notify them in response to the disagreement between you and me in reference to the allotments."

"Do you mean the other four civilized tribes?" the chairman asked.

"I do not mean the other four civilized tribes," Chitto responded, "but I can call on the Spanish government, and the British government, and the French government. I can call on four of the civilized governments across the mother of waters to come in and see that this is right. That is all I have to say." You could have heard a pin drop, the way he had gone to the heart of the matter. He understood that the Creeks had international recognition as a nation of people that had treated with other governments; historically the Creek Nation was on an equal footing with European nations. His was a much more radical stance than Chief Justice John Marshall's definition of domestic dependent nations in the 1830s. And he had just left out the United States of America in his list of civilized governments. It was brilliant.

Chitto had spoken from a different script, one inside himself that came from a sense of what was sacred, the very meaning of words themselves, the Creek Nation's historic connection to Creek land. He was calm; he didn't need any of the speechifying flourishes of the senators, who had to rely on jokes and dramatics rather than the truth of what they had to say. Chitto, speaking from memory and feelings, never lacked for language to express himself, and even with David Hodge interpreting, the words in English carried a spirit of resistance. Harjo's speaking and thinking abilities carried forward the role of the long line of well-known Creek warriors he was descended from. They could have heard a pin drop in the hall, so close was the bond between Chitto and his audience by the time he finished.

HICKORY GROUNDS, THE ILLEGAL STATE OF OKLAHOMA, FORMERLY INDIAN TERRITORY, 1909

Me and Jimmy had gathered at Chitto's house, about a mile from Pierce, along with the other Snakes, because we had planned on going to the council grounds before all the trouble broke out. Now we were holed up, no place to go without getting in trouble. Jimmy had got a little practice stickball going outside since he'd brought some sticks for the real thing when they got to the ball field at the grounds. "Come on out, Josh," he hollered up to the porch. "We need someone to even up the teams." Jimmy passed the ball to Sa-pah-ye, but Lewis Yardica dove for it instead and caught it in the end of the webbed stick. Jimmy let out a blood-curdling whoop and took after Lewis, who ran circles around the well, then hopped over a farm plow and threw the ball at

Chitto's lightning rod, the closest thing they had resembling a ball pole. It struck and rolled down the roof, landing in front of the porch.

Chitto came out of the house to see what all the commotion was about. "Get in here, boys," he said, "and stop fooling around. We got work to do." Sam Herrod and Thomas Ogee came in with a couple of chickens they had killed, and I smiled at the prospect of dumplings for supper. Ben Fife was there, along with Thomas Jones, Legus Jones, Lewis Smith, and Charlie Coker. I went in and made some coffee.

"I wonder if we're the first nation to fight a war over a piece of bacon?" Jimmy asked, chewing on a stick of deer jerky Chitto had set out.

"Most likely a pack of old curs drug it out of their smokehouse, pitiful as the dogs are around there," Thomas said, handing the chickens to Chitto's daughter. "Constable Patty sure got on it quick when he found out those white folks were missing a side of hog out of their smokehouse. You'd think he'd have better things to do than tear up the country looking for bacon thiefs."

"Well, whatever the arrogant bastard said, he sure must have got the black squatters around Hickory riled up for them to take a potshot at a white farmhouse," Jimmy said. "If they were really the ones to do it. The sheriff came back at daybreak with a posse and attacked and killed one of them and put forty-two in jail, including my Uncle Harrison. Now there's gangs of white people roaming the countryside, robbing us and setting houses and buildings on fire, terrorizing women and children if their men are away."

"I rode by the grounds today," Legus Jones said, "and the council house was burned down."

"The Oklahoma City paper brags the posse killed scores of blacks in the 'battle,'" Jimmy added.

"You know what will happen next, don't you?" Chitto asked, looking around the room. "They'll blame the uprising on us, say it was Snake doings."

A squirrel started chirping out past the well, at the edge of the tree line, that high excited chatter like somebody was coming up on the yard, so Chitto got up and opened the door a little and peeked out, not that it did much good in the shadows with night coming on. Like always, we were expecting trouble from the whites; the law seemed close on our heels wherever we were gathered. Where two or more are gathered as Snakes, there's the law in the midst of them. We had been living that way the last eight years, never sitting down without first planning the quickest way out.

The first bullet hit a tin pail, and we heard it fall off the edge of the porch with a little clank. Everbody except Chitto, his boy, Legus Jones, and Jimmy and me lit out the back door, I mean just a-hooking it. Charlie Coker fired a few shots into the dusky night to keep the posse occupied while the rest of them darted toward the trees. Chitto had left his guns in the barn where he'd been cleaning some squirrels, tacking their skins to the barn wall to dry. Inside the house, Jimmy couldn't get Chitto to lay down because he wanted to see whether or not the others had made it out to the woods without getting shot.

We saw a chink of daubing fall from a crack, and Chitto grabbed near his hip. When he lifted his hand, he had blood on his fingers. From the instructions being yelled in the darkness, we figured two posse members were shot down by the well. We couldn't believe our ears since just a little bit before we'd been drinking coffee and laying out plans for the meeting. Charlie Coker must have been giving them hell from the tree line, or, with that bunch of crazy yokels, they could have shot themselves in their own crossfire. Sa-pah-ye had the misfortune of tripping over an old wagon wheel during his mad dash toward the woods; otherwise, they would have never caught him. After they tied up Sa-pah-ye and boosted him up on Ed Baum's horse, since Ed had been one of them shot down, the posse rode off for reinforcements.

We didn't waste any time getting out of there. We rode hard for McAlester where Daniel Bob, a Choctaw nationalist, met us north of town. Charlie Coker had reunited with us on the way, and he was wounded in the chest. We continued to get reports from friends and kin who met us out in the woods at secret springs, riverbanks, and other secluded landmarks where they brought us food, and we rested and tended to Charlie and Chitto, who could only ride a half a day at a spell. They even brought us newspapers, which at first made us cuss,

then laugh. The headlines said, "WAR IN OKLAHOMA"; and "WAR WITH
SNAKES: 2 DEAD. THREE HUNDRED ARMED MEN ARE MOBILIZED AT PIERCE
FOR ATTACK AT DAYBREAK"; and "DEPUTIES ARE SHOT DOWN BY SNAKE
INDIANS IN AMBUSH." Chitto made us laugh, said he always did like
dime-store novels. The *Eufaula Indian Journal* understood the true
nature of these headlines, which did not connect to any real events:
"The Spanish-American War was never more vividly pictured, and
the number killed, wounded and captured is generally larger than was
Taft's majority." What was of more concern was what we heard about
the posse, which had started to attack Indian and black women and
children whose husbands and fathers had to flee since the blame was
being pinned on anybody with red and black skin.

We passed through South McAlester, then north of Wilburton and
through the Winding Stair Mountains by the road leading from
Wilburton to the Kiamichi River. We followed a narrow horse trail
through the Kiamichi Hills until we got to the headwaters of Eagle
Fork, then we had to take a deer trail around Bobtukle Mountain until
Daniel Bob finally got us to his house in the middle of the night. We'd
been run out of the Creek Nation into Choctaw country. Me and
Jimmy, once we got Chitto settled down at Daniel's house and called
on the Indian doctor, rode back to Weleetka. We hadn't been seen in
the shooting, so we had the luxury of returning home.

But not Chitto. He died, two years later, in a foreign land,
amongst the Choctaws, driven out of his own nation by whites. The
federal government kept looking for him over the next couple years,
even after they cleared him for the trouble at Hickory Grounds and
the shootings at his house. They were looking for him because he
owned land in Creek country, and they wanted to settle the title.
Chitto never came back because he refused to accept the allotments or
the bastard state of Oklahoma or the breakup of tribal government.
His house had been burned down by the posse.

Though he had to flee the nation, and died not too long thereafter
amongst the Choctaws from his long-lingering hip wound, Chitto was
still strongly felt at Hickory Grounds. Most important, the resistance
he started continued on long after his death and continues today. In

1924 there were still sixty families living at Hickory Grounds under the old tribal law, and they sent delegates to D.C. until 1930, nineteen years after Chitto passed away. None of us layed down like whupped pups, and I want future generations of Oklahoma Indian kids to know that many tribes, including ours, had these strong holdouts against state government. This is what they ought to teach in Oklahoma schools instead of the history of the boomers, Sooners, and criminal politicians, in other words the glorification of land theft. You tell me which group makes better heroes for young people.

Four years after Chitto's death, Daniel Bob answered a reporter's queries. The reporter was writing an article for the *Kansas City Star*. Daniel Bob, who couldn't write in English, dictated a letter to him that later got printed in the paper. Bob said,

> There was a man by the name of Chitto Harjo were came over at my place. He was stay here while, and he got down in April 5, 1911, and the last few days of his life were spent in bed. One morning in April 11, 1911, at 10 o'clock, his life passed from away. In this April 5, he get down that with indeed distress, as the gunshot wound in his hip, and had died. Then we laid him good in my house yard. That where he lie in grave. This is all about Chitto Harjo death at my place.

There's a story about a Rabbit, call him Jimmy, call him *Choffee,* call him Chebon or Dear Hotgun. This Rabbit liked to mouth off to guys who were a lot bigger than he was. A kick, a shove, and before he knew it, Rabbit was up to his elbows in Tar Baby. You can call this Tar Baby Josh, if you want, or you can even call him Jimmy if it'll make you feel better, or not call him Jimmy if you see that as some kind of racial slur. Because I'm not thinking about that, I'm talking about the birth of the Tar Baby, a story maybe you never heard. Some might say a Tar Baby isn't born, he's made, fashioned from human hands, to scare off crows and other thiefs. But he's born, all right, shaped out of words. An invented history, a history of invention. A choice to invent your own history. As early as birth, there's the danger of getting stuck to a bad story if you stick your hands inside the wrong words. You could wake up inside the belly of a whale, boiling in a black kettle of sin, instead of glued to a Tar Baby. Or you could come unstuck and just float away without changing anything. And there's the real Tar Baby, too, stuck to a Rabbit, but he's a little more tricky to locate. Tar Baby talks Rabbit into a boiling pot by telling him a story. Now, you might ask, given our story inside a story, or stories inside stories, who is the inventor, and who is the invented? You might even wonder which parts I made up and which actually happened.

I didn't know the answer. I only knew at that point that I wanted out of the kettle, especially if someone else was going to be throwing logs on the fire. The way out wasn't by leaning over the side and spitting on the flames. I'd have to climb out, up over the words, and into a new story. I was still here, Jimmy was still in Weleetka, and Creek land was still waiting for us to take it back.

ELEVEN

The Spirit of Resistance

Josh Henneha, Oklahoma City, 1993

I had gone to Project Vision, an Indian-run AIDS center that offered
services and counseling for Native people. Project Vision tries to make
traditional medicine available to guys living with AIDS without making
a big deal out of it, if the person wants such services, and seeks to get
families and communities involved in supporting their members living
with the disease. They also offer housing assistance and job training, as
well as work with Indian communities in presenting positive prevention
messages. I had just come for the test the first time, something I'd put
off for way too long, choosing to live with ignorance rather than facing
grim possible realities. If I didn't know, I didn't have to do anything.
I couldn't be sick if I didn't know I was sick, could I? Did I really
want to start taking massive doses of AZT, introducing a foreign
substance in my body and suffering the side effects, if I ended up
testing positive? Which was worse, knowing or not knowing?

I drove in circles all over the city for an hour, unsure if I'd gotten
lousy directions over the phone or I just didn't want to get there. I
watched the blood drops as the nurse squeezed them one by one from

my fingertip onto the five circles on my card. I had strange thoughts, started obsessing on blood. The counselor had warned me that the test might make me think of things I'd never considered before. When I'd cleaned fish I caught, crouched on the lakeshore at Eufaula and other places, I'd seen the blood compromised from bright to milky red as it filtered out through the shoreline moss. As I stared at my five blotted drops, I imagined my Aunt Lucille standing a good ways off from the lakeshore, up on the blacktop road near the dam, and she pointed toward the water, which was shallow for quite a ways out to the end of the weed beds. Jimmy had stood up in the place of one of these blood clots. If people knew my thoughts they might say I have an overactive imagination, or that I'm a little nuts, but I've always been this way, a dreamer, and the clinic had put me in an even more introspective mood than usual.

I missed Jimmy, maybe even loved him, though I felt foolish harboring such thoughts about someone I'd spent a single night with. Well, only one that really counted, anyway, though sleeping over and that night down by the river had become part of the story, too. What had brought us together that summer night after my Aunt Lucille's funeral was a combination, perhaps a culmination, of a lifetime of love and betrayal that had intensified in the years we'd been apart.

After I talked to the counselor at Project Vision, who I was actually related to through a cousin's marriage, but not by blood, a fact neither of us mentioned because of the clinic's protected confidentiality, I decided to look up Jimmy over the weekend. The counselor had mentioned on my way out something about the possibility of volunteer work helping take care of Indian guys with AIDS, just driving them around, taking them meals, everyday chores.

Friday after work a fellow employee dropped me off at the Ford dealer where I picked up my truck, since he lived out that way. It had never run right ever since Docia and Zadie had worked on it. My co-worker didn't like me much, but I think I was keeping him and the others amused at work as they speculated about what made me tick. When you don't give a shit about the job, people get kind of interested, sometimes more than when you're trying to impress them. I'd never

make it anywhere in the agency, but I had become the guy most likely
to intrigue. I was hoping to work their curiosity to my advantage
somehow, or maybe I'd just quit and leave them wondering forever.
I'd have to find another job first, though. My practical-minded father
always taught me never quit a job until you've got another one lined up.

I got on I-240 and drove across Oklahoma City back to the house,
where I loaded up with Merle Haggard tapes, a new graphite rod I'd
bought, and some plastic worms, spinners, and jigs. If the bass weren't
hitting, I'd get some night crawlers or shad, bait up, and hope for a
big ole cat. The fishing had slowed way the hell down during the heat
spell of the last week, and they tended to be hitting really late evening
on top-water lures after things had cooled off a bit. The fishing was a
contingency plan if I couldn't find Jimmy, given I didn't have much
confidence in regards to my luck with love.

I'd been fishing more and more with my grandpa, and he'd kind
of turned over a new leaf, too, now that he had a regular partner. He
seemed to like discovering new fishing haunts with me, and we started
venturing forth from Eufaula to Arbuckle Lake in the Arbuckle
Mountains, the Muddy Boggy River down near Farris, Tenkiller up
at Tahlequah—that is to say, into the Chickasaw, Choctaw, and
Cherokee Nations. In Oklahoma you can enter many different nations
in just a few hours' drive. I'd even gotten Grandpa to leave home for
a couple days at a time, and we had a better aluminum boat with a
trolling motor we'd picked up at a yard sale in Eufaula, an old tub, but
it floated and the motor worked, and it could be tied down in the back
of the truck and it was cheap enough for a couple of Indians. My fishing
was getting a little better, though I still wasn't that much of a fisherman.
I was pulling in some two- or three-pound bass every now and again,
and my grandfather had started to see me as a suitable fishing buddy.

I stopped for gas in Seminole—I always liked taking state highway
number 9 rather than I-40—and a drunk Indian guy was taking a piss
in front of the convenience store in broad daylight. "We're such a
proud people," I thought to myself and walked in the store grinning at
the 'skin behind the sales counter, who was laughing also. I pulled
back onto 9, and on the outskirts of town two middle-aged white

ladies were coming right at me on the shoulder of the road, matching blond perm jobs bobbing up and down on top of their heads and folds of tight black spandex trying to hold back a lot of flesh that clearly wanted to bust loose. They were power walking, pumping their arms and fixing their eyes dead ahead on Seminole as if it were a prize.

As I got closer to Weleetka and came upon the Highway 75 turnoff, I had an overwhelming urge to just stop in and see Jimmy, come what may, so I headed north. But I weenied out when I got to the little enclave of HUD houses, one of the many unofficial rezzes that existed in many of these Oklahoma towns, a pan-tribal gathering of Indian families, Cherokees, Creeks, Choctaws, and other tribes, living on the same street and sometimes burying, other times throwing down, the old war sticks. Of course, here, there were more Creeks than anybody else. First I just parked at the end of the cul-de-sac, and, wouldn't you know it, a young couple was handing out flyers for an Indian evangelist preaching at a tent meeting in Shawnee. I wasn't listening, mostly watching Jimmy's house to see if anyone came out. There wasn't a car in the driveway, but it could have been in the garage. I wanted to ask the couple if I could bring my boyfriend to the service. What a joke, even apart from the blasphemy; when was I ever gonna find a boyfriend? Anyway, I let the proselytizing break down my focus and chickened out before I had the courage to knock on Jimmy's door.

What was holding me back? If I let him come after me first, maybe I'd be safer. Perhaps I'd know he really wanted me, wouldn't turn away later. Truth is, I didn't know the reasons, just the fear.

I decided to go down to the Canadian River to think and strategize. I parked my pickup next to a fence line and headed out across an open cow field toward the river's edge. As I got closer to the trees, standing among the cows were some soft-brown willowy shapes which turned out to be deer, and they bounded off into the tree line when I was about a hundred yards away from them. I could feel the pull of water drawing me toward the river; I'd always sensed its power to take me under. So I headed upriver from this spot, and I had to cross another fence before I climbed down the steep bank. From the top, before my tricky descent through briars and brush, I could see the sandbars of the Oktahutche, and a couple of turtles on a half-sunk log slid off into the brown water.

I found a felled tree on the sandy bank and sat down. Some sick prankster had buried a gar in the sand so that its long snout was stuck in clean up to its eyeballs. Gar can't be caught with hooks—their sharp teeth snap fishing lines—but they sometimes gaff themselves accidentally on trotlines, and when they're running, fishermen throw out treble hooks and try to hook them in the sides. I saw a nylon line stretching from a tree stump on one side of the bank to a cottonwood on the other; the gar had probably gaffed itself swimming past the hooks which hung off the trotline a few feet below the surface. The river must have fallen considerably because the hooks were dancing above the brown current, blowing in the breeze.

A kingfisher was sitting on a branch beside the river, watching for minnows. I was amazed at its intelligence, its face, bright and alert, the diligence with which it would dive after fish, sometimes hovering for a moment in midair before the final swoop. My grandpa had once had me stop and watch one that speared a small crappie with its long bill, then tossed it into the air, caught it, and swallowed it headfirst.

I wondered what my Aunt Lucy would have done if she were me. I wished that the kingfisher would leave her branch and hover over me, swoop down, and pluck out whatever it was that was ailing me, the loneliness of the last thirty-three years. I saw the kingfisher disappear into the sandbank, probably into a nest which she'd built at the end of a tunnel she'd burrowed into the riverbank. Catching minnows for her brood, I reckoned. Then I had another crazy thought, the kind I'd been having a lot lately, except to me they felt more sane by leaps and bounds than the way I'd been thinking the previous thirty-three years. Why didn't I just have a talk with Lucy right here, sitting on the sandy bank?

So that's what I did, started talking to that old woman. Talked about the last time I'd seen her at the old folks' home. Talked about how nice her funeral was. Talked about how the fish had slowed down considerable in this hot weather, hadn't caught much with

Grandpa the last time out. Talked about Tarbie and Seborn, wished
I knew more about them. Small talk, at first—I was nervous, see,
didn't know how she'd respond to the news. I didn't even know how
to say it in her language, something I regretted terribly. I didn't know
how to explain love and betrayal, hate and desire, in any language.
I decided to go ahead and limp along as best I could in English. I'd
been having a recurring dream that she was trying to tell me something. She'd called up on the phone, but she was talking Indian, and
I couldn't understand a word of it. This was unusual in that, especially
lately, on many fishing trips where there was lots of time for such
things waiting for those elusive bass to strike, Grandpa'd been teaching
me Indian, and I could understand words and phrases now when
I was around the old people. On good days I'd even be able to follow
the gist of what they were saying, and my mind would reach back to
my childhood around Grandpa and Lucy when the only language in
the house would be Muskogee. Grandpa, though proud of my school
education, was generally suspicious of what exactly they taught there
since he was a former boarding school student, and he claimed I was
finally getting some real learning. I think he has something there.

I told Lucy about drowning, the rescue, the betrayal on shore.
About the night I spent over at Jimmy's house when he had touched
me in the night and his dad had burned his jacket in the morning.
I told her about the ghosts along the Canadian River I'd seen with
Jimmy. I tried to explain how I'd ended up over at Jimmy's house last
weekend. And what I found sitting out there on the riverbank was
that for a long time I had wanted to tell these stories to someone.

It had gotten deep in the middle of the afternoon by the end of
all these speakings and musings, and there wasn't a hint of a breeze
anymore reaching the muggy riverbank. I started back up the slope,
sweating and cursing at the vines and bushes impeding my progress.
I ripped the ass end of my Levi's a little crossing the last fence, but
luck prevailed and before it was all over I'd happened upon a patch
of wild onions. Grandpa had taught me how to recognize them when
I was a kid. They almost look like grass, not exactly what you'd expect
onions to resemble. The ongoing arrangement was me and him would

pick them, and Grandma would scramble them up with eggs and commodity cheese, a real treat. I just filled up a big paper soft-drink cup that I'd gotten from the McBurgler Queen, and I grinned at my borrowing of the crazy twins' habit of mixing and matching all the fast-food names together.

Back at Grandpa's house, while Grandma was cooking up the eggs and wild onions, I started putting out feelers for Jimmy, gathering information. Among Indians, you don't have to fabricate much of a pretense to gossip about families, and my inquiry proceeded without a hitch. Actually, all I had to do was mention their last name, and I didn't have to say another word. Both Grandma and Grandpa took the ball and ran with it. I found out Jimmy was trying to lay low from his old man, whose drinking had gotten worse, and he was always hitting Jimmy up for money. Jimmy's mom had moved to Wetumka just to get away from the guy, leaving the house to her husband's devices. They told me Jimmy's family was camped out for the once-a-month "fourth Sunday" of the Indian Baptist church, and most likely Jimmy would be out there, too, since church was one place his father couldn't stomach.

So I ate up and headed out to the country. Fourth Sundays were so named because once a month church members camped in and held services. A couple miles outside of Weleetka, I started down the dirt road toward the church grounds, which comprised several wooded acres with the small concrete church building in the center and about fifteen camp houses along the perimeter of the grounds. The road followed a creek for a little bit, and a bunch of Indian kids were playing by the bridge. An old man was admonishing them, probably for lighting off firecrackers, which I'd heard all the way from up on the blacktop. I imagined that they'd been tossing them over the side of the wooden bridge that stretched the short distance from bank to bank, leftover munitions from the recent Fourth of July. Indian kids, fireworks, and old people harping on them to chill out seemed a part of all Oklahoma summer Indian doings, even church.

Generally, church members started camping-in on Friday nights. Early that Saturday morning they would have had a short service, followed by a day of the women cooking back at the camp houses in preparation for Sunday services and the feed that would follow. This evening there would be a short testimonial service, which I was hoping to miss, to be honest, mostly because I wanted to visit with Jimmy, and also because I didn't know what to make of this Creek Christian stuff. The white Christian stuff had nearly done me in, and I didn't know how much of an improvement I could expect from the red version. I'd decided to go back to the stomp grounds and taking medicine.

My grandpa, God love him, had unknowingly provided me with the perfect alibi for being out at the church grounds. One of my cousins, whose folks were Indian church people, had gotten a ride back to town to pick up some cooking supplies, and her ride had needed to hurry back to the grounds. Sabreena needed a way back out there. If Jimmy's family saw me around, I knew they'd invite me inside to eat. One thing the stomp grounds and church grounds had in common was you went from camp to camp visiting and eating. It would be expected of me to sit with Jimmy's folks for a little while.

At the grounds we parked over behind our auntie's place. I helped Sabreena carry the grocery bags inside the camp house. "Hello, Josh," Aunt Lettie said, "you staying for church with us?"

"I might stay a little bit," I said, keeping my options open in case me and Jimmy could go off someplace. Aunt Lettie was putting stuff up on the wood plank shelves.

"Where's the sugar?" she asked. "Oh, shoot," Sabreena said, "of all the things to forget." Auntie picked up a wooden spatula and faked hitting Breen over the head, clucking in disapproval. "That's the main thing I sent you after, girl."

"I'll go borrow some," I offered.

"Aren't you helpful?" Lettie said, winking. "I know how you young guys like to get around and see who all's in the camps."

"Tipi creeper," Sabreena said, taking the spatula from Lettie and whopping me on the ass.

"Creeks don't have tipis," I shot back. "Maybe the Alexanders have some sugar. I see a car over there."

"Yeah, they been here since last night," Lettie said. "Here, take this." She handed me the measuring cup. I walked across the grounds, and Ben Harjo was on a riding mower cutting the grass. I didn't envy him any, hot as it was, and Ben was wide as a barrel. I handed him my Coke when I went by, which I hadn't opened yet. He took it gratefully and downed half of it before riding off again on the mower. I walked up the front steps of the Alexanders', and my knees felt like they might buckle from fear and anticipation. Inside, the wooden camp house was larger than I expected with a dining room, kitchen, and three bedrooms with various kin stretched out on old steel spring beds. Jimmy wasn't anywhere to be seen, and I was a little relieved at putting off the encounter awhile longer. From outside, the smell of a wood-burning stove had been wonderful, but inside was an inferno, and I began sweating immediately and profusely. Before I could make excuses to go out on the porch to escape the heat, Jimmy's mother said, *"Lekibus,"* and had me sit down, poured me some iced tea, and pointed toward some grape dumplings, which I'm wild about. As I watched everyone else laughing, visiting, and just snoozing, I couldn't believe I was so wimpy, but I still felt like crying uncle and running out onto the porch where even the Oklahoma humidity would feel refreshing.

When Jimmy walked in and saw me, he just about dropped the plate of food he was carrying, but he passed it off as clumsiness. He covered his surprise skillfully, shifting immediately into the customary Creek hospitality, asking about my folks and grandparents and making sure I had enough to eat. "Getcha some more of that," he kept saying, motioning to the corn bread, then the *sofki,* then the fried chicken.

Let me tell you right now, Baptist surroundings and all, the man was looking hot, and I'm not just talking about the dripping heat. He had on overalls with no shirt, and I could see a good portion of his well-developed chest and arms, lean but muscled. His upper body was glistening with sweat inside the cookhouse. He took off his Adidas cap and scratched his head, revealing his short, wiry black hair, buzzed in the back and on the sides, longer on top. The bottoms of his overalls were stuck inside a pair of Air Jordans. I'd been crazy to think I could ever have a man like him. What was I doing here? I wanted to run out of the camp house. "Yeah, get me some more of *that,*" I thought, half afraid immediately afterward of what might come of lusting after a man at a Baptist campground. But then again, maybe the Lord had brought us back together, who knows?

The church service was running on Indian time, hadn't even started up yet, so there was still church to go to. Not unlike the ceremonial grounds, Indian church seemed to have a spirit of its own, a way of running itself apart from human control. The deacon had gone over and began pulling the rope that clanged the church bell, an ancient rite signaling the beginning of the service; it had gotten dark out, and I could see fireflies flickering outside the door of the camp house. Jimmy stepped outside, and I followed, sitting myself down opposite from him on the porch. He winked and whispered, "I'm glad to see you. Why don't you go to church with me? Then we'll talk."

What with the insects humming softly in my ears, the fireflies flashing their small lights in the darkness, the people moving from their camp houses to the church building at the center of the grounds, and Jimmy sitting across from me on the porch, leaning against a post and trying to work up the momentum to rise up in the muggy night, put on a shirt for church, and walk to service, I felt about as good as an Indian boy can feel in this life.

Inside the open-air church building, a roof over a concrete floor with pews to sit in, Jimmy and I took our places with the men, who sat on the left side of the building, the women on the right. In the white church I'd gone to with my parents, couples sat together, and I pondered the meaning of Jimmy and me sitting side by side in this different cultural context with ritual separation of men and women. Whatever it meant, it sure felt good there, as if his presence was casting a blanket of protection over us. I loved the feeling of being subsumed by another man in this way. Surely this had happened before. Two men had sat next to each other, in church, or out under the arbors, who had once been lovers or still were. At any rate, it also felt good to have our place among the men. Of course, they didn't know about us; surely that would change things. Or did they?

The church chairman called upon an older woman to sing a song and say a prayer to begin the service. The singing that ensued carried me deep into other worlds. The songs, sung in Creek, were a stunning combination of Protestant cadences and Indian chant, and with the melodies wafting out through the camp, amplified by cricket and cicada choruses and fireflies bearing silent witness with their flickering lights, I could feel my spirit drifting with the music toward the woods, along with those generations of Creek Christians who had come before, joining their voices—some of whom had sung Creek hymns along the trail during the forced march of Indian Removal in the 1830s.

What struck me most was the expression on the women's faces as they fanned themselves and sang, their eyes half closed, the sorrow in their rising and falling voices as well as the hope for something better. The men looked different somehow, perhaps more resigned, doggedly committed to finishing the race. There was another spirit in the women, traces of resistance, a strain not yet tamed worth learning about.

I was listening to Jimmy's voice closely, trying to pick up words and phrases when so much was happening all at once. These sounds began fading to a quiet backdrop when I heard the distinct percussive sound of a whippoorwill coming very clearly from over by the creek where I'd driven in. You can't miss the cry, and it has a way of predominating the woods, even though the three notes are not loud or piercing. I looked at the women's faces and saw my Aunt Lucille's years of pain carried on their voices throughout the campground, their invitation for her to join in, their willingness to share her burden. I didn't even know what Lucille's pain was, never considered that she had any—too focused on mine, I guess. It occurred to me that the only way left to know her suffering was through my own, and I let my voice go, mostly humming along at first, then, increasingly, joining in on words and phrases, as they became clear through repetition, following closely Jimmy's lead, adding whatever I could to the women's lament. I felt a hunger I'd known before, as Jimmy leaned over to read the words of a hymn. I wanted to slip my arm around his shoulder, claim him as my own. Yet none of the men shared this privilege, separated from their wives as they were, so I contented myself with sitting back, soaking up the night.

The preaching brought me back down to earth. Whenever the preacher would talk about laying aside the sins of the flesh, he'd speak English and turn toward Jimmy and me, the only young people in the small congregation that evening. And there was a sadness as the preaching wound down, a reminder that next time they camped-in, someone who was with them now would be passed on. This was the way of things, and there was acceptance and grief in the preacher's voice. But tomorrow was a different matter, I thought. There would be a lot more folks during the main service when those who couldn't camp-in yet would join their relatives.

After the service we decided to drive back to Jimmy's place to talk and catch up. Jimmy would go back in the morning for church and his family's feed, and he invited me to join them. Driving back in Jimmy's car with the windows down, it was one of *those* Oklahoma summer nights. It had come a big thunderstorm when church let out, and we could see sheet lightning to the southwest toward Lawton. The slow sprinkles, blowing softly through the windows, had lowered the temperature of the muggy night air considerably, though it would be hell tomorrow when it got hot. But tonight it smelled like rain. I slid over on the seat and put my hand on Jimmy's leg.

"Do you know what we look like?" Jimmy laughed. "You know how when you're driving out in the country, and those white farm guys wave at you by barely lifting their index finger off the wheel? They usually got their big-haired blond babe scrunched right up against them."

I laughed, too, then flirted. "Do you reckon I could ever be *your* big-haired blond babe?"

"God, I hope not," he replied, grinning. I dug through his cassettes, mostly hip-hop, some R&B stuff, until I found a Jackson Browne tape, more my style. "Good choice," Jimmy said, as I turned it up, "perfect storm music." Ah, another romantic, I thought, hopefully. While "Running on Empty" started up, I told him about the job, all the fishing with Grandpa recently, everything I could think of. I was a little nervous, but Jimmy listened quietly.

"What took you so long to look me up?" he asked, after we'd

lapsed into silence for a while. I felt my heart rise up in my throat, a little surprised at his directness and a little unsure, really, of the answer.

"You mean this week?" I asked. "Why didn't I phone?"

"No," he said. "All those years you were in Stillwater going to school, then in Oklahoma City when you got out." Looking for Jimmy was something new for me. More than just a happenstance snag at a bar or someplace even seedier, always when I was drunk, seeking out Jimmy required consciously acknowledging I wanted to be with him and purposefully working toward finding him. A couple years ago I couldn't have even conceived of such a thing.

I wasn't ready to say all that, however. "I don't know," I answered back quietly. "Why didn't you look *me* up?" By then we'd gotten to his house. The front door was still unlocked, the same NBA poster was on the wall, and the place was still minimally furnished, just about like I'd left it last week.

He had acquired a couch, so I sat next to him. "My mom threw it out," he laughed. He was shirtless again; he'd pulled off his T-shirt in the truck and rolled down the windows, and I began rubbing his chest, reaching under the straps of his overalls. Needless to say, this was fun, and I had him sit in front of me and massaged his neck and shoulders, just about had him purring like a cat. Then I bent down and kissed him on the cheek.

"What'd you go and do that for?" he said, almost grimacing. Wow, this took me by surprise, the defensiveness, the sudden change. "You sure get right down to business," he added, and I felt something different between us. I didn't know how to read being taken back to his house, which, given that we were two gay guys who were attracted to each other, involved certain assumptions, and then this resistance when we got there. Maybe I was just moving too fast.

"I was fixing to tell you why I haven't looked you up since you got back," he said, pulling away.

My heart sank. "Do you have a boyfriend?"

"No, it's not that. I wanted to find you more than anything else. My life has changed a lot since you've been gone. Nothing is like it was before."

"I haven't been gone very long," I said, puzzled. But what was I talking about? Those four years in school and the USDA job had been an eternity. Maybe for Jimmy, too; I didn't know.

He laid down on the brown shag carpet. All the signals were mixed up now, and I didn't know if I should stay on the sofa and give him some space or join him on the floor. My yearning heart held sway, however, and I lay down next to him and threw my arm across his chest, a move he neither encouraged nor resisted. That's the way we had lain together last time. He lay on his back looking up at the white speckled ceiling and said, "I'm going to tell you something.

"After you went off to college, I spent a wild summer in Tulsa. I moved up there because I wanted to escape my old man. He was going around Eufaula and Weleetka, talking shit with his wino buddies about how he was going to make me move back home and straighten me out, give him the respect he deserved. Just bullshit drunk talk, and he didn't really have any clue, as far as I knew, just how 'unstraight' I really was. You know how I was. I started smoking dope when I was thirteen, pulling some shit, but then backing off enough so I didn't get kicked off the basketball team. My old man, of all people, had no room to talk about sticking to the straight and narrow. After high school, I freaked on myself, but maybe I really tripped on him, looking for some way to get him back. I'd been drinking a little bit, and I'd got in some trouble when some friends of mine ripped off a car in McAlester. I only spent a couple days in jail because my buddies had picked me up after they stole it, and they'd both testified to that effect.

"That's why I moved up to Tulsa. I was sick of my dad's talk around town, and I was a little depressed because I hadn't been able to find work around home after going to school at Bacone for a semester. Just floating, a huge letdown after being a star ball player, then graduating to an Indian around Eufaula with no job and lots of time on his hands. I didn't know what to do with myself anymore. What really sent me packing to Tulsa, though, had to do with not being able to face my dad no more because of the way I'd gotten out of jail.

"My dad, who usually ain't very cashy and is hitting everybody and their cousin up for money, was the one to bail me out. He had some incredible pieces of Southwestern Navajo, Hopi, and Zuni jewelry, rugs, and art that friends had given him when he worked as an auto shop teacher in a vocational program at Navajo Community College years ago, down in Tsaile. Dad was that kind of guy. Everybody but those who had to live with him thought he was the greatest. Anyway, Dad pawned the whole collection for bail money and begged the rest of the money off of kinfolks, who generally felt sorry for me since I hadn't been in any trouble and had gone off to school, then come back home.

"I was ashamed and guilty that my old man had sold off that stuff to bail me out. It just ate my ass up. That summer I'd moved to the northeast side of Tulsa, and I was drunk most of the time, living on limited funds, and just going off in a rage, then picking up tricks almost every day—in the bars on weekends, in the parks during the week. Didn't have any self-esteem, didn't give a shit, often didn't remember the next day. It was like a long ways down from the state championship team with all my buddies and practice every day.

"I got so crazy that I can't really explain all my behavior, but I became obsessed with my father's whereabouts and activities, even though I was living in Tulsa away from home. I started asking about him, calling, and bugging the shit out of my kinfolks, 'Have you seen my dad?' He was still running around talking trash like 'I'm gonna catch that wild boy and tame him.' My life centered on drinking, picking up tricks, and spying on my old man until all this culminated in me actually following him one weekend. I drove all the way home and waited at night up the road from one of his wino buddies' places. Sure enough, here he came, looking surly as hell, and crawling into that old green Impala that he drives. Dad's a pretty good mechanic, and he's still got that piece of shit running like a top; I'll give him that. He's the one who taught me to work on cars, one of the few things we ever did together. This ended up coming in more handy than college, at least in terms of surviving.

"So I followed Dad, and he pulled into the parking lot of the Indian bar between McAlester and Krebs; the Cave, they call it. He never got out of the car, though, just sat there in the back of the parking lot, with his headlights off, in the dark. I didn't have a clue as to what he was up to. Two 'skins staggered out the front door, a married couple it looked like, and they were giving each other some serious shit, shoving and slapping the tar out of one another. My old man picked up something off the seat of the Impala and pointed it out the window. It took a second to register. It was the old 30–30 he used for deer hunting, what we kids had referred to as 'doe hunting,' when we wanted to tease him. An old Winchester lever action. Before I could holler 'duck' or something, Dad had aimed at the couple, staggering arm in arm by then, and he made a firing sound like a kid playing cowboys and Indians, faked the recoil of the rifle, and laid the gun back on the seat and started laughing like a motherfucker. The click I'd heard moments before was the dry firing of an unloaded gun.

"My old man sat in that parking lot until closing time, and he shot every 'skin who came out the front door. He let all the white people go. And every time he shot an Indian, he got a bigger kick out of it than the time before. Every now and then he'd cuss up a blue streak and mumble, 'Goddammit, I fucking missed,' then he'd down another Budweiser from his twelve-pack to steady his aim for his next victim. The ones he knew, he'd talk about as he was gunning them down, telling all their hypocrisies and shortcomings, both individually and those of their relatives and friends: AA assholes, apples who worked for the tribe, Oreos who taught at the black college, drug addicts who went to church. He had the skinny on all of them.

"This is kind of hard to explain, but something turned loose in me that night, and I cracked up at my old man's warped sense of humor. It should have horrified me, but it had the opposite effect. Seeing that made me less pissed at him; I saw something there besides the boozing and bullshitting. A couple weeks later I moved back to Weleetka and stayed there. He talked me into it, one of the many concessions I'd make and then regret.

"Ended up he was still the same leech and pain in the ass he always was, but I stopped thinking about it as much because, for one thing, I got that mechanic job over to McAlester. I was just less bored, less time on my hands to brood over this shit. And every night I'd park

my car over at my Aunt Maudie's, out behind the post oaks, and
walk home, so Dad didn't know I was at the house. If he came by,
sometimes I didn't answer the door, sometimes I did when I felt up
to it. I stopped going to Tulsa and tricking around, though once in a
while I'd go to the bars on Saturday night, hoping to find some nice
man. What a joke. The only thing I've found is homophobic white
guys who'll fuck you or let you suck them off but won't let you touch
them. They like their brown boys kneeling in front of them. And then
the Indian guys all had a monkey on their backs as well, dealing with
substance abuse issues, and I needed to stay away from that shit. I kept
getting fucked, but I wasn't getting kissed. I even placed an ad in the
gay newspaper to look for an Indian guy, but I just got responses from
white Indian lovers. I finally just gave up altogether.

"You know, I had a little 'early exposure,' you might say. I know
you remember the night I took you to the river after the high school
game. I'd gone down there with a drunk teammate who'd shown me
the place and pretended shock and disgust at all we saw. I was smart
enough to figure out that wasn't his first night down there. I went
back on my own, and once I had a taste of that I kept returning. So
by the time I got to Tulsa after high school, I kind of knew the ropes.

"But after I moved back to Weleetka I started to have a funny
feeling about my HIV status. I'd done everything, all of it unprotected,
that drunk summer in Tulsa. I wanted to be clean in case I ever ran
across somebody like you; I wanted an unhindered relationship, and
I didn't want to die.

"I drove back up to Tulsa, this time to be tested instead of to chase
snags, and the test didn't turn out in my favor. I cried all day. That's
why we can't have sex, Josh; I'm not trying to be a prick. If I gave you
the disease, I'd have that to deal with, too."

I could tell you that I had some kind of epiphany lying there next
to Jimmy, that I thought about my own mortality or some such shit.
Truth is, I didn't really think of much of anything other than what
I'd already been thinking, which was that I wanted him. I was lying
there, holding him, and I wanted him. No, I wasn't thinking about the
possibility of loving him and losing him; I was more entranced with

the rising and falling of his chest as he breathed quietly. I said the only thing I could think of, "You're a beautiful man." Yeah, I was a little scared at the strength of my own desire, but none of this lessened my attraction to Jimmy. I'd had thirty-three years of loneliness. I knew I couldn't go back, no matter what.

I fell into my statistician's logic. "There are still things we can do," I said, "with reasonable levels of risk." I talked about oral sex, generally considered a low-risk activity, and anal sex with condoms.

"Nothing is without risk," Jimmy replied. "There's pre-cum during oral sex. Condoms break."

"Have you ever had one break on you?" I joked, to lighten things up a little. "That's exactly my point; nothing is risk free. I could have the disease myself, for all I know. I could fall out of the boat and drown the next time I go fishing with Grandpa. I could get shot by a lone rifleman the next time I walk out of the Indian bar. Let me decide what risks I want to take." Though my argument was sound in logic, Jimmy's was more emotionally compelling, the terrible burden of the possibility of infecting someone else.

I was getting frustrated, the old feeling of holding him for a moment, only to have him turn away. "Then why did we have sex last weekend?" I asked. "What was that all about?"

"There's something else," he said. "One of the guys I was with that summer is dead now. A white guy. Even though he had a lover he lived with, he was seeing me. I think I got infected by him, though I really can't be sure. I was quite fond of him, though I don't know how he felt about me. When he got sick, he told me he had leukemia and moved home to Little Rock. I know now that he had the disease, though. I've been really pissed off this last year, taking it out on friends and family who don't deserve it, and I've just begun realizing where some of this anger comes from. That's why here lately I've been trying to go to church with my mom, things like that. I feel shitty about the way I've been treating them. I just want to be friends with you, Josh. Someone to kick it with. What we did last weekend should have never happened. I let myself get too desperate. I apologize."

"You apologize?" I said. "Thanks a lot. That makes me feel great about myself. An accidental screw when you hit rock bottom. Rejecting me will help you develop your self-discipline. I'm glad to be of some service," I said bitterly. "Last choice once again, only called in to even up the team, so you get to play your precious game."

"It isn't you," he answered, "and this isn't basketball."

I called him after work on Monday night. "Whassup?" he said, cheerfully, like nothing had happened. I'd prepared for a letdown, but not *this* letdown. What did the future hold, anyway, jigging for crappie on the lakeshore, a return to our adolescence where we traipsed all over Eufaula together, winding up everywhere except in each other's beds? Yet I couldn't think of much else to offer him. I didn't want to lose whatever I could salvage.

"Good to hear your voice," Jimmy said, sounding like he missed me. I had no idea how to respond to this intimacy that he offered and held back at the same time. How could I overcome his resistance?

"You wanna go to the show or something this weekend?" I asked. "I know it's kind of early, a week away and all."

"It's not early," he said. "Call anytime."

He drove to the city that weekend. He bought me popcorn at the movie. He took me to the coffee shop afterwards and we talked for hours. He crashed on my sofa at my apartment. We had breakfast together Sunday morning. "Nice place," Jimmy said, walking around my living room while I scrambled eggs in the kitchen. He walked over to the bookshelves. What had bothered me most wasn't Jimmy's decision about sex; it was his body, after all, and I finally had to admit that. It was his total resistance to physicality, even to me touching him or putting my arm around him or lying next to him. At the movies I'd tried to hold his hand, and he'd pulled it away. I don't think he was worried about anyone seeing. It was more like he thought any small act of kindness would lead to sex. Behind his fear, of course, was the fact that I wanted exactly that very thing to happen, and I couldn't let go of this hope. He knew this fully well.

Jimmy started pulling books off the shelf. He brought them over to the kitchen table and sat down. I set a cup of coffee in front of him. Lately I'd been reading all these books on Creek history, comparing them to what my relatives had told me. "Man, I've read all these," he said.

"You read?" I asked, surprised.

"Don't say it like that," he protested.

"Sorry," I replied. "It's just that I always saw my bookishness as a great gulf that separated me from the rest of the world. Especially the Indian world. I thought nobody read but me."

"No, Josh, there are bookstores with volumes of stuff, and other people besides you come in there and buy them. That's how they stay in business. Even out in the country, where we're from, you walk into people's houses and see books on the shelves. Especially these tribal histories. They like looking at pictures of their relatives in them, seeing that someone in their family had some important role in history."

"I guess that's right," I said. "But I thought only dreamers like me were stuck inside books."

"Hell, yeah, you always were a little scary that way," Jimmy said. "I thought if you spent any more time in your room you might crawl inside one of those stories and disappear."

"I almost did," I said, laughing, "but now I think I got it under control."

"I hope so," Jimmy said, "because you creeped people out, man. We were all scared of you."

"What?" I said. Had I heard him right? They were afraid of *me?*

"Yeah," Jimmy went on to say, "I actually read a lot of books as part of my dad's home schooling program. The special Creek version that he invented. He had a theory about taking back Creek land if it could be proven that white title to the state of Oklahoma was illegal. Angie Debo's *And Still the Waters Run* was our bible for home lessons. Remember when I'd show up for class late all the time? My dad made me sit through his history lessons in the morning before school. He said he wanted to get the first word in every day before they started hammering away at my brain.

"I always argued with him, pointed out whites had written all this shit. Dad said even white people could tell the truth sometimes. I could see his point, but there was something missing in all this history.

I couldn't connect it to anything that was happening to me. I could see Oklahoma was still racist, not much had changed. But I couldn't see how the books were going to do much for Creeks."

I knew what was missing. Did I dare tell Jimmy that I had flown as a child and that I was seeking to revive my powers? If sex scared him, what might he think about leaving the earth altogether or touching down in another world? Part of me was still holding out for the return of all-out flight. I hadn't figured out a way to tell him about my dreaming, but I was working on it.

In the days to come, I kept an instant replay going inside my head, trying to figure out what had gone wrong since we'd hooked up after Lucy's funeral. Jimmy had not been standoffish, didn't seem homophobic and resistant to male intimacy; in fact, he was rather a passionate and fiery kind of guy. At the height of my insecurity, I asked him if he simply wasn't attracted to me, and he responded vaguely that sex wasn't the foremost thing on his mind, though he would never actually just say, "No, you're not my type."

At first, being around him involved a period of insanity for me, that close to someone I was falling in love with—someone sitting a foot away on the couch or the bed while we watched movies or listened to his favorite music. He would be shirtless, in cutoffs, and I'd be crazy with desire as the ceiling fan softly blew air down on us. After a while the days he didn't call were a little bit of a relief, a respite from the madness, but still I'd be anxiously craving hearing his voice again by the end of the day.

Every weekend, and even a couple of weekdays, I'd drive down to Weleetka, or he'd come to the city; we were together every possible moment, doing everything from shopping for clothes to going to movies to teaching him how to work bass lures down at the lake with me and Grandpa. He was at my house so often that Jimmy's best friend started calling for him there.

"How'd you get this number?" Jimmy asked the first time. Then he took the call in the bedroom.

"Who was that?" I said.

"Nobody, just C.A." Jimmy said, cryptically.

"What's the big secret?"

"No, secret, man, he's just always up in my business. He wants to know everything."

"About what?" I was really curious and jealous of this shared intimacy. I wanted to hear Jimmy say, "about us," to force him to acknowledge the amount of time we were together, more than he and C.A. had ever spent. But he wouldn't say anything, even if that's what he'd been talking about with C.A. Mostly a minor pest, C.A. had shown up unannounced a few times at Jimmy's house in Weleetka, and Jimmy had hurried me out the door, made up places we had to be, and rushed off. And C.A. would run off pretty quick himself. I think he still held it against me all the times I'd ditched him in junior high. I can't say as I blame him. He was the one person even more pathetic than I was, and I'd taken advantage of the fact.

"Nothing, he's just pissed I been spending so much time down here," Jimmy said, in response to my question. Then I had the depressing thought that maybe Jimmy had taken up with me simply to get away from C.A. He seemed to make dodging him a kind of art form, developed over many years, far surpassing my unsophisticated attempts to simply outrun him in seventh grade.

This friendship thing between the two of us started angering me because it wasn't always consistent with the vibes Jimmy was sending. One Saturday night we were sitting in my pickup in the parking lot at the gay bar in Okie City on 39th Street; we'd smoked a bowlful, and I could tell we were both getting horny because we started talking about sex, at first in an abstract way, then more concretely as we went from talking about good-looking guys to what we liked and didn't like to do, then progressing to fantasies we'd always harbored. Jimmy started up a hypothetical sex game, presenting scenarios, quizzing me as to what I would do in certain situations. We were having phone sex with no phone and both partners within two feet of each other, perfectly capable of uniting word with deed.

"Check this out," Jimmy said, rolling down the window because the car was starting to smell like a hemp factory. "What if we were sitting next to each other on the public dock at Lake Eufaula. It's broad daylight." Though Jimmy didn't make any physical moves, he had a way of teasing me with his voice by making his meaning even more slippery than ever, and sexy too, his voice just short of a growly baritone. "The dock is rocking because there are a couple of ski boats out on the lake. Not rocking hard, just slowly rising and falling. We're dangling our legs off the end, crappie are nibbling at our toes, our backs are toward shore. I dare you—would you jump in and swim in place below me and give me head while the dock was moving?"

"Hell, yeah," I said, "no problem," ignoring the logistics of swimming, the moving dock, one riding the waves, the other below them, a ridiculous act of acrobatic sex. I was hoping the word game was a prelude, and we could move from the hypothetical dock to the very real bedroom I happened to live in, the apartment where we both spent so much time these days. But Jimmy had hit a nerve, since I was a little afraid of water if the truth were known, and he'd chosen the one sexual scenario that might actually scare me off if the dream became reality. In my grandpa's boat I always insisted on wearing a life vest, no matter how hot it was.

The problem was I'd let myself be tricked by Jimmy, let his words pull me under. I should have said, "Why the fuck are you tormenting me like this? Why are you saying you don't want sex, then playing this game?" Instead, I'd been fooled by his storytelling. I wasn't sure of his motivation for such a provocative scenario, but with the weed and the words, I could almost hear the wood creaking and feel the water slapping my legs as I listened to Jimmy's voice. No ambiguity here; clearly Jimmy was making a sexual pass at me. I reached across the car seat toward him, but he batted my hand away and growled, "Back off!"

God, I was mad, and embarrassed, too. I knew I hadn't misread the signs, not exactly nuanced flirtation, yet I'd been made a fool of. I hissed, "I'm fucking leaving. I'll give you a ride back to your car at my place, then you can drive *home* to Weleetka." I started up the car.

Jimmy looked genuinely surprised. "What*ever.* Calm down, man. Sometimes a sexual fantasy is just a sexual fantasy. I didn't mean let's go drive over to the lake and do it. Christ, you're so sensitive. And such a horny toad. Why can't you settle for friendship?" He slumped back in his seat, exasperated. He eventually talked me into staying and said that maybe we shouldn't get high together, blaming it on the dope. "That shit lowers my immunity, anyway," he said. "I ain't smoking no more."

"Yeah, I agree about the dope," I said. "Maybe we shouldn't be smoking together, or maybe not at all, I don't know. Maybe we shouldn't even be hanging out. It's turning into more of a pain in the ass than a good time. I think you like intentionally provoking me. You don't tell a story like that by accident, especially considering our relationship in the past."

"What relationship?" Jimmy shot back. "We're just friends, and it's up to you if we remain friends. I don't really care, one way or another."

Now I was pissed. "If you're that ambivalent about it, if you don't even care one way or the other, then what's the point? Why are we hanging out?" I was screaming now, and Jimmy laughed uncomfortably, trying to pass it off like I was making an unnecessary scene.

I continued, a little calmer, but still pissed and hurt. "The kind of fantasy we just created didn't come out of the blue. We're not two strangers dialing a 900 number. We wouldn't have played it out if we didn't mean it on some level. I have no problem with being friends," I added, "if we're clear that's what we want. You share responsibility in this, too."

Jimmy sighed. "You're right; what I did is wrong." He seemed sorry and a little embarrassed. The tension eased up a little. "I guess we just can't talk about sex or get high together," he said. "You know I want to be friends. I was just being stupid."

"Well, I think it's way more than an interpretation problem," I said. I presented the best offense I could, and I continued to stake my claim to my right to decide for myself what level of risk I wanted to take with an HIV-positive partner, still believing that his need for friendship without sex was related to his fears about spreading the disease. Of course, his point that he had the same right to decide what level of risk he was willing to expose others to, given his HIV status, was also hard to argue against. Ultimately, I had to respect his wishes, given that it was his body we were talking about, as well as mine.

"Josh, do you know what it's like to think to yourself, oh my God, an hour has gone by, and I haven't thought about this disease?"

"How am I supposed to answer that?" I said.

"You can't," Jimmy glared. "That's the point."

We finally just went inside the club and danced our asses off, giving ourselves up to a physical release of our frustrations. We shared a love of dancing, and it felt good because he was one sexy dancer, and I wasn't too bad myself. For the first time in my life I was actually enjoying going to the bar occasionally. It was good being in there with Jimmy rather than alone. No cruising pressure and the inevitable frustration of going home without anybody. Some guys found it exciting that on any given Saturday night their luck might turn; they might find Mr. Right. I just found it depressing, like the concept of a limit in my college calculus classes—no matter how close you get, you're never quite there. I'd seen other Native guys in the bars and other Creeks. The blacks, Asians, Hispanics, and Indians seemed to congregate in their own corner, and I had intuitively found my place there apart from the pretty white boys. Not that white boys wouldn't come over our way to cruise as a last resort when the first pickings had been taken and closing time drew near. I felt pretty much the same as when we chose sides for kickball in grade school, and I'd been picked last. So being there with Jimmy, having someone to dance with and talk to, had made going out now and then bearable. And we were starting to get to know some of the Indian guys there, listening to their stories. It was a good feeling, like we were kind of sticking up for each other, a lot less frustrating than sexual prowling and trying to make eye contact, an all-night promenade back and forth through every dark corner.

One weekend Jimmy stayed the night at my place in Oklahoma City, and we rented the film *Madame Butterfly*. While we were watching it, lying on my bed and resting on big pillows we'd propped up against the wall, Jimmy said, "Man, that Chinese opera singer is *hot*— as both a man and a woman. That gets me off looking at her, even though I ain't bi, or any shit like that."

I'd never really been attracted to anyone in drag, but I started to see his point, the eroticism of the androgyny of the character, the power to change at will. The next thing I knew I was sitting on Jimmy's legs facing him, moving my hands in front of my face and imitating the coy gestures of the singer, making Jimmy laugh. A bad imitation of a worse simulation, my impression of the Chinese woman as imagined by the film character, her French male admirer. While waving one hand in front of my face in a move of exaggerated shyness, I'd let the other fall down to Jimmy's belt buckle, which I was tugging on playfully.

"Your hand's in the wrong place," he said, his head thrown back and the rest of him too far gone to keep up his usual resistance.

"Really?" I said, hardly believing my good fortune, like a schoolkid finally given a piece of candy. Jimmy closed his eyes and began to groan softly as I rubbed his crotch. One thing led to another, and I had Jimmy going pretty good by the time the Frenchman is confronted by his Chinese lover in his male form as they are going off to prison. Not that I was paying much attention to the movie. The next evening, when I called him up for what had become our almost daily phone chats, Jimmy argued that our sexual encounter should have never happened, a moment of weakness for both of us. Why did I keep coming back for more of this?

"You're quite the team player," I said, trying a basketball argument on him. He'd been trying to get me to learn something about the game. "You call the shots, and it's always 'no sex,' but you also reserve the exclusive right to decide when to break the rules."

"I told you; this ain't basketball," he said. I hung up, infuriated.

I had decided to distance myself from Jimmy, get involved on some less personal level. I talked him into going with me to Project Vision to find out about volunteer work. The center wasn't located in the best part of town; in fact, it was just down the street from the Indian bar, the Horse, the local 'skin shorthand for the Crazy Horse. Crazy Horse himself probably would not have been honored to have his name used by a bar which served the very drug that white people had used as chemical warfare against Indians. In my incipient study of Creek culture, I had found out that every time a land cession was made, the treaty signers were first plied with a huge amount of rum.

So I liked the shortened version of the name of the dive, which distanced it from the powerful resistance leader.

We found street parking, and when we passed the entrance to the Horse, a white guy stepped out of the alleyway, holding a capped fruit jar at arm's length and shaking it at us in fury. We jumped back in surprise, and it took Jimmy and me a minute to discern that buzzing around inside it was a yellow jacket wasp. The white man had large blue eyes, sunken in a disturbingly small head the size and shape of a muskmelon, offset by a tall lanky frame. Ichabod Crane in stature, Rasputin in visage, Jonathan Edwards in intensity. He pointed one finger toward the ground, as if it were flaming around his feet. He shouted, "Damn your hides! I'm gonna turn these insects loose on you two! Where's my razor strap?"

A counselor came out of Project Vision and told the homeless guy to stop harassing people coming into the center. He ushered us in. "Damn," Jimmy said, "there's a spook."

"Well, I would say he's harmless," the counselor said, "but it's hard enough for some of our people to come in here without zombies charging them from the alley." The counselor was Wyandotte and Quapaw from Miami, Oklahoma, up in the northeast corner of the state. He was really white-looking. I think a guy who works at a place like that should at least look Indian. But he was nice, and I reconsidered. The director of Project Vision was at a conference in San Francisco, but the counselor explained the volunteer schedule, and he said he needed two guys who could work together because some of the single clients, both men and women, had kids who needed to be watched while the client was driven to the hospital. We got signed up to work on weekends, which was when Jimmy came down from Weleetka to see me, and I agreed to be on call in the evenings for things that might come up occasionally during the week.

I'd made this vow to myself to start pulling back from Jimmy, but he talked me into taking a quick overnight trip, fishing some farm ponds around Shawnee, pitching a tent, and going back in the morning. It was a beautiful day; the damn heat had slackened a little, and I looked out the window at wildflowers still in bloom in the roadside ditches along I-40. I had that fishing buzz I normally got in spring, first time out; perhaps this was because of the new venture we were entering into with our volunteer work, the hope that it would be the breakthrough we needed. We rolled down the windows, let the air in.

As tricky as Jimmy was, I was getting even sneakier. I had surreptitiously stuck *Hank Williams' Greatest Hits* in my coat pocket. Jimmy was a hip-hop, R&B kind of a guy, and he referred to most of the stuff I listened to as "incestuous hillbilly warbling." He'd heard all my Merle Haggard and George Jones and couldn't stomach any of it. I stuck the Hank Williams tape in the player, and he eyed me like, "Okay, what kind of redneck shit are we gonna have to listen to now?" I had to turn it way up since we'd rolled the windows down, and to my astonishment, when the tape kicked in, Jimmy knew every word to "Howling at the Moon," and, in true coyote abandon, started singing along with gusto: "You got me chasing rabbits, scratching fleas, and howling at the moon." He even turned his face up toward the blue sky and wailed along with the coyote chorus at the end. I cracked up at his antics.

Jimmy said, "In high school I used to go with C.A. all the way to Henryetta to get somebody to buy beer for us. We'd get six-packs of Little Kings and listen to Hank Williams, parked at the cemetery north of town." This was a small miracle; I had been listening to Hank Williams all my life. I told Jimmy how my dad sang his songs incessantly; I may have been the only kid my age who knew that Hank started out doing talking blues and calling himself Luke the Drifter, singing sad songs, one that I particularly remembered about the town slut who gets killed saving a little boy from a car wreck, the community realizing too late that they had misjudged her. The name of the song is "Be Careful of Stones that You Throw."

I said to Jimmy, "Yeah, I remember really clearly the day I first heard 'I'm So Lonesome I Could Cry.' That was the purest, rawest, most emotional thing I'd ever listened to. I thought, good God, this isn't an expression of pain, this *is* pain, the stuff of which pain is made."

Jimmy was interested; clearly there was something we could both feel in these songs. He leaned forward, excited, "Yeah, that's it," he said, "those songs have everything to do with being Indian, everything to do with being queer. I don't know quite how to put my finger on it, but it's about loneliness, a shitload of pain, not being able to speak to the one you love, remaining hidden and silent in the shadows for a lifetime, being an outsider everywhere you go. That's some powerful shit, huh? You reckon Hank was queer?"

"Well, he definitely wasn't Indian," I said, and we both laughed.

When the tape got to "Setting the Woods on Fire," we both sang along this time; when you start singing those Hank songs, it's hard to quit.

We got to the fishing hole and unloaded the truck. Jimmy fished like a lot of Indian guys I knew, which is to say he was a bobber-and-worm man, liked to get his line out, keep his hands free for drinking Budweiser. Except Jimmy didn't drink anymore since his Tulsa days; I had to give him that. He just didn't have any faith in lures, that a piece of metal or plastic could catch a fish. I'd tried to show him how to work them, and he'd give it a go for about twenty minutes, but if he didn't catch anything soon, he'd start stringing up his bobber rig. I didn't mind because it meant I usually caught the big ones, though he'd do pretty good catching a lot of little crappie, and he was indispensable if you needed to catch bait for a trotline. He'd now and again catch a big ole cat, too, and at such times he laughed at all the trouble I went through working lures and wandering up and down the bank, searching for that elusive bass hole, the perfect sunken log, the cove where they just *had* to be feeding. On one such occasion, pissed, I retorted, "Obviously, you don't know a goddamn thing about bass fishing," something like what my grandpa had probably always wanted to say to me. I went to the other side of the pond, and it hadn't been five minutes after my bitchy statement that Jimmy hooked three of the biggest bass, in immediate succession, off a night crawler dangling beneath a bobber no less, that I'd ever seen. He'd tricked me once more, and he didn't say a word, though he sure took his time holding them up for me to see while he was putting them on the stringer. This made me madder. We'd been fishing on his uncle's property outside of Weleetka, and I said, "You need to throw those back in so as we ain't taking all the big fish out of your uncle's pond." Jimmy just snickered, though he did turn two of them loose.

But today was a nice day, relaxed, a breeze blowing off the bank, a couple tugs after the first five minutes. In fact, we had more fish than we could eat after an hour and a half, and we decided to release most of them while they were still healthy. We chose a little cat and a couple medium-sized bass, plenty for a fish fry that evening.

In the tent that night, we lay next to each other, stuffed from too much fried potatoes and fish. My pup tent necessitated physical proximity, but I kept my hands to myself, finally having given in to Jimmy's wishes. I was getting sleepy, just about to drift off, when Jimmy got kind of antsy, shifting around in his sleeping bag, acting like he was fixing to tell me something.

"Josh," he said finally, turning toward me, "I have a present for you."

"What?" I asked. Was I dreaming? No, he crawled toward the tent opening and unzipped the bug screen, then the nylon flap. I stuck my head out to watch, dumbfounded, but once he walked past the fire he disappeared. I heard the pickup door open, a pop, and a creak. Ah, something behind the seat. When he walked back past the fire I saw he had a photo in a gold frame. He crawled back into the tent on hands and knees, got seated, and handed me the picture.

"I had it framed," he said.

Lucy is seated in a porch swing, holding a cigarette gayly and the swing chain in the other hand, her legs crossed at the knee. Her husband, Glen, is standing beside the swing, one hand in his front pants pocket, the other arm akimbo. He has on a white starched shirt, a neckerchief, and a black cowboy hat, maybe taken in the fifties. A young boy is standing to the right of Lucy and Glen, leaning at a weird angle, goofing off like Charlie Chaplin. Jimmy points and says, "That's my dad when he was nine." On the back of the photo, in lowercase letters and no punctuation, is written:

> theres alot of them used to sit in front of they houses like that and
> I guess us too that crazy boy come over and Lester took it

I recognized the very small, neat script of Lucy's handwriting, unmistakable. I'd seen it in the "card room" at Zeke and Arlene's house. By then I'd sat up, and I was weeping. Jimmy put his arm around me, and we stared at the photo.

"I went to see my dad after church last Sunday. I told him I'd run into you, and he gave me this old picture after I got to telling him about the night we drove Lucy all over Oklahoma City, looking for a music store, and that she came to my game."

"Yeah, it's my Aunt Lucy all right," I said. "I have a lot to tell you about her."

"Yeah," Jimmy said, and he hugged me closer. I luxuriated in the closeness, the silence, as we held the picture between us. We went to bed, didn't say anything more.

I fell asleep and dreamed I could hear Lucy calling from outside the tent, from the tree line. She was calling for me to join her. The more I listened, the more I could hear her voice, and the more I heard my Aunt Lucy's voice, the more I could hear my own. I said, "Aunt Lucy, I'm coming directly, but let me and Jimmy catch you up some fish for supper."

Jimmy and I got into the little aluminum boat we fished out of with Grandpa, leaving Lucy in the trees and Grandpa on the bank still fishing in the growing darkness of dusk. We waved at them as the boat slapped the waves. "It's too damn choppy out here," Jimmy said. "Let me show you someplace you've never been." He drove the boat over to a streambed on the other side of the lake where a creek fed into the main body of water. Bass were coming up to feed near the shore where the fresh water came in, and we could see their circles rippling out as they jumped on the surface. We pulled the boat on shore and waded into the shallow water of the stream. Jimmy unbuttoned his baggy pirate shirt and pulled it over his head as he stood motionless, ankle deep in the creek running past his feet and into the pond. He pulled my face toward his and brushed his lips against my eyebrows. My face was sore from his beard, as if we'd had sex earlier, maybe the day before.

He whispered in my ear, motioning toward a large school of carp in the shallows. They were turning, rolling over in the water near the mouth of the creek. As I turned to look, he unbuttoned my pants, cupping the bulge in my briefs in his palm, running his hand over the cotton, his thumb massaging a growing damp spot in the material. He dropped his cutoffs to his ankles, and the water started to eddy around them. Jimmy stepped out of them, and they floated off toward the school of writhing carp. He stood there in his underwear. His cock head had slipped out from the elastic band of his shorts, and I laughed, telling him that it reminded me of the turtles we'd seen all day sunning themselves on partially submerged logs, their heads poked out of their shells. Jimmy stood behind me and put his arms around me, kissing me on the back of the neck. He removed his briefs all the way and let them float off; I remained fully clothed. We sat down in the stream, him in front of me now, and I draped my arms lazily around his neck. The water ran around us, around and around in little circles. Jimmy smiled, looking down at the water lapping against our waists.

I'd had my shirt off earlier during the hottest part of the day, and the cool water stung like hell when it hit my sunburned skin. Jimmy's darker arms had a slight pinkish cast, but he wasn't as red as me, and he didn't grimace at the touch of the water. Then he turned his head toward me, and we kissed. Jimmy said, "It's getting almost too dark to see," and I held both his arms, saying, "I can still see the cattails, barely." As I spoke, in spite of the fact that I wasn't touching him below the waist, spurts of white petals fell into the stream, resting on the surface like water lilies carried in a circle by a small eddy.

I dreamed that I came back a year later with him and the pond was no longer there, only a large, shimmering mud flat where small-mouth bass and crappie and old mudhead catfish were flopping around, slowly suffocating in the rays of sunlight hitting the wet red mud. In the dried-up creekbed, at the exact spot where Jimmy had come in the creek, had grown a red cedar. My Aunt Lucy stepped out from behind it, and she laughed at the way she'd startled us. "See, boys," she said, nodding at the cedar, "now you know where those trees come from." I woke up from the dream, and Jimmy's arm was around me, and he was sleeping soundly.

After we got up and around in the morning it took me and
Jimmy a while to get the tent stakes pulled up and the tent itself
folded, the dishes done, which we'd neglected to do the night before
(cold fish is the worst to have to look at in the morning), and the poles
loaded. During these little chores, Jimmy was strange and anxious
like the night before, in a hurry to get packed and going, but hesitating
and lingering like he had something else up his sleeve. Just as he was
about to climb in the truck, he said, "I sure hate the thought of heading
back for the city. Let's have one cup of coffee while it's still early. We
got time."

"But I just packed all that shit," I protested.

"Just get the coffeepot out; the fire embers are still going. We
won't even have to unpack the stove."

I grumbled, more on principle than any real dissatisfaction, and
handed Jimmy the pot. "You're the one who wants coffee," I said.
"You fix it."

He did, and we sat on the small wooden dock and drank it.
Jimmy ate an orange. We enjoyed the morning quiet, the rays of sun
creeping out toward the center of the pond. A raccoon was wandering
up and down the shore, and Jimmy said, "Here, *Wotko*," and threw
him pieces of the leftover fish, which fell short of the bank, but the
raccoon waded in and scooped them up out of the water. Jimmy sat
down behind me.

In the stillness of the morning, as the raccoon waddled back up
the bank into the shade, Jimmy draped his arms over my shoulders
and whispered in my ear, "Josh, I love you."

TWELVE

I'm Gonna Marry Me
That Horse Trader

Lucy, Weleetka, Oklahoma, 1904

The way I see it in my mind is like this here: The horse trader is leaning back against the rail fence cutting off a brown clump of Day's Work and stuffing it in his cheek. I mean he's slick now what with his straw hat pulled down to those slanted Chickasaw eye slits and his pointy-toed black cowhide boots poking outta the legs of his jeans, snugger than acorns in their husks. I call them pointy-toed boots "roaches" on account of you could mash a cockroach in a corner.

After he gets a mouthful of tobacco, he spits a long stream of brown rust outta the side of his mouth, and it hisses and sends up a little explosion when it hits the dust. His pants is so tight he can't hardly get his hands in his pockets when he settles back against the fence. I cover my eyes trying to block out the sun that's coming up behind him over the tree line behind the corral.

He's got that brown mixed-blooded hair, even lighter than mine, and is it ever slicked back when he lifts his hat and wipes the sweat from his dark forehead. Green eyes. He couldn't look less inersted in the menfolk milling about unless he was dead. It's up in the fall, the

cotton and corn's in, and they got a little extry money to spend. This
year they's a fancy price for cotton on account of the boll weevil, but
they ain't too many that made much of a crop. Talk all around every
day about things I don't understand like allotments and whether or
not Indians would be allowed to sell them, and some folks, especially
full-blooded ones, madder than a hornet and don't want nothing to do
with any of it. The white Indians will probably get to sell, but the
others won't is the way Daddy tells it. He don't like it because Mama
won't be able to sell. But that isn't what's made these Snake Indians
mad, he says; Snakes is what white people call them. They go by the
removal treaty that promised them their nation in Oklahoma forever.
Daddy says things have changed so that they cain't count on that no
mores. The Snakes keep going down to Hickory Grounds to talk it
over, and a couple years ago Daddy and a bunch of white folks got the
marshalls and U.S. Cavalry out and throwed 'em all in federal prison
at Muskogee, and they cut off their hair. Then they took Chitto Harjo,
the leader, up to prison in Leavenworth for several months just
because he met with his people at Hickory Grounds to talk about the
corn crop, which was failing out. Daddy thinks the full-bloods was
gonna make white people leave Indian Territory, and that's when he
helped get government folks to round up the Snakes. Daddy makes
fun of them full-bloods and their hickory shirts made out of checked
cotton cloth. He says they're lazy, and they don't grow nothing but a
jar of *sofki* and a hill of sweet potatoes.

The horse trader come in driving a covered wagon, been down to
Texas swapping ponies, then up through Pushmataha, Pittsburgh, and,
finally, McIntosh County until he got here to Weleetka. A pretty setup
if I ever saw one with white canvas spread over the top so as if you was
to lay down in the bed of it, you'd think you was looking up into the
clouds except for the stovepipe, which might be a tree stump or even a
horse, if you pictured it right, standing asleep on three legs—you
know how they hitch up one leg when they're resting? A lot nicer
than the wagon we drive to town. Now, wouldn't that be a nice place
to live? No mess to clean, beds to make, just have you a little place in
there for your dolls and a cot to lay down on.

"I'm gonna grow up and marry that horse trader," I say to myself. I'll learn to swap horses just as good, maybe better than him. "I'm not gonna trade a goddamn thing today," I say, letting on like I'm not inersted in a big solid buckskin, a cow horse, and I turn to walk off, but Mama's standing on the porch behind me, and she hears what I just said. Her hand squeezing my shoulder makes me forget all about horses. "What's that, young lady?" she asks me. I'm so embarrassed at my make-believe that I don't let on, and just let her stand there and get mad. She don't whip you or nothing like Daddy, but she's liable to say something that makes you wish you'd never done it, that's for sure.

She can't sing, either. She goes around the house bellering in the kitchen "When the roll is called up yander," and when she hits that "yander" she looks like a dying cow with its eyes lolled up back of its head. It's the awfullest sight you could imagine. But ever' now and then when we go to the Weleetka Indian Baptist Church she does different on them Indian sings, those songs in minor-sounding keys floating through the camps and off into the hills, the women fanning themselves, eyes closed, every word like all the things that ever hurt them. I think she sounds better at Ind'n church on account of it's outdoors, and the cicadas help to drowned her out.

It's the dance that done it. Got me to thinking about the horse trader. Not a stomp dance out at the grounds but a reg'lar old fiddle dance. It's at Uncle Lem's, Daddy's brother, so it's a white fiddle dance, not like the Indian ones where they play Creek songs on the violin and sing in Indian and make rhythm with sticks on the backs of they chairs. At an Indian fiddle party, they can drink and all what they can't do at the stomp grounds. And there's sure to be one or two good fights. But tonight Mama is playing for white neighbors. It's funny a woman who can't sing can play a fiddle, and play it better than anyone in the territory. Me, I can sing, but I don't play anything, just love listening. I'm getting ready to go on over to Uncle Lem's, and right now I bet he's pushing back furniture. Uncle Lem's place ain't like ours a-tall. We got a sycamore tree in the front yard where the south wind blows down the hills from over Kialeegee way. Daddy sits in the shade and talks politics the times when a neighbor comes by while Mama goes out and picks up some dead wood to start a fire under the *sofki* pot until smoke starts to boil outta the chimley. We got an old squirrel dog who comes out from the fence corner ever' now and then and gets in the way around the kitchen door and keeps order amongst the chickens. We got more on the outside of the house than we do on the inside, what with a crib full of hard yellow corn and a barn and a spring off a little ways that we're always having to keep cleaned out of brush and limbs. Lem, though, has furniture and pitchers hung up on the wall, and a rug, and it just naturally makes you wanna look down at your feet whenever you go in there.

What makes tonight extry unusual is for one thing there's gonna be more than one fiddle player; the Chickasaw horse trader's coming over, and Mama can get him to play second. What a difference another fiddler makes. Twin fiddles on "Soldier's Joy" is beautiful. Uncle Lem will holler, "Take it away, Rachel, take it away," and the horse trader will start out on the melody, and Mama will play the harder part, the harmony, and the cicadas outside will drone like a bagpipe, until you got pert near a whole orchestra.

Those little singing black ink spots pulse from the treetops and you cain't see them, but you have to take their word for it that they're out there. "Faith cometh by hearing," I said one night to Mama while we was sitting out on the porch trying to cool off before going to bed. I'd heard the preacher say that, and I liked the sound of it. But Mama took me by the hand and walked straight toward the grinding hum until she narrowed down all that insect noise to a particular voice and headed toward the exact spot and pulled a cicada off a low branch of a scrub oak and handed it to me. I mean, in the pitch dark. That's the way she talks stories sometimes without saying anything. Sometimes boys likes to catch them and put them on a string, but I just turned her loose.

The other thing that's unusual about this evening is that Bertha Bowlegs, the old woman from over Eufaula way, who folks reckon to be about one hunnerd and one years old, is gonna be there at the dance, watching. Let's put it this way. She tells stories about the day her older brother traveled along the Tallapoosa River with his party of warriors from Upper Creek towns to fight against William McIntosh in the Battle at Horseshoe Bend. Andrew Jackson made Creeks give up 25 million acres because of the treaty that come out of that lost war. Bertha has made a vow. Somebody's been sneaking into her watermelon patch and getting up in there and leaving a mess of busted melons and seeds all over the ground, and she aims to catch him. I don't know what she'll do with him once she gets him caught since she's so old, other than make him feel ashamed of robbing an old lady. Now you'd think she'd stay out on her porch with a barrel full of buckshot, but she's one of those old women who knows things, and she'll be able to tell the culprit when she sees him. Such as is likely to steal watermelons is also likely to come to a dance for a good time.

Sometimes I feel like a rabbit. You ever see a swamp rabbit in a low-down marshy spot? I seen one come running out of a swamp onced with its eyes bugged out like it might die from fright, but, you know, that rabbit was tricky. When the dogs come out of the swamp grass and cattails, they fanned out all over the place because that rabbit had doubled back on his own trail and left them at a dead end.

Me, I'm looking for just the right trick, too. Tonight I'd sure like to get out of babysitting Dave so I could watch the dance. Oh, sure, I'll be inside and hear the music, see the men step up and hold their hands out to the pretty girls and two-step around the floor. But what about taking a turn at it myself? Dave is an orphan boy, and Daddy is his guardian. Dave isn't like the rest of the babies around here who cry ever' time one of their brothers or sisters toddles over and snatches a play-pretty out of their hand. Dave only cries over the basics. Food and such. When Mama gets to cooking he sets up a caterwauling like you wouldn't believe as if you can't get it to him quick enough before it disappears. Rest of the time he's stony-faced and staring. Sits off by himself.

So we head off towards Uncle Lem's; me carrying Dave, Mama carrying her fiddle case and a jar of *sofki,* and Daddy not carrying nothing. It's getting dusky, and Daddy starts to tell how one time when he was little and walking home from the house Lem now lives

in, the devil jumped out of the buckbrush and chased him all the way
to the sandhills and down to the riverbank of the Canadian where
Daddy hid in a pool of stagnant water behind a sandbar. He tells me
this story ever' time someone sends me over to Uncle Lem's, and I sure
do watch the bushes while we walk the road. I hold Dave in one arm
and Mama's hand in the other. I try not to let on I'm a-scared. The
washouts on the side of the road look like white people's faces, always
staring right at you.

It ain't but one section away, so it don't take long to get there, and
I'm glad. I get to spend the night, and we don't have to walk back
until morning when it'll be light out.

At the dance ever'body sets down what they brung to eat on top of
a couple of tables pushed together. We was to eat first, then the adults
was gonna dance inside there while we kids just play outside and run
in and out. Mama took Dave for a while and fed him. Daddy went
outside to roll his Bull Durham and smoke. Now, Uncle Lemuel and
Daddy; there's two brothers different as day and night. Uncle Lem
looked out to the front porch, then whispers to me and Mama, "Lucy,
I got something special I wanna show you." I was afraid of white men,
and I grabbed a-holt of Mama's skirts when he said that to me. "It's in
the bedroom," Lemuel said, and when he went to get it I wrapped my
arms even tighter around her. I was somewhat relieved I didn't have to
go in there with him.

He came out carrying something that looked to me a lot like a
little suitcase and some books. We'd never owned a suitcase, but I seen
it in the Sears and Roebuck. Uncle Lem set the case down on the floor
in front of me, since we'd pushed all the furniture aside. "Open it up,
Lucille," he says. I look at Mama. She nods. With her standing right
there next to me I figure it will be all right just to take a little peek.
I bent down and undid a latch. It popped open. Me and Mama both
jumped. Uncle Lem laughed. "Open up the other one," he said. "It'll
make the same noise." It popped open, too, just like he said, and
I slowly lifted the cover.

Right away my eyes was drawn to the prettiest mess of shiny gold
metal and buttons and twists and turns that laid to shame anything I'd

ever known up to then, including the ivory-skinned doll with the blue eyes deeper than lake water.

"Ain't that pretty?" Mama says. "What is it?"

"They call that a trumpet," Uncle Lem answers.

"White peoples make music on it," I tell Mama. Like I says, I was well versed in that Sears catalog and took to reading at a young age with little to teach me except a day here and there learning the alphabets before the white peoples told my daddy I had to either go to Chilocco with my own kind or quit. You can see I didn't go to Chilocco.

"That's right," Uncle Lem says, smiling. "It's for making music. Lucy, I got that from my daddy when I was little. He hoped I'd turn into something more than a plowboy. He got me some books with music in them, but I could never make sense out of any of it. Looks like I turned into a plowboy anyway in spite of Daddy's best intentions. I want you to have this horn, Lucy. If anyone can figure it out, it's you. Are you able to keep a secret?"

My eyes got big as an old milk cow's, and I'd been rendered plumb speechless. I'd never got much more than an orange for Christmas except for one year when I got a piece of hard candy and a bottle of sody pop. My heart coulda exploded into about a hunnerd pieces any minute the way it took to pounding. The first thing that come into my head was what on earth does this white man wanna make me do to get that trumpet?

"You know how your daddy is," Lem said sadly, shaking his head. "We was all growed up the same; I don't know what turned him so sour. He don't have no use for anything such as a trumpet that might give a body a half a minute of fun. If I give you this horn now, he'll just take it and sell it. But when your mama brings eggs over on Fridays, I'll show you what little I know, which don't amount to much more than a scale or two. You was always quick to latch on; maybe you can make sense of these music books."

Uncle Lem handed me one of the books he'd brought out of the room with the trumpet. I opened it up, but it was no more than shapes and lines, nothing near what I thought music might look like. They was some instructions I might be able to study up on if I put my mind to it.

"Will Mama be here while you're learning me?" I asked.

"Why, sure," Lemuel said. "She can sit right next to you." I don't believe he knew how scared I actually was, but somehow I knew it would be all right because every which way my daddy was my Uncle Lemuel waddn't.

"Well, you decide," Uncle Lem says. "You're the one most likely to learn music; I'm sure of that much. And it's going to waste now, just laying in the case under the bed. If you can figure it out, I'll give you the horn when you're old enough. Between now and the time you might be able to teach your own kids to play it, maybe I can work on your daddy to let you keep it," Lem laughed.

If only I could have that horn *before* then, I thought. You see, I'd already been taken in by the beauty of it, the shine of its metal, the secrets of its workings, the way it wrapped all around itself and then opened up and let out what was trapped inside. My head swum around until I was dizzy with the hope of getting that horn as soon as possible. I had to hold back tears when Uncle Lem put it back in the case on account of Daddy coming in off the porch, and Lem slid it real quick behind the sofa near the wall. Lem winked at me and pushed me toward the door, saying, "Lucy, you go along and play now."

I notice a boy at the bottom of the porch steps. I b'lieve I know this boy from Weleetka, and I wanna ask him if he's one of the Choffee boys, which I think he is. He was in the first grade before I had to quit and start chopping cotton. I go out there and walk up to him slowly and ask, "What's your name?" I don't look right at him 'cause I don't know him for sure. This boy has his bangs cut like his mama stuck a bowl on top of his head, and he covers his face with his fingers and giggles. He's about my age but kindy shy. I repeat again, this time in Creek, *"Naakit chihochifkat?"* At first I think he ain't gonna tell me, but then he mumbles, "Jesse Choffee, *chahochifkat os."* Just like I suspicioned, he's one of them Choffee boys.

"I believe you're kin to Tarbie, ain't it?" I ask.

"Named me after him," he says proudly. "My middle name's Tarbie."

We sit down on the porch steps. We don't say anything, but Jesse keeps turning around and straining to try to watch the grown-ups dancing around inside the house. His foot starts tapping out "Arkansas Traveler," and he looks like he can barely sit still. Jesse is twitching like he's sitting on an anthill. Jesse seems to be shut up tight as a terrapin, but I know he's listening extry close because he's looking away, down at the ground, and he spits. After about ten minutes of silence, I say to him, "You ever tried that?"

"Tried what?" he asks.

"Dancing like that," I say. If he waddn't already looking down at his feet, he sure is now. But then all at once he stands up and puffs up like a rooster shaking out his feathers. He says something funny.

"You think I'm afraid of dancing with you?" he says, and reaches down and takes my hand as if I'd just dared him. His hand is all sticky, and I try to place what he's got all over his fingers and palm. Right away it feels like our hands is glued together.

I put my hand on his shoulder, and the cotton's stiff where I got my fingers on a dried-up pink stain. My palm's sweaty, and the crinkly red spot gets warm and clings to his shoulder. I feel my other hand get stuck to him.

"You think I'm afraid of dancing close with you like they're doing in there?" he asks, then reaches and puts his hand in the small of my back and our faces are cheek-to-cheek. He's got something sticky on his face, too, and our skin is stuck together now.

My hand is on the back of his shirt, and we start moving around in the dirt—slow, slow, quick step; slow, slow, quick step. He steps forward with his left foot; I go back on my right. He sings in my ear, "I'd a been married a long time ago if it had not a-been for Cotton-eyed Joe." Then under my fingers, pressed to his back, I feel three small, hard seeds. I realize I'm dancing with a thief, the one who busted open Bertha's watermelons. My face blushes, and I feel warm all over.

"It ain't no more than walking," he says. "If you can count to two, you can dance." Now he's leading, and I'm following, going backwards, so I can still see inside the house while he's dancing toward the edge of the yard. Old lady Bowlegs herself comes out on the porch and glares around, and before you know it she spots us two-stepping towards the cicadas in the trees. She just hops clean over the porch, and I'm so scared I can't speak like in a dream when you have to say the right words to come awake. I wanna pull apart, but my speechlessness has me glued to the watermelon boy, and before I can say anything she's got him by the collar and me by the ear.

Bertha Bowlegs turns loose of me so she can get a-holt of Jesse by both ears. She has his head under her arm in a headlock and a tweaked ear in each hand. At first I laugh hard because it looks like she's wrastling a Poland China hog towards its pen, with Jesse half bent over and kicking at her skirts, swinging with his free fists, and Bertha walking backwards and pulling with all her might. Who'd of ever thought the old woman had it in her? Bertha got a look on her face of pure motion like a runaway team of horses. Then I notice she's backing toward the storm cellar, a low mound of dirt humped up on the far side of the house. She reaches the trapdoor, keeps Jesse in a headlock with the one arm, and throws the bar that keeps it from blowing open with the other.

Words come flooding out of me. I cain't hold them back. I'm so angry that I might not ever stop hollering now that I've started.

"Turn loose of him, you old bitch," I scream, even though it ain't respectful and that might earn me a whole bar of soap. "All he did was bust open your old rotten melons." Then I name ever'body who I'm gonna run and tell. "I'm a-getting Sonny Boy. Lester and Little George. Ernest, Bill, and Henryetta." I go through ever' one of my brothers and sisters, aunts, uncles, and cousins. "I'm a-getting Ward Coachman"— except I say Co-chi-may—"Gool Coachman, Martha Blue, Willie Whisenhunt, Dona Whisenhunt, Carl Brackett, Wilma Self, Rachel Ausmus, David and Iva Sessions, Tecumseh Blackwell and his brother Thomas," and I name all my relatives, living and dead, far back as I can remember, all the way back to Indian Removal and some before.

Bertha turns to me before kicking Jesse down the steps of the
storm cellar and grins. She looks the happiest I ever seen her. "I'm
gonna boil him alive, girl," she says to me. I figure she's just being
mean, so when she slams the squeaky wood door, throws the bar shut,
and stomps off in the dark toward her house, I suspicion she's gonna
go get a willow switch or a thorn. Sometimes old folks punish kids by
scratching them on their legs or arms. When she gets to the edge of
the yard out by the well, I can barely hear her for Jesse beating the
cellar door with his fist, but she warns me not to let him out or I'll get
boiled, too. Before disappearing into the dark, she tells me to keep
guard until she gets back with her kettle.

Jesse calls to me from down below. I'm afraid of cellars. Remind
me of my nightmares, sinking down to that place of suffocation. Each
concrete step takes me deeper into blackness and silence. The first step,
my tongue goes thick and my head foggy. The next, I'm walking into
spiderwebs and stuttering. At the bottom I can't speak at all and feel
the weight of earth above me. I try to force words out but none come
until I wake up sweating and groaning. The cellar ain't like the
smokehouse, which I kindy like on account of it's aboveground and
inside it smells of hickory, and I like to look at the white swirls of fat
on the bacon middlings hanging from the roof.

"Do you wanna know how to really guard a prisoner?" Jesse asks
from down below.

"No," I say. I wanna go in the house and get Mama is what I want.

"You gotta stand guard down here where you can see him. Can
you see me from out there?"

"I ain't that dumb," I tell him. "I'll let you out, but I ain't about
to get in there. I'll go fetch Mama. Mama won't let Bertha bother us."

Jesse agrees, and I pull off the bar. It's really just a two-by-four
that fits into an arm across the door; keeps the wind from blowing it
open. When I get the bar lifted, before I even fling open the door, Jesse
comes flying out and grabs me by the arms, forces me down the steps,
and has the door shut and locked before I can rush back out. I'm here
in the dark, and Bertha's on the way back. I been in this cellar before
with Mama to get canned goods. I know there's a box of matches and

candles near the top of the stairs. I don't know what scares me more, to sit in the dark or to see what's down there, but I light the candle anyway. I am relieved that it looks the same as during the daytime, except for less light and the shadow of the candle on the wall. I'm plenty scared but not as bad as I would have guessed. Not all that different from the smokehouse except it don't smell as good, more musty. I see it's just a cellar. I try speaking out loud. It echoes a little, but I find I can name my kinfolks just like I could outside when I was hollering at Bertha. I say their names again. I keep telling myself that it cain't take very long for Mama to come outside for some cool air and to check on me. She's sure to look around the side of the house, and I'll tell her I'm down here. Jesse, the little bastard, has run off.

My eyes get used to the dark. In order to pass the time and not think about the time Daddy killed a copperhead snake at the bottom of the stairs in our cellar over home, I find me a rag and dust off the jars of sweet pickles and green beans, wild grape jam and blackberries in syrup. The music is far away, but it eases my mind a little that I can still hear them dancing and laughing. When Mama finally comes around the side of the house, calling for me, I notice the worry in her voice.

"I'm down here, Mama," I cry out, banging on the door with all my might, and before I know it she has the bar off, and I run out and she grabs a-holt of me so that I know everything is all right.

"Josh," he calls, and shakes my shoulder a little, handing me a beer. "Been daydreaming again?" The bar comes back into focus, and I stifle a groan. I'm forced to acknowledge that Jimmy and I have let a friend talk us into a Saturday night at the clubs. Jimmy explains to him we can only stay a little while since we've agreed to provide transportation for a Project Vision client who needs to go to the hospital in the morning. In my boredom with the bar, I had drifted off.

I grow weary of the pretty boy cha-cha palace, so I talk Jimmy and our buddy into going to Saddle Tramps, where we sit and get a kick out of seeing fastidious gay boys dressed as cowboys and two-stepping close together in the same direction around the dance floor. Before

discovering the 39th Street clubs, I had never imagined these kind of cowboys, not what one is led to expect from one of America's most virile and venerable class of heroes.

"Wouldn't it be fun to dance with them—*dancing with the enemy,*" Jimmy says sarcastically.

We watched. These cowboys, I suspected, had never had anything to do with cows. They didn't smell like cowboys, for one thing, any suggestion of the range heavily masked under Aramis or Obsession or Giorgio. The Stetsoned and Wrangler-jeaned dudes were line-dancing with their thumbs in their belt loops, redneck divas. I had always associated cowboy activities with very physical sensations— leather on horse sweat, the sound of a creaking saddle, the feel of a horse's wet flanks soaking your pant legs—and I doubted if these urbane cowboys could cinch up a saddle if you gave them a winch and a come-along.

At ten o'clock, much to my disappointment given its entertainment value, the country music ended and the techno crap began. At least there was something to watch while the cow queens were line-dancing, and now I was ready to go home for sure. Strains of Madonna started up, a prelude to the hardcore machine music generated by computers that would soon follow. Madonna, at least, had lyrics. She was singing that it doesn't matter if you're black or white, and I thought, how ridiculous, of course it matters; it makes all the difference in the world. Only a white person could make such a stupid statement. We said goodbye to our friend and drove home.

When we got back to my place, I pulled Jimmy toward me and apologized for being a stick-in-the-mud. "That's all right, baby," he grinned, "we got our own dance we can do." He put on a CD, Luther Vandross, much, much better. But still I can't seem to bust loose; it's not happening. Jimmy knows how to move everything, to turn, to talk stories with his hands, the dance itself a statement beyond the music. I am constrained in my little square corner, all bunched up, don't know what to do with myself.

"Loosen up," Jimmy says. "*Damn,* Josh. Here, let me show you something different," and he puts his arms around me. I try to follow his movements, and at first I'm a little out of sync, his feet going one way and mine another.

"I don't know what's wrong, tonight. Guess I'm just tired."

"You're not listening close enough," he grins. Playing tricks again, as usual. But I stop thinking and let myself go, and sure enough we start to hear a beat below the music, and we begin dancing for every blue note that ever came out of the end of my Aunt Lucy's horn, and we dance for my Uncle Sonny Boy who died lighting a cigarette after spraying arsenic on a white man's cotton field, and we dance for Jimmy's dad shooting all the 'skins stumbling out of the Cave, and we dance for my Great-Uncle Glen who cleaned up a mess of tobacco spit from his boss's car, and we dance for Dave who turned out the wolf pups from their cages, and we dance for the man we're running over to the hospital in the morning for pentamidine treatments, and we dance for my Uncle Ezequiel Elmer Henneha who left us for Jesus, and we are dancing and dancing and dancing and there is so much at stake and it makes all the difference in the world.

So much difference that our dancing beckons others; they rise up out of the darkness to join us. We begin dancing for a nation of people, Mvskokvalke.

Loca. Shell-shakers. Night dances under the arbors. Fireflies flitting over the willow boughs that roof them. *Shuguta shuguta shuguta,* women stepping toe to heel, the sound of shells shaking, the turtle voices.

About the Author

Craig S. Womack (Oklahoma Creek–Cherokee) is Assistant Professor in the Department of Native American Studies at the University of Lethbridge in Southern Alberta. He is the author of *Red on Red: Native American Literary Separatism.*